Dance Lessons

Dance Lessons

Moving to the Rhythm of a Crazy God

CATHERINE M. WALLACE

MOREHOUSE PUBLISHING

Copyright © 1999 by Catherine M. Wallace

Morehouse Publishing
P.O. Box 1321
Harrisburg, PA 17105

Morehouse Publishing is a division of The Morehouse Group.

All rights reserved. No part of this book may be reproduced or transmitted in any form or by any means, electronic or mechanical, including photocopying, recording, or by any information storage and retrieval system, without written permission from the publisher.

The Scripture quotations are from the Revised Standard Version of the Bible, copyright 1946, 1952, © 1971,1973, and are used by permission.

Every effort has been made to trace the owners of existing copyright material, and apology is made for any copyright inadvertently not cited. Please notify Morehouse Publishing of any errors so they may be corrected in future printings.

Printed in the United States of America

Library of Congress Cataloging-in-Publication Data

Wallace, Catherine Miles.
    Dance Lessons : moving to the rhythms of a crazy god / Catherine M. Wallace.
       p.   cm.
    ISBN 0-8192-1795-6
    1. Wallace, Catherine Miles.   2. Catholics—United States—Biography. 3. Narrative theology.   I. Title
BX4705.W2554A3   1999
282'.092—dc21   98-55276
[B]   CIP

CONTENTS

Preface
vii

Prologue: As Angels Dance
1

1 *Fiat Lux:* April, 1979
5

2 Is There Life after Birth?
43

3 Bonbons and Soap Operas
93

4 A Rainbow in the Sky
137

5 Across the Waters
175

6 A Big Blue Frog
219

Epilogue: Another Leap
251

Notes
255

PREFACE

God is crazy. If I had known that from the beginning, none of this would have happened as it did. I would have been on guard against the sly and deviously underhanded Holy One. But no: sixteen years of Catholic education both convinced me that God is supposed to make sense and equipped me to deconstruct—easily, without guilt—the quaintly medieval metaphysics encoded within conventional belief. One Saturday night, over dinner in my college dorm, I realized that all of it had always been both pointless and highly improbable. So I stopped going to church. The sky didn't fall, and that was that: no problem. How was I to know? How?

Sister Mary Robert, for instance. She was two hundred years old, nine feet tall, and the principal of my high school. She glided around the school as if on metaphysical roller skates, materializing out of thin air when we least expected her, holding up one long bony white finger and making cryptic pronouncements. If you don't know nuns of this sort, imagine the Oracle at Delphi in her later years, except with large, slightly buck teeth. But Mary Robert had had a lot of speech therapy somewhere along the line, and so she did not lisp. She spoke with a clear, distinct not-lisp that gave a hollow, vowel-like quality to certain consonants. I was a headstrong kid, no expiring Ophelia by any measure; but Sister Mary Robert scared the socks off of me (uniform cable-knit knee-highs, navy blue or grey but not black). I especially remember her catching me all alone three or four times and intoning, "Make your mistakes with confidence, Miss Miles! With *confidence*!" God knows what she meant by that. Which is my point. I bet God did. I certainly didn't. But I remembered. That's how it works.

And then of course there was the day Sister Mary Robert appeared in the doorway of Senior Honors English, on a "seminar" day when we had only some of our classes, but each one for ninety minutes. She nodded curtly to the nun who was teaching, her thin lips closed firmly over those teeth. I couldn't figure out whether our teacher was startled or not. Nuns could be an exceedingly inscrutable group. Mary Robert crooked one long finger at the first girl in the first row by the door, who got up and left the room, panic blanching her features. A few minutes later, she returned, eyes downcast, face composed, and demurely took her seat. Proper comportment, in short. No way to read that! Obviously she had been warned not to distract the rest of us.

And Mary Robert crooked that finger at the next girl, and the scene replayed itself exactly. And the next girl. And the next girl. One by one, in alphabetical order, all forty girls in Honors Senior English were called out. All but me. When my turn came, Mary Robert looked me in the eye, turned deliberately to the girl behind me, and crooked a finger at her instead. I settled back into my chair. By the end of ninety minutes, everyone but me knew what was going on, and no one would meet my pleading eyes as she came back into the room.

Each girl had been invited to join the convent. When she refused, each girl had been offered a fairly generous scholarship to attend the college run by this order of nuns. All but me. They didn't want me, not in their convent and not in their college. Years later, I told this story to a Protestant friend, who was not amused but transparently horrified. I couldn't figure out why: it was one of those baffling moments when a familiar funny tale falls short. Protestants can be inscrutable too, for the Catholic bred.

"Didn't you feel rejected?" she explained. "I think that's awful. Singling you out like that! No matter what you had done, that was cruel. And . . . what *did* you do? What had you done?"

Cruel? My stock had skyrocketed. I was famous. Everybody laughed and cheered, as if I had won some convent school equivalent of the Nobel Peace Prize. It had been glorious, so glorious in fact that I secretly suspected that Mary Robert had done it deliberately, as something like a very complicated favor, one final cryptic comment before sending me off to college: "The church has no need of you, God doesn't want you, go in peace to love and serve The World." And I did. I felt not rejected but liberated, liberated beyond question: once and for all I was free of that great and terrible threat, "God's call." God himself would never dare to disagree with Sister Mary Robert. I shed religion as quickly, as easily, as I shed that wretched navy blue blazer and plaid, pleated uniform skirt, the whole nine yards of coarsely woven twill.

Which suggests, I suppose, that God is not only crazy but also exceedingly patient and monumentally nonlinear. I graduated from college in 1972, fully equipped and raring to go, an eighty-year plan in hand. Like most of us at that age, I was omnipotent, omniscient, immortal, invulnerable, and skinny. I outgrew it. We all do. And then what? As omnipotent omniscience starts fading to grey, the multiple demands of our kids and our careers start scrambling our lives into chaos, into a weariness that haunts us. The time bind ties our soul in knots. Once we had all the right answers. Now we'd be happy to have even a couple of the right questions.

This book recounts my battles with two questions that are, if not the right questions, at least good classic ones: Is God real? And, So what if God is real? What difference would *that* make? If God matters, if there is a God who matters, then any of us ought to find God at work within the ordinary perplexities of our own lives. For me, or for the sake of the story given me to tell here, there are two such problems: the work/family conflict and the directions of my own career. The discernment of "call," as Christians say, and with it some complementary vision of my own moral obligations. Alas, I don't have easy answers to give away, no magic wands or patent medicine in brown glass bottles. It is our questions and not our answers that matter the most, our persistent doubts and our skeptical incredulity that keep our lives lively and susceptible to grace. In short, nothing of the Holy that makes much difference will ever be trammeled in the nets of intellect, no matter how fine the mesh we cast. I know. I tried. Let me tell you how hard I tried . . .

But that's getting ahead of myself. First I have to offer thanks. Around here at least, women tell stories to women all of the time. Sitting on park benches, standing at the sides of soccer games, waiting for trains, meeting for lunch: we swap stories. To get to know someone is above all to hear her stories, in an oral tradition as rich, as long, and as wise as any to be found. So first and foremost, I need to acknowledge the blessing of that tradition and the grace bestowed by women who nodded and laughed and so often demanded that I should write a book, so often insisted that my stories are their stories too with simple substitution of inconsequent details. So here it is, ladies, my version of the ordinary story that all of you said one of us should take time to write down. I could not, would not have written without your voices holding me like hands. In all our different circumstances, amidst the unruly details and quirky demands of our particular lives, all of us struggle endlessly to turn the chaos into dancing.

In what follows I have changed names, disguised identities, and left many significant individuals and institutions nameless. I have done so because I respect others' privacy and yet also wish to recount my experience as I experienced it and not in any impartial or objective way. But mostly I have done so because the literally historical details of my story add very little except some potential for local gossip, which I would prefer not to encourage. Our lives are shaped by those who love us, T. S. Eliot says somewhere, and by those who refuse to love us. He is right. And so, thanks are due to all of those whose shadowy, edited images populate these pages. I am glad to be who I am, with my life in the shape it has.

Thanks are due as well to those kind folks who took time to read even the longer, messier drafts that lie behind this neatly printed book: Dabney J. Carr III, Zahava Davidson, Jane Garrett, Nancy Gordon, Stanley Hauerwas, Bob Horine, Deborah Koomjian, Charles

Long, JoElyn Newcomb and several of her friends and their mothers as well, Mary Neuhaus, Philip Rule S.J., Barbara Froman Syverud, Warren Wallace, and Sally-Ann Wolcott. Their encouragement was crucial. I am also grateful for how Stanley Hauerwas and James Griffiss have steadfastly encouraged my literary inquiry into the horizons of narrative theology, scholarly accounts of which Jim has published in *Anglican Theological Review*. An earlier draft of Chapter One was published in 1993 by *Iris*, the women's studies journal at the University of Virginia, in a special issue on women in the academy. I enjoyed that enormously. I'm pleased to acknowledge their support, their permission to reprint, and Chip Tucker's hand in facilitating that connection and his encouragement at a crucial early point. Late in the game, Sherri Curry spent untold hours editing the final manuscript for what film makers call "continuity." Her pages of notes were a priceless gift. Debra Farrington, editorial director at Morehouse, has been a delight to know; particular thanks are due to Jane Garrett, my editor at Knopf, for introducing us.

There are two teachers I need to name, two beloved men who took up where the nuns lefts off. In 1969, Philip Rule S.J. introduced me both to Samuel Taylor Coleridge and to the study of autobiography, brilliantly demonstrating both how permeable the boundaries among poetry, storytelling, and theology, and how writers manage the technical challenges involved in working in the margins of genre. John Wright, who directed my doctoral dissertation on Coleridge's autobiography and his theology at the University of Michigan, introduced me both to William Blake and to mystic philosophy. He insisted that even the most formal and rigorous of philosophic systems be read artistically, as unfolding with the dramatic aesthetic compression and imaginative character of sonnets. And there is no story, no poem, that is not also an argument about what is real, and how we know, and how the world works. What is theology, after all, but the effort to find God's part in the story, to see, to find the trace of grace woven like an elusive gold thread into the fabrics of plot and causal pattern and ordinary lives?

Virginia Woolf argues, in *A Room of One's Own,* that women will inevitably revise the conventional boundaries dividing one genre of writing from the next, because these boundaries reflect the creative choices of men struggling to represent masculine experience. She is right, of course. But I came of age as a writer and as a woman utterly confident that such re-vision of genre has always been under way and that the need for new literary forms is an ongoing part of both human experience and cultural history. It was an extraordinary blessing to have been introduced to the literary and cultural heritage from this inclusivist, visionary perspective, right from the beginning. Such a fluid, flexible sense of form is, of course, characteristically American.

From this perspective, narrative theology, properly so-called, goes all the way back to the earliest written texts we have and descends in a continuous, unbroken, vibrant tradition. Whether as a mom or as a poet or as a theologian, then, I am doing the same work and from the same place: telling stories that are not original in the sense of simply mine but rather originary, primal, the oft-told tales told again, here and now, because the night is dark, the fire warm, and the company weary of work and glad thereby to bide a while and listen. Stories have a truth to tell that can be told in no other way; and we need, in each generation, to find new ways to retell the great improbable tale of God's presence in our lives.

Above all I am grateful for the principal characters of this tale: my husband Warren and my three teenaged children, Tim, Carol, and Mark. There is much more to them than their reflections in these stories, but I am very grateful nonetheless for their permission to reveal so much and for their generosity when I disappeared into my study for the necessary long stints toward the end of work on a long manuscript. At Warren's insistence and with his help, I have always had what Woolf demands: a room of my own and the economic freedom to work, a freedom secured not by independent wealth (as Woolf proposed) but by his quiet, witty, unflagging recognition that my writing is as central a moral obligation as any in this household.

So maybe God's craziness has a certain logic of its own. Be warned, that's all. Don't say I didn't warn you. The Holy One is wholly unscrupulous.

PROLOGUE
As Angels Dance

MARY HAD MOVED. AND WHERE THE STATUE HAD ALWAYS STOOD, BLANDLY surveying my third-grade class, now there was a shrine (I supposed it was a shrine) to Vatican II, going on in Rome in those days. From her new vantage point on the wide grey sill, Mary could see out the window; but I was not tall enough to read the newspaper clippings posted in her place. One, outlined in blue pen, said something about women. But it was too high, and time allowed away from our seats was far too short. Angrily, I wondered why the nun had posted this stuff where we couldn't see it. And then I wondered, 'til she poked me with her ruler for staring blankly out the window, Do nuns hang up such stuff for other nuns? Or do they hope the pastor might come in and see?

One of the purposes of Vatican II, she was explaining, was to put an end to such foolish theology as had wondered how many angels could dance on the head of a pin.

Why put an end to that? The nascent philosopher in me leapt for joy. Surely it would depend upon how they were dancing. How many aunts and uncles and cousins had fit around the edges of Aunt Laurine's dining room last weekend, doing the bunny hop? The hokey-pokey takes a circle: that's lots of wasted space. Or what about how my parents danced when cousin Kathleen got married? They had the whole floor to themseves—everybody else stopped and watched. Of course angels would never dance like *that*. Even though everybody clapped. Not angels.

And was the head of a pin the pointy or the other end?

She poked me with her ruler again. I supposed it was sacrilegious for her to depose Mary like that. Maybe if the pastor came in she'd get in trouble.

> Walking, like prose, has a definite aim. It is an act directed at something we wish to reach. . . . The dance is quite another matter. It is, of course, a system of actions; but of actions whose end is in themselves. It goes nowhere. If it pursues an object, it is only an ideal object . . . But please note this very simple observation, that however different the dance may be from walking and utilitarian movements, it uses the same organs, the same bones, the same muscles, only differently coordinated and aroused.
>
> —PAUL VALERY, *from "Poetry and Abstract Thought"*

> *Labour is blossoming or dancing where*
> *The body is not bruised to pleasure soul,*
> *Nor beauty born out of its own despair,*
> *Nor blear-eyed wisdom out of midnight oil.*
> *O chestnut-tree, great-rooted blossomer,*
> *Are you the leaf, the blossom or the bole?*
> *O body swayed to music, O brightening glance,*
> *How can we know the dancer from the dance?*
>
> —WILLIAM BUTLER YEATS, *from "Among School Children"*

Let us consider what we do when we leap. We first resist the gravitating power by an act purely voluntary, and then by another act, voluntary in part, we yield to it in order to light on the spot which we had previously proposed to ourselves. Now let a man watch his mind while he is composing; or, to take a still more common case, while he is trying to recollect a name;

and he will find the process completely analogous. . . . There are evidently two powers at work, which relatively to each other are active and passive; and this is not possible without an intermediate faculty, which is at once both active and passive. (In philosophical language we must denominate this intermediate faculty in all its degrees and determinations the *imagination*. But in common language, and especially on the subject of poetry, we appropriate the name to a superior degree of the faculty, joined to a superior voluntary controul over it.)

—SAMUEL TAYLOR COLERIDGE, *from Biographia Literaria*

1

Fiat Lux
APRIL, 1979

IT WAS A LEAP ALL RIGHT: AROUND THE PERIMETER OF THAT ENORMOUS bed, down the hall, past the footed tub with its patched-in shower head. Surely I had not touched down once. I sat shaking on the cold hexagon-tile floor, leaning back against the small radiator. I had, I had . . . what? What had I done? I had rolled over. My breasts hurt so much that then I sat up again, recoiling in pain. And then this nausea.

Oh damn. A pattern. Gastritis again. It must be back. A couple of days before, we had gone out to eat at a familiar campus place; and after dinner I had felt the same sudden wave of nausea. Panicked, I ran to the street rather than try to wend my way back to the bathroom. But in the cold late-winter air, I was suddenly fine. Cigarette smoke, we had decided. But as the radiator softly clanged to life, I admitted that this nausea was getting chronic. Nothing tasted right. Everything left me slightly queasy.

Slowly, dimly, the pain in my breasts repeated its wordless question. I could hardly climb stairs without holding both my breath and my breasts. Who was I fooling? Pigheaded denial had always aroused that gastritis. I tried to feel for lumps, but it hurt too much. I closed my eyes against the nausea, thinking pH-corrected thoughts.

And I remembered our packing for a spring break vacation, just ten days before. I complained of *mittelsmirch*. Warren said nothing. But later he tossed aside the contraceptives I had set out.

"You're pregnant already," he laughed. I didn't. Yes, we were planning a child—but at some time in the far uncertain future. *Me, pregnant now?* Nonsense. I knew a metaphysical impossibility when I saw one. I packed the contraceptives, which we dutifully used.

The radiator clanged loudly: surely soon there would be heat. Me? Pregnant? Who? No. I'm a hotshot young professor with a heavy schedule: I don't have time for this. Furthermore, English professors are balding men in their fifties, with pipes and herringbone tweed jackets—and not, for God's sake, PREGNANT WOMEN. Oh, but in some dark, beleaguered corner of my soul, a hitherto-silent voice cheered wildly, a warm, inarticulate delight making a primitive, potent, sexual claim. A brilliant flower opened slowly and with exquisite grace, a time-lapse Georgia O'Keeffe. I sat flat on the cold floor, bewildered. Ah yes, I thought, Motherhood 101: queasy and conflicted at five A.M.

The radiator was warming at last, but now I was shaking too hard to lean back against it. I dragged myself and this growing panic into the living room. Warren covered me with a bathrobe and brought tea.

"Could I be pregnant?" I asked. His serious medical professor look dissolved. He beamed. He laughed—loudly. He reminded me of his earlier prediction, and he laughed again. I wondered whether I could heave my teacup at him without splashing myself, and if so whether there was more tea in the kitchen. Then I noticed that in fact I held a real tea cup with a saucer—should I fling the saucer, Frisbee style?—from *Warren,* who so emphatically preferred mugs to cups and saucers. An old argument between us, long settled: server's choice. What? Just in time, he sobered; and we sat there staring at me. Slowly, I warmed up.

I'm Not Pregnant: I'm Crazy

I wasn't even late yet. Surely this was all a mistake. On the way in to campus, I bought a jug of antacid, the brand recently taste-tested in the *New England Journal of Medicine*. Gastritis, no doubt about it.

What about the full professor of gynecology who had so solemnly, so gently told me that my test results were "incompatible with fertility"? What about that, huh? Huh? Treatable, he had said—but don't wait until you are 35 before you start. I zipped the jug into my briefcase and strode on, resolving to buy myself a herringbone tweed jacket.

I walked into my first spring quarter class and thought, "These were each someone's baby." My eyes filled with tears. Shock and outrage brimmed in me as well: tears withered, blood drained from my face. But then I blushed and fumbled and couldn't find my voice or my notes. I should have been able to do that introductory presentation in my sleep. But I was, heaven help me, not asleep. This was not just a first-day nightmare. No, this was certainly real. Twenty-five ex-babies were sitting in a circle staring at me.

I handed out the syllabus, read their names off a list, and let them go. I crept queasily back to my office, determined more than ever to get control of myself. I drank some Mylanta (regular mint). I drank some tea (Keemun). If thinking I might be pregnant did this to me, what would the real thing be like? Or is this the real thing, and if so what does that portend? And I drank some more tea, and I realized that if I were not pregnant then I would mourn this phantom child who had driven me crazy for days. I sat in a huddle, terrified of being pregnant and equally terrified that I might not be. I drank some more Mylanta, straight from the jug.

My abdomen soon felt leaden, and I was sure I would menstruate momentarily. And a week passed, and another week passed, and this insanity continued. Warren began calling every few hours to know if anything had "happened." I stared unabashedly at every pregnant woman I saw, and the world was suddenly full of them. What about childbirth? I remembered each of the awful stories I had heard at cousins' wedding showers, then fought the urge to run screaming down the street—and then panicked all the more profoundly. I don't have urges like that. I'm a rational, scholarly sort, an intelligent woman who makes well-planned decisions and copes adeptly with contingencies and complications. I know how to lead my life. Furthermore, for eighteen months we have been planning a family—or at least planning to start trying, prior to the expected infertility work-up. What then is going on here?

If this is not pregnancy, I worried, it is probably a nervous breakdown. Every sad story brought tears. I could not open the newspaper without finding some morbid account of maimed, abused, or dying children. Strangers on the train unnerved me with gruesome tales. One description of the lability of pregnancy neatly matched everything I knew about schizophrenia: women, kids, and crazies, beyond a doubt. Sudden, "inappropriate" responses were nearly unstoppable, as if my professional demeanor had evaporated. Obsessive thinking—"Am I pregnant? Am I? Am I?"—interfered with concentration. No line of thought could be pursued: they all got away, sometimes mid-sentence; colleagues stared.

"But of course it is not really this bad," I told myself. "It just feels this bad because mature judgment and a broad perspective are impossible."

"Or maybe it is this bad," I countered, "and I just don't see it." Having been professionally trained in the philosophic pursuit of my tail, I could keep this up for days. And I did.

In comparison with all this, the classic nausea was far less disconcerting—although as the days inched past, my stomach problems rapidly developed from chronic to acute. Or maybe, I worried, worrying about being pregnant was in fact giving me the ulcer I had flirted with all these years. My mother had always teased me that with a stomach like mine, I'd never know when I was pregnant. One morning that spring I lay in bed, tears running down my face as I listened to Warren get the crackers I needed to eat before I dare lift my head. Our eyes met as he handed them to me; he startled lightly.

"Your crackers," he said, his inflection proposing an apostrophe if I were willing to admit the possibility of a verb on the semantic horizon. I laughed so hard I choked on the silly things, spewing crumbs all over the bedsheets. He looked down at me in mild-mannered professorial surprise at my misreading of his wholly innocent comment.

"Well, that's what you get," he said, "sleeping with crumbs . . ."

I nailed him with a pillow. And then I got up and got sick.

Reading Lists

At one point during the endless days of wondering if I were pregnant, Warren looked up an exotic, early, expensive pregnancy test. If we really *had* to know, we could. But we decided that we would be embarrassed to ask one of his colleagues to run it for us. It would look anxious. And if we were not pregnant, then someone would know about our anxiety. But as The Date moved further and further into the past, the truth became plain enough. All the signs and symptoms checked out. It became important to be certain on our own, to be certain as people had been certain for centuries before us. Lab results are convenient affirmation. But one also has a body, which is in its own way quite articulate. I felt passionately, stubbornly committed to believing my body, to making up my own mind that I was pregnant before submitting to some test.

But finally came the day when I could submit a morning urine sample, get a blood test, and thereby get myself established with an obstetrician. Unfortunately, we had had asparagus with dinner the night before. The urine smelled awful. I almost spilled the precious stuff when I leapt off the toilet to vomit. Warren, who was showering at the time, struggled but failed to contain his amusement. I clutched the rim of the toilet and imagined headlines about the police finding him naked in a pool of his own blood. Crimes of passion. Dementia of pregnancy. I flushed and made some tea and accepted his humble and guilty apology with no grace whatsoever. If I am truly pregnant, I thought, it will be a long nine months.

I delivered the holy stuff to the HMO clinic, then headed—still fasting—across the street to the local public library. Since I was certain I was pregnant, since this lab test was just a formality, I should of course begin where one always begins: a bibliography. But there were no stools by the card catalogue, no chairs in sight anywhere: I muttered to myself about community libraries and exerted all my scholarly self-discipline to fight off the dizzy nausea. I climbed the stairs to the appropriate ranges, then sat on the floor trying to force the wrought-iron railings to stand still. I was not about to faint in the public library! But the only way to combat such lightheadedness is to lie flat—and I was not about to do that either.

Once the railings stopped shimmering, I went to look for the books. But they were all gone. Other people wanted them. What a thought! I could not imagine who. Emboldened by this news, I walked over to the local franchise bookstore, where the manager offered me a chair and a glass of water. I really should have stopped for breakfast, but eating felt out of the question. What I needed most was a reading list.

But here I might be seen. What if—I selected a few likely titles, then edged quickly down the aisle to stand by some safer category than "Pregnancy and Child Care." I kept the yet-unexamined selections spine-down, face-in under my arm. How would I get through the checkout? Oh, no! I hadn't thought of that! I scanned the racks and grabbed the first safe title I saw, a safe title beneath which to hide my choices for the exposed moment when they would sit on the countertop. It was the Dover edition of Blake's *Songs of Innocence,* shelved under "The Occult." What would Professor Wright say! I laughed, and in one bright labile flash Wright's whole seminar appeared in consciousness.

Fortified by the memory, I stood for a moment in the aisle remembering a seminar paper I had abandoned. In Blake's *The Book of Thel,* a young virgin laments the transience of her life. Various naturally transient elements—a cloud, a clump of clay in the road, a flower—respond to her lament. They urge that her life will achieve meaning only if she gives of herself to others. In the end, she flees. Critical consensus condemned her for fleeing, for refusing the self-sacrifice inherent in mature feminine sexuality.

But one of the supposed models of mature womanhood is a lily of the valley, who willingly allows the innocent lamb to crop its fragrant flowers. Except, of course, that lily of the valley contains potent amounts of digitalis. Such an altruistic, self-sacrificing flower would poison the heart of any lamb who accepted its gift. I wanted to write a paper arguing that Thel rejects not mature feminine sexuality but rather various images of self-destruction and self-denial. Unfortunately, Blake was as ideologically misogynist as most men of his day. But there was no question that he denounced self-destruction parading as morality and maturity. Furthermore, Blake elsewhere describes the effects of such behavior as "poisonous."

I spent weeks on the phone and in the library, seeking good evidence that Blake believed that lilies of the valley are poisonous to sheep. The relatively easy first step in such an inquiry is to verify that they are poisonous to sheep. Is the digitalis bio-available? Or is it broken down by sheep digestion? Sheep have been domesticated for millennia: somebody, somewhere, would know if you could kill your whole flock by letting them graze on *Convallaria majalis*. And facts that somebody knows and others need to know eventually show up in print. But where? There would be no point in tracking down the details of Blake's knowledge of sheep, after all, if in fact the critters can eat all the lilies they want without harm.

What this means, of course, is that I had to ask, over and over again, whether lilies of the valley are poisonous to sheep. Such questions are hard on one's professional self-image at such a tender age. Even my friends among the reference librarians laughed at me: the Rackham Graduate Library at The University of Michigan is not noted for its holdings in animal husbandry. That sort of stuff belongs over in East Lansing, at Michigan State. When they were done laughing, they wanted to know why I wanted to know. The more I tried summarizing Blake's symbolism, the more I tried repeating my argument, the less comfortable I felt. I bogged down altogether one dreadful afternoon, trying to summarize the poem to the switchboard operator at the University of Illinois School of Veterinary Medicine.

"Is there a veterinary medical library?" I asked. "Or a reference desk where collections include animal husbandry?" She connected me to a phone line into the sheep barns, where a gruff annoyed voice insisted that any fool knew that the flowers were poisonous. I asked for the title of a reference book to which I could refer—or the name of a library?—one cannot footnote to a voice on the phone, after all—and the man hung up on me.

All I had were crumbs. A headnote in a pharmacology book explained that lilies of the valley contain enough digitalis to rank among effective herbalist remedies for congestive heart failure, and to have been recognized as a potentially poisonous heart tonic since antiquity. A reference text in the history of gardening lamented that wild lilies of the valley have been eradicated from cultivated areas of Europe for centuries—but never said why. Various Blake scholars noted that Blake knew herbalist lore well, but without documenting their claim: how was I to find Blake's sources and check them for lilies of the valley? And even if he knew about lilies of the valley and digitalis, did he know about sheep? I could not find the gold-standard proof I wanted before facing the hostile scorn and ritual combat of seminar presentations—especially since I was taking on a well-established critical consensus, and from a feminist viewpoint no less. And I was running out of time. After the guy in the sheep barn hung up on me, I found myself unwilling to pursue the matter further. This whole business of poisonous self-sacrifice was too complicated.

Rousing myself from memories of Thel, I got through the checkout line without incident. I was only mildly embarrassed by the fact that I already had two illuminated versions of Blake's *Songs of Innocence,* and three more copies that were text-only. I didn't need this book. Maybe it could be a Christmas present for someone? I stashed the pregnancy books deep in my briefcase and treated myself to a ride home on the train—flipping idly through this new copy of Blake.

It was as if I had never read these poems before. His *Songs of Experience* played their extraordinary counterpoint in my head as the trained swayed along. Never had I felt so keenly the truth of Blake's impassioned arguments about childhood, about psychological development, about denied passions, about a warped society transmitting the lethal disorders that arise from its own repressions. I wondered, with a heart-sickening thud, if now every literary work would be different, if now I would have to reread everything.

In comparison to Blake, the prosaic pregnancy books I had so furtively selected were unredeemable trash. I had learned as much biology and physiology in fifth-grade sex-ed. "The pregnant woman" was portrayed throughout as fat, whiny, self-indulgent, and irrationally, stupidly anxious. She was a needy, insecure "other" whose petty needs the authors condescended to meet only so that she would be better motivated to obey them.

Poor Thel. She had a point. So where was I to go for the books I needed? What bibliography was going to guide me through this next project? And in my head, lines appeared:

I may not hope from outward forms to win
The passion and the life, whose fountains are within!
O Lady! we receive but what we give . . .
  And would we aught behold, of higher worth
Than that inanimate cold world allowed
To the poor loveless ever-anxious crowd,
  Ah! from the soul itself must issue forth
A light, a glory, a fair luminous cloud
    Enveloping the Earth—
And from the soul itself must there be sent
  A sweet and potent voice, of its own birth,
Of all sweet sounds the life and element!

It was hard to inhale: a repeat of that heart-sickening thud had closed my airways altogether. And Coleridge's voice continued, this time in prose: "It could not be intellectually more evident without becoming morally less effective; without counteracting its own end by sacrificing the *life* of faith to the cold mechanism of a worthless because compulsory assent."

And from that small dark corner, the hitherto-silent voice cheered wildly again, the flower preened her feathers and sang.

"Do you set upon a golden bough?" I asked of her, not understanding why. There was no reply. Enough and more than enough, I decided—settling on the couch for a nap. It was late afternoon, I had eaten almost nothing all day, and I was obviously incapable of serious work.

Just as oblivion settled over me, the phone rang.

I was pregnant.

Telling Times

When my father was dying and my mother was after me about grandchildren and I was fighting desperately to finish my dissertation, I had told her I was infertile. That was, after all, what we had been told. I just left off the part about possible treatment. We were driving together on a crowded urban expressway, and I hoped that her need to watch traffic would mute her expression of grief at this news.

"God provides," she assured me, with her unflappable, matriarchal, Irish faith in the triumph of all things female. Men—even full professors holding endowed chairs—were not worthy of regard in such matters. What could a man possibly know? Such tests measured only the feeblest realms of reality.

"Just wait," she promised, and pulled out to pass a semitrailer.

I winced as I realized my mistake: now she would pray. Sophisticated theologians may have discarded the notion that God is omnipotent and omniscient, but there is no possible question about the omnipotence and omniscience of the late great Grandma Murphy. I didn't hold much stock in God, but Katie Murphy is altogether another matter. I am her namesake, the umpteenth in a line of Kates, heir of dozens and dozens of highly improbable but quite real stories about friends and relations praying to Katie Murphy and then finding a lost needle in some haystack or at least retrieving a lost wedding ring from a condominium dumpster. She is a whiz at finding things: if I had a fertile egg hiding anywhere, she would find it. And then generations of ancestral Catherines would directly persuade my pituitary to behave itself more productively, the better to achieve for themselves yet another woman in the lineage. I could see it all in an instant. Mom was going to pray to her mother? Oh no!

Warren and I had always continued to use contraceptives, just to be safe. But my mother's omnipotent Mother Almighty is not a well-behaved Greek axiom. She has no respect whatever for statistics and probability and the stability of causal patterns. She is not an Enlightenment deity: logic has never prevailed in rural Ireland. I clutched my knees together.

Until that moment, I had never given much thought to the news that I was infertile. When we got that news, we were twenty-three and ambitious for other things. I did not want children. I had decided that much when I was ten, sitting on the library steps coping with a nosebleed. I did not want to be a mother. I wanted to make a name for myself. I would be a scholar when I grew up, a physicist, and I would go on space flights to do my physics.

I figured it all out, there on the library steps. I would get into the space program by publishing under my initials. That way no one would ever know I was a woman. I would be the best physicist in the country. By then, they would be sending real scientists up, not just test pilots. But they would want the very best physicist and so they would call me. They might be mad when they found out I was a woman, but they would have to let me go anyhow. They'd be embarrassed then to say no. I had it all mapped, sitting there in the July sunlight. It was 1960: the times felt right for dreams like these. All I had to do was work hard and hide the fact of my femininity. What a snap. (This was, of course, before I discovered sex.) My premenarchal hyper-estrogenic nosebleed ended, and I went back into the library and checked out a biography of Madame Curie.

As I neared thirty, I discovered two additional facts about my own reproductive capabilities. First, human beings are not actually equipped to make rational decisions about having babies. No sober, analytical person would freely choose on logical grounds to have a child. The burdens, the risks, the expense: how impossible. All we are really equipped to decide is whether or not to have sex. And that's an easy call.

The second thing I learned is that I was, despite all probability, going to have a baby. The collective grandmothers Kate, rallied by Grandma Murphy, had proven the nuns right: all it takes is a single instance of unprotected sex.

Shortly before the fit of my clothes was going to declare matters for me, about a third of the way through the pregnancy, we began to make The Announcement. My mother leapt to her feet and screamed and starting crying: I wondered if our immigrant Japanese neighbors would call the police. Reactions at school were no less vivid, albeit the volume was set a bit lower.

"Have you heard my news?" I ventured nonchalantly to one of the modernists as we sat together in the department lounge, sorting through the debris from our mailboxes. "I'm going to have a baby." He stared at me, speechless for far too long.

"You know," he said in a tight little voice. "I can't do that. *I* write books. My wife, my wife, *she* has the babies. I have—books." And he went on to talk about foods that nauseated her, about how much she slept, about how incapacitated she became, about how inconvenient all of it was, how pregnancy and babies had terribly interfered with his writing of books. I smiled and nodded and watched him become progressively more distraught.

My second attempt was, I felt, a bit safer. I should never have resolved to tell the first person who came into the lounge for mail and coffee. I spoke to one of the other women, single and probably a dozen years older than I. Her face fell.

"Oh my God *no!*" she said. "Is this a mistake?"

"I don't think so," I replied mildly, but meeting her dismay squarely, with the confident manner honed over years of ritual combat in graduate seminars. I held her gaze for a moment, waiting for her to speak again; and when she didn't, I walked out. In the dark hall, I felt an overwhelming surge of combativeness. I also realized I had left my briefcase in the lounge, and with it my wallet and keys. I stalked out of the building anyhow: I was going for a walk lest I slug someone.

That night, the phone rang during dinner: the other senior woman, also single and older.

"I hear you are pregnant," she said, questioningly. "Are you going to get an abortion? And why didn't you tell *me*?"

It was a brief and gracious conversation, but I did not return to the table.

So this was how it was to be. Okay then. I made no further announcements, and no one else asked me about the matter. The spring term was almost over anyhow, and my scandalous lapse from Academic Womanhood apparently did not merit much repetition on whatever amounted to the gossip circuit on campus. When I reappeared in October, almost eight months pregnant, no one would ask me then about having an abortion. I hoped.

I remembered, reluctantly, my first interview with my advisor in the fall of my first year in graduate school, here in the same department where I was now an assistant professor. We shook hands, I sat down, and he asked if I was married. I replied that I expected to marry sometime in the next year or so.

"Do you expect to have children?" he demanded. I stared at him a moment, so astounded and offended that words failed me. This man's office mate sat behind him and to my right, directly in my line of sight. He had not glanced up. Steadied for the moment by the protective presence of a witness, I collected my wits enough to choose to make no verbal reply at all, to let my startled stare open out into a clearly deliberate silence.

"If you expect to get anywhere in this profession," my advisor continued, "you had better be prepared to strip naked in front of any search committee, to show them the scars of your tubal ligation. This profession is not open to women with children!" I met his eyes and let my silence hold; the office mate continued placidly reading. But I felt a dark purple flush begin accumulating on my face. Finally, I asked him to review both my course selections for the fall and the worksheet illustrating my preparation for the comprehensive exams in the spring.

"You want four *graduate* courses?" he objected with sarcastic incredulity. "You can take undergraduate courses for credit, you know. Don't you think this is too much?"

"Obviously not," I retorted. "That's how I filled out the form. Do *you* think it's too much?" With a contemptuous snort, he scribbled his signature, tossed the papers across the desk at me, and returned to his typewriter. I walked out without another word. I did not report the incident: the office mate had heard, even if he had not looked up; and furthermore, there was no way to know whether my advisor was expressing an attitude he agreed with, or whether he was simply warning me—as one junior person to another, even more junior person—about a misogyny that he had observed permeating the profession. I knew better than to look for trouble, and so I said nothing to anyone.

I began instead the process of transferring to the University of Michigan, where programs in my major interest were staffed by far more senior people than this jerk of an assistant professor. And years later, I chortled gleefully at the poetic justice of my return as an assistant professor to replace him: he had been denied tenure.

But the memory of that interview returned to haunt me. I told myself that I was being silly, I reminded myself of all I was reading about the lability of pregnancy, I told myself over and over that I had gotten through the remainder of that master's year without incident. But meanwhile, I kept my suit jackets on to hide the safety pins across the open back zippers of my skirts, and I culled from my wardrobe those blouses that now gaped across my growing breasts.

I had never seen a pregnant professor. I had never even seen a married woman professor—except one philosophy professor, in my undergraduate college. She had been untenured; she resigned prior to her hearing. October would be interesting indeed.

Choices and Dreams

But I brooded a lot that spring, both in body and in spirit. If my ordinary feminine sexuality was somehow taboo in this profession, then nuts to them. I had never wanted or expected an academic job anyhow. And if this feisty anger was but more estrogenic lability, that was fine too. I would be sure to hang onto it. In Ann Arbor, I had watched a mother mallard chase off a dumb but innocently friendly German shepherd who had ambled curiously down the riverbank toward her flock of tiny yellow ducklings. She grabbed his nose in her beak, beat her wings over his face, and hung on while he ran, yipping, half a block back from the waterfront. "There's motherhood for you!" I had thought, laughing. But I remembered her now. And I remembered other things as well from those days in graduate school.

The winter that I achieved candidacy—passing orals despite choking on my coffee, getting my dissertation prospectus approved by various committees—my campus mailbox started to fill with Placement Center announcements: meetings, workshops, all-day seminars, weekend-long events. Graduate school 999: Sell Yourself. We scruffy mid-seventies Ph.D. candidates, formerly '60s undergrads, were to be dressed for success and taught a new set of scholarly skills: resumes, cover letters, interview techniques, dossier design, Statements of Scholarly Plans, networking the old-boy circuit by soliciting the help of well-connected senior professors. "Soliciting" on behalf of our beautiful young brains. The English department itself chimed in, offering analyses and presentations and helpful hints to standing-room-only crowds in the biggest classrooms Haven Hall had to offer.

I stood, briefly, in the back of one, near the door—as close, in fact, as the crowd would allow to a latecomer. We were in the same lecture hall where I first had met all these folks, when the famous Professor Sheridan himself had showed us how to grade papers—the department's one effort at teacher education before throwing us to the wolves. Once again, I craned to see around the shoulders of the men. Unlike last time, the man up front in his herringbone tweeds and khaki twills offered no easy tricks with red pens.

The air was thick with anxiety and ambition, and the message was the same one that had laced my mailbox for weeks: Being smart won't work this time. We were all smart, after all. But far less than ten percent of us would make tenure in this profession: the lucky fraction, not the better part. And "making it" includes an exclusive diet of remedial literacy to the desperate victims of a collapsed system of secondary education: perhaps six hundred pages to grade each week, for far less than half the starting salary of a Chicago bus driver.

Per hour, I would earn far more packing grocery bags than in such a job—and I would have evenings free for reading. My sister was an executive at a big Chicago grocery chain: maybe I might have a chance at service manager after a few years. But that would interfere with free evenings for study. Or if I used yet other family connections, I might become an apprentice electrician—did they allow women? The skilled trades earned more than bus drivers. My father-in-law was a master tool-and-die maker in the proud and somber tradition of Central European craftsmen. What would he say about these men around whose shoulders I could not see?

I left before the panel of speakers was introduced. Whatever I did for a living, it had to support me and yet leave time for my work. The academic market had too little to offer.

Graduate school had been increasingly tainted with a bitter, destructive competitiveness. We did not argue with some intellectual equivalent of good sportsmanship, later to shake hands and go out for a beer. It was as if we were fighting for our very lives, as if defeat in logic or ignorance of fact were shameful death. I hated it. I no longer could remember what I had enjoyed about being a student. I especially hated how well I fought when cornered, and what that cruel skill showed me about myself. I could pretend a moral superiority to that sour-smelling anxiety, but I too had based all too much of my life on one narrow set of skills—now honed to a very fine edge, while other parts of my soul languished.

After seven long hard years at universities and brutal summer sessions to contract my program to match Warren's, I had gotten so adept at deferred gratification that I was no longer sure what desire felt like. So if anyone threatened what was left of me, I was quite capable of quick and nimble counterattack. Women were chronically underestimated and dismissed, after all, and I had learned how to make such blindness into a fatal mistake. Very few underestimated or patronized me more than once. Although I had earned myself some enemies, particularly among those who were close scholarly rivals, I also had at least my share of good friends—especially among the likes of medievalists and Americanists, folks who were safely remote from my own specialty. I had, I felt, some measure of quiet respect within the program generally. And carrying the weight of that sterile, futile, costly success left me feeling dirty.

Thereafter, I pitched all such announcements and turned away from the knots of job market gossip among the other doctoral candidates. I did not establish a dossier, I solicited no letters or phone calls, I sketched no Statements of Scholarly Plans. I made no announcements to my faculty or my classmates, but my feelings were clear. I would not seek an academic job. I would do my dissertation—there, at least, joyous light shone in my life—and then I would look about me in the world and see what was possible. *Then.* Now would be for now, for my dissertation, for pages of manuscript scattered with breadcrumbs and coffee drips, for decks of 3×5s, for hours and hours at the keyboard of my new avocado green electric typewriter facing the back window overlooking the little creek where the ducks swam up to mate each spring. I would bake bread, brew big pots of soup, write, and watch the sunset behind the Huron River cliffs. I would settle down to my one, first, last, real scholarly project.

And as I set up the file folders and outlines and bibliographies of that project, I also began a long black grief for the parties I had skipped, for the vacations I had not taken, for all the countless sacrifices behind the dream of scholarship. And the writing went well, and my research went well.

At the only really unnerving trouble with my research, I dreamed that Coleridge himself walked into my apartment, sat in my favorite armchair, chuckled quietly at me, and told me to keep working. Tears and anger competed for my face as Coleridge and I stared at each other across more than a century and a half. Goddammit, what did he mean by "hylozoism"? I had searched high and low for a definition of that word. And his comments about Spinoza and Descartes were off the wall. What was he getting at? Who could make sense of this man, and why was he smiling at me so warmly, and why couldn't I talk to him? What good is it to know when I am dreaming, if I can't do anything with the dream? When I woke up that morning, I took the day off to go hiking in the arboretum.

Exhausted by more than just the long hike, I slept very soundly that night. But over and over again I dreamed wordlessly about a beautiful engraving of Spinoza that I had once seen in a history book and about the particularly handsome binding of my new eight-volume *Encyclopedia of Philosophy*—as if the engraving were printed on that fine blue leather with its gold lettering and sexy red pin stripes. Puzzled but hopelessly Irish, I read through the encyclopedia entry on Spinoza as I ate my breakfast the next morning.

And there I found a passing reference to the fact that one of Coleridge's favorite seventeenth-century theologians had attacked both Spinoza and Descartes as advocates of philosophical errors this theologian called "hylozoism." He had coined the word himself—awkwardly and inaccurately, etymologically speaking, and, as history proved, quite unsuccessfully as well. No wonder I had not been able to figure this out! But the theologian's critique beautifully opened out Coleridge's dense and cryptic argument. Bingo! I offered a grateful glance heavenwards to Grandma Murphy, finder of all improbable items, and took myself up to the library to find the collected works of this theologian and double-check the encyclopedia's claim. What a footnote this would be!

The Mirrored Wall

To get home each day from the Rackham Graduate Library, I had to walk past the Power Center for the Performing Arts. Home was down across the Huron River, down in the medical ghetto just beyond the hospital, which perched quite improbably at the highest point of the east cliffs. We lived snug up against the western cliffs, which is to say I had to cross the river itself on a narrow, creaky wooden bridge whose railings anchored huge, symmetrical spider webs that glinted in the dew on summer mornings.

Just before heading down the cliffs toward the river, I had to pass the Power Center for the Performing Arts. The Power Center is paneled in long mirrored strips set slightly at angles to one another. Reflected in these mirrors is a large square lawn with irregularly spaced high old elm trees, a lawn cut into two right triangles by a strip of concrete that lies in the lawn like an arrow directing traffic between the medical campus and the main campus. Walking here twice a day, I saw dozens of images of myself in those angled mirrors, my image of myself shattered into dozens, all trudging in the same direction, stooped slightly under a bulging and tattered red backpack. Even when I watched my feet, these shattered self-images danced along on the periphery of my vision for that whole long block. So I tried to close my mind altogether as I walked.

And that walk, with my mind so firmly closed to the pain of those images, provoked my first visionary encounter with a figure I came to think of as "The Lady Behind the Desk." She was, it seemed to me later, like a secretary to the dean—one of those white-haired ladies who for decades, maybe for centuries, did all the real administrative work of any university: enforcing rules, setting dispensations, leaving pointed reminders in mailboxes, solving all problems with the competence and common sense and wry humor that academics so notably lack. As the daughter of a steely-eyed, white-haired secretary (now turned executive, I was proud to say), I had always cultivated the goodwill of such women and heeded their shrewd advice.

This particular lady was not in academia—that much was clear, somehow—but nonetheless she sat behind a long rectangular desk of a rich and glistening golden oak. Behind her were bookcases of the same oak, or maybe just elaborate paneling on the wall. I couldn't quite see such details, but I certainly felt the aura of tradition, the glow of something powerful. There was some small square of natural light from quite high on the right, but the artificial light in the room was softly yellow and localized, as if from table lamps set somehow beyond my rather narrow line of vision.

I had just finished explaining to her, in what I felt as hesitant and clumsy ways—I had not been expecting this interview—what my essential skills are. I can find words for things. I can name. I can provide the words people are unable to find for themselves. I can stand at the edge of something, some highly complex activity, and as if I were a translator I can find words for what needs to be said. It's an odd skill, I was saying apologetically. But even smart people with good ideas can feel inarticulate and lonely. Most of us are so terribly isolated that it is a blessing to name accurately even the ordinary experiences and feelings. But I listen to people, I listen and then I can name. Words always come. And then we don't feel so alone.

In the vision, I finished speaking to her and stood there, feeling all the grief and all the hopeless stupidity of what passed for my career plans. What had I described, after all, but a ponderous and self-important account of public relations or speech writing? But what choice had I? An academic dossier? Somehow I knew there had to be an alternative both to academia and to advertising. I swallowed hard.

I looked up from the front right corner of her desk, forcing myself to meet her eyes. "Does anyone here need skills like these?" I asked. She was smiling that competent wise-old-woman smile.

"Aren't you the answer to prayers!" she exclaimed and started to stand up and to reach ahead of herself toward something. I'm not quite sure what she was about to do.

My comeback was as swift as my answering grin: "Your prayers or mine?"

I found myself poised on the curb of Plymouth Road as if I were my own Seeing Eye dog. Four lanes of traffic roared past. I stepped back a pace or two from fear of that traffic and started to turn to sit on the theater steps. But too many of me watched me turn, and I was afraid to meet my own gaze. I turned aside abruptly, the mirrored wall of Power behind me, and stared out instead toward the ragged rooflines of medical offices and dormitories backing their way down the high east cliffs.

I had really meant what I had said: "Your prayers or mine?" Pray? I didn't pray. "Prayer" was part of the working-class world I had left behind years ago, part of the blarney permeating my urban-ethnic Irish-Catholic childhood—and that was all. It was as remote from my present life as those tediously ugly Catholic school uniforms or the watery brogue and silly lilt I had worked so hard to scrub from my enunciation. *Prayer?* How, how *quaint*. What could it possibly mean to pray about my career questions? Even if there were a "God," "He" wouldn't care about my career. "Praying for a job" would be silly at best and at worst superstitious.

What an odd notion. What a strange daydream. I held and examined the experience, turning it this way and that over and over again as I crossed those four lanes of traffic and trudged down those east cliffs, along the edge of the flood plain, across the decrepit wooden bridge, back along the west bank of the river itself and up the stairs to my sunny apartment hard against the northwesterly cliffs, to my desk overlooking the creek. I could make no sense of it. But I had sure meant what I had said about prayer. And that's what bothered me. I had, at least in daydream, honestly spoken as a believer. But I was not a believer. But but but—where then had the daydream come from?

I shrugged and tossed the question aside as I unpacked my backpack and set about making dinner. Dreams are goofy, that's all, waking or sleeping. So a bit of blarney surfaced and sounded convincing: forget it. But I couldn't. The memory of The Lady Behind the Desk kept intruding every time I looked up to stare blindly out a window or down some dusty library range. Who was she? What was she? Who was I, facing her? Why was that simple daydream all so real, so overwhelming?

I began to find other routes home, longer and steeper ones that blistered my toes going down the cliffs and set off my asthma going up. I did not want to risk seeing her again. With slowly growing certainty, however, I felt a new confidence in my decision not to look for an academic job, not to put myself through that destructive and humiliating process in order to play out my very slim chance to stay in an academic setting that seemed—even at this elite university—less and less congenial.

My intellectual ambitions had always been a very private part of me, not something that had ever found much resonance or support either in the world of my growing up or even in college, except from a very few faculty mentors and trusted friends. So I would just keep poetry and all that it meant as my own private affair. I would let these years be my own investment in me before I joined the "real" grown-up world of ordinary jobs providing for the ordinary needs of rent and grocery bills. Yes, the English department would be shocked and then variously disapproving. A quitter! Another one of these spineless silly women who never belonged here in the first place! But I had never ever been a quitter, I knew. In fact, I was liable instead to witless tenacity.

As the weeks went by, I began to feel that I had some emotionally incontrovertible evidence that everything would work out fine, that all manner of things would be well in the end. How many impossible problems had academic secretaries solved for me over the years? Nobody messed with those gutsy and self-assured middle-aged women. They knew the score—and the scorekeepers. Not much in my academic world had encouraged the broad streak of daring and whimsy I had inherited from my father, as visible an inheritance as his thin and wiry build. But I knew it was there, under all these heaps of books and papers, all these years of earnest study among men constitutionally cautious. And now I felt permission to trust this bold heritage of irreverent peasant daring, the whimsy found most often among those who know they have little to lose under any circumstances. "Nothing ventured, nothing gained"—how often my parents had countered my introverted reticence with that line!

And so, in this new confidence, I went back to walking past the Power Center. I still watched my feet and not the mirrored wall, but I was much less bothered by the dance of shattered reflections beside me. Nonetheless, I stayed away from the fully withdrawn mental state that had provoked the vision. After all, I told myself, one needed to be careful not to wander blindly out into Plymouth Road. Daydreams could be dangerous. And silly. I was no Walter Mitty. I had figured this out, my grief was bearing fruit, so good for me: just keep going.

Calls

So I did keep going. And a few weeks later I was unnerved by a phone call essentially offering me a tenure-track job at the university where I had done my M.A. The job was perfectly tailored to my scholarly interests: Romanticism, literary theory 1550–1900, Victorian poetry, and a comparative literature classics course. Homer? I might get to teach Homer? Dante? The prospect of Dante did me in: I stumbled into the dining room, stretching the phone cord to its limits so that I could sit down before I fainted. If I could promise to complete my dissertation, say, a year early? If I understood that there would nonetheless be a national search, that no guarantee was possible, that departmental politics and the dean might interfere, etc., etc. But could they interest me in applying? Would I send my dossier? There were people in the department who felt that the array of open courses added up to a job that had my name on it.

"Let me think," I answered and did not add: what dossier?

I stood the next morning amid the mirrors, looking at an array of me, angrily trying to summon The Lady Behind the Desk. What is this? I begin, finally, to come to peace with leaving academia, I "agree" somehow to go with the flow, to "trust" that all will be well, that all manner of things will be well, for no reason that I understand—and then this! For a couple of days I deliberately watched all of me stalking along under the elms, shoulders set and square under my heavy backpack, angrily meeting all of those eyes meeting mine. Nothing. I stopped and sat on the steps facing Plymouth Road, staring as before out over the chimneys and along the noisy sweep of traffic down the hill and around the corner in back of Power and in front of the long row of red brick dorms, trying to find that lady and her confidence somewhere in the recesses of my imagination. In bed at night, I pictured the scene and saw again how little I had seen clearly but how powerfully clear the feelings had been. Nonetheless, I did not dream.

And what about Warren? What about his internship plans? I had said to him that where he would go, I would follow, that by internship my dissertation would no longer be dependent upon the Rackham Graduate Library, that my dissertation and his internship would be the last great ordeal of our academic trainings—and in his choice of towns. We had laughed over maps showing pollen distribution, over *Weather In U.S. Cities:* his credentials could take him anyplace in the whole country.

After a few days of meditative confusion, Warren and I went out for ice cream. In long silences over hot fudge sundaes, we agreed that I would assemble a dossier and apply. Given the odds—despite my connections, this was not a sure thing—it was a completely unreasonable career-development compromise for him. He had spoken at length to his advisor, who had ranted and raved that he must apply to top programs nationwide. His advisor had been outraged that he would even consider limiting himself to one city. We spent a lot of time staring at each other, trying not to choke on our desserts.

In memory, we have eaten those sundaes dozens and dozens of times and tried to imagine reaching other conclusions honestly and tried to imagine radically different lives for ourselves in smaller cities with delightful climates and cheap real estate. It was that rare gift, a crossroad we recognized as a crossroad. Was I turning away from the imaginary future offered by The Lady Behind the Desk? I was being solicited for a job by the Old Boy Network: was I also being "solicited"?

But somehow, the ultimate message of the vision had been to trust, to go along with life, to take the whimsical path, the path of least resistance. Abandoning my academic career had been unspeakably painful even to contemplate: surely applying for the job would be easier, if only because it would rescue me from this depression for the next year and thereby help me to get the thesis through its difficult adolescence.

Because Warren was so plainly, painfully willing to compromise his own plans, I had to face my own conflicts all too directly. In one of our long silences, there in the Dairy Queen, I could hear a favorite line from Blake echoed over and over in my soul: "Prudence is a rich ugly old maid courted by Incapacity." So with a deep hard breath I decided that quitting academia really meant welcoming the prospect of gift horses but not feeling that my moral life depended upon the gift showing up in my barn some afternoon. Nothing ventured, nothing gained. All things work out for the best in the end. No harm in trying. Feeling almost pursued by lines like these, I went into Placement and got the dossier forms.

And, almost a whole year later, I did get the job. I still remember exactly where I stood in the kitchen, staring at an array of dirty dishes on the sink, clutching the phone, and listening to the deep round voice and its unbelievable words. And twenty-four hours later, what we had feared would be Warren's career compromise landed him instead in a top-notch training program where he flourished—eventually joining the faculty.

This time we did not go out for ice cream: we were both shaking too hard to want anything so cold. I made a big pot of tea, which we drank slowly, in a sacramental silence. Something felt inevitable.

But something in me stiffened, and I did not know what it was. I did not go up to face the mirrored wall of the Power Center: I was more than ever afraid to go through that looking glass again. I did not tell my friends nor even my dissertation director about the job, until the national gossip mill fed the information back to the Director of Graduate Studies. His secretary caught me on the Quad and demanded to know.

What Dances in the Mirror

And so, I supposed to myself, this pregnancy merely confirmed my willingness to improvise my way through life rather than follow some set choreography. I had seen that in myself during graduate school, and it was certainly a familiar truth even then. And yet, I admitted to myself, ruefully, almost apprehensively, I had certainly been delighted that the fates had not called my bluff: I had refused to walk the straight-and-narrow, sure—but wow I had been pleased to reach the conventional goal nonetheless. Clutching that job contract to my heart, I had leaped gleefully back into my dissertation, utterly thrilled that my own style of scholarship had won such unexpected approbation. But once the thrill of it wore off, I could not deny the honesty of my account to The Lady Behind the Desk of what I felt my talents really were. More and more, the core of that experience felt clear: at heart, I was simply not an academic in the ordinary way. I was headed somewhere else, however indirect the route. Somehow or other, I felt, I would someday find myself facing her desk once again, struggling once again incoherently to name myself, to say or to know what I am at the core of me. The only question was what I might yet discover of that truth in the place to which I was now headed. But I was not really a scholar. Who then was I? Around that question, I had felt pain the like of which I had not known to exist, pain that now stood in the shadows of my memory, distant, aloof, and mysterious.

When we left Ann Arbor, seven long years to tenure stretched ahead of me, just as those eight years of college and graduate school stretched their weary way into my past. But I knew, as we unpacked boxes of books in our new apartment, that whoever had decided to escape this trek had certainly been real enough. I began to worry that if I did not provide *lebensraum* to some of the selves dancing in the Power Center mirrors, then I might never see them again after seven more years of this self-sacrificing austerity.

I was barely twenty-six when I was hired as an assistant professor. I was so slight and so youthful-looking that even the undergraduates took me for an undergraduate. One day a librarian thought I was even younger than that: when I asked for a book from a closed carrel, she demanded to know if my father was on the faculty. If I could not take chances at this point in my life, if even with such youth I could not gamble nor risk, then God help me but something was seriously wrong.

Well then, I thought, as I struggled with the safety pins at my waist, getting pregnant before I had tenure was a gamble. Maybe it was an unthinkable gamble. So what? I had already taken the craziest leap of my life, away out over the east cliffs of the Huron River, that day when I discovered my own unruly, unreasonable faith in that ephemeral, visionary Lady Behind the Desk. I had, for a while and with her help, faced the prospect of not being a scholar when I grew up. Maybe this baby was not the only new life I needed to find the courage to celebrate.

What Virgins Conceive

When spring quarter drew to its weary end, I spent a week or two napping and futzing around the apartment. I cleared odd stacks of things from the corners of the dining room where such clutter was spontaneously generated during the usual course of an academic year. I scrubbed the mold out of the grout in the tile around the shower, so that I could bathe without setting off my asthma. I threw away all the papers that students had not bothered to collect; I filed memos and minutes into the folders labeled with committee titles. I emptied the black crumbs from the bottom of the toaster and wiped inky fingerprints from the white plastic handle of the coffee carafe. I looked over my research plans and outlines concerning Coleridge's mature theology and his linguistics, for the ongoing revisions of my book manuscript on his autobiography. But mostly I slept.

I dreamed over and over about our waiting, naked in some public place, for the arrival of some stranger. Our nakedness was incongruous—everyone else was wearing clothes in the usual way—but it was neither embarrassing nor wrong. We were simply waiting, commonly at the foot of some stairwell or the entrance to some long hall. Such transparent dreams! I have never been a particularly creative dreamer: maybe I use too much of my creative energies just trying to survive the ordinary perplexities of the day, perplexities that other people seem to manage with a rationality and ease that has always eluded me. For whatever reason, such dreams and this estrogenic willingness to nap easily demonstrated to me that I was spending this week Getting Used to Being Pregnant: *here, take a week, adjust; then get back to work.*

After all, we knew what we were getting into. We had read all those '70s magazine articles celebrating the new two-career couple. Perhaps you remember: "professional women" were hot stuff in the popular media in those days. Such articles always showed a picture of her in a dark and elegant business suit, sitting behind a gleaming fruitwood desk, gazing directly into the camera. The caption below would say something like, "It's quite a challenge—I have to be very organized—but I love my work and I love my family and I wouldn't have it any other way." The correlative paternal picture shows him wearing a crewneck Shetland sweater over a dress shirt. He sits on the living room floor, leaning back against a coffee table and surrounded by beaming children. His caption says something like, "I'm more involved with my kids than a lot of guys are. But that's how I want it. We're a real team in this house."

And of course such good cheer was not limited to periodicals. Bookstores were giving prominent space to a paperback titled something like *How to Raise Children on Weekends and in Your Spare Time*. We had questions about details, of course. But we never wavered in our conviction that there would be space in our lives for both a family and our careers.

So we knew that we knew what we were getting into. We knew. We would work it out, we knew, because motherhood is a lark. Women who stayed home with their kids spent their lives either eating bonbons and watching soap operas or else maniacally "keeping house." I had higher ambitions than that. I had a greater sense of responsibility to my talents. Granted, we might both get a bit less professional reading done in the evenings—at first anyhow, until we developed workable routines—but one or two little people couldn't possibly make *that* much difference. Kids go to bed early, for heaven's sake! We usually spent an hour or so after dinner in quiet conviviality before hauling out our briefcases. So we would share that time with a child. Quality time, the magazines called it. What could be simpler? We shared housework equitably; we would share parenting as well. And then the kid would go to bed and we would get our briefcases out, as always.

Furthermore, everyone that I spoke to about baby-sitting arrangements carried on at great length about "how wonderful my sitter is." Everyone admitted marvelous luck in having such great care, in exactly the same tones with which graduate students admit to having been terrified before the prelims on which, however, they earned first honors. Those few who had themselves been raised by housekeepers talked with Dickensian nostalgia about their love for dear sweet Molly, who baked bread every week and stayed with the family for twenty years before retiring to live with her grandchildren in North Carolina.

I understood. Finding good care was obviously not easy; but academics are, after all, specifically trained in the finding of needles in haystacks. With a little diligence and persistence, we too would find Mary Poppins. Not a problem. Finding whether lilies of the valley are poisonous to sheep had defeated me, but networking to a good sitter was obviously a much simpler and less esoteric quest. And sure enough: I met a grad student in the women's room one day, and to my delight she volunteered to sit for us. She was doing her dissertation and teaching a night school class, so she had plenty of free time during the day. And her fiancé was eager for kids and she was, well, curious . . .

And so I spent that couple of weeks, napping and dreaming and tidying a bit before taking up my usual summer routine of ten- or twelve-hour days at my desk or in the library. I read all of Coleridge's mature theology and sociology that summer, plus several thick volumes of notebooks and letters. I came upon spectacular evidence for my arguments about the theological substructure of his literary theory; I collected witty little remarks from the *Table Talk* to use as epigraphs for each chapter. "Truth is a good dog;" he said on 7 June 1830, "but beware of barking too close to the heels of an error, lest you get your brains kicked out."

And all summer long it was never too hot and never too rainy, and my pen never ran out of ink.

Prenatal Vitamins

I was out of vitamins. And it was lovely outside, August with a hint of September in its drier air and the ambiguous fecundity of the smell of moldering lilac foliage, moldering *Phlox paniculata*, moldering anything at all that faced the coming season blithely unaware. The almost-empty vitamin bottle offered an excuse that I needed to go for a walk. I was, I suppose, a bit embarrassed—once again—by my own inability to shut down such self-discipline as needed an excuse for a walk. But mostly I was awash in estrogenic earth-mother beneficence toward all of creation. If sometimes I felt grateful for an excuse to get out of the house, after so many years of forcing myself to stay in and work, what did it matter? I waddled cautiously down four long flights of stairs.

It was an ordinary evening in the urban midwest: Big Wheels blocking the sidewalks, little kids chasing fireflies, people sitting on stoops or leaning against the split-rail fence in the park, young couples meandering about, neighbors conversing with neighbors about nothing in particular. None of these old houses and big brownstone six-flats had central air conditioning: we all still took to the streets in the cool of dusk. It could have been Oak Park in the '50s, when all these yuppies were youngsters. My belly caught an occasional knowing, sympathetic glance, and I walked without haste.

Carrying my gaudy blue plastic bottle of prenatal vitamins-plus-iron, I wandered idly toward the aisle of "infant needs" to survey again the astounding array of ointments and diapers and accessories that babies were said to need. It felt not unlike cruising campus bookstores, years before, surveying the texts assigned for courses I would be taking in the semesters ahead. And to my surprise I met a graduate student—a particular favorite, in fact—clutching the same blue bottle. Her skin was queasy green, her stunning hazel eyes were encircled in black, and her small flat breasts were now high and most boldly rounded. Quick, she shifted the bottle out of sight to her other hand.

I had ready words to tease her, but they were swept aside by her surprised and delighted proclamations at my pregnancy.

"And so are you," I hazarded when I could get a word in edgewise. She almost fell into my arms; and I stared speechlessly at the bottles of baby oil as I realized she was sobbing. I held her and waited and remembered, wondering what it would have done to me, last April, to find that a favorite senior colleague was also pregnant. The baby kicked vigorously against us both, and I wondered if she could feel that.

By the time she disentangled herself and began to rummage in her pockets for a tissue, the pharmacist was peering around the corner at us, over the edge of his Plexiglas and rows of little boxes.

"Joyce," I ventured uncertainly. "What's . . . ? Are you . . . ? You look awful. Tell me."

Her face fell apart again. Bill had left her, walked out. He wanted no part of babies or pregnancy. He had gone through that with his first wife, and it had been the ruination of the relationship. They had agreed. They had agreed not to have kids. Now he was furious.

They had agreed because Joyce had some pretty serious medical problems that meant she should not, in fact, try to have children. The pregnancy was unexpected, unwanted, accidental—and possibly a mortal threat to her. And Bill had walked out, telling her at that point about his other lover, a clandestine affair of some months' duration. I folded Joyce back into my arms, her wiry, athletic frame bony against my own new soft roundness. She had done brilliant work in my class, astounding stuff that challenged and changed my views of the poems she had engaged. For a moment, the bottles of baby oil disappeared: all I could see were pages of her footnotes and the mature historical acumen they had demonstrated. I am a philosophical critic, not an historical one; she is an historian to the very bones, and she had wowed me. And what in the name of God was I supposed to say or to do now?

She lifted her wet face from my shoulder.

"It's *real*," she said over and over again. "Everybody is telling me to get an abortion, but this baby is *real*. They don't understand. This is a real baby. I'm never supposed to do this and it shouldn't have happened but it happened and it's *real*."

I remembered the perhaps-phantom baby who had ruined my first-day lecture last spring. And when Joyce finally looked me in the eye, I had to agree. The baby was real. We held that look for a minute, as if I had tossed a line that she clutched lest she drown.

"I don't live in such a world," she said at last, very softly. "I don't live in a world where men walk out on their pregnant wives because they don't want diapers. I don't live in a world where I'm having a baby but he's having an affair." She glared at me, forceful and defiant, all of her formidable intelligence aglint. I held her gaze, feeling her incredulity echo and re-echo into depths of anger within me.

"And I'm not walking out on this baby!" her voice rose firmly, then cracked. "Oh Katie, what am I going to do??"

I took her arm and steered her out the door.

"C'mon, c'mon, let's get out of here. Let's go someplace—" She wheeled on me.

"*Where* am I going to go? Who's going to take care of me?" Those hazel eyes I had so often admired were wide with panic and not really focused on my face.

"How will I do this *alone?* You should have heard the doctor—he wouldn't hear of my living alone." She turned away and I reached after her, knowing all too well what such verbal dissociations signaled in folks like us. She pushed my hand away.

"Go home. Go home to your husband. Let me alone."

I watched her go. The August night was dark; the toddlers and their Big Wheels were inside now, the grownups were visible inside yellow windows as they puttered around getting ready for the day to come. At home Warren waited, watching a baseball game or reading a novel or a journal; the sheets on our bed were cool and white and crisp.

"I do not live in such a world." The line lingered on the fragrant air, an indictment of chill terror that bore down on the weight of my womb.

Doors

October, when it came, began auspiciously: the door to the English department building banged shut in my face. I gave a more determined tug, and this time the door opened a full two inches before falling closed. My new center of gravity—aided by a canvas briefcase jammed with books—was no match for these enormous old oak doors. I set my briefcase down and glowered at the polished brass handles, set just about shoulder high. An undergraduate male brushed past, but I couldn't stoop fast enough to retrieve my books and slip in behind him—a trick I mastered in the weeks ahead. But my own building! Good grief! I tried one more time, incredulous and—slowly, almost reluctantly—amused by my predicament. And then very amused, until I was laughing hard enough to set off a contraction.

I gave up, circling around to the front doors. The front doors had been rehabbed to less Brobdingnagian proportions in hollow-core pine, the veneer now warped and splitting. But by then the 9:50 bell had rung: I had to swim against the flow of bodies pouring out the front doors and south toward the history building. As I bellied out into the crowd, a student from the previous year caught my eye and waved and headed toward me, cross-currents, with a delighted grin. I watched her delight erupt into something more than delight as she saw my new girth.

"Oh Ms. Wallace, Ms. Wallace," she babbled. "You're, you're, you're . . . " she stumbled into silence. "You've cut your hair." She held her chin high, as if to keep my belly out of sight.

"Not really," I replied. "But I am pregnant . . . Did you notice?"

She laughed and I laughed with her; we hugged clumsily around all that we carried and then she ran off, late, to her next class. I watched her go, slim and brown and unbearably sexy in a tall, lithe, leggy way. Surely I had never been lithe and sexy like that: I was small and wiry and intense, with coppery-brown hair far too curly to billow like hers in black silky waves over broad, bare shoulders. The baby stirred in response to my uncertain yearning. Her glee, her stunned and youthful glee at my pregnancy, remains a blessing I will carry into paradise.

In those first few warm October days, that scene replayed almost exactly five or six times. I had never before realized how closely my students watched the exact cut and curl of my bushy hair—or just how unspeakable feminine sexuality remained, even in 1979.

No one, it seemed, had ever seen a pregnant professor. I met the slack-jawed looks and garbled, inarticulate remarks with the mildest possible surprise, as if the real fact of mature and sexual women on the faculty had actually been known and accepted all along. I wished some social anthropologist could follow me around. Failing that, I ached to write heroic couplets upon academic pregnancy. I was not, as Pope might have wished, "a softer man," but I did yearn at times for his venomous wit. This gracious self-possession took too great a toll on the lining of my stomach.

Furthermore, I lacked the common decency to be embarrassed by my rotund fecundity: I loved it, gawking at myself admiringly in every mirror or plateglass window I passed. I was perpetually a bit high on estrogen, and like all who are somewhat drunk I was just a bit disinhibited. My long-standing effort to curtail my own combativeness was distinctly diminished. The distress I caused amused me, angered me some, and then amused me even more. After all, there is simply no way to be massively pregnant without seeming to flaunt one's powerful, creative femininity, one's earth-mother authority. And so I felt—at times quite distinctly—that while I had this embodied power I was in fact almost willing to flaunt it, almost willing to play life's ultimate one-upmanship card against these guys who could not do it themselves.

When I finally got inside the building on that first day, I met a particularly self-important, terribly repressed colleague by the mailboxes. He would not have been more distressed had I stood there stark naked.

"You're you're you're" he spluttered, unable even to say the word.

"Yes," I replied beatifically. "I'm *pregnant*." I smiled with sweet maternity. He turned bright pink and fled.

Publish or Perish

Doors were not the only problem. I was also too big to walk to campus. It was twenty-five minutes of brisk walking under the best of circumstances. But now this baby seemed to occupy one-third of my lung space and to demand at least half of the oxygen I managed to inhale. And those hazy, fragrant, autumnal molds had always shut down my twitchy airways. So Warren drove me up to campus before he left for the hospital each day. At six-thirty in the morning, it was quiet in the old converted house I shared with half-a-dozen or so English department colleagues. The dissertation revisions were almost complete, the two gestations proceeding side by side as I reached awkwardly around myself to the manuscript in front of me. In those long, silent, productive hours, in that gorgeous, timeless, golden autumn, I had it all.

So I was not about to take any guff from a traveling acquisitions editor now late for his appointment with me. One of the full professors—no doubt the real reason for this visitor—had given the man my name and suggested a conversation. I was entirely convinced that no academic press editor would be able to see the quality of my work around the impressive girth of my belly. Women were tolerable in this world only while men could sustain the fantasy that we were actually men—or at least sexless. That bland, sexless Academic Woman, creeping like a nun. Instead I looked like a diminutive Irish version of a fertility goddess, bright green eyes and curly hair rampant in the autumn mist.

And now this editor was late for our appointment. I fought back a tide of resentment, counseling myself that I needed experience being interviewed by editors and above all that I owed courtesy to the senior male colleague who had offered me this plum. Be strategic, Kate, I counseled myself sternly. Not all the men here are boors: you owe this guy. Get control.

The editor finally flustered in, just minutes before I had to leave to teach, brimming with frustration and embarrassed apologies and telling stories of lost cabbies charging exorbitant fares. He was not much older than I, disarmingly openhearted, and apparently quite oblivious both to my sex and my sexuality. I tore a campus map out of a catalogue, steered him to his next appointment and then to a good but cheap lunch place, and set up a second appointment. And before he returned, I sketched maps for the public trains back to the central city. The temperature was plummeting, snow was starting to fall, cabs would be hard to find, and this foolish man with neither an overcoat nor an adequate expense account clearly needed some help. Stupid maternalism, I thought to myself. Stupid estrogen. Quite unprofessorial. Sigh . . .

Annoyed so with myself, I was instead annoyed with him when he returned, a long-necked Englishman, thin, the stubble of his beard darkly shadowing his long and shapely jaw in the grey light of a snowy afternoon in early November. Thick eyebrows too, just barely touched with grey—quite dramatic, actually—over very dark blue eyes. Beautiful, expressive hands; white shirt sleeves at a graceful length over his wrists; the glint of cufflinks. More estrogen poisoning. I made myself stop admiring his body and tried listening instead to his spiel. I found myself arguing with him about why he should not be interested in my book: I was very young and it was just a first book. It would be very controversial and liable to attack—particularly given my sex and youth—from several quarters, all of which I described. I couldn't promise when I could send a finished manuscript: I was obviously at work on other projects. He looked very frankly at my belly for a long moment of warm and admiring appreciation. Yes, he grinned, he could see that.

No male on campus had ever looked at me like that. The room was suddenly electric with the complementary sexuality of a man and a woman. So much for professorial poise: I went slackjawed. He seemed not to notice. No hurry to submit a finished manuscript, he said. And carried on a bit about how his press had a distinguished reputation for controversial but permanent works. And he told me all about his new baby.

I gave him the maps. He was charmed, and I caught him looking again at my girth with that same ordinary and very richly masculine admiration. When I stood to shake hands, he met my gaze and I saw just a hint of surprise in the depths of his eyes. Not the English professor type he had come to expect, by golly. But he was clearly pleased by that fact.

The Birth of Athena

I taught a Great Books course that fall, in the fall of 1979, on the third floor of a classroom building across a pocked gravel alley in back of the old house converted into faculty offices. Three flights of stairs left me breathless—and thus entirely speechless—so I got to class ten minutes early each day. I sat gasping asthmatically on a low, creaky old folding chair behind a high, rickety conference table, pretending to review my notes. The students learned not to bother me with questions, because I was genuinely unable to speak. They were a very sweet group of kids.

This particular day, I looked up at the bell to find a whole row of parents in the back. Parents' Weekend! Oh no! I should have done something better with my hair!

But class was off and running with questions about the recent lecture by one of my team teachers. We were doing the Pentateuch, and Joseph's interview with his brothers in the Pharaoh's palace, and someone had lost track of who Joseph was. Ordinarily, I had no patience with such difficulties. But this course had an impossible reading list—an epic every ten days or so—and the row of watchful parents also urged compassion. So I stood up and turned to the blackboard, sketching the generations of begats from Adam and Eve onward to Joseph. I turned back to the students, chalk in one hand and, as usual, the other hand on my waist (or, where my waist once was). I looked out at them and asked for questions.

In that back row, four fathers were bug-eyed and pale; four mothers were beaming triumphantly. I met the mothers' eyes and felt a deep blush start creeping up my neck.

"Yeah, I know," I wanted to say. "English professors didn't look like this when you were in school, did they?"

But whence that ferocious approval from these women? The class hurried on, however, as that group predictably did; and I had to catch up with them.

As the term wore on, and my big belly became bigger and then some, people started wondering about due dates. So did I, in fact, particularly when the official day waddled on past without remark. One day, one of the Great Books kids responded with a high-flung arm to my standard opening invitation for questions.

"When is that baby *due*!!" she demanded. There was a small gasp from some of her classmates, but a more general look of pleased conspiracy on their faces.

"A week ago Tuesday," I said, as if in scholarly reply to any other question about dates. As a group, they eyed the door: I suspected stampede at any moment. I laughed at them, crossing that magic line of impersonality.

"Stop staring! I won't do it here!" We laughed together and got down to work. Or, they did. I had some trouble concentrating around that thought of giving birth on campus. Birthing on campus: what an impossible clash of categories.

After class, the same student proposed that the baby should come as Athena did, from my forehead. I objected, of course, that the forehead in question would then have to be my husband's. The circle of observers erupted in yet another laugh, but their faces were shadowed with thought: miraculous, bloodless, cerebral birthing obviously felt better somehow, obviously it matched better with some visceral dimension of their perceptions of me. Musing and amused, I followed them down the stairs and recrossed that treacherous gravel alley, unable to see where I was stepping.

Late Papers Not Accepted

At two weeks late and counting, the problem finally became clear. As a colleague pointed out, I couldn't possibly give birth until after my grades were submitted. How unlike me it would be, he explained, to dump forty exams and twenty-five papers onto the desks of my generous friends among the other assistant professors.

"I knew I could offer," he confided, "because I knew you would be here. You would never let pregnancy interfere like that."

That did it. I sat up until three A.M., clutching my red pen and reaching around my enormous belly to the calculator and the mess of papers and blue books on the dining room table. I fell into bed queasy with exhaustion, but labor did not start. The next morning, I walked almost two miles up to campus. It was ten degrees below zero but windless and brilliantly sunny: not a bad day for a walk, actually, when you carry your own little furnace with you. Unfortunately, I still had to breathe the cold air, and so I walked very very slowly. I arrived extremely pink and too breathless to unzip my briefcase.

"Are you still here?" the secretary fumed. "What do you want? Why are you here?" I sat wordlessly for several minutes while two more support staff came in and worried collectively about my health and sanity. Something deep within me stirred at the depths of their concern, at the edge of anger in their voices.

"You have no business walking all that way!" one of them finally asserted.

I wanted to argue that grade lists *were* my business. But suddenly my belly felt huge and full and hard; my head started to swim, and my eyes stung with tears held back. I did not know how to ask one of them to take me home, so I slept on the floor of my office for two hours.

Grading better not count as nesting, I thought to myself when I awakened, alert enough but now very tired indeed. It was a long and even slower walk home, haunted by the glowering look from the secretary who saw me leave.

But labor still did not start. It waited another ten days. It waited until after I had done all the mending and balanced five months' worth of bank statements, until after all the Christmas presents were wrapped and tagged and then opened, until after the fridge was full of soups and stews and frozen sacrifices to some ancient goddess. It waited until the gynecologist gave me twenty minutes before he would declare the induction a failure and begin preparations for a cesarean.

But finally unto us a child was born, arriving as all babies do with firm hold of the upper hand. He was long and big and scrawny, beautifully prepared to wreak ongoing havoc in our tidy academic lives. When they plopped him onto my chest, he picked up his wet and wobbly head to stare right into my eyes, self-possessed and wise and quizzical. His eyes were a dark and brilliant blue, just like his father's. Like his father's, his chin was deeply cleft. Infinity and eternity intersected in the depths of that gaze: the sacred mystery of the universe, there on my chest. My eyes clouded with tears, and then my brain fogged over as a bolus of intravenous analgesia hit my brain. The docs needed to begin some emergency repairs: no time now for spirituality. Faceless hands took him away.

"It's done," was all I could think as the room itself faded from consciousness. "It's a baby." I let myself be enveloped by that full-blown Georgia O'Keeffe, while silent trumpets played an invisible fanfare in brilliant golds and yellows.

2
Is There Life after Birth?

ANY MOTHER KNOWS THAT THE BOOKS DON'T REALLY TELL YOU ABOUT postpartum. Lots of new mothers resolve to write books that will tell that truth—after the baby starts sleeping through the night, or after the baby stops nursing, or after the Second Coming in one form or another. I'm sure that many mothers have in fact written the books as they resolved: bookstores now have exponentially more titles on pregnancy and childbirth than I found in 1979. The problem is not that the books cannot be found. It's that postpartum is too irrational to be explained to outsiders. Every woman discovers it for herself, a great psychic *terra incognita*. And most of us feel terribly isolated—not to say somewhat deranged—as we explore its terrain.

I have three archetypal memories of the first few weeks after Mark was born. The first is a bright morning, perhaps ten or fifteen degrees below zero. I am on campus, very briefly, for something that in memory feels very important. Collecting my paycheck, perhaps? I am greeted warmly by one of the oldest men in the department, himself a new grandfather.

"How are you *doing*?" he asks, his face alight with a personal concern for me that stops me in my tracks. I don't know what to say. Or at least not to *him*. But his warmth melts the morning air around us.

"We are having the time of our lives!" I say at last, more than a bit astounded at my own confidence and glee. He thinks about hugging me and thinks the better of it. I realize, with a bit of a start, what a very handsome man he is—snow white hair, rich gold complexion, beautifully proportioned rectangular face. We bow, as people bow when it is just too cold to remove gloves and shake hands, and continue our walk in opposite directions.

The second memory is in a grocery store. I am in tears. I am not merely fighting tears: I am hoping no one will see me there with tears running down my face. I'm in tears because I cannot choose between cream of chicken soup and creamy chicken soup with mushrooms.

But in a few weeks I will begin teaching a course that includes such fluffy delights as Kant's *Critique of Pure Reason*. Will it still make sense? How will I ever manage a seminar room full of aggressive graduate students? No matter what the course topic, there were always one or two cocky young males whose a priori contempt for "lady intellectuals" forced some nasty showdown over their refusal seriously to engage difficult material. Theory courses were worse. And this was a theory course, sixteenth through eighteenth centuries. Theory courses always managed to have a couple of dingbat males who knew that they knew the answers to all the theoretical and metatheoretical issues. If I didn't know what properly characterizes the act of critical reading, if I couldn't comprehensively define the nature and the value of literature or the character of the "real world," then they would set me straight lest I waste any more of everyone's time. She who cannot choose a canned soup will never succeed in graduate seminars.

I am terrified, there in the grocery aisle. I grab two cans of soup (one of each kind), dash through the short-order checkout, and sit weeping in the car. Warren perks an eyebrow at my appearance when I get home, but I am far too embarrassed to tell him. And I am far far too tired to pursue the implications of that experience. Others had gone back to work successfully. So would I. If pregnancy rotted your brains—*it will change you*, conventional wisdom had warned me, *it will change you and you will never want to go back to work*—then dammit my brains will somehow have to heal themselves. The world was full of competently functioning women-with-children. I will not give in to this, I resolve. I stay up late reviewing my notes on the *Critique.*

The third memory is very clear and yet from this distance I have trouble believing its prescience. Warren calls late one January afternoon, and I am again in tears as I tell him that four times that day I had fixed myself something hot to drink, only to have Mark need some attention before I could so much as take a sip. Each time, the drink was cold when I returned to it. Reliably the practical partner in this marriage, Warren came home shortly thereafter with a microwave oven—the newest yuppie toy—so I could reheat such cups of tea. With exquisite clarity I remember sitting with one such reheated cup, thinking to myself that I could not wait to go back to work because working was so much less work than being home. The implications of the desire stun me. Maybe I had underestimated motherhood. Maybe I had underestimated babies. Maybe I had miscalculated, muddled some equation, failed to recognize the essential form of the work before me. The thought seems to hang in the air, as if in a balloon over the head of some cartoon character.

With a mental slowness born of estrogen poisoning and sleep deprivation, I wonder whether to pursue the implications of the thought. I decide not to. "Working is much less work than being home" hangs a moment longer in the air, in its cartoon-dialogue balloon, then floats through the front door and down the long flight of stairs to the cold dark January afternoon. I let it go.

Postpartum was full of moments like these, moments when the inability to think consecutively intersected in hazardous ways with my highly disciplined capacity to concentrate on some immediate task and ignore everything else, absolutely everything else. And when those two realities intersected, my brains simply locked up, like a computer with too little random-access memory. As my winter quarter maternity leave drew toward its close, every morning I awakened hoping that today my mind would function properly, just as for all those December weeks I had awakened hoping that today the baby would be born. In the last two weeks before my maternity leave ended, I went up to campus twice, each time for four or five hours, gingerly testing my mental functions. Superwoman incarnate, I was thrilled to find myself working easily and fruitfully on difficult revisions to a philosophically technical and particularly complex chapter of my book manuscript. In comparison with my own life, Schelling's construction of self-consciousness seemed remarkably straightforward, even simple in its radical abstraction from the visceral realities of breastfeeding and diapers and recovery from childbirth.

Elated, I waved the first such page at a colleague who stopped by my doorway to welcome me back. He congratulated me on the page, albeit with the perplexed look that Shakespeareans tend to reserve for Romanticists. I did not explain that my brains seemed to be working again—as long as I did not try to think about home.

The First Day of a New Term

Unfortunately, spring quarter—and *The Critique of Pure Reason*—was soon upon me. I set aside my book manuscript and set up files for ungraded papers, graded but not returned papers, old teaching notes, current and prospective teaching notes, memos and meeting notes from various committees, memos and reports to write for various committees, forms to fill out for undergraduate advisees, graduate advisees, and dissertation writers—all the silly debris of academic life. I worried, but not too much—the courses were familiar ones in which I planned no innovations.

I have always hated the first day of class. The skeptical faces, the arguments of students who hope to evade prerequisites, the embarrassed apologies of students who want to drop, the pressure from several directions to admit more students than the room will hold: toxic levels of anxiety inundate the whole campus. Nor was the first day of this spring quarter any exception—except that I had not had an uninterrupted night's sleep since some time before Thanksgiving.

On that toxic Monday afternoon, I dragged myself home through the dark and the snow, exhausted and despondent and amorphously anxious. I was not prepared for the next class, on Wednesday:

handouts needed updating but there had been a continual stream of students to my office. When I had left that day, a piece of paper still sat blankly in my typewriter. Furthermore, I had to collect enrollment data for certain introductory courses over the last ten years: my analysis of enrollment trends would be presented to the appropriate committee in just a few days. Contrary to my confident plans, I had not gotten over to the dean's office to begin collecting these numbers. And Ruth would not return to baby-sit until an hour before my next class: I would have just time enough to walk to campus, check my mail, and have a few minutes for the inevitable gaggle of students waiting outside my office. So would Mark nap well tomorrow, and would I get something done? Or would the night and the day be the usual cold-tea chaos—and then what?

Ruth met me at the door in tears. She had counted on Mark's napping so that she could finish grading papers for her night school class downtown. Instead he had fussed endlessly, then vomited all over the red polyester crêpe de Chine blouse in which she planned to teach. She had washed it out in the bathroom sink, resolving as she did so not to baby-sit again on the day she taught. She walked out the door in her damp blouse. I stood there in my coat, listening to Mark screaming in his crib, my briefcase heavy in my hand.

Cuddled in my lap and fed again and consoled, Mark sat quietly admiring his own very long and graceful fingers, each hand grasping the other. Pianist's hands, everyone said. I struggled to ease my own grip on myself. Someday, I thought, this will be funny. I tried to imagine how Barbara Streisand would handle this scene, how she might stare at Ruth's damp and tear-stained exit. Or Goldie Hawn. Or, I think now, Whoopee Goldberg. Yes! Whoopee Goldberg. Someday this will be a great funny story, starring some woman who knows the comic resources of helpless painful silence.

Someday. Meanwhile, however, I had no sitter for next Monday and no protected time before my next class. I had planned childcare only for minimal on-campus classroom and office hours: five hours on campus three days a week, plus an hour each day for the walk back and forth. I had planned such limited hours because I knew that babies mostly sleep—until they are old enough to play by themselves for equally predictable long stretches of time. Kids sleep and play. What else is there, for a kid? At first, we had set up Mark's crib in my study: after all, as a little kid I had always gone to sleep with one of the older kids typing or practicing the piano. That arrangement didn't last long. But working at home even more than I did already had been an entirely self-evident plan, which ten weeks at home with a newborn had somehow never called into question.

Slowly it began to dawn on me that I had always worked at least from seven in the morning until five every day and for at least two or three hours every evening. My routine silence-and-solitude workweek was between sixty and seventy hours—excluding regular weekend sessions that added at least another five or six hours to the minimal workweek. What had I been thinking? Had I been thinking at all? More estrogenic brain rot?

I looked down at Mark, asleep at last. Ten-hour days? At what I was paying Ruth, that would be half of my paycheck. Ten-hour days in some group care situation? If I could find one! People signed up on waiting lists for infant care the moment they found out they were pregnant. But ten hours in a group of three or four babies in the care of a single woman? As if he were one of triplets or quadruplets? What sort of woman takes a job like that, for the minimum wage no less?

I could call the famous Judy who cared for a couple of toddlers whose fathers were in my department. But that would be like hoping for someone to vacate a parking place right in front of you: day care homes were everyone's choice of choices; demand was so high that—unlike the corporate centers—such women refused to keep waiting lists. Maybe I should pray to Grandma Murphy to find me a baby-sitter?

But what about Mark? What about me? Ten hours? What? What? I couldn't think: my mind locked up, the screen fizzled audibly and blanked out. Mark and I rocked quietly as the grey room faded into full darkness and Warren came home. I handed Mark to him and went off to my study. I redid my handout and prepared my classes and, sometime well after midnight, I stopped to eat a carton of yogurt before falling into bed.

Late Tuesday morning, Mark and I took a cab to Judy's. She had space, she had said, and no other infant—just two toddlers and her own child, who was four years old—if we could buy her a crib? (If we could buy a second car, to get Mark over there.) I could hardly hear what she was saying: *what if, what if* had been reverberating in my head for so many hours I felt almost deaf. Before I had called Judy, I had phoned the various social service agencies in the area and then called my way down all the numbers they gave me. The shortest waiting list I found had five kids on it. Judy had to be it. Or else I'd teach next Monday with Mark in his corduroy babypack strapped to my chest?

Worst of all, worst worst of all, was the undeniable, unwelcome fact that some obscure corner of my soul was hoping that no child care could be found. Something in me—something most unscholarly indeed—was agitating for unpredictable adventure. The Harris-tweed hotshot professorial self was sternly ignoring her, but I was frightened nonetheless. I had heard that still small voice before. "Silence, reprobate!" I wanted to shout. But in that bare fraction of an angry flash I had admitted that she was real. And then she laughed at me and settled into an obtrusive, cocksure silence. I paid off the cabby, lugged Mark up the stairs into our apartment, settled him for a nap, picked out some reading to do, and settled into my armchair with a big mug of tea—and then sat shaking and miserable and unable to concentrate. I fell asleep.

I slept in the chair until Warren came home. Mark had napped for five hours.

Journal Excerpt, May 1980: The White Rabbit

What am I doing wrong? The magazine articles say "Organize!" Organize and be saved. But by golly I *am* organized. Weeks' worth of dirty clothes are sorted into color-coded barrels lined up on the closet floor. In fact, we have just gone to Sears to buy taller barrels— and more underwear. My spices are in alphabetical order in a cute little rack, mounted above a sink heaped with dirty dishes slowly growing mold. On the fridge hang lists of things to do for each of us, the tasks categorized neatly, priority items starred. The paper is yellow with age. Unwashed baby bottles line the counter in straight rows. My research files all have typed labels and cross-reference cards, but my desk is an impossible heap of unfiled pages. My life is exquisitely organized. My life is almost pathologically alphabetized and ordered.

It's my mind that's chaos. I'm dizzy from changing hats. No matter where I am, I need to be somewhere else. My attention to one task competes with my anxiety about the tasks I am ignoring. Nothing happens, nothing gets done, except at what feels like the crack of doom. And there is no longer any satisfaction in completing a task: I leap over that moment like a cross-country runner broadjumping a brook, and take off after the next task. Or as if I were a muzzled greyhound after a mechanical bunny, unaware of the impossibility of ever catching up.

"There is only one of me!" I want to scream. But I'm not sure that's true any more. I feel like a hostile committee, thoroughly at odds with itself, never doing anything wisely or well or with glad heart and single purpose.

I remember reading *Zen in the Art of Archery* and *Zen and the Art of Motorcycle Maintenance*. I could imagine what a Zen master would say about my life. But if some Zen master male dared to rebuke me, I'd shoot him—plink!—square between the eyes. I would not even have to aim: an arrow possessed of such justice would find its own way. How many, do you suppose, of Zen masters have tried to balance babies and laundry and housework and scholarship and teaching and marriage?

"Before enlightenment, chop wood and carry water," they say; "after enlightenment, chop wood and carry water."

I know. That sounds great, doesn't it? But my life is a lot more complex than that sort of rural-purity utopianism. I'm not living in a remote hut with wind chimes and one spare saffron robe and a small pot of lentils. I'm in the middle of a modern university. And I am doing a big presentation of my research to the interdepartmental humanities faculty colloquia tomorrow, dammit, and two minutes ago I realized that there is baby spit-up down the back of my good blue suit. The car insurance agent called this evening to ask why we are late paying the bill and to warn us that we are now driving without insurance. Who knows what else is buried on my desk? Any enlightenment that I might find needs to lighten the life I really lead, here and now—not on some Colorado mountaintop.

And how many, do you suppose, of scholars in The Great Tradition washed and ironed their own clothes, bought and cooked their own food—and then did the dishes and swept the floor and bathed the baby—before sitting down to read of an evening?

Warren does his part in that routine. Clearly, we are in this mess together. But the fact remains that his professional life is rigidly scheduled and mine is not. He works in a community, as part of a very complex and interdependent team. I don't. I work alone most of the day for most of the week. I have choices. I'm not teaching tomorrow, so I could work on my four o'clock presentation, on which I have spent no time whatever. Or I could maybe find the insurance bill. Or wash some baby bottles, since we used the last clean one at bed time tonight. Or grade some papers—their next paper is due in a week and the students are complaining loudly that this one has not been returned. Or I could read the several hundred lines of Wordsworth I assigned for my ten o'clock class and spend some quiet time thinking about that course and about those kids. Or I could get something done on my own research. Yes. Everybody knows what a great life college profs have: all this free time and independence.

Theoretically, anyhow. Instead, I feel like a Walt Disney heroine besieged by ungraded papers, by unwashed dishes, by unread books. And by babies turned overnight into sullen adolescents and then hopelessly unhappy adults, like *A Christmas Carol* without the happy ending.

But neither is there time for serious brooding. I'm much more likely to dash off like the White Rabbit, late and clutching my pocket watch. But now it is past two in the morning, which proves I guess there's not really time for all this guilt either. If I don't get to bed soon, tomorrow morning I won't have the wits to do whatever it is I will decide to do.

Scholarly Molds

My face itched. It burned and tingled with an intensity known only to the allergic or to sleepless, homesick eight-year-olds suffering from mosquito bites late on hot summer nights at camp. Hives had bloomed and merged into one long white welt all along my jawline and up toward my right eye, which was beginning to twitch and to swell. The palms of my hands tingled and yet felt numb. I sat on the cold stone stairs and leaned the right side of my face against the brass newel post, closing my eyes to absorb its coldness. What kind of scholar am I, to be so allergic to the molds that grow on three-hundred-year-old books? I knew I had not touched it: *one does not touch rare books.* One uses little rubber-tipped gadgets, very very carefully, to turn pages. Molds must have gone airborne. How many years had it been, do you suppose, since John Wilkins's pages had been turned?

I opened my eyes, though I did not move my hot face from the newel post. Now what? I could go home and take some antihistamines. Then I would sleep for four hours. But it was three already: by the time I packed up and got home and the meds helped and I was heading to sleep, it would be four. And Mark needed to be picked up from the sitter's at five. By then I'd be too sleepy to drive. I couldn't get him, go home, get the meds, and then sleep: I dare not leave a mobile infant to his own devices while I floated off into a chemical haze. He'd slither under the coffee table and clunk his head again. Or who knows what. Every day now he found something new to explore: no more of this "contented baby lying on a blanket" routine.

I would have to tough this out. But if this inflamation involved the remains of that tumor on my right eye, my whole head would start to throb. Tears started to burn tracks across my burning face. I forced them to stop by sitting up—a colleague might come by, after all—and surveying the scene as if merely giving my eyes a break from small print.

Atop a broad, square pedestal sat a bronze figure with a book, a scholarly monk whose robes and crucifix still did not disguise an ancestry that must have included gargoyles. He guarded this transitory hall from the new library to the old one. The ambiance of the new library was set by starkly abstract modern art, by poured concrete, and by the latest electronic wizardry of information management. But the tone of Special Collections was set by its quirky bronzes, oak paneling, and stained glass. It could have been a church, if you rescued the bronzes from their nooks on window ledges and among the books in glass-fronted bookcases, if you set up the small reading tables as altars, with rows of votive candles. Light a candle before getting down to work, and say a prayer to Descartes or to Dante or to Molière: what a thought!

Furthermore, the new library had cheap and ugly industrial-grey carpet—to match its poured concrete walls, I supposed—carpet already patched with duct tape at the seams. Here, the old slate floor was worn but still beautiful, its patina enhanced by a gleaming matte finish that bespoke how Buildings and Grounds people can love the places for which they care. This university had its faults, but its B&G people had both excellent taste and a strong sense of their own independence. B&G didn't like the new library either.

Nope. No doubt about it. Special Collections was homey, presided over by crackerjack librarians who knew and could find absolutely everything every time. I loved them and I loved their cluttered space. I just hated old books. One day, the principal curator knelt next to my chair to praise in a whisper my care and consistency with the rubber-tipped tongs for turning pages. What an example I set! I accepted his praise with a pink-faced humility that I suspect he interpreted as true scholarly reticence—not the fear of urticaria.

I felt less fond, suddenly, of that presiding gargoyle of a scholarly monk. My twitchy right eye was beginning to water and my temple to throb. All this for two or three sentences and one lousy footnote to John Wilkins's 1668 opus in theoretical linguistics, to his speculation that it was in fact impossible to invent a language in which obscurity, equivocation, and polysemy would be impossible. In no language, Wilkins contends, not even an invented one, is it possible to say just what you mean—and absolutely nothing else. Poor Wilkins: after years and years of work, he lost his manuscript in the Great Fire of London. Must have had a copy, though. He doesn't say. Scholarship has always had its bad moments, I supposed. Three hundred years from now, would some scholar itch and wheeze over *my* book, held as a treasure in Special Collections? Fat chance! For all I knew, no one would ever—ever—look up footnote nine in chapter six and then get to a library that still preserved one of Wilkins's huge old books.

The monk sat with his back to me, but I could feel a sneer in the set of his shoulders. What an idiot I was, how unable to manage priorities intelligently. Instead of itchy debates about whether two more hours would suffice to finish with John Wilkins—or whether I'd be courting disaster to risk more exposure—I could have taken my baby to the park on a perfectly beautiful summer afternoon. Such a clear and comprehensive thinker was I, such rational discernment of values. Wilkins and the problem of clarity. But what would celibate males know of my life? Their reading was never disrupted by a baby.

Truth be told, the only linguistics that really mattered to me at the moment was my baby-sitter's grammar. Every time she said, "between you and I," I flinched. She was loving and conscientious; I was jealous and elitist. One Saturday morning, Mark had crawled to the front door, stretched his hand up toward the doorknob, and asked eagerly, "Judy? Judy?" And I had fought tears. Judy loved him, he loved her, and he was obviously flourishing. I was not. And if he ever said, "between you and I," I'd never survive. What really mattered, in his life or in mine? Was the proper use of the objective case the authentic issue or was this—as Wilkins discovered was inescapable—but one dimension of a multidimensional meaning?

I leaned my hot face back against the newel post, shifting my weight a bit on the worn depression of the stair and admiring still the soft glow on the slate floor. How fallacious the scholarly premise—equally gorgeous, but wrong—that with enough hard work one can in fact come to The Truth about something. True or False: Mothers and babies deeply or authentically need to spend most of their time together. True or False: Women must not be forced to choose between motherhood and an intellectual life or meaningful career. Yeah, the premise of libraries like this is that we can find answers to the questions that we ask, and—furthermore—that all our itchy labor collectively has built the mighty edifice of western humanism, each small sacrifice of a summer day counting toward the whole, just like the cumulative anonymous craftsmanship of the great medieval cathedrals.

How much I had staked on this dream that we can, somehow, *know*—actually know—the crucial dimensions of what it means to be human in our own time and place, and how one ought to live.

Keats: "'Beauty is truth, truth beauty'—that is all/ Ye know on earth, and all ye need to know." And: "A thing of beauty is a joy forever:/ Its loveliness increases; it will never/ Pass into nothingness." And here is Wilkins, in 1668: we cannot say just what we mean. Like Prufrock. And the sarcastic shoulders of celibate scholars, cast in bronze. "'That is not what I meant at all./ That is not it, at all.'" So what is it, after all, I wondered, what is it that brings me here, keeps me here, even on summer afternoons? And what twentieth-century images would persist or be recovered and cherished, like campus gargoyles or the "sacred art" in Special Collections? What image captured my experience of university life in this last quarter of the twentieth century?

A picture came to mind, a life-sized statue of me on some future campus, like statues of Newton or Galileo: I'm clutching a baby, a book-laden briefcase, and a diaper bag; I'm trying to close a car door with my knee without falling over backwards. In a cold November downpour, ideally; or maybe in ten inches of new snow. Suddenly my statue was amidst a fountain to mimic that November rain, and I could see a Latin inscription. But, alas, I can't read Latin very well—and certainly not without a dictionary. The vision started to blur: one cannot envision much beyond what one already knows in more ordinary ways, even if as-yet unconsciously. No point, in short, in trying to parse the unreadable text. So am I, I wondered, a noble moment in the grand entrance of women to the full and ancient scholarly tradition? Or a dead end, a failed evolutionary experiment, doomed to falling over backwards? Maybe Mommy and monument will just never make it together.

And at my back I always hear that "Mommy" will not be forever. "Mommy" would carry through my tenure hearing, of course. But he would only be a baby once, for such brief years. Yet I would only be an assistant professor here once too. We each have but one life to live; one does not step into the same river twice. "The grave's a fine and quiet place," I thought, surveying again the tomb-like silence of remote, arcane libraries on beautiful summer days, "but none, I think, do here embrace."

I felt Mark's arms around my neck, the sweet smell of his skin and hair, the small puffs of his breathing near my ear, the wonderful warm roundness of his sturdy little body in my arms. And at my back—literally—the inviting beaches of a nearby lake, with its sandy beach and quiet little waves for a baby to play with. I could hear Mark's unbelievably beautiful chortling laugh, the clarity and the truth of immediate grace: *this is fun.*

I felt like Odysseus on Kalypso's island, in Book Five of the *Odyssey,* refusing the goddess's offer of eternal youth because he wants to go home to Telemachus and faithful Penelope. Kalypso warns him that the journey home will include terrible trials and much suffering, but he replies, "I will endure it, keeping a stubborn spirit inside me, for already I have suffered much and done much hard work." Me too, I thought, I hoped, me too: whatever this might take, maybe I have it in me. Maybe. I've proved myself more than capable of one hell of a lot already: maybe—maybe??—I could manage (or had somehow already traversed?) my own version of sailing 'twixt Skylla and Charybdis, neither losing myself to the incessant demands of work nor to the incessant demands of family life. I am a scholar, and I am a mother, and surely there is much more to me than either term can name. Surely. Somewhere. Isn't there?

And I thought of Achilles in Book Nine of the *Iliad,* arguing with Odysseus and the others who came out to his tent to persuade him to rejoin the battle against Troy despite his anger at Agamemnon. He reminds them that he knows his destiny already: if he stays to fight, he will win immortal glory but die young; if he leaves, he will live a long but obscure life. But "no riches can compare with being alive," he explains. "To all the rest of you I say: 'Sail home.'" Two destinies. Like me: a scholar's life, and given my ambitions and abilities, no doubt rich with achievements; some other life, an obscure and quiet life, playing with my baby but—not merely captive to *kinder und kuche*—doing something else. I had no idea what.

Beyond a doubt: here was another tradition, profoundly questioning the value of heroic achievement and the glory it can provide. Here was an ancient and daring poetic claim that prestige and possessions and worldly success are not the only measures of life. Homer's tales go back nearly three millennia: as a culture, we have been struggling with this question for a very long time. Achilles does eventually rejoin the battle, of course, after Patroklos dies while disguised as Achilles. But he does so for the love of Patroklos, to avenge the death of his friend—not for the love of glory.

Wordsworth too had stood on a beach, asking questions about the purposes of life.

> *The world is too much with us: late and soon,*
> *Getting and spending, we lay waste our powers:*
> *Little we see in nature that is ours;*
> *We have given our hearts away, a sordid boon.*

It is not given us to know for sure, to say with certainty and singleness of meaning. But it is indeed given us to yearn, to dream and to desire and to choose what dreams will matter. To sell our souls, or to give them away, or to trade them for a mess of pottage to soothe some immediate hunger. I could not find my heart, that afternoon: it was beyond the recall even of the crackerjack librarians in Special Collections. I had enough for footnote #6.9, I decided, and gave the rest of John Wilkins but a cursory skim to his conclusion. In the bathroom, afterward, I bathed my face with smelly, stinging, liquid soap and dried off with cheap brown paper towels. Hives were now all up and down my arms, and the side of my head was pounding as the tumor began to swell in earnest: #6.9 was one footnote I would *not* recheck later.

Mark and I did not stop by the beach that afternoon. I resolved to take some afternoons off; but it never worked out, because theoretical linguistics in the seventeenth and eighteenth centuries proved a far richer and more complex matter than I had ever imagined—particularly since I had never studied linguistics. To master so much of a new domain, I needed those long weeks of long days of utterly nonstop reading that only summers offer. That reading turned into a whole separate journal article, in fact, later published in *Philological Quarterly*. In my book manuscript, footnote #6.9 then referred both to Wilkins and to that article.

In short, note #6.9 became my first chance to cite myself. And it remains the only footnote among hundreds I have written that has its own imaginary subtitle: "How I Spent My Summer Vacation."

Having It All

News came one dark and rainy Tuesday early in November of 1980: my book manuscript had been accepted for publication by the English press of Allen & Unwin, whose editor had been snookered by a cabbie and then ambushed by a snowstorm blowing down from Canada. I was thrilled. Getting a book published is one of life's major transitions for bookish sorts: to go from reading books to writing books—I might as well have sprouted wings. To find my own name on the shelves or among the battered yellow cards in the catalogue: what a thought! I had dreamed for ten years about writing a book on the *Biographia Literaria,* ever since I had first read it as a sophomore. And that dream had come true. I detoured to buy champagne on the way home; we hired a sitter for the next weekend and planned a proper celebratory dinner.

By Thursday, people I barely knew from other departments were stopping me on the sidewalks and in the library to shake hands and offer congratulations. Talk started immediately about my team-teaching graduate courses in other departments or lending a hand on various of their dissertation committees. There were rumors from several quarters that I might teach the whole required sequence in the history of literary theory in the new interdepartmental Ph.D. program in literary theory. I had always taught one course in this survey, but all of it? Good heavens! What an improbable plum.

And yet, the men who taught the other two courses were both leaving: one had another job and the other was retiring. I had been hired, after all, in part because I had done my prelims in the history of theory. There were various people interested in teaching contemporary literary theory, but there was no one else with credentials—or interests—parallel to mine in the history of theory. My specialty was very new stuff, the leading edge of new developments in the field generally. Despite the relatively lower prestige of survey courses, teaching all of the only required course sequence would give me tremendous influence over that whole batch of graduate students. This wasn't just tenure: it was a niche of my own, a major niche in a high-prestige, well-funded program. And it was hope for escape from the exhausting—albeit rewarding—work of teaching composition. I bought another bottle of champagne, to have on hand in case the rumors proved right.

Within the week, an associate dean came up to my lunch table to say how pleased everyone was over in Student Affairs. Another from Freshman Advising expressed similar delight. Both of them hoped I could now be persuaded to trade some teaching for some administration. Ah yes: the contest for resources between graduate and undergraduate programs, the contest for power between scholars and administrators. Were I ambitious to be a dean one day, this was the route—not brooding over my own little flock of graduate students in literary theory. I knew that my original dossier from the University of Michigan had warmly praised my potential for leadership and for administration. At the time I was startled by those comments; but clearly, now, other people seemed to be agreeing.

I felt dizzy for days, astounded by this visible shift in my status: I had made it. "Of course this means tenure," people kept saying. And maybe I belonged here after all. Perhaps, after all, I could be—as Joyce had once put it—a "normal woman" and a professor too. Maybe the awkwardness I felt was merely the personal cost of a larger transition in the public roles of women. Surely there was a substantial cohort of good-humored, capable people here, folks for whom academic pettiness was simply part of the human condition. Surely some of my graduate-school contempt had been youthful—even immature—idealism, expecting Edenic reality. The English department had plenty of people who were decent and conscientious and humane. And there were jerks. But there would be jerks in any job.

So I was not surprised, nor did I take visible notice, that not everyone in my department was pleased with the news that I had hurdled the principal barrier of assistant professorship. Although some of my departmental colleagues were gleeful—as close to boisterous in their congratulations as somber middle-aged academics ever get—others were icily formulaic in their acknowledgments. Dismay was quite visible around the corners of their eyes. Neither women nor literary theory were welcome in some circles both in the department and in the college: in the spring of 1976, when I had my final on-campus interview, mail from the dean to faculty came addressed "Mr. Mary Smith" and the inside salutation was

"Gentlemen." When that was changed, in the fall of 1976, my mail started coming not to Mr. Catherine Wallace but to Mrs. Warren Wallace. It had been quite a fight to get that changed: the Provost himself had said hello to me on the street one day, calling me "Ms. Wallace" in an exaggerated, sarcastic way.

Furthermore, Romanticism as an historical and literary movement was severely underrepresented in the college, in accordance with academic intellectual trends in the first half of the twentieth century. But nationwide, that neglect was now being reversed, and English departments were leading the way. Romanticism was the hot new field in cultural studies. But not at this university, not yet anyhow, and that's why I was being recruited to serve on dissertation committees in other departments. As a romanticist and an interdisciplinary cultural historian of literary theory, I was very clearly needed. So I stepped demurely across a variety of power lines, pleased—not for the first time—that the nuns had taught me what they called "chaste deportment." People would be not dismayed, after all, unless this publication did in fact insure my future in the place. I could afford to be demure. History was clearly on my side.

In my mind's eye, I stood again at the edge of Plymouth Road, with the mirrored Power Center and the weight of Central Campus behind me, looking out across the chimneys of the buildings that backed their way gingerly down the steep cliffs of the Huron River. All those fractured images of me looked out over my shoulder. There was a lot of rich golden oak at this university, by golly. Even the open carrels in the library were oak. And there were tradition and power to spare. Did I belong here? The inexplicable job, the improbable editor, the quick book contract: were these evidence of fitness? An answer to prayers I still had not said?

To get from my own office to the departmental offices, I had to walk up toward the foreign language building through a long formal rose garden. The flower beds were flanked by double rows of ancient flowering crab trees that bloomed just before the roses unfolded into their early peak. At the end of that rose garden, I would turn left between the last crab tree and the most beautiful ginkgo I had ever seen.

In November there was not much to admire on this walk. But one morning I slowed as I approached that ginkgo, as if to do it homage once again, so as not to hurry a very elderly professor as he hobbled across the irregularly triangular courtyard flanked by English, by history, and by foreign languages. Like him, I might teach on this campus and walk past these roses for nearly fifty years. I bet he had known this towering ginkgo as a sapling. For a flicker of a moment, his rough gait was the ragged, fractured dance of mirrored images. All the weight of the university slammed down on me, and for that moment I could not move.

Or Maybe Not

As my initial elation settled back to earth, I found myself exhausted. Like Wordsworth scaling the Alps, I found that I had gone from struggling uphill to heading downhill without an intermediary moment, as if I had somehow missed the peak about which I had dreamed. The wife of a colleague began to put the situation into words for me.

"You really have it all," Barbara said, her dark eyes bright with some inscrutable mix of envy and affection. Her own career in commercial art was on lean times around the demands of their daughter, who was almost a year older than Mark. But I felt vaguely bereft that afternoon. Yes, I seemed to have both a glorious career and a gorgeous baby. But I had no time to savor either of them. Like Wordsworth's Alps, everything in my life seemed fogbound. I did not stand triumphant at some peak.

But I recognized Barbara's ambivalence in the face of a woman who was regularly out for a walk with her children at about the time Mark and I arrived home. She was always comfortably dressed in sweats or jeans or shorts; she eyed my hosiery and uncomfortable little pumps and tailored wool suits. She watched me struggle with diaper bag and briefcase and tired, cranky, opinionated baby. We never spoke. I suspect that neither of us had any idea what to say.

On campus that week, an associate professor from another department called my name and ran to catch up with me. We stood a moment as she caught her breath; the shadowy November sun angled between black clouds. She is one of those women whose glossy hair is always flawlessly groomed, whose clothes somehow never look rumpled or dusty with chalk. People who seem so effortlessly beautiful have always intimidated me: I stood there feeling the unruly curl of my hair in such damp weather, lamenting how pink my complexion gets when the wind is raw and how any makeup at all simply gives me hives.

"Y'know," she said, "a lot of us are watching you. A lot of us are thinking about doing it too. And I just heard about your book! You are doing it all. You are doing it all so *well*." She stopped, suddenly, embarrassed.

"You're an *inspiration*," she said, her voice almost edging into irony. I smiled, ready to laugh. But her smile was gone; her mouth was taut and her eyes were bright with unshed tears. At that moment the bell rang: she turned away abruptly, late to her class. I watched her go, then trudged slowly up the stairs to my office. I brewed a cup of tea and tried to inspire myself into grading freshman essays. I didn't feel "inspirational." I felt haunted.

I did in fact seem to have it all. A book. A baby. A husband who enjoyed long slow walks with his befuddled and wheezy philosopher wife. I had everything, it seemed, except peace of mind. "I have set before you this day life and death," goes some Bible verse we had read in the Great Books course. "Therefore choose life, that you may have life everlasting." But as far as I could tell, there were set before me two very different choices. I could be guilty, or I could be crazy. I could neglect my baby's needs, or I could neglect my own. I could be exhausted and strung out and overworked, or I could be bored and restless and "underutilized." Just a housewife? Not me!

I had been bouncing off the walls of this little box for months. For months Warren had been responding that it was both false and stupid to frame the issue as Mommy vs. Baby, that Mark's most basic need was for a happy and well-integrated mother, not for a mother who spent every single hour in the house. He was right. And I was right. These were tough times, we agreed; but there was simply no reasonable way out. This was one of those situations in which we had to rely upon our unquestionable, even excessive capacity for delayed gratification. We had toughed our way together through all kinds of tough times—gross anatomy, German qualifiers, internship, and dissertation. And so, dammit, what was wrong *this* time? Why was that dependable old act failing us now?

Maybe this is what people mean, Warren had quipped, when they say we "have it all." Yeah, we can do it all, we can have it all—at a cost. And the cost is life itself. The cost is a life with all of everything and none of the simple silence of time to do nothing together, nothing at all. We had so much of everything, he had proposed, that we had no time for nothing. And, he grinned down at me, it was nothing that we needed. I took a swing at him, but he danced lightly out of reach.

On the horizon before me lay neither life nor death but dissertations to direct, increased administrative responsibility, graduate exams to devise. Another book to write. And I wanted all of it, and I wanted none of it. Warren's career in the medical school was at a parallel juncture. Now we could see that the success we had craved came only to those who sacrificed most of their personal lives to their careers. Now we had seen big-time academia up close. And we could see what it offered and what it asked of us. And we were tempted, and we were horrified, and mostly we were tired and lonely and depressed.

The Arsenic Hour

When we were first considering pregnancy, we had admired studies showing that women at home full-time with their children spend most of their time and energy on housework, household management, and such baby maintenance tasks as changing diapers and changing outfits, tasks that are usually done without significant interaction. Around such mindless scutwork, there are amazingly few moments of quality time. Any reasonably organized pair of parents, we had read, can hire out the housework—or continue to let housework fall into the nooks and crannies of the week—and concentrate an equal measure of quality time into evenings and weekends. Fathers, after all, have always had only evenings and weekends with their children; and devoted men have always succeeded at loving, effective fathering. Children need to know they are cherished, but they probably don't need Mommy to wash every sock and mop every floor with her own two hands. Self-evident truths. QED. Of course of course of course.

But as that autumn gave way to winter again, and winter turned slowly to spring, it was increasingly obvious that we were still not managing to make it work. Or, perhaps, we seldom succeeded in getting Mark to go along with our tightly disciplined schedules. Like most babies, he was born with limited management skills: all he knew was My Way, and usually My Way Now. I tried again, as the weather warmed again in the spring of 1981, to leave work a couple of hours early, so as to walk the two short half-blocks from our apartment to a darling little Tot Lot playground—all pine bark chips and miniature swings and benches painted in high gloss primary colors. In the very late afternoon, those benches were littered with rich leather briefcases carefully stacked atop diaper bags. Mark and I needed to meet these women and their toddlers, I resolved. Maybe I could pick up some tricks to managing this routine. Who knows: maybe I'd even make some friends . . . For whatever array of reasons, then, the long bright afternoons beckoned me out of the library a bit early and off to the park when Mark and I got home.

Mark was puzzled when I kept blocking his way into the apartment courtyard. This was a game he played with Warren—early football training? I had wondered—but Warren and I were always careful not to usurp one another's forms of play. With a laugh, Mark realized that I was playing Daddy's game; he turned willingly back toward the street—and straight back to the car door. I pleaded. I explained. I enticed. I picked him up and walked a few yards and set him down, stepping a few paces ahead and holding out my hand. C'mon kid, I thought to myself. This is called "a walk." We are going to walk to the park. *C'mon, dammit!* Mark beelined to the nearest car and waited earnestly for me to catch up and buckle him into a car seat. I tried again. This time, Mark selected a gorgeous red sportscar. Nice try, kid. *No.*

I could not comfortably tote thirty pounds of books and papers, plus thirty pounds of toddler. Nor could I reasonably leave my briefcase in sight in our little station wagon. Our apartment was on a high third floor—four flights up, actually—of a brownstone with ten-foot ceilings, servant's quarters, and real fireplaces. If I carried Mark and diaper bag and briefcase up all those stairs, we would never come back down. It had been a horrible day at work and—really, God—all I wanted was to sit on a park bench and watch my baby play in the sand, or push him in one of those cute little swings. Really now, God: that's not so much to ask.

Maybe God was willing, but Mark was clearly not. "Outside" was merely transit-to-car. One did not *stay* outside. People belonged either in apartments or in cars—or else maybe asleep in strollers. "Walking outside" was beyond his conceptual universe. And furthermore, he began to suspect that I had lost the car or maybe misplaced the apartment—or my wits. When I pulled him away from yet another vehicle, he flung himself on the grass and screamed. No hiker lost in the Himalayas ever felt such despair. The car had been right here someplace, just a minute ago!

I picked him up. He kicked me. I set him down, facing back toward the courtyard—still quite visible, only fifty feet away. He charged off to the next closest car. I picked him up again, and we were both in tears by the time I got the front door unlocked. He refused to climb the stairs. Instead of carrying him up first and stashing him safe (albeit angry) in his crib, I left him wailing at the bottom of the long stairwell shaft as I trudged up with briefcase and diaper bag. When I went back down to get him, neighbors peeped out of two different apartments to watch me going past, tear-stained and steely-jawed.

I tried again the next day, and the next. I tried one Saturday morning. Warren tried one Sunday afternoon. No question about it: this kid was convinced that walking outside was only to get in the car to go to Judy's or to run errands. He was warped already, deprived of his toddlerish birthright by the ambitions of his parents.

I tried another tack. Judy was to give him a bigger snack after his afternoon nap, so that I could play with him in the apartment right after work—rather than beginning immediately to fix his supper and thus getting trapped into cooking and dishes. We kept his toys to the left of the fireplace, on shelves built in between the fireplace and a generous bay of big, south-facing windows. The yellow sun gleamed through the trees onto the toys scattered across the honey-colored oak floor. I set him down amid this inviting clutter and stretched out on the floor myself, sun on my back, wishing for a moment that I were a cat and could just sleep in this welcome yellow warmth.

Mark glowered at me and crawled away to pull newspapers off the coffee table and to tear the covers off of expensive professional journals. He pouted and wailed inexplicably. I tried every trick known to ingenious creative motherhood, but Mark was equally clear and determined. He wanted no part of me, none whatsoever. He wanted to be left alone. I should go fix dinner. I did, glancing out now and then to watch him play, alone, with the clutter of toys. If I wanted to play with Mark, it had to be on his terms and on his schedule. And his terms, as I knew so well, meant the half hour just before we had to leave in the morning. His efforts to engage me in charming play at that point left me guilty and rushed and barely prepared for my ten o'clock class, day after day after day. I wanted him to want me when it suited my schedule but—as in any love relationship—"schedule" was both alien and alienating. Only the Buddha could have had such implacable self-possession: when Mark wanted no part of me, he wanted no part of me.

Mark and I had, unbeknownst, encountered a central mystery of life between parents and small children: the Arsenic Hour. I didn't even know it had a name until years later. A friend's great-grandmother—a tiny, frail woman well into her nineties—sat watching her struggle to get dinner around the whiney demands of her two small ones.

"Ah yes," Granny laughed suddenly. "'Tis the Arsenic Hour: and y'don't know whither ta give it, or ta take it!" Such benediction from the matriarchs of old! There is a stretch, from three-thirty or four each afternoon until shortly before bedtime, when children are insufferable and parents are convinced that instead of getting pregnant they should have gotten a ceramic Dalmatian to sit by the fireplace.

Shortly before bedtime, of course—and acutely so on nights when Mommy and Daddy have brought home particularly bulging briefcases—one encounters another seldom-described phenomenon.

The glossy baby books never warn you about this one: I'm Too Cute to Put to Bed. Babies who are adept enough at this maneuver can train their parents to delay baby bedtime for hours on end. Quality time, yes? Parenting on the evenings and weekends, yes? Besides, what remotely normal human being can resist the engagements and stratagems of a playful baby who has—for the preceding several hours—resolutely refused every playful initiative of the eager parents? The cranky fussing finally stops, and the kid turns on the charm: hearts of stone would melt. And guilty, conflicted, lonely parents have notoriously unstony hearts.

So there I was all too many nights, up very late reading or ever-so-softly tapping out the scansions I would need for my prosody class. Mark had charmed my socks off once again, or I had been unable to concentrate on this week's Greek tragedy around the antics of Mark and Warren together on the floor, fooling around and mugging for my approval. Nor had anyone washed the dishes.

I loved my baby, I loved my work, I had never been so gleefully in love with my husband. It was my life that I could not endure. Slowly, something deep within me started to corrode in the acid of that reality.

Like the Tin Man

One despondent Sunday in the spring of 1981, Warren and I walked along for blocks in thoughtful silence, listening to the back left wheel of the stroller squeak with every revolution. For how many months now had we been too busy, too preoccupied, to dig out the oil can and fix that squeak?

Something else was squeaking too, and in that long windy silence I began to hear it. Academia is fun because success is fun. Academia is fun because there is something undeniably gratifying when two hundred people sit there writing down your every word, when students stand in line to plead for admission into your courses, when journal editors send prompt letters that begin, "We are pleased to accept for publication your essay entitled . . ." Academia is fun because there is in me some broad streak of plain Irish blarney: teaching is performance, and I love it.

Above all, academia is fun because it is an excuse to sit reading poetry. Not just an excuse: a paycheck! I had spent all of one August reading Dante, feeling blessed beyond what I had words to express. I could spend ten hour days in the library, and no one would dare to say, "Get your nose out of that book and go play!" Of course I loved academia. It would take a cast-iron ego to resist such gratification.

And that was exactly the problem. There's nothing wrong with the gratification we were enjoying. But something is wrong when feeding a single dimension of your own ego begins to crowd out attention to other needs, as certain kinds of perennials will overwhelm a whole flower bed in just a few seasons. Something in our lives was crowded out. And listening to that incessant skrreee skrreee skrreee of the stroller, I could feel the rusty rubbing of some fundamental personal need edged almost out of existence.

Finally, I began to find words to replace that squeaking, words to name the rust. "Maybe," I heard myself saying, "maybe I want to quit. Set sail for home and stay there, full time." Warren's head snapped up; he stared down at me, amazed and skeptical.

"A sabbatical," I backtracked—no less startled than he by what I had said. "A year off, a year from now, after I get tenure."

Warren nodded speculatively, noncommittally. He gets cautious when I get metaphysical; he worries that I orient myself more to the potential and the theoretical than to the actual and the pragmatic. And he's right, of course: I do. But then he laughed and it was my turn to look up startled.

"In a year we'll be having another baby!" he observed dryly. "Doing this with a toddler *and* an infant would be undeniably crazy!"

It was easy to agree with that. And, counting months and years, I knew he was right about our schedule for a second pregnancy: this was April—and good Lord we had planned to start trying to get pregnant again in July! I was thirty-one and my biological clock was ticking fast—and louder no doubt in his head than mine. He did too much consulting for the high-risk obstetricians, too many referrals for people just older than we who found themselves unable to conceive a child. But the thought of a second baby somehow moved the whole afternoon into the realm of the entirely and purely speculative. Another baby?

We both felt better, having agreed not to look seriously into this particular mirror. We turned at last into the manicured courtyard of our apartment. Yes, something in our lives needed to be changed—unless of course this was just reality again, failing to be what we dreamt it should be. Lousy reality. What a crazy world. Who designed this system anyhow?

But there was no more time for speculation. We had been out all afternoon, and there were papers to grade and classes to prepare and reports to write and reading to do and laundry to do and dishes to do, and, and, and . . . We hauled Mark and his collection of blankets up those four long flights of stairs, with their gleaming waxed handrails and the lurid green "oriental" carpeting on the treads. We put the cold and silent walk behind us and settled into the evening's chores. We would worry about it tomorrow.

Moses and Me

That spring I was once again teaching the first term of the Great Books class: Homer, Sophocles, Ovid, Virgil, the Pentateuch, and the Gospel of Luke. Four epics, three plays, the "Metamorphoses," and Luke. Not excerpts: all of all of it. And in twenty-seven fifty-minute hours, minus the classes lost to the taking of exams. It was an impossible reading list, the kind of course devised by senior faculty who just want the material covered and foisted off onto junior faculty too dumb to know what they are getting into. But this particular bit of academic grandiosity was taught by the very best teachers from several departments and jammed with the best students the place had to offer: we had a great time, even though it felt something like the intellectual equivalent of an insane but unforgettable canoe trip I had once taken at summer camp. Or, a colleague proposed, this course was like riding a motorcycle through a museum. Except, another quipped, we were leading a troop of motorcyclists.

And so it was again. Mark was now sleeping through the night, but it hardly mattered. I was up until two or three o'clock night after night, trying to keep up with the reading and to write the weekly reading exams or to prepare my share of the formal Monday lectures. I hadn't kept such hours since I had been an undergrad myself. But such poetry as this sustained me. It kept my eyes open at two in the morning as if I had never read it before. And once again, the Jewish YHWH leapt off the page-crazy, caring, nameless. In comparison to the Greek divinities, YHWH was stunning in his complex and vital humanity. Only Odysseus is drawn as well, I thought. Once again I howled when Sara laughed behind his back, when Abraham dickered over the cost of saving Sodom and Gomorrah. I marveled at the poetic grace and economy of Jacob's getting up with a limp after fighting "the angel of the Lord" to a standstill as dawn threatens. Above all was I touched by how YHWH pleads and argues with Moses. No self-respecting Greek or Roman god would plead like that. Homer has thunderbolts for just such situations; Ovid has metamorphoses by the score.

At one point in YHWH's long argument with Moses, he promises that he will put words in Moses' mouth when the need arises. Reading in my office at nine one morning, I found myself cheering Moses onward.

"Maybe all this sticks and snakes business is a trick," I thought to myself, advising Moses. "But you can certainly trust the business of finding words. Yeah, God does this all the time. Trust me. All the time."

I stopped reading. What? But I knew, I knew at once and in a blinding flash. All my life I had been haunted by a powerful aura of the numinous when meaning was moving into words. My best writing arose from a dense inward silence of not-knowing and my confident but costly faith in that wordless unknowingness. I called it "imagination," as for centuries poets have. The prologue to the gospel of John calls it *logos,* incarnate as Jesus of Nazareth—a word from which Coleridge took the title of his famous, unfinished *Logosophia.* I had grown up hearing the fine poetic mysticism of that prologue at the end of every single Mass, as the old pre-Vatican II "Last Gospel." Literary theory and psychodynamic psychologies alike had taught me to call it "imagination," but for me it had never lost its metaphoric resonance as the light from some sacred fire. Nor had it for Coleridge, of course, and that was why I had become a

Coleridgean—but a Coleridgean, not a Christian. I believe in the unconscious, I argued, not the incredible.

But maybe these moments were not just my imagination at work in the levels below ordinary consciousness. Maybe it really was God—and God *within me*. What a thought . . .

What an absolutely impossible, wholly undeniable fact. I was dumbstruck, literally bereft of words. I turned, as I had turned so often, to the silent, nameless, darkly invisible core, shimmered round about with my years and years of work on all that the poets and all the philosophers had tried to explain, and all that the visionaries had described "as if." Perhaps this was my experience of God, this impenetrable, lucid obscurity, this darkness into which I could step or that would at times step out to envelop me. This was the silence from contact with which I had found the words that underlay not only my career but my identity. This was that paradoxical core of terror and of blessing to which I had learned, with such patient, agonized discipline, to be open whenever I struggled to write, to listen to students or to read their papers, whenever my studies confused me. This was the reality music revealed, the power and abiding solace of music that Warren and I shared so profoundly in those rare, crucial evenings of doing nothing.

Oh, no. *No*. I sat in my cold and funky office, in the yellow light of spring, as the hour I had set aside to prepare for my class slowly dribbled away. I left my office at the usual time, cut across the gravel alley, and hustled up the back stairs to my classroom, still unable to think and without the least glimpse of how I might teach in the next hour.

The students looked at me, expectantly, as I took a deep breath—and found I still could not speak, nor could I summon words to mind. If words were a gift, it was as if the gift had been rewrapped in some original silence that demonstrated again its etiology. I set my shoulder against that silence and shoved, as if against a recalcitrant door; but the blankness had taken over and it would not budge. Access was denied. The faintest ripple spread across the faces of the most attentive students. I flipped a page of my unreadable notebook, took another breath, and tried again:

nothing. Again that ripple across the students' faces, deeper and broader this time.

So with an inward laugh that would have made Sara smile, I consented. *Okay, God. You win.* Words came instantly: "Well . . . what did *you* think of these readings?" The class simply erupted with their own responses to the text; all I had to do for the next hour was keep order.

Back in my office after class, I closed and locked the door, turned out the light, and made myself some tea. The papers waiting to be graded could wait for awhile. This had been yet another of my Blakean visions, Wordsworthian spots of time, I told myself. But powerful enough to steal my voice for a few seconds in front of a class? Passionate, imaginative sensitivity is one thing. The depth of my own response to literature was familiar stuff. But the inability to think—and then to speak? That was something else again. My own moment, like Sara's, of laughing at God: *You must be kidding!* But God wasn't joking, the Genesis poets argued: not at all. Our God YHWH is like this.

Maybe. Maybe I'd have made a good Jew? In my experience, in the urban-ethnic Roman Catholicism of my childhood, Christianity's God, despite his putative origin as the God of the Jews, has no such wit, no such witty intimacy with creation. Or no such poets in "his" service? Unless, of course, you count Blake. Or Wordsworth and Coleridge. Or Donne, or Dante, or Hopkins, or, or, well, plenty of poets, especially once you get past the anthology classics and off on your own into "the collected works of." But as far as I could tell, no one in any church I'd ever known had ever taken such poets seriously. The social function of churches was to get people to obey the culturally dominant group—not to awaken us from our "dogmatic slumber." Nah. Dogma was the very stuff of religion. I could still explicate early Church heresies by the handful and recite the principal findings of major church councils; by the age of ten or twelve, I had dutifully memorized the first 367 questions of the 499 published as the "Baltimore" catechism. I'd been a real hit once upon a time with the instructor of a graduate Joyce course, because I could still rattle off the doctrines and definitions that underlie parts of *Dubliners*. The nuns had never succeeded in teaching me trigonometry. Even my spelling was scandalous. But I learned all that doctrine.

And so there was no question: nobody ever laughed at God, and God bore no resemblance whatsoever to this entirely enchanting, dangerously unpredictable, passionately Jewish character YHWH. YHWH was a character someone might love or hate—or both, quite as if "he" were a real person. The God I had grown up around was the sort of compulsive, small-minded bureaucrat that one approaches only in the company of an expensive lawyer: "God" was powerful, vindictive, violent, and the ultimately insignificant image of our own psychological projections. I had seen through "him" in an instant the first time I had read the great Enlightenment deconstructions of religiosity.

Having thus reminded myself of my own long-standing atheism, I felt a lot better. But what was I to do about my extraordinary reaction to this business of finding words in one's mouth? Surely language was the real issue here, not God. Despite the heaps of work on my desk, I continued to sit, silent and alone, the lights off, the door locked, just sitting, waiting patiently with the question in mind to see what would come to mind, as if I were merely baffled by some puzzle in my scholarly research.

And the Nuns

What came to mind was a story I wrote as a freshman in high school, a story about a girl who plays the piano. I called her Sally because I had always liked the name—especially after *sally* as an intransitive verb had appeared on a recent vocabulary list. Writing such a story—or at least turning it in—felt like a bold leap, for me. At any rate, Sally wants to play jazz in addition to the standard classical repertoire. Her parents have a fit. She feels miserable, defiant, and trapped.

An uncle visits, encourages her, responds sympathetically to her passionate response to jazz, to her refusing the demands of her parents' desires for her, which were of course merely their desires for themselves. He takes her part. At the end the doors to the cage stand open. He has bought her an expensive collection of the right music. It sits on a shelf over the piano, awaiting her touch. The uncle leaves. Sally is determined to master this new stuff, but I wanted my readers to wonder whether she will be able to sustain her resolve all by herself. I wanted my readers to share her fear at the uncle's departing shoulders.

What I remembered best about the story is what fun I had describing the very early spring weather—the color of grass as it begins to green, the pale and delicate angularity of grass seedlings new-sprouted in fine black soil, the soft round smell of the air, such a blessing after the sharp grit of winter. My heroine has a friend, whose mother takes this fine spring Saturday to wash screens: that was fun writing too. Black screens against a dark green picket fence, the water from the hose still cold enough to deserve caution, to make the girl dream of summer water fights but not—not *really*—want to grab the hose and start one.

This mother is a Phi Beta Kappa. I wasn't sure what that was, actually; but I knew it meant "smart." I'd seen this guy once, with madras-plaid Bermudas and a little gold square thing dangling from a gold chain attached to a belt loop and disappearing into his pocket. He had sat next to me at the soda fountain at the corner drugstore, drinking a Coke. I asked him what it was, and then later I had to ask my oldest brother what a Phi Beta Kappa key was. It didn't look like a key at all, actually. But my brother had been very impressed, and I had remembered. So anyhow, this mother in my story has a Phi Beta Kappa key on her madras-plaid Bermuda shorts.

My heroine likes her friend's mother. This lady makes great apple pies and decides for herself that she wants the screens up and sets about doing it, nonchalantly competent. She is the rare sort of mother who might join a water fight—or even start one. Sally's mother would never wash screens or fight with the hose. She disapproved of such behavior in a woman. Furthermore, outstanding academic attainments, like homemade pie crust, were the sorts of behavior she condemned as ostentatious. A woman need be nothing more than a credit to her husband, a modest, unobtrusive support to him in his endeavors. My heroine watches this woman washing screens and feels her own entrapment all the more keenly. That's why she erupts when, later that afternoon, her uncle the musician sits at the piano with her and asks an innocent, avuncular question about what she enjoys playing.

I wrote the story for a literary magazine that my English teacher and her pal, the sophomore honors English nun, were trying to get started. They were ambitious, those two: fiery and devoted as perhaps only young nuns can be. I remember them as tall and strongly built: I saw breasts and hips despite the yards of white wool that made up the Dominican habit. I could no more talk to them than Sally to her friend's mother, but I did leave my story on the corner of Sister Monica's desk.

She summoned me with an abrupt word, and my heart strangled my voice. The story was accepted; could I condense it? I dropped out the spring grass and the smell of the air and the washing of screens; I dropped my girl's delight in finally mastering how to grab the newel post and swing down five steps at once without losing her balance—despite how her parents yelled whenever they heard her try.

I was summoned again. *No*, I was told. I had taken the life out of it, I was told. I had taken out everything that had made them accept the piece to begin with. I had fought tears to drop those parts, and now I was guilty of exactly the death I had suffered. I could not ask what to do instead.

"Look at me when I talk to you!" the nun demanded. "Do you understand?"

I did not want to look up: she would see my tears and then I would really be in trouble. They would never take the piece. But I did as I was told. Her face abruptly softened—such an abrupt person, Sister Monica—but she said nothing. And I said nothing back. I had never before noticed what large, beautiful grey eyes she had, luminously flecked with blue. I almost let myself wonder if in fact she understood. But I stopped myself. I knew better than that. She just had pretty eyes. And what's pretty eyes—in a *nun*? I took the manuscript she handed me, bowed politely, and left.

I got back inside my story, over and over again: what was life, in a story? Where was what you could call "alive" in these pages? As I recall, eventually I trimmed a bunch of dialogue, and thus the story was published. I don't have a copy. But for a long time I cherished that still unanswered question. What is "life," in a story? Some stories do, clearly, come to "life." What is that? What does it feel like, when you are storytelling? Or listening? Lord knows I was growing up in a compulsively verbal clan of Irish storytellers. I had lots of stories and lots of experience watching the listeners. The listeners' faces were fun even when the stories themselves were baffling to a kid. Whatever "life" was, by golly, it was *real*—and it made even small, plain stories into something important. People listened.

And I remembered sonnets. Sister Monica read them to us. We had no books with poetry: I'm sure of that. Our classroom was a windowless basement room, dank and noisy with the clump of the steam boiler and brilliant with Monica's art museum posters. (Nobody else had stuff from the Art Institute. Nobody else had *anything* worth looking at. I had known immediately to look out for this nun: she was strange.) When she read these sonnets, no one breathed and no one moved. No one was distracted from her voice by the usual noises and sights of the room. Or if anyone was, I sure didn't notice. Quatrains, octaves, sestets, rhyme schemes— the delight all had *names*. Nothing anywhere in my life had prepared me for this. This was not the same stuff as the verses printed between stories in my grade school reader, as the verses inside greeting cards. I had never dreamed that words could do that, that words could be so . . . *alive*.

Whatever "life" is, sonnets had it. Not in places, as stories did, but everywhere. Sister Monica was watching me. She had been watching me, I realized. (That wasn't hard. I was second from the front, in the second row from the far wall.) I checked that the collar of my blouse was properly folded over the collar of my jacket, that my feet were together and flat and my knees touching. She started reading again the poems with which she had begun the hour, and I looked up from the corner of my desk, from the little hole designed to hold an ink bottle where I always stared when I needed to concentrate on what I was hearing. I watched her face, looking down at her book. She knew these poems. She had a whole thick book—was it all poetry? *She knew poetry.* As she read, her stern abrupt nunface, held in that vise of starched white linen, was soft and round and suffused with unexpected pink.

She looked up at the end of a couplet right into my eyes. And there were just the two of us, and these incredible words in the air around us; and there was only the most enormous space imaginable and the softest most inviting light. But I could not see. And I could not breathe.

Our eyes met again, again willingly, as I left the room in the usual silent single file. It was as if she were not a nun at all, not even a grownup, as if somehow, in some impossibly crazy way, none of that really mattered.

But I knew better. In my heart, I knew better. And so I was taken aback by the grief in her voice when she summoned me again, months and months later, at the far end of the year.

"Sister Quintilian tells me you plan to be a biologist," Sister Monica said, as if I had been arrested for vandalism. Quintilian—another blazingly young nun—taught freshman biology. I tried to explain that biologists can write poetry on the side, but poets cannot do biology without access to microscopes and petri dishes and all that stuff. You know. Laboratories. Nobody had a lab in her house. I did not try to explain that things like photosynthesis or mitosis and meiosis had the same heartbreaking beauty, the same austere grandeur that sonnets had—and that I could do biology and talk about biology without strangling, without that wrenching transit to someplace too bright to see and too dense to breathe. Until I had encountered sonnets, I had always wanted to be a writer. But my response to sonnets was more than I could manage: I wanted to keep a safe distance from words.

"But you can't," she objected again. "You just can't. Literature is—" She stopped. And I saw tears in her eyes, her large grey eyes with their deep blue flecks.

Embarrassed, I dropped my gaze, dumbfounded and disoriented by the possibility that she had in fact understood, that she felt what I felt, that she was herself as lonely and as hungry for words as I was.

"Yes, S'ter," I said, and bowed the formal, proper little half-bow, half-curtsey that was expected of us. "Yes, S'ter, I understand, S'ter," I said. And ran. Thank God it was almost the end of the year.

And I remembered Shakespeare, heaven help me. Sophomore English began with *Julius Caesar.* I took the crisp new paperback with me baby-sitting one Saturday night, never imagining that a play might be poetry and knowing only, vaguely, that "Shakespeare" was a famous name. I remember reluctantly giving way to sleep much much later that night, long after I had returned from baby-sitting. I had read the first act five times: I was beginning to get it.

Several weeks later, we took the classic Shakespeare exam: for selected passages, we were to identify the speaker, the spoken-to, and the immediate context; then we were to comment at greater length on the significance of these lines for plot, theme, setting, language, and character development. Sister Mary Charles lambasted the class as a whole for its miserable performance and announced that there would be a retest. She stalked around the silent room, glowering at each girl in turn as she slapped the test paper—face down—on each desk.

Mine was last. I remember, because I had obviously been pulled out from my usual place in the middle of the alphabetical order.

"You!" she hissed, in a whisper. "You're going to be a *biologist?*"

I had missed only one part of one question, on some exchange with a soldier about military events.

The class filed out in particular silence and order; but I stopped by her desk, still brimming with delight. Never had I worked so hard, rereading and rereading night after night. My inkwell hole should have been hot to the touch, so closely had I listened to every word in class. No A I was ever to earn would mean as much as that one. And never had a test been so absolutely satisfying. Only one who both understands the work and respects her students could write such a test. No wonder she and Monica were pals.

I felt the despair and the loneliness behind her anger, and I easily forgave her contempt for the class. She had worked so hard. I had worked so hard. We needed, both of us, to delight in my A before either one of us had to face the rest of the class. I wasn't the only one, after all, who had noticed my displacement from the alphabet. Kids would be asking me. I would have to hide my exuberance and lie convincingly.

"Do I have to retake the test?" I asked, remembering Monica's beautiful eyes and daring, now, a convivial grin.

"Yes!" she snapped, her face livid with anger and contempt.

"Yes, S'ter," I bowed and left. I made a point, after that, of rereading and rereading so as to be certain to ace every one of her tests: she was a worthy opponent who continued to write extremely difficult exams. Eventually, I made her glad to have me in her class, when she absolutely had to have the right answer from someone.

But I never raised my hand. I met her eyes and waited for her to call on me, to *ask* for the answer she needed. And I did not write a story for the literary magazine. I did not even pull a poem out of my poetry folder. Monica caught me in the hall to ask why, but I shrugged and said nothing.

And I remembered—of course!—writing for the school newspaper. In January of sophomore year, I changed to another Catholic girls' school, run by a different order of nuns. My parents, outspoken liberals who were keen on the Jesuits, had been suspicious of a Dominican school from the very start. Catholics have long memories on such matters. The new nuns were cutting-edge Catholic liberals in a brand new school with a sharply progressive curriculum. The principal was appropriately ancient, but the rest seemed to me unspeakably young. The sophomore religion nun— she was doing a dissertation on Chardin, as I recall—was still wearing an orthodontic retainer. Her braces had only come off the previous spring, the girls told me. As far as I could tell, half of the faculty were graduate students at the University of Chicago or at one of the divinity schools clustered in Hyde Park. We had a substitute for two weeks once, because the junior algebra nun was studying for some big test she had to take. I thought that was seriously weird. Nuns with braces? Nuns *taking* tests? But I liked the big mosaic by the front door: "Every girl has the obligation to become what she has the ability to become." And I was made welcome by teachers and students alike . . .

. . . Except by the sophomore English nun, Sister Julian Margaret. SJM, as they called her, looked up at me sourly when I appeared at her desk.

"Coming midyear like this—" she paused, letting her ordinarily sour face pucker down a bit further. "You know you are coming in at a disadvantage."

I was beginning to tire of this bow-and-nod business. I did not answer. I looked right into her colorless grey eyes and decided she was one of the rudest people I had ever met. And she was the assistant principal! I was in trouble already, dammit. She waved her hand, dismissively, to the desk that had been vacated for me in the middle of the room, thus to preserve alphabetical seating. I collected a few sympathetic looks as I took my seat, enough to bring a blush creeping up my neck and a glint of tears stinging to my eyes. I busied myself digging a pen out of my pencil case and looked up in terror to see her bearing down on me.

"Here," she said. "We have just started this." And she put a paperback copy of *Julius Caesar* on my desk. I gloated but did not look up.

In the spring of my junior year, Sister Julian Margaret resigned as moderator of the student newspaper. The official explanation was that she had become too busy as assistant principal to teach a full load and moderate the newspaper as well. From the students who wrote regularly for the newspaper, however, I heard rumors that she was angry at the principal's decision. But SJM was not a woman to be trifled with. When angry she could, we were certain, turn eighteen-wheel semitrailers into stone with a single, curt, dismissive gesture. None could imagine how the principal—a tall, aged, increasingly frail woman—had ever managed to impose her own will.

The new moderator was to be the new freshman English nun, Sister Patrice. We agreed that she didn't stand a chance. Patrice was too young, too uncertain of herself, too new to the place. She might do moderator-type scutwork with pasteup and such, but SJM would no doubt still call the shots. For instance, most kids were sure that SJM would keep control of making the writing assignments.

But I rather hoped Patrice would give out assignments. Eventually I had earned SJM's grudging and sour respect—and, I suppose, offered her my own in return. But we had never gotten along, and I had never understood why so many of my classmates enjoyed and admired her so genuinely.

In particular, we had crossed swords about my part-time job in a grocery store. Mom had come home with the application the week that I turned sixteen. Despite my protests, within ten days I was working sixteen hours a week: two short evenings—3:30 to 7:30—and Saturday from ten in the morning until seven P.M. Soon it stretched to eighteen hours: every Friday night I would work until 9:30, every single Friday night for the rest of my years in high school. I hated that job, but it paid for my monthly bus pass: $68 each month. That was a lot of money in 1966. It was everything I earned in a month, it was all the parties I did not get invited to, all the movies I did not see, all the dances that, even on Saturdays, I got home too late to attend. And when SJM had found out I was working, she was livid.

I stood silent when she berated me in the hall one morning for working when I should have been studying, just to buy myself more clothes and go the movies. But when she repeated the tirade in our English class, I jumped to my feet—without permission—to speak heatedly in defense of economic reality. I was working not for clothes but for a bus pass. I was fighting tears, furious both with her and with this filthy, exhausting, stupid job. SJM did not chastise me afterwards for lack of humility and proper deference—though I felt I probably had that coming—but neither, after that, had I gotten a second writing assignment for the school newspaper. When I had asked for one, she had retorted that I had homework to do.

I did not ask again—especially after she came up behind me at lunch one day just as I was regaling classmates with a parody of her. The girl opposite me gestured frantically, surreptitiously, as the table fell silent and pale. I looked up over my right shoulder, locking eyes for a long, silent few seconds. Then to hide my own urge to laugh—wondering, astounded, at a small almost repressed twinkle in her flat grey eyes—I turned back and took a large bite of my sandwich.

SJM glided wordlessly away, that silent nun-glide they teach to all nuns. I barely managed to swallow. And then no one else thought the episode was funny. They were all thoroughly chastised. I finished my lunch in silence.

Curious about the new moderator, I lingered after class one day to query the junior honors English nun, Sister Mary Hope. Mary Hope was a diminutive, utterly formidable Americanist and a maniac about good writing. I thought she would have been a sensible choice as moderator—although I suppose the principal might have worried that every issue would be late because every article would have to be rewritten sixteen times to meet Mary Hope's exacting standards. Mary Hope was not content with evidence that we had understood the poem or the novel in question. She was infamous for returning papers unread if the first paragraph failed to present a fully predicated thesis supportable by appropriate evidence and argument. I have never known anyone so passionate about the aesthetic power of good clear hard argument, nor as patient and loving and ruthlessly demanding with her students. One learned to think or died. My survival had been most uncertain for a very long time: seeing my first book in print was not as satisfying an event as the first time I earned some praise from this batty little nun.

When she was not talking about literature, Mary Hope was quite apt to stammer. As a result, she was a woman of few words, apparently little invested in the politics and gossip of the place. She would not talk to me about the newspaper, insisting—with a long deliberate look—that I should go talk to Sister Patrice.

So I did. Reluctantly. I explained that I wanted to be a journalist. I explained that trouble with math had cooled my passion for a career in science, and so I had gone back to thinking I would be a writer—a journalist (no poetry in journalism, I was thinking: maybe I could do it). I explained about why I worked and how SJM didn't think I should write for the paper. All I wanted, I explained, was some small bit once in a while. I promised that my regular work would not suffer and offered Sister Mary Hope as a reference on my reliability and skill. And, well, everybody knew that Nancy would be the new student editor—but even Nancy didn't know which

Sister would be assigning articles. So I wanted to ask who would be. And I wanted to ask for assignments, next year, if that were possible. I floundered to a halt.

I had been prepared for anything except her relaxed, silent, keenly attentive listening. When I stopped talking, Sister Patrice said that she would think about what I had said; she thanked me for stopping by and nodded to dismiss me. I bowed twice, just for good measure, and left convinced that I had once again made myself look like a dolt. But it probably didn't matter. This sweet young nun would never wrest real control of the newspaper away from SJM.

So I was certainly not prepared to be named the new student editor. Various nuns congratulated me in ways that seemed freighted with meanings beyond what I understood. Mary Hope caught my attention with a wave of her hand, then turned bright pink and nodded repeatedly, wordlessly, her large brown bird-like eyes sparkling inexplicably.

Between the grocery job and my new duties, I had no time to puzzle out my bafflement: neither the new editor nor the new moderator had the least inkling of how to get an issue pasted up and to press on time. I watched dumbfounded as Patrice reached up under the cape of her habit to unbutton the long loose outer sleeves of her habit, folded them neatly over the back of a chair, pushed up her inner sleeves, and started asking questions. I had never seen such a nun. She would eat Cheetos and lick the orange stuff from her fingers just as the rest of us did. One day she spilled Coke on her habit and swore. And almost every time I cited one of my Grandma Murphy's famous sayings, Patrice could name the poem from which the line came. I had grown up thinking this was ancient Celtic wisdom: most of it turned out to be Keats, Wordsworth, or Blake. So who had Kate Murphy really been? She had not gone beyond the fourth or fifth grade in rural Ireland, in Ulster, where schools for Catholic kids were hard put: where had she read these poets? And who in heaven's name was this nun, and what was she up to?

But there was no time to wonder about that either. I was far too embarrassed to ask Nancy for help—although she was, eventually, to prove herself kind and gracious far beyond her years. And in loyalty to Nancy's terrible disappointment, SJM's trained cohort of student journalists were keeping their distance. Panicky, I had corralled a miscellaneous group of bright-but-shy kids who were mostly outsiders to everything. Suddenly, these girls were willing to walk on water for this nun, to go ask anything of anybody, to spend some part of some evening doing something besides study. Suddenly we were a newspaper staff: the miracle of loaves and fishes didn't beat that.

When the first issue came out on time and reasonably correct, both Sister Patrice and I had lovely notes of congratulations from SJM. As a propitiatory offering, my first editorial criticized part-time jobs when they were not required by family finances. Nancy herself starting coming around, explicating to Patrice the more arcane points of pasteup and the magical incantations required before changing ribbons and typeface balls on the huge humming IBM Selectric typewriter. Nancy proved a whiz at short witty headlines, at the headliner's puns and wordplays of the sort that—legend had it—used to reduce SJM to apoplexy. I remember one night, much later in the year, when I got Nancy out of bed at ten-thirty to read her an article over the phone, give her a character count, and plead for help. Instantly, she had the headline we needed. I hung up the phone overwhelmed all over again at having a job that was rightly hers.

I lost ten pounds before Thanksgiving of my senior year, as the newspaper and senior humanities competed for my attention. In both junior and senior years, I was working thirty-two or, usually, thirty-five hours a week at the grocery store. That meant I could pay all of my own tuition and the bus fare besides, although I had no more than two or three dollars left after each monthly payment. But it also meant working four nights (going to the store straight from school) until 9:30 or 10:00 P.M. and every Saturday until 7:00. Sunday afternoons and the fifth weeknight—usually Wednesday—I spent at school on the paper. Six nights a week, then, I did not eat dinner: by the time I got home, I was far too exhausted to fix myself something to eat. The ten-minute breaks on weeknights were barely enough time to wolf a sandwich, particularly since waiting at the store's deli for a sandwich to be made and then waiting to pay for it used up at least half the break time. And those sandwiches were expensive. Usually I had nothing more than yet another mug of coffee, which was available for free. Furthermore, I have never been able to eat when I have too much on my mind. And the demands of the newspaper plus the delights of senior humanities—Dante and Homer and Sophocles, Shakespeare and Milton, Marx and Mao Tse-tung, Hobbes and Locke, glimpses of a world I had never known to exist—it all added up to much too much. I was overwhelmed, and I was hungry, and I was cold, tired, frustrated, and confused.

Did I want to be a journalist after all? I was haunted by a lifelong image of my mother wrapping today's wet garbage in yesterday's newspaper. The coffee grounds got several pages to themselves: the small aluminum percolator basket made a hollow wet "clunk" on the counter as it delivered its neat round packet of grounds. (It took me years to master Mom's adept wrist action, and by then the world was beginning to make drip coffee and to use tidy paper filters: no more of this potent brew that had boiled for seven or eight minutes.) I was haunted by words obscured by coffee grounds, by eggshells, by leftover noodles congealing in Mom's rich brown gravy. Night after night in my dreams, someone's writing was obscured by garbage.

But I had also lost ten pounds or so at the beginning of junior year, when I had first started working thirty-five hours. Keeping my summer work schedule into the school year was one thing. But it was something else again to work that much when I was trying to learn to write for Mary Hope, and to read my first long narrative poem, Stephen Vincent Benet's epic on the civil war, and above all to understand from the inside out how a poem does what it does. I now had a copy of X. J. Kennedy's famous little anthology of poetry, which concludes with Coleridge's "The Rime of the Ancient Mariner." I sat up night after night, reading and rereading and rereading that poem, astounded that anything could make so much emotional sense and so little intellectual sense at all—at least none that I yet could understand. And between bouts of "The Ancient Mariner," I wandered freely in that book, as gleefully obsessed as only a teenager can be. And so I lost weight that I had never regained, especially not after an appendectomy over Christmas break that year. I also didn't do very well in algebra, and I stopped reading history. I just listened in class and on tests relied upon my growing facility as a writer. But I felt very guilty about all of it.

Losing this second set of ten pounds left my uniform distinctly droopy. I had always been very lightly built—as the Irish often are—but minus twenty pounds I looked a bit peculiar. Customers and co-workers both took to commenting.

And I hated the job more than ever, complaining to my friends about subsisting endlessly on coffee and cookies and Cheetos, about staying up half the night to get papers written. I shared a locker with another honors student, one of the very organized worriers; I scandalized her but I was grateful when she added me to her list of things to worry about. More than once, her questions reminded me of some assignment or exam I had forgotten. Under the pressure of my job, I had entirely given up studying for exams. But I always wanted to get my written work in on time, pounding out papers on a big old black cast-metal typewriter left over from my grandfather's trucking business.

More than once my friends covered for me when I cut out of gym class to finish a paper or to prepare some oral presentation I had forgotten about. In an odd but, in memory, very touching display of motherliness, at times they even insisted I had to cut gym to study for some test. And I would. Or I would take a nap, curled up on the floor of the locker room. I was lousy at volleyball anyhow: captains happily agreed to do without me. Once I got an A on such a gym-class-based oral presentation when the others presenting with me all got Bs. They were annoyed: they had come to me as we went in to gym that day, just to make sure I was ready as the assigned moderator of the panel, which I had entirely forgotten. They were afraid I would screw things up for *them*. They were willing to lie to the gym teacher, if she asked where I was; but I was not to use my guilty adrenaline to outshine them.

I began to suspect that the nuns knew what was going on. Soon after that infamous oral presentation, SJM cornered me outside the cafeteria. She commented on my loss of weight and demanded to know if I still had "that job." I did not reply—although I was certainly thinking it—"Do you still charge tuition?" I simply looked straight at her with much more angry defiance than I actually felt, answering "Yes, Sister" with a slow, proper, sarcastic bow. She glowered at me, silently, shook her head and turned sharply away.

The last issue of the school paper was a nightmare of pasting: we had to get 2"×3" pictures of each graduating senior—all 367 of us—glued down in straight lines. Once again we missed the printer's scheduled pickup. And once again I got to drive the convent car to the printer's, because of course nuns were not allowed to drive. Sister Patrice always came along, because of course girls were not allowed to drive without nunly supervision. Life was like that in 1968.

Driving back that May afternoon, we were caught in evening traffic blocked by a freight train crossing the roadway. As we sat waiting, the sun sharp in our eyes, Patrice tried once again to dissuade me from journalism. Mom and SJM had colluded to get me a full-ride five-year scholarship from the *Chicago Tribune* to Northwestern's Medill School of Journalism, to a combined B.A./M.A. program. To their considerable dismay—and if you added Mom and SJM, that really added up—I had at the last moment turned it down when I discovered that I could not change majors if I changed my career plans. But I was still planning to begin in journalism, at the University of Detroit—a Jesuit place in a neighborhood that would be torn by the riots later that summer. The university had added to my National Merit Scholarship: tuition was covered. All I had to pay for was housing, food, and books. But I was terrified about trying to earn that much money—the $500 I had saved from summers at my grocery store job would not cover even the first semester.

Furthermore, I was weary to tears of pressure from grownups about my plans: everybody had always been so damn sure about what I should do with my life. We had gotten into this *Tribune* scholarship fiasco because I had failed to win one of the scholarships given by the grocery store. The scholarship included summer jobs: it was, essentially, a recruitment program. But I had not won their scholarship—although my sister had—and I wanted no part of a future in the grocery business. No one had told me that the store manager had to write a recommendation. I hated that woman and I had never made the least attempt to disguise my feelings: when she asked me if I wanted a career with the company, I had laughed at her contemptuously and said something rude. Failing to win that scholarship, and then turning down the *Tribune* scholarship: my parents were baffled. And now Patrice. Now Patrice was after me with her version of my future.

"But Catherine," she pleaded—she is one of the two or three people who have ever called me Catherine—"literature touches life so directly!"

I imagined literature, like a pole or a kitchen mitt between me and life; and I retorted that *I* wanted to get my hands on life.

My retort hung in the air as if an unintended accusation while tears rolled down my face. I loved this young nun: I didn't quite mean what I had said. And yet I did—or did I? She sat back abruptly, her face hidden behind the veil and starched linen of her head-dress, staring out the window at the First Avenue forest preserves along the Des Plaines River. The sun-silvered asphalt ahead of me felt like life itself, taking me who-knows-where. All I understood was that I wanted to be in control of it. I wanted to live my own life, directly and immediately and not to please all these insistent Everyones. I did not want to spend my life trying to get sophomores to understand *Julius Caesar* and to stop splitting infinitives or dangling participles. Surely there was more to life than these sheltered classrooms and all their petty rules about uniforms and demure comportment and humility.

Sister Patrice turned to me again, silencing my thoughts with the pain on her face. "But Catherine," she began again. "But, Catherine, you have such a gift, such a gift for words . . ."

I wondered, *what does* that *have to do with being an English teacher!* But before I could ask, the line of cars began at last to move, forcing my eyes away from her tear-streaked face, blinding me to whatever revelation it might have held. We rode in silence, her phrase electric in the air between us. I parked the car in the convent lot, we bowed to each other in the proper way, and I went out to the bus stop to get myself home.

A gift for words. But we were done with the last issue, and I have no memory of ever speaking to her again.

And here I was, all these years later, correcting split infinitives and dangling participles. My "gift for words"? I wrote well enough, evidence suggested; I enjoyed writing as much as ever. Of course I had stopped writing poetry at some point in college—the more I read of "real" poets, the fewer illusions I had about my own literary talent. Nor did I write fiction: storytelling had reverted to a purely oral form, to witty historical anecdotes to keep my students entertained. But it was probably true that, at some level, I had a certain gift for words if you wanted to use that sort of rhetoric. Why, then, had Moses blown me away like that? Why had I lost my voice, lost language altogether?

I hovered on the brink of panic as the memories of the nuns faded away and I was left face to face with my original question: what had just happened to me?

And then it was—almost as if gently—that whatever was pushing me to the brink of panic backed up. Blood not ice returned to my veins and there I was, just sitting in my office ignoring a stack of papers that needed to be graded. The proper explanation appeared in my mind, self-evident and easy. The Genesis poets were among the world's best, that's all. Of course I had found myself for a moment entirely within the fictive world that they create. And then, overwhelmed and exhausted as I was, I had found myself trapped inside. "Poetic faith," Coleridge calls it: when a literary work engages us successfully, we simply ignore the fact that it's "only a story," or that it's "just a movie." We react "as if" whatever happens is entirely real. I just needed to get some rest, I told myself calmly. That's all. I'm tired.

And stress does funny things to creative introverts like me. I was born to love Blake, I suppose, who said, "that called Body is a portion of the Soul discerned by the five senses, the chief inlets of Soul in this age." I have more than my share of the other inlets, the subordinate intuitive and imaginative ones. And that's a hazard when I am weary: imaginary things can start to feel astoundingly real, even imaginary characters like YHWH. I did not give the experience another thought. It did not occur to me to consider that YHWH of the Jews is portrayed as both persistent and very very patient and—most dangerously—utterly nonlinear in thought and behavior. I resolved to send Sister Mary Hope a copy of my book on Coleridge when it was published, and I closed the door—firmly—upon the whole experience.

I stopped staring out the window, rinsed my empty teacup, turned on the lights, and got out my red pen. I had work to do.

July 1981: News and More News

The sound of a door opening awakened me; startled, I could not remember where I was until the doctor put a gentle hand on my shoulder, urging me to lie still again. I had fallen asleep in an examining room, on the padded examining table with its paper cover. I remember staring, disoriented still, at the grey plastic buttons on his lab coat and the two slips of paper in his left hand.

He sat down heavily on the small wheeled stool, looking silently into my eyes for a moment, giving me time to collect my scattered wits. I was pregnant again. And, and, I had mononucleosis. He did not know what that combination might portend. He had looked it up, he had called around, and nobody seemed to know. The next night, Warren came home from work with the same report from his high-risk obstetrics pals. They didn't know either. Nor did the infectious disease docs. One of them called the Centers for Disease Control in Atlanta, and then the National Institutes of Health: we could not even find a study in progress. Computerized literature searches by the reference staff found nothing either. Nobody knew. The only grim hope was that if the infection caused problems, they would probably be catastrophic problems because they came so early in the pregnancy. I might not be pregnant for long.

And I was far too sick to care. Warren stayed home to take care of me, until he came down with mono two weeks later. Then we both stayed home, taking turns sleeping while Mark was awake.

Once a week my sister and mother brought in groceries and frozen casseroles. They washed our pajamas and bedsheets and left again.

After endless weeks of lying in bed, not even wearing my glasses much less trying to read, I felt well enough to put on my glasses and read a little between naps in my big yellow recliner. I tried Derrida—the same paragraph four times in one day. And then gave up. I spent August and September reading Dickens, reading Dickens a few pages at a time before I went back to sleep. My book was in press. Nothing more could possibly get accepted for publication prior to my tenure hearing that fall. I could afford a summer reading novels. And I did not have energy enough to concentrate on anything else. Neither of us left the apartment until late August, when stifling heat drove us to the lakefront a block away. It was a terrible mistake. We sat on the grass for an hour, then struggled home and, very slowly, up all those stairs.

By the end of September I could dress and drive to campus, although the exhausting walk from the parking lot left me in tears. I had lunch with the chairman of the department, hoping to persuade him to persuade the dean to let me shift my "light" teaching quarter from spring into fall. He didn't understand why I was not asking for a medical leave, just taking fall quarter off altogether. I had to explain that I was pregnant again, that if I did not miscarry then I would be off in the spring on maternity leave. This was not welcome news. Accommodations were not possible. I was falling into the gap between medical leave and disability insurance: the dean's only suggestion was that my colleagues teach at least one of my fall courses for me as overloads to their own schedules. The chair regarded this suggestion as patent foolishness from the dean.

For the first time, I taught from old notes. My comments on papers were minimal. My most vivid memory is how incredibly high and steep the stairwells felt, how often my classes started a few minutes late because I still had not caught my breath. And how forgiving my students were, and how dark and somber the eyes of my gynecologist. I had not lost the baby, but between the nausea of mono and the nausea of pregnancy I had lost a lot of weight. I was down to a hundred pounds or less, and at best losing weight more slowly than I had at first.

We figured that we ought to buy a house, that two babies meant we needed a washing machine, that we needed to be able to walk out the front door and into the car rather than negotiating both the stairwells and the parking problems of our densely populated neighborhood. Interest rates were at 18.5 percent. We would not be able to afford much, but by golly there was plenty to chose from. We had no energy for much shopping: we just picked one, a solid, small, well-located, entirely undistinguished '50s ranch in a modest neighborhood not too far from campus.

We signed a contract on Sunday night in the second week of November of 1981. By Thursday, the final negotiating was completed: the house was ours. On Friday, the pregnancy reached twenty weeks: I had gained four pounds and the gynecologist was jubilant—this baby was probably ours too. We were scheduled for an ultrasound at three on Friday afternoon. Judy was planning to keep Mark until six, feeding him dinner while we went out for one of our ritual celebratory dinners.

The ultrasound technician finally dropped her elbow out of my line of sight, and I craned to see the little monitor. "There's two babies in there," she said in that neutral medical voice. "Twins."

3
Bonbons and Soap Operas

ONCE THE FALL QUARTER ENDED, I WAS PUT TO BED REST. ACTUALLY, BED rest began even before the end of the fall term: one of the senior women astounded me by offering to take my classes for the last ten days or so, an offer I accepted through tears. Once home full time, I ate and slept and ate and ate some more. I got up in the middle of the night to eat; and I dozed through every broadcast of *Sesame Street* or *Mr. Rogers' Neighborhood,* both of them broadcast four times a day. In no time at all, I attained a truly spectacular girth and an utterly hilarious shape. I could not drive because I no longer fit behind the wheel of the car. But that was the only thing approaching a problem: no doubt rallied by Grandma Murphy, my fertile feminine heritage resumed its flawless control, and the pregnancy went full term without the least complication.

And thus it was that the next April, on our first night home with Carol and Tim, the first midnight feeding began in the usual way, with the thin bleating wail of a newborn. And immediately, the wail of two newborns. We were both awake instantly, which proves I suppose that we had actually managed to fall asleep. I remember, vaguely, being proud of that fact—neither of us had slept at all our first night home with Mark. I wondered how long we had slept, but

I couldn't read the alarm clock without my glasses. We both got up, each to change a baby and see about the feeding.

"So how do we do this?" Warren asked, unduly bright-eyed and organized from all his midnight experience as a medical intern and resident. Some vague problem nagged at my dopey brains, but did not succeed in reaching me. I climbed back into bed with one infant, unbuttoning my nightgown.

"Uh, *how* do we do this?" Warren asked again, holding the other baby in his arms. Then it dawned on me.

"Easy," I replied. "Go get a couple of nurses. Then put up the head of the bed and bring about six pillows." That was how I had nursed both babies at once in the hospital, after all—with the help of two nurses and their artful skill at arranging an apparently infinite supply of pillows. It was his turn to look dopey. For a second or two I debated being sensible and going to a chair in the living room. But nursing in bed is so much warmer and nicer in the middle of the night, even in April. Surely we could figure this out.

Milk was starting to dribble down my chest; the babies were beginning to whimper as they smelled it. I settled back flat on the bed, pulling a pillow under each elbow, and craning my head to try to settle one infant on one side as Warren bent over me with the other one. But I couldn't get the kid arranged properly, lying flat as I was.

At this point I suppose I should admit that in my fullest-chested glory, breast-feeding two babies, I almost completely filled out my double-A nursing bra. My lack of largess meant that the babies needed to be positioned in such a way that only a woman with triple-hinged arms—or maybe two nurses, six pillows, and a hospital bed—can breast-feed snug in her bed. What we were attempting was completely impossible.

But we were still trying. I was not quite awake enough to admit defeat, and Warren was too much the gentleman to declare defeat on my behalf. One baby would almost get settled barely long enough to taste a bit of the stuff, and then he or she would be somehow dislodged by our attempts to settle the other. Their whimpers quickly turned to purple-faced howls and then they were too hysterical to latch on even when we had repositioned them properly. With much effort we each calmed one baby and then tried again. We almost succeeded, in fact. But then I giggled and dislodged them both. Warren was not sharing my amusement. He was wadding up his bathrobe as an additional mechanical aid when Mark appeared in the doorway.

"Hey you guys!" he protested. "I was asweep!" His sleepy dismay opened out into full-fledged grief when he saw both babies in bed with us.

Well, that did it. Warren gathered Mark into his arms and the two of them curled up under the blankets on Warren's side of the bed. I tucked one hysterical baby under each arm and headed off to nurse in an armchair in the living room. Nobody ate much: their hysteria had exhausted them, and they went back to sleep fairly quickly. I put them back in the crib, carried Mark back to his own bed, and took his place under the crook of Warren's right arm—until the next time a infant wailed angrily, awake now and still hungry, half an hour later.

Warren moaned softly. This time I put on a heavy bathrobe and warm slippers before retrieving the wailer and nursing him or her (I don't remember which) in solitary glory. The other baby had sense enough to wait, or maybe some supervisory angel took pity upon us. Once the first baby was well fed and content, I awakened the second, who was in fact far too sleepy and new-baby disorganized to nurse with much energy or skill. After half an hour of trying, I gave up and returned that baby to bed—and explained again to Mark, who was again wandering around, why it is that babies are awake in the night. I got Mark back to bed and got back into bed myself. Fifteen or twenty minutes later, however, that second baby was now thoroughly awake and indeed hungry. After a second, successful attempt at feeding, I climbed back into bed, again for twenty minutes, because the first baby was now ready for its next meal. I settled again into bed just as Mark got up demanding breakfast.

But the night at last gave way to a lovely, sunny April morning. Warren fixed eggs and orange juice while I showered. For a while, the babies were both quiet and content at the same time: as if it were any Sunday morning at all, we took turns playing with Mark and reading the newspaper while a second pot of coffee slowly gurgled its way into existence. Despite their distress during the night, these three babies welcomed the morning and the sunlight as if it were the first dawn of some new creation.

I remember, I remember as one of the most powerful memories I will ever have, the color of that yellow sunlight angling through the south-facing dining room windows, and the taste of orange juice, and the soft fuzziness of the curve of a new baby's head, so small it cups easily in the palm of your hand.

"Look at this!" I pleaded to Warren. "Look!" Every inch the beaming *paterfamilias,* he looked over the top of the *Tribune* at his alert, contented offspring. "Do you suppose we can do this?" I asked.

"Well," he pondered, professorially, "it's not new babies who are the fragile ones. It's new parents. *They* are the fragile ones. But not us." Over and over again, in the months to come, on that baby cycle of three or four hours, in the planet's fundamental quotidian rhythm of dark and light, over and over again we found elusive moments like these, two or three minutes altogether of the incredible wonder of birth and life and living together.

Bottled Brew

Meanwhile, however, there were all the other moments waiting to be survived. I began to time midnight feedings. The shortest was ninety minutes; the longest was two hours and fifteen minutes. Since they were eating every two or three hours, the interval between feedings sometimes felt almost nonexistent. It averaged thirty to forty minutes: time enough to shower or to fix and eat a meal—but not both. And neither eating nor bathing nor napping was possible if Mark needed my attention. I also kept track of how much sleep I got: I went six weeks without sleeping more than three hours in twenty-four, and that three hours was commonly subdivided into two or three pieces. The first waker sometimes ate well and quickly; the second baby, whom I awakened, almost always ate slowly, as if I were some fancy French restaurant. But either baby would object, angrily, if I declared a slow feeding over and tried to return him or her to bed.

After our first week home, the visiting nurse declared that my blood pressure was high, my pulse was fast, my weight was down precipitously, and the babies had failed to gain. I decided to nurse both babies every two hours, no matter what. One week later, I was running a fever and we had all lost weight. The visiting nurse made emergency appointments with physicians for the lot of us.

Afterward, Warren dropped me and the babies at the house and took Mark with him to buy formula. I began to spend ninety minutes every night washing bottles and mixing formula, night after night filling the whole top shelf in the fridge with baby bottles. After a day or two of this, I called Barbara, who had nursed her daughter so successfully and happily. That's what the nursing books said, after all: call a friend for encouragement.

"You are crazy," Barbara assured me. "You are nuts. I wouldn't dream of trying to breast-feed two! Are you trying to prove something?"

She stood in the doorway a few hours later with four bottles of Guinness Stout. She walked in on Warren feeding someone while I half dozed on the sofa.

"Sensible man!" she said approvingly as I sat up and reached for my glasses. "You married a sensible man," she repeated, and then she went into the kitchen to open a bottle of beer. She put the beer in my hands and a can of nuts on the coffee table.

"B_{12} vitamin complexes," she explained to Warren. "Real ale has lots. For somebody smart," she concluded, "you can be really dumb, Katie Wallace. And you look awful. Drink your beer and go get some sleep. In *bed*." She settled down to feed the other baby; I guzzled the beer and did as I was told.

The babies quickly gained weight, now that they were being properly fed. For a while I persisted in breast-feeding: the closeness of nursing comforted me. I had so little energy for all these babies, for all their needs and for my own need to engage the full reality of how my life had been transformed. The simple physical reality of nursing felt so good, so direct and uncomplicated, in comparison to the complex emotional realities of the household. Despite our best efforts, Mark had taken to sitting huddled and disconsolate at the corner of the sofa, crying angrily and unwilling to be touched or comforted in any way. I was scared.

Another Call from the Chairman

The babies were to be baptized on a Sunday afternoon in early May, when they were five weeks old. I called the local Catholic church to arrange the ceremony—and the pastor, an old man with a considerable brogue, let me arrange everything over the phone. I also called a deli that would deliver a tray of meat and cheese; then I called a liquor store to deliver some champagne. This would not be the fancy spread we had when Mark was baptized, but my guilt over that fact was buried in my guilt over everything else. My sole priority now was survival.

Warren's parents arrived for a visit in the middle of the week before the baptism. By then, it was clear that Tim had himself a bad case of classic new-baby colic. He was to spend most of his first year screaming, unless of course I carried him on my chest in one of those soft corduroy babypacks. I was astounded, that Thursday, to hear Warren's father giggling—Warren's somber, very reserved father, giggling—giggling while Timmy wailed. Not a laugh, but a high-pitched, unmistakable giggle, better suited to a ten-year-old girl than a big-shouldered, muscular sixty-year-old man.

No wonder I had never heard him laugh! And then Warren's mother was giggling too. I stayed in the kitchen, listening and marveling. I had seen Hank smile perhaps two or three times in more than a dozen years; I had never heard anything like this from either of them. When the laughter died down, Wanda came into the kitchen for a piece of tissue to wipe her eyes and blow her nose.

"That baby has *colic*," she said, in a not very convincing imitation of sympathy. She tried to hide her smile behind another piece of tissue. "Warren had colic, you know," she said, breaking out into a loving grin, giving up on the pretense altogether. "He screamed for a whole year. I'll have to tell him when he gets home tonight." She went back out to the living room, to the still-screaming Tim, her shoulders beginning to shake with soft laughter. I kept my own laughter silent, but I replayed the sound of theirs every time Tim's inconsolable distress threatened to drive me crazy. And in fact the two of them proved incredibly adept at calming Tim. They had him quiet in minutes, that day.

And then the phone rang. It was my chairman. Tenure had been denied; he was sorry; would I please call the dean and schedule an exit interview. From the living room, Tim screamed as if he had been stabbed. The chairman said good-bye and hung up. I stood, listening to Tim scream as I felt like screaming, listening to Wanda and Hank talking softly to one another. And then I hung up the phone too and listened to Tim. I tied up the plastic trash bag holding kitchen garbage and carried it out to the alley, standing there dizzy and holding the back gate for balance.

My Delicate Condition

I told myself sternly that this news was not unexpected. The evening labor had begun, in that very earliest stage of labor when contractions are at most slightly distracting, the phone had rung and I had gone out to the kitchen to answer it. A friend on the Tenure and Promotions Committee was calling surreptitiously, guiltily, to ask if I had heard from my chairman. A preliminary vote taken several weeks earlier had gone against me, he explained, despite my superb dossier and outside referees, because the department's recommendation, although supportive, had looked equivocal. The formal departmental defense of me was scheduled in a few days. He and unnamed others on the committee were beginning to worry that the department might not defend me at all, concentrating its efforts instead on one of the two men up with me whose vote had also been negative. I should, my friend advised abruptly, merely call the chairman and inquire about the progress of my hearing. I should not mention this conversation, which violated propriety. His nervous secrecy reminded me of old Watergate hearings: I wanted to laugh, somehow, but instead I solemnly agreed. According to the kitchen clock, the conversation had lasted exactly fifteen minutes; I had had three contractions lasting a solid two minutes each.

I returned to the living room, puzzled but quite unable to think clearly about anything except the contractions. Why were they so frequent, so regular, so well organized—but so entirely painless? And why was my brain so dysfunctional? I couldn't think. Instead I spent half an hour telling Warren about the phone call. But in that half hour I had six more of these strange contractions. Finally I told him that my belly seemed to be up to something odd.

He pointed out, in a not-unkindly way, that two minute contractions beginning every five minutes constituted three-minute intervals. And this had been going on for more than an hour? He even got up and dialed the phone for me. Shortly thereafter we went to the hospital, where the doctors announced that labor was in fact very far advanced. But an X-ray revealed that the babies were very badly positioned, and so I was wheeled in for emergency surgery.

Tim and Carol were born at two that morning to a standing-room-only crowd of high-risk gynecologists, high-risk neonatologists, nurses, residents, interns, medical students, and student nurses. I think there was also a janitor or two at the back, but it was hard to see around the crowd. The babies were big and pink and lusty, born smack on their due date. To everyone's delight, they looked around with fully conjugate gaze at the gleeful celebration, the happy congratulations flowing back and forth among the doctors and the nurses and us. I felt like the hostess of the world's most spectacularly successful party: our terror in this pregnancy had been widely shared indeed. I asked Warren to leave his place beside me to be with the babies, but when I found myself alone I started to cry. The anesthesiology resident sitting behind me cradled my face and stroked my hair as one would stroke a child's. He wiped away my tears with his gloved thumb.

I awakened the next morning feeling briefly, deceptively lucid and unbearably ecstatic. I called the English department to tell Mrs. Gilligan, the departmental secretary whose daughter—also named Catherine—was also pregnant. Mrs. Gilligan had mothered me all through this pregnancy, providing all the practical help that a generous major administrator can supply. I wanted to talk to Mrs. G., to tell her myself that we were all fine and breathing on our own and to thank her again.

She handed the phone to the chairman as he passed by her desk. He offered his congratulations politely, but the sound of his voice set off a deafening clash of categories. Then he said something about chapter two—and I realized that my mind was free-floating in a chemical and hormonal fog: chapter two? What? Huh? Not two *chapters,* two *babies,* a boy and a girl, early this morning. I floundered wildly in the murk, trying to made sense of my mind. He apologized, and that cleared the air momentarily; then he said something about not asking "before," but needing answers now. I stood in clear air just for a minute and thought, "Oh of course, oh how Victorian: my delicate condition." *Sorry, pal, not a chance, not a chance in hell.*

But I don't think that is what I said. He was the chairman, after all; and I am (I try to be) a lady in the traditional sense. I think I demurred politely as the murk arose around me once again. I explained for the second time—I tried to explain—that I had had major surgery six hours before. I was, I said, still quite heavily sedated. He should call me in a couple of weeks, when I would be able to explain chapter two more coherently than I could at the moment. Something in me protested or muttered dimly, far off in the haze, that if he had said the defense was in three days, then two weeks would be too late. But I lost sight of the thought before I could say anything.

I made myself say good-bye politely before I slammed the handset onto its base. I swore at length, with a vulgar inebriated eloquence I did not know I possessed; from behind the curtains, the woman in the other bed made a startled, strangled-sounding noise. I started to sob, but the enormous incision up the midline of my belly put a quick stop to that. I lay there, staring at the metal brackets holding up the curtains around my bed, little brackets like legs, brackets broken like broken legs, imagining breaking his legs and quizzing him on scholarly issues within hours of orthopaedic surgery. Delicate condition indeed!

And then the phone rang: it was Warren, suddenly startled from sleep by inexplicable anxiety. Was I okay?

And Other Calls

Yes, I remembered all this. So why was I so stunned by the news? After a while of clinging to the gate by the garbage cans, I dried my face on my tee shirt and went back into the house, pretending not to notice the neighbors Jack and Millie watching from their kitchen window. The baptism was three days hence, and I had to hand wash and iron the fancy little inherited outfits. No time for this now: there was work to do. Work is always comfort, after all. Once I had taken refuge in libraries. Now it was the laundry room, cold and grey but clean and quite unambiguous. There would be plenty of such consoling work in the months and years ahead.

And in the days following this phone call, there were other calls. Senior people from other departments were outraged by what they had discovered about a whole series of scandalous irregularities in the conduct of my departmental hearings. Eventually there was an angry delegation to the provost of full professors from each of the other humanities departments. My internal appeal to the university collected an unprecedented outpouring of supportive letters from the faculty generally; eventually, the appeals committee issued a stinging indictment of both the English department and the dean.

None of that, however, led to tenure for me. I was not surprised: ultimately, universities are a cross between mindless dinosaurs and imbecile bureaucracies, unable to respond even to their own realities. Like the medieval church, a university is likely to admit its errors—and then carry on regardless. Nonetheless, I was deeply touched by such broad and unexpected support from so many fine scholars. Getting tenure can be a wonderful affirmation by one's peers. Such expenditure of political capital, however, said even more about my standing with my colleagues. No one, not even a full professor, opposes the dean lightly.

Meanwhile, my own reality argued forcefully for a sabbatical of undefined duration. I was exhausted by the multiple gestation and its concluding surgery; I had still not recovered fully from the mono; and I was what they called "deconditioned" from so many months of bed rest. Soon enough, I developed a persistent bronchitis: I hacked consumptively for three years, often sleeping in armchairs because I could not lie flat without coughing. Most of the time, that hardly mattered: both of the twins also had asthma and thus—predictably— repeated bouts of pneumonia. Two or three of us spent plenty of nights dozing together in my big pale yellow recliner, tipped back about forty-five degrees and covered with a quilt.

Partly because they were so often so sick, and partly because I was, my decision to stay home had none of the moral complexity of our earlier agonizing about Mark and childcare. Now we did no philosophic fussing; we took no long cold walks. I was just too sick to work. I would just stay home and rest and take care of the babies. I felt the grit of flawed thinking somewhere, but I was too tired to look for the error. Nope. I would just stay home and rest, and when I was better we would figure out what to do. I would worry about my career tomorrow.

Tomorrow. It had to wait until tomorrow. I could not think about my career today or any day in which I found myself, because every time I tried to think through my feelings about the tenure decision, the hyper-empathic Timmy would scream. I could awaken him from naps; I could interrupt Warren's feeding him. In that utterly mysterious bond between mothers and infants, he was terrified by my grief. I had to learn not to think about it when we were in the house together, or he would start screaming and end up with another asthma attack.

Nonetheless I caught myself at times staring out the window and staring numbly into an enormous hollow ache. I didn't want to teach full time. Not with three such little kids and for a salary that would not cover child care. But I certainly did expect them to tenure me, even if they were not willing to accommodate some part-time schedule. My record deserved tenure. I'd earned it.

My grief felt quite reasonable and it felt quite inexplicable; and mostly I took some care not to feel it at all because Tim would scream sympathetically. His screams sounded all too much as mine might have sounded.

Let Us Pray

In my memory, the twins' baptismal ceremony is a blur. My only clear picture is how warmly the old Irish priest fussed over Mark, and how delighted Mark was by the flame of the candle he was given to hold. And how mesmerized all the adults were by the hazards involved in handing one candle to Mark and another to his toddler cousin with her great clouds of long curly hair. But it worked. No one had ever seen two two-year-olds stand so still, so proudly and attentively, for so long.

At one dim point I realized that all the prayers seemed to be for the parents and not the babies. And I felt grateful, suddenly, for whoever had rewritten this liturgy in the two years since we went through it with Mark. We were going to need all the prayers we could get. By golly, for once in my life the church seemed to have the right thing to say. "Get me through this, God," something deep inside me growled. "Get me through this and I'll owe you one." It was a plea—or a promise? or a threat?—that I found myself repeating over and over again in those first few years.

At home again, I downed an entire glass of champagne and let other people fuss with the food and tend to the children. Warren and his family of sneaky photographers were sneaking around taking pictures. My family of talkers were all talking. Our photo albums suggest that it was in fact a great party. I had another glass of champagne—always a mistake—and sat silent and glassy-eyed, wondering if anyone would care if I fell asleep sitting propped with a pillow at the end of the sofa. If I did fall asleep, at least no one took a picture of me.

By the time all the guests departed, I realized that I had not nursed anyone all the whole long day—and my breasts were not hard with milk. I felt bitter tears somewhere in the distance, but they stayed distant. At most, I felt a slow, disgusted anger; but that too felt remote. The champagne had worn off, replaced by a nasty headache.

I nursed only one last time, the next day, crying so hard that the baby soon was frantic and unable to suckle. I put the screaming baby back in its crib and curled for a little bit on my own bed, struggling to get ahold of myself and listening while one crying baby awakened the other and all this grief undid Mark, who had been entertaining himself in the living room. He appeared in the bedroom door once again, quizzical and concerned.

"They *crying*," he objected.

"Yeah, well, so am I," I admitted, sitting up. He climbed up on the bed and into my lap and we held each other. He was such a tall and thriving two-year-old. He had failed to gain at first too, but he had survived quite nicely on formula. Carol and Tim would survive it too. But would we make it through the next year? Warren's two-week paternity leave was ended; helpful grandmothers had come and gone again. We were on our own. I was on my own, with the three of them.

We could not afford household help—we could barely afford the house itself without my salary. I had refused the termination year contract offered to failed candidates for tenure, so my last paycheck was on the immediate horizon. Warren meanwhile had talked to his chairman to reverse his plan to go part-time so as to keep the children home with a parent and yet keep both careers going—albeit slowly—during these difficult years of infancy. That would not have worked anyhow, we discovered: my chair had refused to schedule my classes in the morning, as I had requested. So Warren was back on the academic fast track in a very big way: we had an 18.5 percent mortgage to pay. He was feeling just as overwhelmed by his solo obligations as I was by mine.

I let the babies scream while I got some cookies and milk for Mark and me. We shared our dismay at life as we shared the treats, in convivial empathic silence, ignoring the babies. We both began to feel a bit better about life. In fact, it proved to be a major emotional turning point for Mark. I gave him—he let me give him—a great hug and a kiss, and I told him he was wonderful; then I headed back down the long dim hall to get them. Walking down the hall, I faced a large plateglass mirror that the previous owners had left mounted on the wall. I looked grimly at my sagging abdomen, at my red-rimmed eyes and my disheveled grey hair. I looked so much older. I looked dreadfully middle-aged. And with a brutal start I realized something.

I did not recognize myself. The slim, green-eyed beauty with freckles and thick auburn hair was gone. In her stead, some stranger stared back at me, some haggard grey-eyed stranger.

The grey-eyed stranger. Grey-eyed. I stood there a moment, not quite knowing why, not sure what to make of not knowing myself. Grey-eyed. My eyes are green. Or they were green, once.

Athena. Athena, goddess of wisdom. Grey-eyed Athena.

"Look," I prayed silently to the stranger in the mirror, "hold this raft together, because I've left Kalypso. My immortal youth is over with. And it will be a long and hard sail home."

The figure in the mirror made no gesture of reply, but day after day there she was. And I never did get used to seeing her.

The Triumph of Alien Reality

Once I had lived by the implacable measure of clock and calendar, the endlessly repeating patterns of the academic year. There were teaching days and not-teaching days, times for course proposals and times for grading papers, times to send my students to the library and times to go there myself, times to read books and times to write them. Clock and calendar provided the commonsense structure of ordinary reality; they underlay the pattern of duties and deadlines that shape adult experience.

Now I found myself mired outside of time altogether. Mothers live by a rhythm of eating and sleeping, of play-outside days and play-inside days. I cared whether it was raining, not whether it was Tuesday. Hungry or sleepy measured the hours, not numerical displays. And I learned—mothers learn—to attend to this new system just as keenly as stockbrokers watch the Dow Jones, just as keenly as attorneys who bill by the hour clock their little three-minute tidbits in steno pads on the corners of their desks. If we were to go to the park for a couple of hours, then everyone's needs had to be eased into congruence such that everyone would be awake and not-hungry simultaneously—not only not-hungry but also not-hostile from having been muscled into conformity. It's an extraordinary art. Like all real art, it has a huge intuitive component.

But the art of mothering is not something honored by museums or libraries. It is not hung on a wall or set on a bookshelf or performed at predictable times to thunderous applause. Nor can it be left "in progress" in study or in studio, not even when the artist needs a shower or the creative élan has evaporated. Living my life entirely within this art—without my office, without colleagues, without the work that had always anchored my sense of self—my sense of linear time unraveled into a timeless present tense. And surviving within the present tense demanded that I attend as never before to my own small ebb and flow of hunger and energy. It is one thing, after all, to know you are hungry but to keep working until a more convenient moment. Adult self-control is very handy stuff. It's something else again not to know that you are hungry. Or, more dangerously yet, not to know when you are frustrated or angry. I had learned, I realized, not to know when I was hungry. And not to admit very much of my own angry frustration.

But I started to notice. I had to notice. My own reserves of physical energy and emotional stability were terribly shallow. I had to begin to face what I no longer had the stamina to deny. And in doing so I discovered an utterly bewildering new world.

Life lived exclusively in the present tense proved bewildering not intellectually but emotionally. The omnipresent present is an ancient philosophic position: I knew Heraclitus, Parmenides, Zeno. In teaching Blake, I had explained to row after row of undergraduates that here and now is all that can genuinely claim to be real. That's an interesting and even a tidy and elegant concept to consider in fifty minute segments, in three-day-a-week courses, in ten-week quarters.

It's not quite so elegant and consoling when it takes over your life, when the omnipresent present becomes not an elegant ontological claim but an inescapable emotional reality. When the omnipresent present becomes the governing emotional reality, all of the linear, logical, cause-and-effect structures of life dissolve into the illusory mist they have always been anyway. But as a result, all the things that had always structured my life no longer felt real. Success. Achievement. Goals and objectives and plans, even little lists of things to do. As every parent discovers, infants deconstruct their parents' lists of things to do with astounding ease. And when you very seldom get away from your infants, the list itself stops feeling real because it stops feeling important. What feels important are the immediate variables of a child's life. What's for lunch? Who is sleepy? Can we go to the park?

Maybe Blake and the Buddhists have it right, I thought. Maybe the mystics and the visionaries—east or west—live closer to the fundamental biological and spiritual realities. Life in the here and now, shaped only by the rhythms of biology and the weavings of delight and desire, gradually but thoroughly discredited all that I thought I knew about myself and about the world around me. All my finely honed intellectual drive suddenly felt quite irrelevant, and I had no idea what might take its central place within me.

Although there might seem to be something attractively countercultural about such escape from ambitious drive, its absence left a palpable emptiness in my life. And I grieved that loss. There are no Graduate Record Examinations for motherhood, after all, and I worried whether I had what mothering so relentlessly demands. And there are no report cards, no teaching evaluations and vita updates, no annual performance reviews. There are no paychecks, no promotions, no status or prestige with which to comfort your ego on bad days. Day after day, all you get is another day. You fix a meal, and then another one, and then another one; wash the clothes, and wash them again, and wash them again. And as I watched the sun come up every morning, I felt lost, grief-stricken and threatened beyond measure.

How was I to respond, for instance, to Mark's inexplicable love for the long row of young arborvitae at the park? He would stroke each tree in turn as if it were a large, affectionate, inanimate cat. They seemed almost to purr in response to his delight. There was no dissuading him, and I did not have the strength to carry him and push the twin stroller as well. So he stroked his trees, gently, one by one, until the air was fragrant. He forced me to acknowledge the depths of my dependence upon goals and plans and organization, the angry fire of my own commitment to control and priorities and achievements. Why was I in such a hurry? What was so important about my plans for the afternoon? Was I hurrying home to a once-in-a-lifetime opportunity to mop the kitchen floor?

On good days, I tried to joke that life with small children has considerable potential as a spiritual discipline. Maybe I should offer New Age weekend retreats: here, have three babies for two days and two nights. I promise that you will go back to your own life with a new and deeper gratitude. But it proved increasingly difficult to joke about such things. I didn't want to see what I was coming to see about the importance of what mothers can offer to babies. For instance, Carol proved herself a precociously athletic infant: she spent that whole first July able to roll from her stomach to her back but not the other way. She drove herself to learn with an angry frustrated persistence that I recognized and admired but regretted—in equal measures. But sitting with her on the floor one afternoon, I wondered whether God watches us like this, whether God regards our moral struggles not with the angry judgment of "Sinners in the Hands of an Angry God" but tolerantly, affectionately, trying now and then to help, trying mostly to keep us sane, always confident that sooner or later we will develop the strength we need or figure out what baffles us so. It was as if that thought sat with me on the floor, having surfaced in the usual inexplicable way, just keeping me company. I watched it as I watched Carol; I kept an eye on it as I kept an eye on Mark and on Tim. And I marveled for a while at how self-evidently true it was and how utterly incapable I was of pursuing its implications. Maybe God was with me as I was with Carol, there on the floor, just trying to keep her angry frustration within tolerable limits. Oh.

But on bad days, I was just angry and frustrated and depressed: home alone in a house in the suburb with three infants, no car, and neither a friend nor a neighbor who was also home with kids. "Just a housewife," my career in disarray, too exhausted to do anything much but get through the day, one day at a time.

Negotiating with Aliens

"I want a gorilla for breakfast," Mark announced at six o'clock one Monday morning. I looked up from spooning oatmeal into two hungry infants, politely explaining that gorillas were like very big monkeys. People don't eat gorillas, I explained. We had taken the kids out to the zoo that weekend. How, I wondered, had he come away wanting gorillas for breakfast? Or did anybody have a stuffed toy in the form of a gorilla, whom Mark wanted to invite to the breakfast table? I set the oatmeal aside and, before starting on applesauce, retrieved a beloved monkey made from a heavy red sock—a gift to Mark in his infancy. If the kid wanted a gorilla for breakfast, fine. All sorts of creatures, real and imaginary, joined us for meals at times.

Mark was not pleased. He was not impressed with my amazing ability to find the right toy, by my flexibility in joining his imaginative world, by my willingness to attempt to function in a competent, motherly way in the dark at six in the morning. He continued insisting on a gorilla for breakfast, rather more loudly and with an edge of hysteria in his voice. A screamy fit was en route, a screamy two-year-old's fit, in the dark of a November morning.

I closed my eyes to think. That trip to the zoo had been such a disaster. In the monkey house, Mark had inquired most anxiously about why all these kids were in cages. We tried to explain, but he would have none of it.

"These kids in *cages*!!" he bellowed. "No!" Carol and Tim were instantly hysterical with him. It had been a long walk back to the car: my thighs were black with bruises from his flailing legs. We had muscled them into their car seats and driven off, the din undiminished. Eventually all three had fallen asleep, but it was a grim, silent drive nonetheless. Maybe we should have let him climb over the fence into some exhibit with a large predator?

And now gorillas for breakfast. I finished feeding applesauce to the babies, feeling my own energy and patience dissolving by the minute.

"Look," I said, opening the cabinet where I kept breakfast cereals. "If I had gorillas you could have some. But we don't have any gorillas for breakfast today. All we have is Cheerios, or Kix, or—"

"Gorilla!" Mark shouted in angry triumph, pointing. "Gorilla! Daddy got gorilla!"

Granola. A small yellow box of granola. Mark ate in that silent self-possession of children who know what incompetent idiots their parents really are, visibly pondering how he might best survive the next two decades without ending up in a cage himself.

I felt better about this episode when I heard the story of Bartholomew's frog. Bartholomew awakened night after night terrified of a frog he imagined to be in his closet. His parents consulted far and wide and thoughtfully. They tried everything. But night after night Bartholomew would awaken, screaming. In frustration one night, his mother flung open the closet door and screamed at the damned frog to go away and never come back. Bartholomew went back to sleep; the mother made embarrassed apologies to her husband after she resettled the other child, also awakened by her bellow.

But in the morning her son gave her an enormous hug.

"You were *great* last night!" he insisted. "That frog will *never* come back."

And, y'know, it didn't.

We remembered Bartholomew's frog later on, when Tim started wakening at night, terrified of dinosaurs and, we suspected, inconsolably anxious as a side effect of new asthma medications. One night he insisted that Warren stay up, keeping watch and guarding the house against attack. I listened from the living room as Warren listened earnestly to Tim's directions. I could only imagine Warren's full professorial bearing as, in his deepest and rumbliest voice, he insisted that all the dinosaurs already knew that this was the Wallace house and they would never ever dare to bother us.

"Oh *gooooood*," Tim sighed, and slept through the night for the first time in a week. At breakfast the next morning, I glanced out the kitchen window and then fixed Warren with my sturdiest gaze.

"There is a unicorn in the garden," I announced.

"The unicorn is a mythical beast," he responded, right on cue.

"Yep, and dinosaurs are extinct. Except in this house." We laughed but then drank our coffee in silence, wondering what we had set loose in our lives.

Such empathic affirmation of the child's alien worldview buys temporary peace, but only at a price—a price that became more evident as they became more mobile and more articulate. Physically outnumbered and psychologically overwhelmed by the utter confidence of the unself-conscious child, we found ourselves as immobilized at times as Gulliver, held down by the silken threads of munchkin metaphysics.

There were all too many days like the Saturday on which we lost two-year-old Timmy in the Field Museum.

We needed lunch. Taking the three of them into a cafeteria line proved an incredible mistake: they were starved and they immediately understood (a) that you could take anything you wanted from the display and (b) that they wanted everything they saw. Warren rounded up the kids and moved them out toward the seating area, leaving me to heap enough food for the five of us onto a single tray.

But when I got out to where they were seated, Tim was missing. He had insisted on staying with me, Warren said, but I had not heard him. And now he was gone. And the other two were absolutely not going to abandon their lunches: they were already fighting over who got Tim's share. In a panic, Warren and I were hastily mapping strategy when a security guard appeared with Tim in his arms. The guard was very tall and muscular, as big and gleamingly black as Tim was thin and dazzlingly blond.

"There you are!" Tim chastised us sternly. "I found him and I told him you were lost and he helped me! Where did you go?" The guard set him down, chuckling and gracious in accepting our profuse thanks. "Don't do that again!" Tim concluded, reaching for his hotdog.

"Three of them?" the guard smiled softly, with the experienced eye and reassuring confidence of an older parent. "You folks take care, now." If we survived these kids, we decided on the way home, we would expect nothing less than a museum exhibit on our astounding accomplishment.

English as a Second Language

Nor were kiddie metaphysics the only problem. Once words had been my business, my way of dealing with the world, my way to make myself noticed and listened to. But now I was trapped in the house with three small and very determined creatures, none of whom really spoke English. Furthermore, by the time Carol and Tim came along, I was very tired of my own line of baby talk. I decided it was a serious challenge to my sanity to keep up a running one-sided conversation with a person who could answer only in gurgles and funny noises.

So I began to answer in gurgles and funny noises. The babies were quite impressed: an adult who can talk! To their intense delight, I would imitate any sound they made. Their faces would furrow with effort as they struggled to make exactly the same sound again.

Eventually, we could keep the same sound going for three or four such exchanges until, with glinty-eyed delight, they made a new sound and watched eagerly for my reaction. I got pretty good at this over some period of months. Warren, with his hyperacute hearing, was even better than I. Mark joined the game when he discovered that they were a highly receptive audience for his toddlerish delight in making odd sounds. He taught them to blow loud raspberries: the three of them laughed for days, overcome with admiration for themselves.

As the babies began to string sounds together into whole sentences of gobbledegook, I expanded my repertoire to match. If the baby's gabble ended with a rising inflection, as if a question, I repeated the line with an exaggerated falling inflection, as if in answer. If he or she made what sounded like a surprised assertion, I colored my repetition to sound like impressed agreement. Foreign language qualifiers were never as much fun as this: if only I could have had a German-speaking baby to play with! Warren and I can still engage an outgoing baby in several minutes of very strange conversation.

But as a habit this too has its drawbacks. Shopping one day, I left the big stroller in the store's aisle. I could see the babies' heads over the display of little sweatshirts, but the babies could not see me. Carol shouted an anxious-sounding interrogatory line of gabble, roughly translatable as "Are you still here?" I called back, tonally, something like "Yes, I'm right here, don't worry." But it was all gabble. The lady next to me looked up cautiously and edged away swiftly. I decided not to try to explain.

But empathic linguistic attunement further exacerbates the inherent conflict between kids' perspectives on life and adults' perspectives. As Barbara pointed out, just because a kid can talk does not mean the kid will make any sense at all. Billy's mother was driven slowly to distraction by his delight in his own ability to identify air conditioners. Sue was fond of long walks about the neighborhood, until Billy started loudly proclaiming "Noosh-ah, noosh-ah" every time he spotted a condenser in someone's yard. Such proclamations would be no problem, I suppose, but like any kid this boy demanded that his mother confirm his observation by repeating every single time, "Yes. Condenser!" Ten years later, she cringed at the memory—although, she told me with a hearty laugh, her kids still eat "gorilla" for breakfast.

We never fixated on noosh-ahs, thank God; but we did spend some months very attached to naming the colors of passing cars. This might be reasonably benign, I suppose, if you had one child, or if you lived in an area with very little traffic. But no. Three kids, looking out three different windows, would spot three different cars. And bedlam would erupt in the back seat.

"Boo ca, Mommy, boo ca," one kid would shout. Another, looking up from his efforts to remove a shoe, would disagree.

"Geeka, Mommy!" would come the angry corrective. "Geeka!"

"Dat's a wed cow," Mark would object, his hearing muddled by yet another ear infection. "Mommy, tell dem dat's a wed cow."

But by then the first kid had seen yet another vehicle.

"Poopaca! Poopaca!"

Or two would side against one, who would be loudly condemned for error and burst into angry, frustrated tears.

And none would be quiet and none would be content until I responded affirmatively to every observation. I soon realized that I no longer cared about teaching my children their colors. They could learn their colors when they went to college, as far as I was concerned. Whatever they thought they saw, I just agreed. I had to watch traffic. I would agree to anything. I startled my mother pretty badly, one day, by calling affirmatively, "Boofuck, yes, boofuck."

Billy could do not only colors but makes and models—especially the expensive sports cars his father admired. Alas, Sue knew little and cared less about the names of cars. But Billy knew that having verbal confirmation from his mother was among the central rights of a child. He demanded that she repeat the name of whatever car he had spotted. I passed her on the street one day: she drove with her shoulders hunched, clutching the steering wheel. In the backseat, Billy was waving his arms and shouting something.

Double Vision

One day there was a front-page report in the papers that Prince Charles's firstborn son had fouled up the plumbing in Buckingham Palace by throwing one of his father's shoes down the toilet. Warren in particular took great comfort in this notice: even the Prince of Wales, he chortled, sometimes loses out to Attila the Toddler. Every parent we knew was laughing to every other parent we knew. No matter how vigilant you may be, there is no way protect your kid—or your plumbing—every single moment.

I know my share of such stories. Everyone does. And over the years we have had at least our share of injuries, some of them pretty serious. But I did not realize how much such accidents cost me emotionally until I had to get myself to the emergency room. I was weeding by an open casement window, stood up carelessly, and hit the top of my head on the metal corner of the window frame. I ricocheted to the ground, smacking the back of my head; I lay there several minutes arguing angrily with myself to keep my eyes open as the world faded in and out, swirling and colorless. I got to my feet, finally, when I realized from the blood running into my ear and down my neck that maybe I had gashed my head—a gash that took seventeen stitches to close. It left me with a scar that runs at a narrow angle across the line at which I part my hair, memorializing the mishap with unruly wisps of hair that keep curling in the wrong direction.

That day, the emergency room nurse looked at me curiously and asked if I were a physician. Or, perhaps, a nurse? I said "No" a second time.

"Then why are you so calm?" she demanded. "You're sitting here, covered in blood, as calm as anything!"

I replied apologetically, my speech slightly slurred: "It's just my head." She turned sharply back from the doorway, visibly prepared to repeat her assessment of my mental status. She reached for my wrist to recheck my pulse.

"No," I protested blurrily. "I mean, it's not one of my kids again. *I* know I'm okay! This is just blood." She backed off, looked at me sharply, and then laughed long and hard, as only a parent can laugh.

"Are you Dr. Wallace's wife?" the resident demanded when he came in to sew me up. "Dr. Warren Wallace?" I admitted it. "And this is just your head, huh? Not one of your kids. What do *you* do for a living?"

"Oh, I'm just a housewife," I answered, fighting to keep my speech crisp and my sentences coherent.

"Oh yeah," he said. "Sure." He looked at me a moment from behind the little flashlight he had been shining in my eyes. "'Just a housewife.' Right. How did this happen? No double vision?" He reached aside for a syringe. "Hold still, this is going to hurt."

Oh, I have double vision all the time, I thought with sudden, absolute clarity. *And I'm not sure how it happened.*

"No double vision," I said.

"Only your head," he chuckled again, as he began sewing.

Zahava, Which Means, in Hebrew, "Gold"

Our suburb boasted that no resident is more than a fifteen-minute walk from a park, and sure enough, we could walk to three different playgrounds once I persuaded Mark to walk anywhere with me. That took about a year. But rolling out one afternoon with Tim and Carol in their big twin stroller, I turned a corner with a high hedge and locked stroller wheels with a woman headed the other way. She looked at my three dumbfounded: she had heard of me, she later admitted, but the reality of three children under four was still quite impressive.

"How—how—how—how do you find time to *read*?" she gasped, looking from me to them and back again.

I had met Zahava. As Jewish as I am Irish, she has long, thick, curly black hair and equally black eyes that contrast dramatically with her creamy white skin. Her eyebrows are long and dramatically arched, her features strong, her build athletic and generously curved: you would cast her as Esther in a minute. I have always felt somewhat elfin next to her, although she is probably no more than two or three inches taller than I.

Furthermore, Zahava was as had-been Orthodox as I was had-been Roman Catholic. In no time at all we discovered that we shared a heritage of crazy urban ethnicity, a passion for books and music and ideas, and a commitment to the hope that what we were trying to do for our kids would make some worthy difference in their lives. Together we could admit to being bored and crazed and exhausted by the demands of motherhood. It's easy enough to be miserable, after all. Genuine commisery, on the other hand, is one of the highest achievements of the well-lived life.

So over the years we have shared untold gallons of tea and uncounted hours in the local parks. Together we struggled both to teach our kids not to go headfirst down the slides and to catch them when they did. One would push the kids who wanted to swing; the other would keep the loose ones from running into the street or chasing stray dogs. We agreed upon systems of sharing and turns, we learned what each other's kids ate for lunch, and we spent hours entertaining each other with zany tales about our birth families and religious schooling. Such childhoods had provided us more in common with each other, we discovered, than either of us shared with those of similar heritage who had grown up secular or even casual about religion.

In the park almost every pleasant afternoon, Zahava and I watched the nannies fervently, conspiring darkly to make friends with some nanny who was unappreciated by her employers and thus gradually to win her away. We were guilty at the plan but tempted—like Hans in the famous ethical quandary—to steal what we needed if we could find it. I would keep a kosher kitchen if the nanny needed it, we laughed; she would let a nanny feed her kids cheeseburgers and Twinkies. Surely somehow we could hire loving, competent substitutes for ourselves and return—with what shreds of our sanity we might still possess—to our careers in the real world.

To our bleak dismay, however, the nannies were quite easy to spot because of how seldom or how shallowly they interacted with their charges. Unlike some mothers whom we also watched, the nannies were never negligent, or inattentive, or emotionally abusive. Clearly, some kids would have been better off with a nanny than with their mothers! Nonetheless, the nannies and their kids made my heart ache.

I will never forget the day Zahava and I shared the playground with a nanny in a crisp white uniform who was pushing an infant swing that held a little boy about nine months old. Both of them seemed bored and lonely. But he was warmly dressed, and she had remembered to pull his pants legs down over his calves after seating him in the swing. He was very fair, and she had put on the right kind of hat to protect him from the spring sun. She made sure to lift the brim when it fell over his eyes. Surreptitiously, I watched her for at least an hour. She did absolutely nothing wrong.

Except that she never spoke to him. Nor did he attempt to engage her. Nor could I catch his eye, nor did he look around as eagerly as most kids his age on a lovely afternoon. He bellowed once, briefly, and she moved him quite skillfully from the swing to a spring-mounted riding toy. He sat on the green dragon with the same blank, withdrawn, expressionless face as before. He did not enjoy the day, the scene, the other kids, nor the toys on which he sat. Kids that age look like 1920s bankers, with full round cheeks—but this kid had the demeanor of a loan officer.

In the swing next to this couple was another boy, almost the same age. The contrast was excruciating. When the swing arced toward her, the mother rounded her eyes in laughing surprise; the baby chortled in response. When the baby looked away, intrigued for a moment by something he had spotted behind his mother's back, she would turn to find and name for him whatever it was. I am sure she was just guessing at times. But they were having a wonderful time together, engaging in a complex and passionate dance.

Parks can be really boring, Zahava and I admitted. It's our babies that engage us. And it's not because babies as such are innately all that interesting. It's because we love them. Such love can neither be hired nor sold, but no quantity of competent child care can make up for its absence in the long hours of a baby's ordinary day.

Zahava and I rolled out of the park that afternoon in disconsolate silence, our nanny fantasies starting to fragment. Maybe we were as important as we tried to claim to each other in what had seemed like merely self-aggrandizing compensatory moments. Maybe we really did matter after all. We walked on in silence for another block. I swore, a long string of Anglo-Saxon epithets characterizing reality in general. Zahava said something in Yiddish that sounded even more satisfying.

I did not ask her to translate. There was no need.

Not the Inanimate Cold World

Day after day after day, seasons slowly turned into years spent at the park, regularly watching how profoundly different adults are in how we interact with children. We are as various in our behavior toward children as we are in our behavior toward one another—except that children are much more vulnerable to adults than adults are to one another. I began to understand and profoundly to grieve how incredibly much we surrender—and thus how much we risk—when our children spend as many hours in substitute care as most executives or professionals will spend working and commuting.

Unhappy with the realities this revealed, I began to marvel all over again at William Blake. I could see for myself now the truth of Blake's contention that the work of parents is the work of creating a moral universe. He was right: all these little decisions, all these actions petty in themselves, added up to a massively powerful definition of what it means to be human. Children must learn to be human because humanity is, in quite substantial ways, a creation of culture, culture transmitted in a thousand unconscious ways by the small everyday decisions and actions of adults. And in that great artistic endeavor of child rearing, the details count. Details count in every form of art. How your kid behaves at the park, how he or she learns to behave that way, how motives are elicited and shaped—all of this matters. It matters profoundly, because we are shaping motivations and desires that will remain, for the child and for the adult she becomes, utterly unconscious and therefore utterly powerful, for good or for ill. It doesn't matter at all that we too, in turn, remain largely unconscious of the most centrally important pressures we are exerting on our kids. But that's exactly why it does matter—why we risk so very much—when we hand our children over for the majority of their days to the unconscious complexities of some stranger's psyche. Or to some changing array of strangers. There is no way to guess what we might be risking.

Adults deal with children from within the very depths of their own identity and history. Blake had argued that as well. For better and for worse, our children's experience of us and thus their growing experience of themselves reveals the pressure of our own experience and our accumulation of both family history and cultural tradition. Never had I felt so keenly the strength and passion and pragmatism of the immigrant working-class ethos that Warren and I shared. For the first time I began to understand and to value the inherent poetry and mysticism of the Irish. But having lived all my life battling that Celtic mist, I was also deeply grateful at times for the clarity and subtle wit of the Poles. Our kids were apt to be very interesting people indeed. But meanwhile, Warren and I both had the inestimable advantage of knowing now, of seeing, of having some chance at least to glimpse and to cope creatively with the unconscious dynamics of the ancestry that had shaped us.

Zahava, I learned, had grown up in a family of highly cultured intellectuals, her father a professor of French and her mother a psychotherapist. She would hum snatches of opera in witty commentary upon the playground scene; she would pun across any of several languages, especially when she was sleep-deprived. Like her mother before her, she is an incredibly splendid and generous cook who would make any sensible person yearn for a Jewish mother.

But Zahava's mother spent several years of her middle childhood in Auschwitz, where her parents, brothers, and sisters died. Zahava and her three siblings carry the names of only four of what had been an enormous extended family, most of whom died in the camps. Watching Zahava's ongoing struggle with that reality left me cold with terror. She had grown up in a Jewish neighborhood, in a large cohort of the children of death camp survivors; everyone she knew, growing up, lived with this, shared this, struggled together to heal, to hope again, to love and trust and live again. From Zahava I heard such stories for the first time at first hand, and I did not hear them as the familiar reality they had always been for her.

After such stories, we spent a lot of time looking quietly at one another and almost reverently at the oblivious children given into our care. Zahava began to talk about someday beginning again to keep kosher just as, once or twice, I hauled myself to the early Sunday Mass that was always celebrated by the old Irish priest. Parenthood was beginning to feel like far too much moral responsibility to face on our own. The radical individualism we once had adopted, willy-nilly, heedlessly, was beginning to feel like an adult version of the toddler's demand, "Do it self."

Rolling home from the park one day, bumping the big twin stroller up and down over curbs, calling to Mark to stop at the alleys until I could catch up with his tricycle, I found myself haunted yet again by lines from Coleridge's "dejection" ode:

> . . . would we aught behold, of higher worth,
> Than that inanimate cold world allowed
> To the poor loveless ever-anxious crowd,
>   Ah! from the soul itself must issue forth
> A light, a glory, a fair luminous cloud
>   Enveloping the Earth— . . .
>   A new Earth and new Heaven,
> Undreamt of by the sensual and the proud.

The poor, loveless, ever-anxious crowd. I remembered belonging to that crowd. Ever-anxious. To be promoted or not to be promoted, as if my career were the only question. I didn't feel anxious now. Crazy, maybe. Tired, certainly. Frustrated and bored at times. Beyond a doubt underutilized both professionally and intellectually. But my initial depression was dissolving. I was beginning to stand up straight once again. There were plenty of unsolved problems in my life, but something here was right that had been wrong. If something ahead was as yet undreamt of, that was okay: I'd dream those dreams when I got there.

The First Day of Preschool

One day it happened. It actually happened. They started going to school. The fall that Tim and Carol were two and a half, I enrolled them three mornings a week in a preschool that functioned as a lab for the child development courses at the local high school. Mark, meanwhile, was in kindergarten. I dropped him off at 8:30 and the twins at 9, then I collected Mark again at 11:30 and the twins at 12. From 9:30 until 11 or so, three mornings a week, I was free. I had "nothing" to do, unless of course I wanted the luxury of a grocery run without three imperious supervisors, or the speed of a circuit to the cleaners, the pharmacy, and the hardware store without the repeated bucklings and unbucklings of three sets of car seat straps and the battle to unfold that massive double stroller. Or I could wash the kitchen floor and let it dry without anyone walking across it.

But on the very first of these days—September 17, 1984—I did not give in to such temptations. I went right home, to a silent house, to a blank piece of paper, to the wheezy hum of my old avocado green electric typewriter. Home *alone*. The silence rang in my ear, a carillon gone mad. It had been so long that I might have been tempted to sit in my rocker drinking tea, just listening and savoring the stillness in my ears. Ninety minutes. An eternity of silence and solitude. But no. I could not sit with my tea. I went down to the basement, where Warren had built a small room that served as my study. I rolled a blank white piece of paper and a yellow second sheet into my typewriter, and sat there as if before an altar.

In that silence there was also space, space that they claimed first within me and then everywhere in my life. I could now stretch from here to there and find no one impinging, no other occupant, no set of insistent demands. Did I once occupy all this space all by myself? I remembered doing so, I remembered hours and weeks, months and years of day after day in an empty place with a blank page and the wheeze of this machine and nothing else. Nothing else there at all, a resonant silence into which words would come.

And there I was, in this silence and in this space, like an old friend met unexpectedly in a dim, echoing hallway. *Hello? Am I really here, after all?* I had not thought this might happen, I had not imagined it to be possible. I remembered her well—we worked together for such a long time—but she had seemed irretrievably lost to me. And I had been lost without her, afraid with new fears, grieving, lonely, angry. But here we are, by golly. *Can I make you some tea?*

All I needed—"*all*"—*what a facile word!*—all I needed was some time to myself while I was also awake enough to function intellectually. Time not for some dreadfully overdue family obligation, but time for a clear desk and blank paper and no special obligation to anything in particular. *So now what?* The question of the day, beyond a doubt.

But by then the ninety minutes were gone, the paper still blank before me. I unrolled the paper from the platen and returned both sheets to a drawer, turned off the machine, covered it with its plastic cover, and went back upstairs.

Wordsmith for Hire

This tiny bit of free time served mostly to convince me that unused analytic skills were accumulating like toxic waste in my soul. My own needs were not being met, and you can't give away more than you are getting—or at least not for long. I answered an ad in the paper and began working at home during school time and nap time and after bedtime to write grammar exercises for a local textbook publisher. Eventually I worked my way up to teachers' manuals, to footnotes for *Beowulf,* to annotated editions of *Macbeth* and *Canterbury Tales,* and finally to sixty-page monographs on the *Odyssey* and on *Antigone.* It was good work for a hardworking, friendly, intellectually responsible house. It paid well enough: at one point, I did a teachers' guide for a 900-page anthology, and we completely redecorated the living room. But paradoxically I found myself far more restless and unhappy than I had been before. Life was more pressured, the kids and I had far less time for fun stuff, and somehow my own needs still were not met.

I went rummaging in the basement one day, sorting through the dozens of cartons of books brought home from my academic office. I wanted the small green teapot I had once kept in a desk drawer. The book cartons were all properly labeled, but five or six unlabeled boxes confronted me. With a sigh, I cut into the nearest of them. It was, alas, some of my Coleridge files—neat manila folders with typed labels, all in alphabetic order. I sat on the cold stone floor and cried. Had my life really been so orderly once, so tidy and predictable and under control? I carried the carton upstairs as gently as if it were a wounded animal.

And in the mail came a notice, forwarded to me by a friend, about an upcoming conference on the *Biographia*. I should go, Warren insisted, blocking the days out of his schedule and pestering me incessantly. Finally I made plane reservations. When I saw what that would cost, I decided to call my friend Estelle. Estelle was an American studies pal from grad school days, now in women's studies and doing quite well for herself. We had stayed in touch over the years, gossiping in the usual ways—not very often, I suppose, but often enough that I could easily accept her long-standing invitation to come for a visit.

On the first morning of the conference, I settled into a lightly upholstered chair in a small, elegant lecture hall and flipped through the list of presenters. An astounding percentage of the major scholars in the field were there: the list of names read like a couple of pages taken straight from some imaginary Coleridge studies edition of *Who's Who*. As I listened to the lectures, the influence of my work was unmistakable. And there were no children. It was exhilarating. Or it was exhilarating until I realized that the discussion moderators were selectively ignoring the women. I raised my hand over and over, but I was invisible. There were very few of us, but we were all invisible, except for two women from the host department. They were allowed to speak, but usually only after all the men who were to be recognized had spoken. At the breaks between sessions, I tried to talk to people, but the male conversational dyads consistently refused to open into a triad that included me. I was quite pointedly ignored. Trying to engage the other women was just as futile: they didn't want to be seen talking to women either. I certainly remembered that particular dynamic!

I stopped trying. I drank my coffee from the periphery, struggling to feel all that I felt and still stand quietly, struggling to understand all that I felt and all that I saw and all that I had for so long previously hidden from myself. Late on the second day two young women approached me, graduate students peering at my name tag and presuming I was also a graduate student. I explained, politely, that I had completed my Ph.D. nine years earlier. Maybe my hair wasn't so grey! I was only thirty-five, after all. I introduced myself and watched the color fade from their faces. They knew my book on the *Biographia:* they had just read it in a seminar with a man who had just done a brilliant but highly technical presentation on Fichte's understanding of consciousness. We talked briefly about their seminar, but then they floated off.

That evening there was a dinner, with a host department professor presiding at each table. I found myself seated to his right. He asked each scholar to introduce himself and identify his home institution and briefly explain his interest in Coleridge. He began the circuit with the man to his left. When the man on my right finished, however, when my own turn came, the host took over with some account of his work with the French consulate to begin planning for a local celebration of the bicentennial of the French Revolution—an event still several years distant. I was astounded and I was not astounded. The man to my right turned to me in a quiet scholarly rage.

"He thinks you're my wife!" he fumed. "Did you see? He skipped right over you! Aren't you going to say something? He doesn't know who you are!" The couple to the right of the man to my right, a pair of almost-retired bibliographers, looked on with demure alarm. I watched the fellow go from babbling about the French Revolution to babbling about how carefully they had selected the wine being poured. Nope. I shrugged.

"It is his loss," I said, with a most unmotherly edge to my voice. If the man were a proper late-eighteenth-century gentleman, he would engage me in conversation at that break point in a formal meal where everyone is expected to change conversation partners. I would introduce myself properly when the main course was served. And if he failed to observe that propriety, well, this man to my right was indeed handsome and furthermore the colleague of a particularly dear friend at the University of Virginia. He promised to be an engaging dinner partner. I never did succeed in getting our host to acknowledge my presence, but the fellow on my right and the bibliographers and I spent a pleasant evening talking about our work on Coleridge.

At the first break in the morning session, I was cornered by one of the conference organizers, the Coleridge-as-philosopher fellow who had done the talk on Fichte.

"You're Catherine Wallace!" he said accusingly, as if preparing to arrest me.

"I know," I replied.

"How could you sit here silent all this time!" he demanded. "You have not said a thing! You have not talked to anyone! No one even knows you are here! If I had dreamed you were in the country, we'd have asked you for a paper—but the dean refused to pay airfare from England."

I observed that I lived in the Midwest, not England. Perhaps he was thinking of Katherine Wheeler? (She had published a book on the *Biographia* just a few months before mine, and she was at Cambridge.) But no. He meant me; he knew whose book was whose.

I explained that I had been not silent but rebuffed. And as I described the events of the week, I felt the warm color slowly drain from my face. My shoulders grew more and more square; my voice became ever more clear and quiet and crisp with anger. I had never felt so articulate, never so strongly felt the power of exactly the right words coming to mind at the right moment. When I was done, all he could do was mutter, "Oh, I had no idea, I had no idea, oh how appalling . . ." I turned and left, spending the rest of that coffee break wandering elsewhere in the building trying to steady my heartbeat and calm my stomach.

At the lunch break, however, I was a center of attention. Several of the presenters sought me out. Dyads immediately paused in their talk to include me, at times in fact to welcome me deferentially. My work was generously praised, my opinions sought, my advice solicited. At some distant cerebral level, the recognition felt glorious. These were the people whose judgment mattered, the scholarly peers whose nearly unanimous judgment that I would be tenured at their institutions (fourteen out of fifteen) had failed to persuade my dean. The conference organizers asked me to contribute a paper, belatedly, to the conference proceedings. They hoped to get the collection published, they said, and including me would strengthen their case with academic presses.

I smelled flattery—or at least politics. A scholarly subspecialty operates like a single small town: despite geographical dispersion, the essential social dynamic can be remarkably intimate because scholars review one another's books, referee one another's papers, and hire one another's graduate students. So as in a small town, it does not pay to offend anyone who is someone. Much effort was expended to redress the offense. It was pointed out that my host of the evening before had been a Byron man, not properly one of us at all. From his grave, I felt Byron spit some contemptuous profanity. But I had made my point, and so I maintained my gracious poise as a scholar and a lady: Sister Julian Margaret herself could not have faulted my deportment, and John Dryden would certainly have approved.

Yet meanwhile I marveled at the deep psychic resonance of another role altogether—the Mother Almighty. A self-possessed, sexually mature woman wields a spectacular emotional authority that I had never before experienced in quite this way. A restrained but very angry mother gives grown men pause. If I wanted an academic job, by golly, here was the perfect opportunity to network into one. What a chance, what a *felix culpa* had I been handed!

But I couldn't. I no longer wanted any part of this club, thank you. These guys had a corner on much that I cherished very deeply. But life with kids had taught me to see and to feel too much more of what people were feeling. I still loved literature, I was still intrigued by the character of creativity or by the operations of imagination—but I did not want to work in a field where, until my talents made their inexorable claim, I could be so rudely dismissed as just a woman. "Just a woman," like "just a housewife"—what pernicious nonsense! My sexuality had been a problem from the very first day of graduate school, but it was their problem not mine. I had absorbed all that I could tolerate of sexually insecure compensatory derogation.

I felt like Miriam, singing and dancing on the far shore of the Red Sea. These guys did not look like drowned men, but the sour competitiveness of high-power academia was deadly, far deadlier and far more decadent than they seemed to know.

But I knew. My vision had changed. It was wider and deeper now. Loving poetry had nothing at all to do with academia's exceedingly narrow slice of reality. When we reassembled in the lecture hall, Shakespeare's Sonnet 29 echoed in my head, as if the very bricks were reciting it in unison.

> *When, in disgrace with Fortune and men's eyes,*
> *I all alone beweep my outcast state,*
> *And trouble deaf heaven with my bootless cries,*
> *And look upon myself and curse my fate,*
> *Wishing me like to one more rich in hope,*
> *Featured like him, like him with friends possess'd*
> *Desiring this man's art and that man's scope,*
> *With what I most enjoy contented least;*
> *Yet in these thoughts myself almost despising*
> *Haply I think on thee—and then my state,*
> *Like to the lark at break of day arising*
> *From sullen earth, sings hymns at heaven's gate;*
> *For thy sweet love remembered such wealth brings*
> *That then I scorn to change my state with kings.*

But who is the "thee" here? Who? I couldn't tell. But I felt myself reclaiming my love of literature from its enslavement in the bondage of academia. The dean as Pharaoh! I laughed to myself. But I sat there a moment looking at the bricks, wondering what else they might recite, hoping for some further enlightenment, some explanation of what I was feeling. In the far psychic distance I heard the murmuring of T. S. Eliot's "Ash Wednesday," which begins with dense allusion to Sonnet 29. In college I had memorized most of "Ash Wednesday," although not for any reason I could explain; the two texts always tended to show up together in my head like this. But the bricks were silent: Eliot did not rise to distinct audibility, perhaps because up in the front, some man was lecturing again about Coleridge. Having come all this way, I decided to listen.

When the last session ended, I went back to Estelle's house, where I had been staying all week. I curled up on a futon in her study and gave way to my long-pent grief over the tenure decision. Tears so stifled for so long had mostly dried out, but it felt good in some paradoxical way to lie there amid the futility of all I had sacrificed, all I had hoped for, all I had dreamed. And to remember other dreams, obscure dreams, dreams I had never really understood, and to wonder what truth that dreaming might still hold for me. And I realized, after a while, that under any of the dreams lay both my passionate love of words and my illusion that life is fair, that the race is to the swift and victory to the righteous. And then I could weep, silent tears soaking the collar of my nightgown. And then I could sleep, soundly and without dreams.

Not Telling Her

Bright and early the next day, we merged into heavy morning traffic on the freeway. Estelle checked the mirrors that final time, relaxed the ropey muscles in her neck, and asked, "So, when are you going to stop wasting your life?"

How far was it to the airport, I wondered grimly.

She was still at it.

"And don't tell me that they need you. Mothers always say that. It's an excuse."

I was offended. I could do better than that tattered cliché. Instead of the shoulder strap of her small sedan, I felt the warm and sweaty weight of babies asleep at last, feverish and wheezing, shallow quick little breaths not in unison with mine or with each other, ribs tight and hard with the effort, whole rows of hard little ribs under my slack hand. Carol and Tim had pneumonia for the first time before they were a year old, and at least a couple of times a year for ten years thereafter. They were chronic lung-ers, pint-sized. And the three of them had had more ear infections than anyone could count. No one could breathe or hear without an array of medications. She knew all this, at least at the factual level.

What then could I say of subtler needs, of games with kitchen towels or paper cups? She was right: don't tell her. She was not ready developmentally, her reasonable political convictions as yet uncomplicated by the realities of childhood.

Perhaps amusement had shadowed my face, perhaps the pain. For whatever reason, she started shouting, pounding the steering wheel, fingers outstretched, the long and muscular fingers of a dedicated pianist.

"You're in a trap! You're a scholar! You have obligations!"

Right on all counts, I thought, and I turned to admire vines rampaging across the fences and trees on my right. A trap indeed—

Because I could not stop for Death—
He kindly stopped for me—
The Carriage held but just Ourselves—
And Immortality.

LAX NEXT RIGHT. Is that eternity? Would Dante have put the airport terminal in some circle of his hell? And if so, which? And why? Or will it merely be the light at the end of this particular tunnel? We pass yet another sign, just an arrow and "LAX." LAX/ lux/ Lucifer:

The mind is its own place, and in itself
Can make a Heaven of Hell, a Hell of Heaven. . . .
To reign is worth ambition, though in Hell:
Better to reign in Hell than serve in Heaven.

And if the mind be its own place, each in its own place, "We think of the key, each in his prison/ Thinking of the key, each confirms a prison/ only at nightfall"—what then? Is this heaven or hell? And do I reign or serve? Or wake or sleep? If it matters at all—Keats: "Adieu! The fancy cannot cheat so well/ As she is famed to do, deceiving elf." Or maybe both at once, simultaneously: Blake, of course. "The tygers of wrath are wiser than the horses of instruction."

No doubt they are, but I was far beyond either wrath or wisdom. My face was wet with tears; drips had spattered here and there down the front of my red trenchcoat. I should stop hiding in the Norton anthology, I thought to myself; we are almost at the airport. I need to stop these voices and pay attention.

As I turned away from the passenger window, I realized that she had stopped shouting some minutes previously. She glanced at me in quick concerned twitches. She watched for a parking place and I watched her. Our eyes met only in flickers.

The silence had not softened as we reached the gate. I had nothing to say to relieve the pain and regret distorting her face. She apologized awkwardly (and, later, eloquently indeed). I still had no voice, no words for this moment. We embraced stiffly, across the gulfs between and within each of us, all of us, these searing ragged canyons torn by love we cannot explain, by love we do not understand.

She shifted the garment bag onto my shoulder without looking me in the eye. Laden, I felt Coleridge's leaden iambics in my own footfall onto the plane—the "dejection" ode once again:

> *A grief without a pang, void, dark, and drear,*
> *A stifled, drowsy, unimpassioned grief,*
> *Which finds no natural outlet, no relief,*
>   *In word, or sigh, or tear—*

Unbidden, a stewardess wrapped a blanket around my shaking shoulders. Our eyes met, just for a moment; and she did not say a word.

And when I got home, Warren took another week of his vacation to mind the kids while I wrote my belated contribution to the conference proceedings. I could still do it, by golly: forty pages, eighty footnotes all in proper form. And so much easier on a computer! And when I was done, I taped the cartons of notes closed again and buried them in a far dark corner the basement. I could almost hear some tenor singing the *Ave Maria*. It sounded right and proper, a good and holy thing: the familiar stuff of Irish funerals. And it was as if, on the sidewalk outside, funeral bagpipes wailed, bagpipes too pagan ever to be allowed inside the church.

Enough of that, enough too of lit-crit for textbook houses. I did a short course of career counseling and began to experiment a bit with medical editing. That proved challenging work: medical research dwells at some considerable distance from Chaucer and Shakespeare, from Homer and Sophocles. The kind of copyediting I was doing demanded no particular appreciation of content: all I needed was a strong sense of language and the ability to distinguish nouns from verbs and singulars from plurals. I did not need to be able to savor the elegance of the chemistry in order to fix a dangling participle, repair a failure of agreement, turn prepositional phrases back into adjectives or adverbs, or cut monumental compound-complex sentences into digestible pieces. Failures of paragraph unity are self-evident to the logical mind, however distant her appreciation of the content.

Medical editing was exhausting work, in fact—as good as cutting up sod to establish new perennial beds. I bought an electric pencil sharpener, feeling as I had felt buying a sod cutter like the one I had rented over and over again from the rental place around the corner. And furthermore, the people I met were lovely folks—at least on the phone. I never actually *met* anyone, except at the annual meetings of the American Medical Writers Association. Manuscripts came in the mail and departed again, festooned with Post-it notes and scribbled over with my English teacher corrections.

And it paid well. And it felt easier, somehow, to say "Well, I do some freelance editing, but mostly I take care of my kids." Easier than to say I was writing monographs on Homer or footnotes for *Beowulf*. I wanted no questions about my scholarly training.

Sacramental Feasts

Despite what the dean thought of me, despite the shenanigans in the English department or the judgment of the college Tenure and Promotions Committee, despite my feelings about academia, despite all this, the essential scholarly disposition is nonetheless deeply seated in my soul. In Aristotle's metaphor, it is stamped firmly in my character as a signet might be stamped in warm wax. Since everyone knows that housewives spend their days eating bonbons and watching soap operas, I decided to undertake some research into these topics.

My early research met the usual early-research problems with finding access to appropriate materials—just as with *Thel* so many years before. For instance, the television remained tuned exclusively to public TV, to a steady diet of *Sesame Street* and *Mr. Rogers' Neighborhood*. Mark also fell in love with Julia Child, whom he called "the cooking lady." Exceedingly ancient reruns were broadcast just after *Sesame Street* and just before naptime each afternoon: Mark sat fully engaged while I got the twins settled each day. I never did figure out what that meant to him. And I never did manage to watch a soap opera.

The newspaper did begin printing summaries of the previous day's soap operas, however. I read those for a few days. But they reminded me of the three or four weeks I spent one summer reading Restoration dramas and then, as the comps deadline drew near, reading plot summaries of minor Restoration drama. The great seventeenth-century farces are marvelous in their own way, but the minor stuff had marked a real low point in my academic career, far lower than the lows provoked by three-volume Victorian novels. I decided that research into soap operas could wait.

Bonbons, however, were another matter. In pediatricians' waiting rooms, on park benches, in suburban malls in bad weather—any place women with small children congregate—I took to starting conversations about bonbons. I felt more like a high school journalist than a scholar, I admit, or maybe more like a poet than a social scientist. But I was intrigued to discover that no one had ever seen a bonbon. Yet everyone had a strong visceral sense of what these confections had to be. Those who like chocolate imagined them chocolate; those who like fruit imagined fruit; those who prefer coconut or macadamia nuts obligingly supplied them.

Once I encouraged folks with my sense that the bonbon might be a mythical confection, a certain lighthearted creativity came to the fore. Women would sit back, eyes half closed, imagining some frothy antidote to life amid the fish-oil stink of Desitin diaper rash ointment. Whole waiting rooms of women with sick and cranky babies would slowly dissolve into giggles and then into hilarity. Nurses would look out over the desk, uncertain whether to be pleased or whether to worry about the maternal effects of sleep deprivation.

Certain conventions rapidly appeared, as I suppose any good social psychologist might have predicted. The bonbon must be too large to pop in your mouth. And the piece that you must hold while you chew the first mouthful must somehow melt on your fingers or dribble something sticky all over your hand, or better yet onto your clothes. Imagine, if you will, the dynamics involved in consuming an improbably large chocolate-covered cherry. Imagining sustaining your dignity as you try to bite all the way through the cherry while struggling to keep the remaining half safely in its chocolate shell— meanwhile keeping an eye out for the drips of sweet syrup and hoping the shell hasn't crumbled into several pieces. Clearly the bonbon was a candy designed for women who have acquired a certain mature and unflappable serenity. Parents who bellow abusively at their hysterical children in shopping malls late on Saturday afternoons—those are parents who lack the disposition of soul to which the bonbon answers. There is an art to this parenting business, an art compacted of the improbable, the excessive, the chaotic, and that which threatens all sense of reasonable propriety. Eating a bonbon with grace testifies to mastery of this art.

Furthermore, there is something necessarily decadent about the bonbon. For some, this meant expense. For others, calories. Some imagined exotic ingredients available only in minute quantities and at great effort. The image of a housewife eating bonbons, then, was comfort for the actual reality of being unable to go to the bathroom alone, or being unable to shower or bathe without interruption. Never eating a meal without stopping at least once to mop spilled milk off the floor. The exotic luxury of a bonbon offers mythopoetic comfort for a life in which the ordinary rights and comforts of adulthood are suddenly elusive if not illusory.

Once, when all three kids had the stomach flu, I realized that I had not eaten for three days. One or the other of the three had vomited all over me every few hours, after all: that does dampen the appetite. And they were big enough toddlers to be extremely unhappy at me for not letting them eat an ordinary diet. So I was not about to eat in front of them. But mid-morning on the third day, I realized that, despite my best efforts the night before, I still had not managed to eat. Everybody had been sick again all evening, and finally I had fallen into bed too tired to care about the stew I had surreptitiously stirred all afternoon. And then the babies had been up and sick early in the morning, before Warren had left for work. When he called mid-morning to check on us, I complained about being hungry.

I don't remember exactly what I said, but he left his office and drove an hour across the city to bring me a sack of stuff from Burger King. I locked myself in the bathroom to eat it and then slept on the floor for half an hour, until he knocked on the locked door to plead about needing to get back to the hospital for teaching rounds. Burger King wasn't bonbons, but it's the thought that counts. There are days, any mother will testify, when a burger and fries and a chocolate shake—eaten in solitude, no less—can seem like unspeakable luxury.

The next time the kids had the flu, he sent me out for dinner to a local restaurant with firm orders to get myself a proper meal. I sat there alone, cold and needing a shower, wondering whether I smelled of baby vomitus and hoping nobody would get sick all over Warren's last clean pair of wool slacks. The menu was revolting, the waitress gentle and kind.

By then, I knew I needed a bonbon. I ordered a chocolate eclair instead of dinner. And then I ordered another one. I probably drank half a gallon of good black coffee too. Perhaps this was undue strain on my uncertain sugar metabolism, but it was great for my soul. I stayed up half the night making a huge pot of thick soup to freeze in small portions, as insurance against the next round of viruses. I still keep little boxes of good soup in my freezer—like Californians maintaining their earthquake kits even after they move to Kansas. Some part of me endlessly expects to answer the summons of some baby in the middle of the night, only to have him vomit down the front of my nightgown.

One day I went in to the local Fannie May outlet, asking about bonbons. The clerk—a new hire—had no idea what I meant. I decided that the confection was probably better left to its mythic status, so it was ten years before I phoned the corporate headquarters to ask about bonbons. I was handed off to the director of advertising, but it turned out that she was home with the chicken pox. But one day when she was feeling bored and itchy, she called me from her home to answer the question I had left on her voice mail. We talked about bonbons, and then we talked about how to deal with chicken pox, and I hung up feeling very motherly indeed.

In fact, the Fannie May bonbon is not quite a two-bite blessing and not messy enough: I know, because Warren bought me a box for Christmas last year. But it is hand-dipped—a prestigious job on their production lines. The candy has such a short shelf life—or corporate standards are so high—that the company refuses to distribute them routinely to stores too far away from headquarters in Chicago. As a result, many customers special order their favorite flavors.

As for what the bonbon is—well, decide that for yourself. Literal-minded inquiry is pointless here, as it is with the Eucharist: it is an error of misplaced concreteness to ask how it is that God is present in the blessing and sharing of bread and wine. The reality is that every woman home with small children needs some mythic support for the moral demands of her life, some creature comfort to console her sacrifices. Bonbons are a sacramental reality, a communal act to nourish both body and soul.

4

A Rainbow in the Sky

IN SEPTEMBER OF 1988, CAROL AND TIM STARTED FIRST GRADE. BY THE middle of October, they were settled into familiar routines and beginning to thrive. Like bell peppers transplanted into the spring garden, they had sat, erect and cautious and perfectly beautiful in their small, gracious symmetry. But now I was beginning to see new leaves and the early buds of first flowers: the miracle of life and growth and timely development, the unreasonable, endlessly astounding tenacity of life once again. All the bedtimes on time, all the mornings carefully orchestrated, the packing of lunches, the listening to their accounts of their days, all the patient consultation about school supplies and sneakers and tee shirts, all the textbooks covered in brown paper cut from sides of grocery bags, all the utterly endless rituals of September that everyone remembers so plainly: we had gotten through September and all was well. September had not changed in generations, I supposed—and once again it had happened, like the turning of the spheres.

I watched them eating their dinners, talking animatedly or intent upon cutting the blossom end from a broccoli spear. My babies. Lord oh Lord I had made it. My babies were in first grade. All three would be gone all day long—well, at least from 8:30 to 3:15. We were settled in a new house, a bigger house—interest rates had come down!—cheerfully distant from the university where I had worked. Warren had a new position that allowed for greater opportunity to teach: he too had settled in happily, finding himself thoroughly at home in the new place. And now all three kids in school. It felt like the beginning of a whole new phase of family life. And, God willing, a new time in my life as well.

But my dinner was getting cold and I was—after gardening all afternoon—more than ready to eat. Then it was as if something asked for my attention by tapping on my shoulder. I glanced around, food in my mouth, startled. And there, in the eastern sky across the street, was the brilliant arch of a rainbow, perfectly encircling the long-needled Austrian pine centered on our front lawn.

We thundered out the front door. A small lake-effect rainstorm had blown in during the late afternoon, sprinkling the first few miles of shore and piling up dark rumpled clouds in the eastern sky. But from zenith to west, the sky was still entirely clear. As we watched, our rainbow grew even brighter, until I could see its echo. I knelt beside each child in turn, pointing out this fainter arch. Mark brought out my camera, demanding snapshots. As I took the pictures he wanted—the full arch took no less than six frames—the rainbow felt like a benediction upon the house. Could I have moved it closer, the pots of gold anchoring its ends would just have fit at either side of our circular drive. I imagined negotiating with the guardian leprechauns, who of course would never have believed that I had no designs on their gold, that I merely wanted to delight my kids.

Oh well. I shot the last frame of film and set the camera to its clackety rewinding, thinking neither of Noah nor of Wordsworth but of my mother. Rainbows follow her around, each affirming a gift from God. In all my life I have seen rainbows less than half a dozen times, but so help me she cannot balance a bank statement or find a parking place without seeing a rainbow and feeling the hand of the Almighty smoothing her way. I stood there on the porch, holding down the rewind button, replaying some of Mom's rainbow stories, noticing that the light rain had not reached around the shelter of the porch to dampen the ground cover that struggled along in the square space beside the porch and outside the kitchen window.

And I realized, as I dimly considered installing a soaker hose amid the periwinkle, that I was using considerable energy to keep some thought below the edges of consciousness. I looked in the kitchen window to our dinners, now thoroughly cold; I looked over to the kids now playing tag around the pine tree. Now really. What was this intuition that I was holding so very firmly at bay?

The camera's clack had turned to click, so I let up on the rewind button. And I eased up too on this other obscure downward pressure, somewhat more tentatively.

Words rose, like a thought finding formulation, like finding at last the words one needs to express an elusive notion.

[The conflict is over.]

Now really. What mythopoetic nonsense. I must be getting hypoglycemic: I turned to go back in to my dinner. Or I tried to turn. Somehow I felt rooted to the spot, my eyes fixed on the dusty wilted periwinkle behind the forsythia. I "heard" it again:

[The conflict is over.]

More definitely this time, more distinctly and—to my confoundment—from what felt like an originating point outside my own consciousness. "Someone"—"someone else"—seemed to be saying this.

What conflict? What? What? Ended how? There was only one conflict: my needs versus the kids' needs. I want to be home with them; I need to be here for them. They need my mothering. But I can't give them what they need unless I have what I need. And I don't know what that is. Yes I'm bored. But I had a prestigious, rewarding career once upon a time: it drove me crazy. Meanwhile I'm trapped in a zero-sum game: when I make a solid professional commitment to some project, they just do without that measure of my energy and care. And I see what that costs them. And me, ultimately: I still love them more than any work I'll ever do. So what else is new? Over with? Bullshit. First grade is a milestone to be celebrated, sure. But ended? I still have to cut their meat, for heaven's sake. Six is hardly the end of childhood!

I was shouting silently, shouting within the deep echoing silence of my own head, where that proclamation of peace lingered fragrant in the air, like incense long after the church has emptied. I was shouting and waving my hands at nothing whatever. At a random thought, at a thoroughly garbled allusion, at a moment of my own wishful thinking, brushing unrecognized across the edges of my mind, at a fine romantic bit of insignificant, contra-factual wishful thinking. It was a nice thought, like the delicate beauty of bird tracks in shallow snow on the driveway, neat little stars, all in a row. But not fallen from the sky, thank you.

But despite all my incredulous shouting, I could not deny the aura of promise, nor the lurch in the beating of my heart.

Nor, worse yet, could I deny the simple otherness of the words, the oddest possible sensation of *listening*. Instead I shook the Celtic cobwebs from my hungry brains, offered a promise of water to the thirsty periwinkle, and called the kids back in to dinner.

It was away past time to eat. And I was starved. I gave the fading rainbow no backward glance, but I recited Wordsworth to them as we settled back at the table: "My heart leaps up when I behold/ A rainbow in the sky . . ." The kids listened with the polite endurance of kids who know their English major mothers. But I hoped they would remember, years later, such impulsive screwiness as leaping up from the dinner table.

Boston

I put the rainbow out of mind and set out one weekend late in October for a four-day trip to Boston. I would stay with Jody, an old friend and former student, who had a good-humored husband and a baby I'd never met. And I'd go to the annual meeting of the American Medical Writers Association. AMWA offers cross-cultural education for medical folks who now have to write for a living, and for garden-variety wordsmiths like me who need to know something about the arcana of tables and graphs and statistics. It's a great organization of people who can think with both sides of their brains, interesting and very creative people who are used to being and feeling a bit out of step with the rest of their organizations. On the third evening there was a poetry reading—"poetry" broadly or traditionally defined as synonymous with "literature." I didn't know whether to be more impressed with the quality of the work presented or with the quality of the attention sustained by the group. That density of aesthetic response was balm to my befuddled soul.

One reading was by a physician, a woman with snow-white hair and square shoulders and gold-brown eyes that echoed and deepened the exquisite dark gold of her complexion. She stood with absolutely centered physical composure to read a painfully vivid account of one night on call when she had been an intern: to lie on a narrow cot, exhausted but taut with anxiety, waiting for a summons from phone or beeper; to walk through cold, echoing hallways to a room or a curtained cubicle dense with some stranger's pain and fear; to catch a glimpse of early morning traffic through a window, watching people head off into another day oblivious to their own terrible vulnerability, to the fragility and the tragedy that stalk us all. This time there was no approving murmur as she returned to her chair: the silence itself was thunderous tribute. We sat together in that silence as if in some cathedral.

Just as the group began with small squirms to acknowledge the muscular cost of such attentiveness, the convener proposed a ten-minute break. A small procession of people went over to the physician, laying a hand on her shoulder or her head or her hands before they moved out to the hallway. I watched them, I watched this roomful of writers, and I felt more at home than I knew it was possible to feel. The laying on of hands: what an ancient, ancient gesture of healing and affirmation. The physician accepted their silent plaudits with equally silent tears, her square shoulders stiff and still.

In the hall I was hailed by a few of the folks I had met during the preceding days.

"I hope *you* brought something," one of them said to me with unexpected intensity. Three or four women turned somberly to listen for my answer. One very tiny, very intuitive woman from Texas smiled encouragingly. I was dumbfounded. And then dumbfounded again, at myself this time, as if at the beginning of some infinite regress. What, me? Who? No. Well yes, actually. But no. But but but . . .

"You do write," asked a Yale Shakespearean now working in pediatrics. "You do. Don't you?" Her gaze was too penetrating, her confidence too discerning: I might have well as tried to lie to God Almighty. All I could do was shrug, holding up my empty hands.

"I hope you bring some next year," she concluded. The circle of listeners seconded her request.

Life-Work

When the readings ended, it was too late to take the subway back to Jody's town house, where I was sleeping on a futon on the living room floor. I hailed a cab. I let myself into the dark house as quietly as I could, folded my clothes neatly over an armchair, and, without ever turning on a light, I climbed under a lofty quilt wearing just my slip. I was so exhausted I was dizzy. But I awakened some time later in the night to watch the moon's moving shadow. And then I was terribly, violently sick to my stomach.

I awakened in the morning to Jody's year-old daughter patting my forehead curiously. "Kate *sick*," she announced to me when I opened an eye. She was trying to decide if I had a fever. I borrowed a warm bathrobe from Jody and let her brew me some herbal tea. I would skip the morning's first session, I decided. The workshop I had signed up for didn't count toward my medical editor accreditation anyhow. And Jody's motherliness felt awfully good. Amelia brought me a puzzle, which we worked together as the tea steeped and Amelia's breakfast oatmeal simmered.

Jody turned from the stove, wooden spoon in her hand. "What *are* you doing here?" she demanded. "What are you doing with this, this medical stuff? What about your real work? What about that? You can't do that and copyedit and have three kids, Katie. What was that, last night? What was it *really*? Did you read your poetry? Did you bring new stuff? Copies for me?"

My throat had closed. When finally I managed to meet Jody's eyes, there were tears on her face. "You can't," she insisted softly. "You can't do this medical stuff. You have your own writing to do."

And I remembered hearing that physician the night before, speaking softly to a friend by the upholstered chairs in the hallway, about how many decades she had waited before beginning to write what she knew she had to write, about writing and remembering what every intern goes through, about realities so few people are willing to look at plainly, about how much and how deeply we suffer and how intimate all suffering is to all other suffering. It had not felt wrong to listen; it had felt impossible to move away from the sound of that voice.

I stirred some honey into my tea, amber swirling lines slowly dissolving. I still could not speak. I sat and held the mug until its warmth was gone, then climbed the stairs to take a very long hot shower. When I returned, Jody was contrite. I began by admitting that she was right about the limits of my time. As always, I was writing poems here and there, as always keeping a journal—but otherwise nothing sustained, nothing intentional. My sustained work was all for pay, all for other people. Between freelance work and the kids, I had no time and energy for any other writing projects of my own.

We had had this argument before, but I explained myself yet again. Writing is fun, I pleaded, but the work of life is work not fun. Orthodontic bills. Sneakers they outgrow in three months. Twins to put through college—all of that grownup responsibility routine. My creative writing is fun but that's all that it is. None of it will ever pay a tuition bill.

I'm a grownup, I pleaded. I have grey hair and lines around my eyes and three kids who depend on me. If the world were fair and responsible and reasonable, I would have gotten tenure. But the world is not fair. It was time to be hard-nosed and realistic. Ten years studying literature full-time is more than most people get!

"I don't care," Jody retorted, her energies high and her contrite tones evaporated. "I don't give a damn that you're not Dante. You have a gift," her voice started to crack. "You're not sharing it. You've got to. I showed that last poem to my friends—" Her voice broke and she fell silent.

She turned back to doing the breakfast dishes, her long blond hair veiling her face, her dark blue bathrobe like a nun's habit, hanging loosely from her long and narrow waist. I went off to the afternoon session still fasting.

Comfort

I took myself one Sunday to an Episcopal church. I'm not really sure why, or how I picked this place from among the entries in the Yellow Pages: it was not the nearest Episcopal church. Maybe I just wanted to go to a church where I knew I'd run no risk of seeing anyone I knew. I had been to several Episcopal weddings, I suppose, where I had been most impressed with the *Book of Common Prayer*. In some vague way, having had the kind of upbringing we both had had, we wished now and then for a church community to help us raise our kids to care about other people. So every few years I meandered out on one of these pointless forays, sat through a sermon complaining about the budget or misreading a text, and gave up until next time.

Once in the door of this new parish, I dodged a gauntlet of ushers by turning down a side aisle. I had barely settled into my seat when the choir processed in the front left side door, singing a familiar selection from *The Messiah*.

> *Comfort ye, comfort ye my people*
> *saith your God.*
> *Speak ye comfortably to Jerusalem,*
> *and cry unto her, that her warfare is accomplished,*
> *that her iniquity is pardoned.*
> *The voice of him that crieth in the wilderness:*
> *prepare ye the way of the Lord;*
> *make straight in the desert*
> *a highway for our God.*
> *Every valley shall be exalted,*
> *and ev'ry mountain and hill made low;*
> *the crooked straight and the rough places plain.*

Oh, I had never expected Handel. The tenor was obviously a professional.

I settled back into the pew, delightedly losing myself in the music, and the spectacular blues of the stained glass windows, and a liturgy high on pomp and circumstance. Six acolytes in procession, carrying crosses and candles. Six! And forty people in the choir, all in proper black cassock and plain white surplice. Two priests. The celebrating priest was a woman in her middle fifties, small and dark and visibly delighted to be up there. Her "Lift up your hearts" was a warmly personal invitation; the congregational response, "We lift them up to the Lord," felt like an equally personal claim.

This felt like church; it felt like holy ground. How many years had it been since I had felt that? Decades? When the whole congregation began to sing the psalm in Gregorian chant, I was awash in religious nostalgia. I had not heard Gregorian in more than thirty years. I had learned to sight-read music by singing Gregorian chant, and I remembered a genuinely mystical moment when there blazed before me the concept of musical notation. I could hear what I saw, I could feel it in my throat and hear it, just looking.

It felt like a show put on just for me, like a mother fixing favorite foods for a kid's birthday dinner. That feeling, once admitted to consciousness, quickly developed an unkindly edge, as if someone were in fact asserting that this was in fact laid out just for me. "As some to church repair/ Not for the doctrine, but the music there," I retorted to myself snidely.

[Okay then. Come for the music.]

I wanted to bolt for the door. But this was not a good moment to run out: that woman was about to preach. Walking out might look like a political statement: Dr. Johnson's nasty dictum felt too close at hand. In full-fledged self-possession therefore, with a posture and attentiveness to satisfy the most critical nun of my childhood, I sat there oblivious to everything but the sound of my pulse in my ears and the circle of sweat gathering around my waist.

The Known and the Unknown

To my dismay, when the service ended two priests stood in the doorway as if in a receiving line as the congregation filed out. The first of the two, a man in his middle-to-late forties, shook my hand as if he knew me, then startled slightly.

"I *don't* know you!"

It was my turn to startle: What? Does this guy expect to *know* his whole congregation? But then he misread my startled look. He flashed bright pink and apologized profusely for failing to recognize me. The Irish face trap once again: I have such incredibly classic Irish looks that people always think they know me. He still had ahold of my hand as I assured him that he did not know me. We introduced ourselves; his name, he said, was Pete. Meanwhile, the departing congregation was piling up behind us. Having embarrassed each other sufficiently, we let the matter drop.

"I don't *know* you!" the other priest exclaimed, turning innocently away from some conversation with the couple in line ahead of me. "That's right; good day," I replied briskly, trying to free my hand and continuing to move resolutely toward the door. She followed me outside without letting go, her brilliant purple vestments billowing in the November wind. We introduced ourselves; her name was Elaine and she stared at me with the penetrating gaze of a grandmother who misses nothing and never forgets a name.

"How was church?" Warren asked over the top of his newspaper.

"Terrific music," I replied. "And six altar boys—half of whom were *girls*."

The Gifts of God

During this time, one of my best and worst clients was a business books-on-tape subscription service. They paid me handsomely to write 26–28 page audio script summaries of best-selling management books. The texts were how-to manuals that spun two or three modest ideas into 250 pages of improbable anecdote and meaningless repetition. It was like the bad writing of sophomores. But this outfit offered a great service to their subscribers: its chief editor had far higher standards than some of the publishing houses responsible for these books. She hired people like me to reorganize these awful books into something concise while preserving the tone and color of the author's voice. The audio scripts I wrote were recorded professionally, and subscribers received two such "books" on tape each month.

I could bat out one of these audio scripts in one very long weekend, reading attentively and then reorganizing ruthlessly. Done at top speed, the work was both more challenging and more profitable. By the end of the third such job, however, I was feeling oddly guilty. Although my high analytical skills had mostly lain dormant for years, it just didn't seem right to be using them to make so much money for a project that aimed primarily to help other people make more money. I was working, at the time, on a guide to interviewing. The book was in its fifth or sixth edition—obviously a classic text. But from cover to cover, it struck me as sleazy and manipulative. It was far more substantial than the usual stuff, but far less innocently banal.

When Warren came up to my study to look in on me, I confessed these misgivings. I was not given these talents for *this,* I insisted, waving at the book typescript spread across my desk and at the printer clattering its way through my audio script. And I became uncomfortably aware that I was sitting behind a long, plain, golden-oak table, like the Lady in that vision so long ago. She had not had a computer, I reminded myself with a feeble chuckle. But my unpleasant sense of moral accountability could not be banished, not once I had formulated it out loud.

I Fed-Exed my script the next morning, brewed a second pot of coffee, and settled back for some quiet, serious staring out the window. Such weekends were exhausting, but they left behind no exhilaration—just the grim satisfaction of a fat check sent out promptly. A most reliable client. But I felt empty, bleak, and sad. And into the silence of my weary ambivalence there came a line: "the gifts of God, for the people of God."

What did that mean? And who had said it? I scanned it prosodically: two iambs followed by two anapests? Or could you elide "people of" to get iamb, iamb, anapest, iamb? Would anyone be so deaf as to try that? Even Wordsworth, at his worst? But where would Wordsworth talk about "the people of God"? No, no, it felt in my mind like an isolated line, in fact a line isolated so as to *acquire* emphasis. A prose line with some very slight rhythmic structure? No. Surely it was an old Anglo-Saxon four-stress line, with a medial caesura. Lord, how many years had it been since I had read that old accentual verse? In memory, I skimmed the ballad sections of the usual anthologies, looking for anything explicitly religious among the blood-and-guts soap opera of traditional ballads.

Nothing there. Could Milton or Donne or any of those seventeenth-century religious poets be guilty of such a line? No, I decided. They did a lot of strange things prosodically, but nothing like this. Surely not. And none of the big Victorians would tolerate all those blurry slack syllables. Browne? What about Sir Thomas Browne? There was a musical prose writer, and concerned with religious themes in his own quirky way. Or Bacon? I had read stacks of both of them, long ago and far away—perhaps too far away to find. But this line had sure enough found me, from no matter how far away it had come.

I stopped myself, embarrassed. Neither Browne nor Bacon would say such a thing. What silliness is this, wasting energy in such an improbable chase.

And it dawned on me that *far away* was exactly where I was trying to get: as far away from that line as I could possibly get, hiding in the thickets of scholarly habits from what was obviously the crucial question: What did the line *mean*? Why did it feel so much like a command, like an insight consequent upon my feeling guilty about hackwork? Why was it in my head in the first place?

I stopped and turned and faced the line, as so many times before I had faced a fact or an insight or a passage that had challenged some argument I was trying to advance. I had learned not to hide from or try to elude these uncomfortable intruders upon my consciousness. Such intrusions were gifts, they had always been gifts, gifts from some deep well of my own abiding craziness. But this time the intruding line refused to amplify into a challenge, into a counterargument, or into a commentary. It remained one small, simple, resonant line: "the gifts of God, for the people of God." I should be doing *that*—whatever *that* was—and not this lucrative hackwork.

"I was not given these talents for this," I had said last night, "not for earning this kind of money on schlock." I had these gifts for a reason, apparently? For some *other* reason than earning a modest and perfectly respectable living as a competent wordsmith? What do you suppose? I stared out the window, drinking coffee, for quite a while.

Communion

The line continued to haunt me. I gave up and spent several hours reading through every Anglo-Saxon poem in my collection, without success. But three weeks later, I found it. I was in church. Just before communion, the priest holds up the bread and the chalice of wine. He or she looks firmly out at the congregation, speaking the line as an invitation to come forward. My heart started pounding so loudly I expected the whole congregation to turn and stare at me. Beginning as an infant in my father's arms, I had grown up attending Mass at least two or three times every week. Although incense now sets off my asthma intolerably, the smell of it reliably triggers a tremendously vivid memory of struggling to stay awake in his arms rather than lay my face on the scratchy wool of his shoulder. I remember giving way to sleep at last but struggling to nuzzle my face into the soft skin of his neck and the smooth starchy taste of his collar just as unconsciousness wells up around me. The symbolic reality of communion was laid just as deep in my soul, inaccessibly deep.

"Baffled" doesn't name what I felt. "Terror," maybe. Everything in me wanted to run for the door, but somehow my muscles would not answer to that desire. I felt increasingly blank and empty as the line resonated into a simple, profound, direct command. Whatever the line meant, it felt like the answer to a question I had been carrying around with me for one very long time.

I took communion, bracing for a bolt of sudden enlightenment that of course did not come. Nope, the little grainy wafer tasted exactly as it had all my life, the sip of sweet red wine just a sip of sweet red wine. Communion was the cacophony of a potluck supper in the church basement, the taste of chicken soup brought in by a neighbor in times of trouble, the smell of someone's shoulder when you needed a hug, or the smell of pine trees after a warm rain. Communion was the memory of my resentful anger when I had to carry a warm and precious loaf of homemade bread out to some neighbor, just because Mom was so unreasonably convinced that it was wrong to bake bread without giving a loaf away. To be blessed, bread had to be shared, and would ye be eating unblessed bread?

I swear that I spent half of my childhood with a bowl of salad or a hot casserole balanced on my knees, as my mother brought her share of dinner to some family with a new baby or a sick parent. When I was in fourth grade, the mother of a classmate—the mother of five, including two-year-old twins—was hospitalized for most of a year with active tuberculosis. The parish organized itself to keep her family together, to care for her children all day and to bring dinner to her family every single night so that the father could spend his time fathering and not fixing meals or doing laundry. I grew up taking that sort of community for granted.

Communion was so intricate to the structure of life in my neighborhood that I had been too many years figuring out that the rest of the world is not really like this. In the ordinary world, your problems are your own and your resources are your own. And if you make an extra loaf so as to give one away, you will only embarrass the neighbor and yourself as well. I showed up once at a house where a child had died, just to drop off homemade soup and bread and brownies. We were merely neighbors—but I thought that this was merely neighborly. But my gift was an intrusion: it seemed nosy or voyeuristic; it seemed to imply that I thought they could not cope on their own. I only made their pain worse. By tradition Zahava and I had traded pans of lasagna (mine made without meat for them; hers made with meat for us) whenever trouble struck; but it was an exercise in nostalgia, an edible version of our allusions to a literary heritage now almost equally lost.

In the primitive Christian socialism of my childhood, as in her equally tight-knit Jewish community of camp survivors and their kids, we were not expected to cope on our own, and none of "this"—however you might define "this"—really belonged to any of us. Academic abilities like mine were nothing more nor less than a car that would start no matter how cold the night, or the ability to fix a washing machine or bake a good angel food cake, or a strong clear voice to keep the choir on pitch. When I had been named a National Merit Scholar, Sister Mary Robert caught me in the hall one day and repeated again the familiar warning, "'Of those to whom much is given, much will be required.'" My talents were merely something I had a duty to care for properly, like cranky elderly relatives living upstairs. Their wealth was simply not mine.

If you think that it is, I was taught, ultimately you will starve. Ultimately, the day will come when you too need to be given the help or the resources that now you are rich enough to share. We are all frail and vulnerable: bad times will always come—and when life seems easy and secure, you have all the more reason to be both alert and generous. "The day will come," my mother would intone sternly, never finishing the phrase. "Your grandmother always said that the day will always come . . ." And then she would hand me the hot loaf wrapped in a dish towel and open the back door. Despite the days that had come and gone in my own life, I grew up feeling that we do not live alone.

The *Book of Common Prayer* explains this ancient vision in a prayer said just before that electric invitation to communion:

> Open our eyes to see your hand in the world about us. Deliver us from the presumption of coming to this table for solace only, and not for strength; for pardon only, and not for renewal. Let the grace of this Holy Communion make us one body, one Spirit in Christ, that we may worthily serve the world in his name.

But that was a time and place remote from here and now, I told myself. Parents weave certain kinds of spells, and my parents and their friends had woven a pretty good one as such things go. But there were darker realities, even then.

So in the tougher, more mature, more bitterly realistic here and now, I got up from my knees. It had been a terrible and excruciating battle to outgrow what time had demonstrated was probably just a naive idealizing of "the neighborhood" and its communal heart, "the church." I was not about to fall back into that sentimentality amidst some vague midlife crisis. I was blessed beyond reason to have even a couple of friends like Zahava. I would be a fool to look for more. Communities like the parish of my childhood—if it had ever existed as I remembered it now—were not part of any reality I had ever known since. As I drove home that day, another line appeared: "I am the master of my fate;/ I am the captain of my soul." The dreadful Victorian hairy-chest-beating of "Invictus."

"Oh jeez," I thought to myself. "Can't I do better than t*hat*?"

It seemed that I could not. The line about "gifts" persisted in its obscure resonance. And the familiar coherence of the mythopoetic ritual drew me back each week even though—or perhaps exactly because—I did not know what the line meant. At times it turned itself inside out: a blessing upon me, a gift to be accepted and enjoyed rather than one to be given. But the moment of its enunciation remained a dangerously charged event, a liturgical reenactment of some original creative act.

Professor of English, Fairy Godmother University

The priest stared at me, with deep vertical lines between her brown eyes, eyes of such a depth of color as to give the word "inscrutable" its resonance. She sat straight in a small stenographer's chair, a computer humming softly to her left and a large, well-organized desk between us. Neither ordination nor grandchildren, it seemed, had changed certain habits of a successful entrepreneur. I held her gaze, feeling her taking my measure as I was taking hers, aware yet again of the disparity between my own version of that level steely gaze and my delicate build and more-delicate-yet pink complexion.

"Tell me," she demanded abruptly, tapping a pencil on her desk, "if I had a magic wand and could wave it"—she waved the yellow pencil in small circles—"if I were your fairy godmother, what would you want from me?"

I answered without thinking, too swiftly to recall the words or reconsider them before stepping into what felt like a trap.

"I'd be a professor of English," I replied. "A full professor, at Fairy Godmother University."

She laughed, but my words sank within me like a leaden weight, like hot molten lead burning and heavy in my belly. I would never have guessed that the dream could still hurt so much. Her face abruptly softened. When shortly thereafter I made for the door, she let me go. No trap, after all. I had never intended to engage that sordid tale: all I had wanted was some explication of that liturgical line about "the gifts of God."

I betook myself and this pain in my gut home to lie on the sofa, to lie on the sofa eyeing the dappled sunlight angling through the window blinds. I could not fathom why being an English professor still felt so important. Most people would rather make friends with dentists or undertakers than with English teachers. Whenever I had said to some stranger at a party that I was an English professor, he or she had edged away swiftly, making small anxious remarks about grammar mistakes. On subway trains, of course, I have made good use of that fear of Miss Grundy: even drunks and lechers seem to grow up afraid of English teachers. I sit up very straight and say, to whatever it is he has said, "I am an English teacher." The bum reliably gets up and moves away, usually mumbling an apology.

A friend once watched me make a car salesman back down, and commented—admiringly, in fact—that I had an uncanny command of the Terrible Teacher Archetype. He wanted me to negotiate the purchase of *his* next car. I glowered but he laughed, howling, "Yes, yes, that's it, that's the look."

Or one day I confided to a good friend that a benign but essentially inoperable tumor on the white of my eye had again developed hair follicles. Tiny hairs were painfully abrading the inside of my eyelid. She struggled to look sympathetic, but then her face crumpled.

"Oh, Kate, oh no. You have, you really do have The Hairy Eyeball!" She laughed. She laughed, and she turned pink and then purple, and then she laughed some more.

"Yeah, I guess I do," I mumbled, trying to laugh along. She took that as permission.

"Oh you *do* and you always always have! The Hairy Eyeball!"

Who wants to give friends such straight lines? But perhaps something in me *was* indelibly stamped "English professor." I had, reluctantly, come to see in myself some measure of that central trait of academics: I too am something of a pathological explainer. Give me half a chance, and I'll explain to total strangers the cellular mechanisms whereby forsythia fail to bloom when spring weather is late or erratic. I know the Latin names of every perennial in my garden and I'm apt to explain the features of competing varieties to anyone who dares to admire a single bloom. I'm even worse on etymologies and holiday traditions and local history.

Pathological explaining is worse, in some ways, than life-threatening allergic reactions or maybe epileptic fits in public: anybody smart enough to know all this blather ought to be smart enough to be at least moderately appropriate in its display. But a chance to explain is like beer in the fridge to a drunk or fragrant popcorn to a dieter: it's a temptation whose power only the afflicted truly understand. My tongue is scarred from the biting of it, but I suspect that no one around me would ever know.

"Can't a kid ask a simple question and get a simple answer!" Tim erupted at me one day. "Can't you answer anything without trying to teach me two new words?"

Probably not, I admitted. He stomped off. And for months, he'd moan, "There she goes. There she goes again, look at her!" any time I tried to answer any kid's question or to explain something I felt they should know. The children of pathological explainers are a well-informed but long-suffering lot: heaven help kids like ours whose parents are both afflicted. The first-grade teachers marveled at Tim's and Carol's near-perfect scores on some national test of general knowledge. But behind their praise of our parenting, I heard loud sarcastic sighs from children held captive in car seats.

Not just full professor at FGU. Why not chair of the English department? Dean of the college? Please, please, world, give me a socially appropriate outlet for pathological explanitoriness and a place where my face belongs.

But underneath such reflections, some greater truth lurked. I had left the university for good and solemn reasons, after all: to nourish that in me which academia had almost starved to death. But what had academia fed? Or what essential nutrients were missing at the moment? The obvious answers—prestige, paychecks, rows and rows of deferential students politely taking notes—none of them had that ring of truth.

Over and over, I had worked full-time for weeks or even months at a stretch when I had a big contract to fulfill. The money had always been very welcome, but the cost to family life had always been proportionally unpleasant. All the fun stuff disappeared. Suddenly all of every weekend was chores and errands and exhaustion. The kids quit talking to me about all the apparently inconsequential stuff, all the kid-consciousness associational flow that kept me in touch with what their lives really felt like and what their needs really were, this week. Such work was great for my ego, great for my sense of self—but the loss of my attention and Warren's, as we struggled to stay up with housework, proportionally diminished theirs. And those who grow up malnourished, whether physically or emotionally, suffer a deficit that cannot easily be remedied.

I am the grownup in this situation, I felt. If someone has to do without—if this parenting business really is a zero-sum game at base—I am far better able to take that loss without real harm. Life's fourth decade is less crucial developmentally than its first. So each time I finished a major contract, I recognized all over again what a huge job I already had in running this household and mothering these three kids. On bad days, I figured that on the whole I worked just enough to have the worst of both worlds.

Maybe I was more or less bored with freelance editing, then, but full-time work in some office would nonetheless be full-time insanity. I knew myself, I knew my own desires and my own limits well enough to be sure that getting a "real job" was no solution. I needed something I could do right here, even with a sick kid sleeping on the sofa. And that meant writing of some sort, and that's what I was already doing—in great variety, no less.

Fairy godmothers, real or imagined, ask all the most dangerous questions.

Unremembered Dreams

In the newspaper one morning I saw a picture of an Irish wolfhound. Such dogs were bred, the caption explained, to hunt deer and elk by running them to ground. The photograph showed a huge, ugly creature, tall and lanky and rough-coated. I felt for a moment deeply moved to drive down to the dog show to take a look for myself. This animal felt—*felt*—like a vision from an old dream that had hovered for decades at the very edges of consciousness. I had never exactly asked myself what the animal in the dream looked like—I'm just not a particularly visual person—but surely this beast in the newspaper had the right looks.

As a young girl, or in these unremembered dreams, I encountered certain aspects of my own consciousness under the guise of a shoulder-high dog bred to run long distances tracking large game. This creature is not a pet. She is not something one ought to have in a suburban backyard, not something to pose with the children in front of the fireplace for Christmas card pictures. No. Not that, but a tough, unruly work animal.

I had not wanted this beast, but somehow she is mine. Because in the cosmos of my childhood God was in minute-to-minute control of every last chirping sparrow and every stray lock of hair and every bud on the lilac bushes by the back fence, I grew up knowing that God was somehow responsible for this impossible, unruly animal who kept trashing my life. Why me, God? Why did you dump this animal in *my* lap? Oh God, what am I going to do with this beast?

But God never seemed to answer. I just kept getting myself into trouble for asking questions, for answering questions, for noticing what was not supposed to be noticed, and all too often for refusing to go along with something or other. But eventually, since I had to live with this creature, so to speak, I began to pay some attention to her needs. I discovered her abilities, honed them, exercised and taught this animal, and learned to live safely alongside her overwhelming passions and energies.

I looked again at the cheap grainy picture in the newspaper. How exceedingly odd to feel so clearly that this is what she looks like! I had not thought of her in decades. What was she up to, really, these days? Were we both now round and grey, not lean and dark and hungry? I looked within me, wondering, but there was nothing to see. Maybe a beast bred to track such big game as metaphysics and metatheoretical constructs in literary criticism will never be a visible or embodied creature, I thought to myself with a laugh.

But was she really bred for that? Suddenly I wondered. I'd always thought so before. But surely what elicited her best work was poetry, not theory. I began to feel that theory had merely been my way to keep up with her, to understand what she was about in ways that kept me out of her path, safe from being trampled. It was like teaching Prince—by far the biggest and unruliest of our collies—not to run circles around me when he was on his leash, or not to jump on me as I opened the back gate, thereby knocking me down into the icy puddle that collected by the garbage cans. Theory had felt like that. "No, Prince! Down!"

Prince would stay down—but only for me. No one else in the family had ever learned how to keep his huge muddy paws off their shoulders. Everybody else just got mad at him. They never figured out that you had to look him in the eye and accept his eager love before you commanded, "Down!" And I was only seven or eight: I couldn't explain it. Eventually, my father gave Prince to a friend of his with a farm—because I couldn't explain. What is theory, after all, but explaining what it is you do by instinct, by instinct and through love? Soon enough, we got another collie. She too obeyed me flawlessly and ignored everyone else. I taught her hand signals, which she learned with the ease of her herding instincts. And then I taught the rest of the family. It worked. Sparky stayed.

Maybe this creature was for poetry, not for theory? Theory is all logic and detail and simple mechanical smarts. But she was so much more than merely smart. She was so quick, so intuitive, so passionate, so outspoken and heedlessly foolhardy. All she really cared about were words, not being reasonable or responsible or getting work done on time. I remembered the day I had discovered the *Oxford English Dictionary:* nine pages of definitions of "green." The rest of the afternoon was lost. When hunger finally drove me out of the library, I could no longer remember why I had needed to look up the word. And I no longer cared. My life with her was like that. I had always struggled to keep up with her, to direct her enormous energy without getting knocked into some icy puddle or bruised against some fence.

And I thought: all this freelance stuff. Of course. Small game—but better than nothing. Using a wolfhound to track rabbits. That's what I have been doing. Yeah, this is wordcraft. But there is nothing poetic about it.

Maybe—do you suppose—could I imagine—that she was the "gift" in "gifts of God"? In my imagination, she and God and I gathered around the kitchen table as I set the newspaper aside and brewed another pot of coffee. In my mind's eye, I also brought to the table all the writing and editing and talking I had done as a freelance over the years—work on apolipoproteins and HIV and the management of post-surgical cardiac problems; work on how-to business books; presentations to architectural firms and chemical firms and engineering firms. This had all been hard work. But mostly, I realized, it had been scouring some intellectual landscape in search of sustenance, a desperate hunger for words, a physically and emotionally exhausting work with an animal whose teeth had turned against me at times.

I had tried resuming literary-critical research; I had tried to pick up with my professional reading again. But it had bored me intolerably; it had felt so terribly self-centered and distant from the real lives of anyone at all. I no longer really cared what Coleridge had thought about imagination between 1815 and 1819—as opposed to, say, between 1798 and 1804. Furthermore, I knew that criticism as a profession had taken off after even less interesting questions, convinced that words mean nothing, that meaning itself is merely a front for political oppression.

I still cared deeply about imagination, of course. But what mattered was imagination itself, not Coleridge's theory of imagination and its place among theories of imagination and its roots among theories of language and theories of consciousness and how these are inevitably refracted through our own contemporary theories—what a weary regression! More than ever I knew that imagination matters, that there are absolutely crucial choices to be made in how we imagine our lives, how we imagine our children and our children's lives, how we imagine our lives together as families and as communities. I still read poetry: if anything, it haunted me more than it ever had. But no one earns a living from poetry—not even poets. Even the poets I knew—and I knew several—earned a living as an academic literary critics. And scholarly careers, I knew so well, meant reading and teaching less and less of poetry but more and more of other scholars as the years went by. Literary theory, once a cutting edge, once an outpost, had taken over the whole discipline: no one any longer studied poetry as once poetry had been studied. And poetry was what I wanted. It was all I had ever wanted, really, ever since that first afternoon with sonnets and Sister Monica, in that damp and funky basement classroom.

Okay God, I wanted to say firmly, what is going on here? What do you want from me? I am doing the best I can, dammit; and this is all fine honest work. It is not enough. I know that. But it's not my fault I'm starving. My intellectual life isn't exactly bulging with options. There is no Fairy Godmother University, and if I had a job in its English department I'd probably be miserable. There's not an English department anywhere that would let me alone to read poetry with kids in the way I want to read poetry with kids, ways that presuppose that meaning and value are moral achievements—not illusions. I've outgrown literary "professionalism," God. I don't think I could do that anymore. So what are you up to?

But there were no answers. She seemed to climb into my lap like an unhappy child. I sat there feeling her size and power and—yet again—holding back inexplicable tears.

Staring out the Window

More and more often, as the weeks went by, I found myself sitting quietly, not thinking about anything, just breathing and staring out the window and trying to stay in touch with some elusive something I glimpsed from time to time. Of course, sitting quietly, just breathing, is not all that hard for an asthmatic to do. It's like asking someone with a gimpy knee to sit and be aware of her knee: breathing is a complicated, sometimes noisy task that I will never take for granted. Any time I get too enthusiastic about carrying laundry baskets up stairs, or carrying groceries in from the car, then I am indeed likely to find myself sitting quietly, staring blankly, attending to every breath as I wait for my breathing to deepen and slow. And after my breathing slows and the dizziness subsides again, it can feel quite nice to continue sitting quietly, breathing deeply, settling into some equivalent depths, some calmer place below the floating debris of the quotidian consciousness that had tricked me—once again—into mindless haste.

In graduate school, I had been enormously amused to learn that sitting, breathing, staring out the window like this counts as "meditation." I was very pleased. My parents and the nuns had been apt to call it "doing nothing." I watched astounded as my friends paid good money for courses to teach them how to sit and do nothing, and I was quite impressed—not for the first time—with what hyperachievers populate good graduate schools. But sure enough: in the mid-seventies, Transcendental Meditation was the trendy way to cope with stress, itself a trendy new topic. Surely, I told myself, I know how to breathe and stare out a window: I grew up with a dog and a father who smoked! I am an old hand at this sit-and-watch-your-breathing stuff!

But soon the whole campus was talking about Herbert Benson, a Harvard professor and physician who had taught his medical students to meditate and demonstrated correlative changes in such basic measures as brain wave activity and blood pressure. Here was good scientific proof that the benefits of such comforting behavior were available without any religious mumbo-jumbo. Soon enough I found myself sidestepping guys who were sitting crosslegged on the floor in the library or in the hallways, eyes closed, thumb and forefinger touching. Women who took meditation breaks, I observed, more often tended to stay seated inconspicuously in their carrels or at the long monastic tables in the reference room. Mildly curious—graduate school was certainly stressful at times—I read a tattered photocopied account of Benson's research that Warren had been given by his lab partner one semester.

I was unnerved to recognize the origins of Benson's techniques. What everyone in Ann Arbor in the 1970s was calling "meditation" was merely what the Christian tradition called "contemplation." According to the nuns, contemplation was the Chivas Regal of pious practice. It was only for the exceedingly wise and holy (not, for instance, for the likes of Franny and Zooey), because it was a direct route to the immediate awareness of the omnipresence of God. And finding one's way to the immediate awareness of the Sacred was dangerous except under careful, professional supervision. So it was advised for lay folks only in small sips diluted with a lot of water and probably ice cubes, to mute the taste. And only on special occasions, like retreats at a monastery or a convent: I knew it happened there, because I'd heard grownups talking about it. But the straight stuff—pure *contemplatio*—was only for clergy. Maybe not even ordinary priests, maybe only bishops and cardinals. The Pope, for sure. The descriptions of how to do it were as vague as what we got in sex ed and considerably less tantalizing: Catholic laypeople are discouraged from direct encounters with the Holy. We are too liable to heresy and rebellion and the sin of intellectual pride. But reading Benson—like reading *The Joy of Sex,* another recent publication—was both a startling revelation and an unnervingly direct depiction of immediate, familiar experience. The techniques were so simple! And such an inevitable, familiar part of my life for as long as I could remember: ack! It didn't feel dangerous! And it didn't feel holy at all. It just felt, well, *good.* It just felt *good* once in a while to unplug the intensity that drove my inner life and to let my twitchy airways calm down. Had the desert fathers been asthmatic? All that desert dust?

Dangerous or not, here was this guy Benson, teaching it to anybody. I tried closing my eyes, as he suggests; but I'd fall asleep or get dizzy. I went back to staring but not seeing, an equally withdrawn trick I'd developed in grade school during that long stretch when my undiagnosed myopia had turned much of the world into an unintelligible blur anyhow. No matter what, a lot of my ordinary life in graduate school was spent staring out the window. Silence would suddenly intrude upon reading, and I would come to, to realize I had been staring blindly into space. Or when I tried to write, the right word would hide itself in the depths below the lowest depths of conscious wordcraft. I would have to sit back from the typewriter, stare blankly, breathe and relax and wait. And now I had these wonderful arguments that I was not guilty of not-working. I was not-thinking, which is an essential nurture of one's creativity. What a deal! Being an intellectual sure was fun. If Sister Julian Margaret were to pounce on me now, I could smile sweetly and respond that I was merely meditating.

And not only that. I discovered that such creative indolence was appropriate to my particular academic specialty. Like Zen Buddhists, or mystic Christians, or Gnostics, or Neoplatonists, the English Romantic poets also insisted that all consciousness is ultimately one, that any individual consciousness exists in communion with a unitary structure that informs all of reality. This unitary whatever—some called it "God"—is the life of all that lives and the being of all that is. The various groups who believe such things argue vehemently with one another about the details, of course—arguments with undeniably massive implications for the living of one's life. I wasn't all that interested in the whole lot of them, however, or in the technique as such. I just wanted to sort my way through the particular subset of arguments about these issues that were current in England in the late eighteenth and early nineteenth century. But I was undeniably pleased at the new status that suddenly accrued to my sitting doing nothing, staring blankly; and so I became less inclined to stop myself.

All these years later, however, in my almost-forty befuddlement, those eighteenth-century arguments on which I had worked so hard came to feel like word games, like intricate little philosophic jewels strung upon a primary intuitive recognition: there is a unity here; and I am part of that unity. The arguments about this intuition are gorgeous and I still loved their intricacy and their intricately faceted history in western culture. But now I felt much more engaged by the psychic string that united them.

I had no idea what this unity might be—to define it meant to engage the word games, to return to the scholarly philosophic endeavor I had left behind. In the end, no one definition commended itself to me as more real, as more trustworthy than any of the others. Each particular definition crested at a particular cultural moment, like an instrumental solo within a concerto, then settled back into the orchestral whole, perhaps forever to blend its voice with all the others or perhaps only until the right moment for another solo. I had never felt any need to decide whether I believed in the flutes more than I believed in the violins, whether I believed in what some called "God" or others called harmonic brain waves.

But now I did feel something. Now I felt a powerful need to do more of this quiet sitting, this mindless staring out of windows, not because my writing was triggering it—I was still only doing medical editing and such—but because doing so helped to calm and to comfort this new chaos in my soul.

"What are you doing when you stare like that?" Mark demanded one day.

"Nothing," I replied. "Just looking out the window. Why? What do I look like I'm doing?"

"You look like you're staring into some other dimension!" he retorted, with that characteristically preadolescent mix of curiosity and disdain.

"Nope," I replied, wryly, to his departing shoulders. "It's just the back yard."

Adding It Up

Not that full-time mothering and a small but thriving freelance business leaves all that much time for meditative sitting around. But running a household involves as much essentially mindless scut work as any other job. And the scut of weeding or washing clothes or waiting in the dentist's waiting room or the soccer field parking lot is actually far less brutalizing than the scut of grading freshman essays or attending tedious, contentious meetings. An attorney friend concluded much the same thing one summer: listening to good music and matching your kids' socks, she declared, was not intrinsically less interesting than skimming hundreds and hundreds of pages looking for applicable legal precedents whereby a client you find despicable can sue some other sleazebag. And when you were done washing and pairing socks, at least you had clean socks. A whole day in the law library was never as predictably fruitful. I discovered that I could fold laundry without seeing it, just as I could stare into the yard. And there was some odd comfort in doing so.

That spring, I started working with an accountant, helping him write his Securities Exchange Commission reports within sentences of approximately tolerable length. He was explaining to me one day about the people who actually read these reports, the sub-sub-analysts in the sub-sub-basements of investment houses in New York, and what those analysts already knew about various accounting options whereby a company might comply with new regulations about its reporting of the cost of health care for retired workers. It was a lovely day outside. At least his office had a window—a splendid view, in fact, befitting a senior executive. I noticed the view because he had stopped talking to stare out the window.

"I don't want to write it, and they don't want to read it," he concluded at last. "You know what matters to me? You know what matters?" He turned from the window to face me, his strong face stern and slightly flushed. "My kid was elected captain of her soccer team. *That's* what matters. My kid is *good* at soccer, she's good and I was never that good, and she loves it. And *that* counts." He sat very still, absolutely tough and angry in his self-composure, as men so often seem to do when they are fighting tears. I had noticed that the muscles of his thighs were big and well defined, that even at forty-something he still had an athlete's loose and graceful walk. As I held his gaze, I felt the power of his paternal masculinity in ways that belied the disembodied abstraction of accountancy.

I had been working with this guy for several weeks, around his travel schedule. I wondered how many games he got to see, how many practices he made it home to watch, and how—as an accountant—he added it all up. He had to buy soccer cleats for this kid, after all. And broccoli, and toothbrushes. And the mortgage, and property taxes, and good medical insurance. College tuition. She needed what his working provided, and yet surely she also needed this passionate and devoted man as a real presence in her life. And he clearly needed someone who needed him as the sub-sub-analysts—or even his colleagues—never would.

We talked, for a few minutes, about kids and soccer. And then we got back to work. I could help him with split infinitives, but not a divided heart. Maybe there is never "world enough, and time."

Not-Thinking Two Entirely Impossible Thoughts

Whether I was sitting and staring or mindlessly doing mindless scut work, no matter what I was doing or not-doing that season, two thoughts kept returning no matter how often I patted them on the head and sent them politely on their way downstream toward some deep psychic ocean.

Why was I going to church? I can't possibly depict how many times that question fished itself out of the stream of consciousness, and how many times I tossed it right back in. *Habit* was certainly one of the best and strongest dismissive answers. After all, I was twenty-two and in graduate school before I had a close friend who had not been raised Roman Catholic and sent to Roman Catholic schools. I had grown up in a city of seven million people from all over the world, but "the neighborhood" had been as well bounded and as definite a psychic space as any small town in South Carolina. Even at the grocery store, all the other kids had been Catholic. One of the stock boys was Italian, as I recall, but everyone else was Irish.

Such cultural homogeneity leaves its mark—its scars, no doubt—so deep within consciousness as to be irretrievable later. So what that I had skipped church for twenty years: the older we get, the more we discover of mortality and responsibility and pain, the more weight our heritage brings to bear upon the directions of our lives. Everybody knows that. We drove a station wagon too. So what? It's immature to panic when you find yourself resembling the middle-aged parents you remember from your own adolescence.

And the reformed Catholicism of the Episcopal Church was not, liturgically speaking, much of a departure from the unreformed Catholicism of my upbringing. Yes, it was in English not Latin. And the altar boys could be girls. Even the priest! But despite these inclusivist and liberal intellectual tendencies, the Episcopal Church has the same essential ceremony. And my childhood had been interwoven with it, enmeshed in what is undeniably among the oldest liturgical and symbolic languages of spiritual experience in the West. Going to church, I told myself, like buying a station wagon, really doesn't mean all that much. It's probably just part of middle age.

Some go to the opera, I kept telling myself; I'm apt to go to church. That's all. Our pledge to the church was no greater an expenditure than two good subscriptions to the Lyric, plus parking and baby-sitters. And the Lyric series was seven or eight performances—not every single Sunday all the year 'round. I was going merely for all the archetypal symbolism submerged within any great art—symbolism which the Mass complexly and powerfully enacts. Furthermore, I prefer Gregorian chant to opera—and besides, this church choir has section leaders from the symphony chorus and a superb director. And parking is easy and we can bring the kids . . . that's all. I need the poetry. There's just not enough poetry in my life.

Plop. Splash. Back into the water with that question. Take a breath. Inhale slowly; exhale easily. Feel the weight of gravity and remember how many billion creatures on this planet are respiring and feeling gravity right now right along with me. The cosmos is a grand unity, but there is no need to embroider that fact with the vague superstitions and magical causality rampant within institutionalized religion—no matter how pleasant the aesthetic experience.

Unfortunately for this particular line of deconstruction, Pete's and Elaine's sermons were never "vague superstitions and magical causality." Their sermons were riveting, week after week after week: glimpses of what was obviously an enormous tradition of subtle, intelligent, rigorous engagement with all of life's most important and difficult questions. Pete was rigorously philosophical—a Jesuit in disguise, we teased him. Elaine was a storyteller: she played a devious counterpoint to all the same tunes. Between the two of them, they kept me incessantly off balance yet utterly engaged.

Career changes can be the work of the Spirit, came the argument one Sunday. So be careful about praying about how unhappy you are in your job, because God just might listen. A story: sending a parishioner to a monastery for the weekend, a parishioner agonizing about a big promotion that would demand a lot of travel. And the monk asks him, "To whom do you have to account for this decision? And why . . . ?" Start praying, we were warned, and maybe God will listen. Worse yet, perhaps, you might just start listening to yourselves, as the monk taught this guy to do. And that's when the Spirit begins to wreak her havoc.

Or another week, a map flipped open from the pulpit, an hilarious tale about arguments between husbands and wives about checking maps and asking for directions. Being lost, we were told, is the central moral experience. Look at what happened to Abraham: Go to a land I will show you, God says. Which means that Abraham never really knew where he was going—or, soon enough, even where he was. Being lost is like that. And that's the Promised Land, the land God promises to the faithful: feeling as lost and as invisible as a black cat on a dark night. Look around you, God says to Abraham, because this is it. And who knows where this is? Or forty years in the desert, led by this guy Moses, who never wanted to lead anybody to anything, who just wanted to be left alone out there with the sheep. What kind of God is this anyhow? If this is spiritual growth, maybe it's safer to tune out God's promises, to stay home and safe—with the sheep, of course.

The whole congregation sat motionless. No one seemed to be breathing. Pete stood looking at us for a long, silent, scorching few seconds, then turned from the pulpit and crossed the sanctuary—with a small, honest bow to the altar—to stand by the benches on the left side. "We believe in one God," he said, in his rich and effortlessly projected voice. And the congregation picked right up with the rest of the Nicene Creed. I looked around, wondering how many of them understood the truly Byzantine issues involved in that creed—or how many of them were simply glad to move on with the liturgy, to get away from the challenges Pete had presented, to let the music of the old familiar words comfort them without their listening to what they were saying.

What kind of God indeed, I wondered, driving home. And what am I doing in "his" church? Abraham, lost. Like Dante, of course. Or more precisely, I suppose, Dante like Abraham, alone and lost in the middle of the woods of middle age, on the verge of drowning in terrors that wrack the lake of his heart. *"Nel lago del cor."* No doubt about it: Dante knew about feeling lost. For Dante as for the poets writing about Abraham or Moses, about exodus or exile or any of it, being lost is indeed the central spiritual experience, the first step toward enlightenment, toward the sunrise glazing the shoulders of Dante's hills.

Dante admires that sunrise just for a moment, and then he is attacked by a leopard, a lion, and a bear, traditional images of lust, pride, and covetousness. And before I had reached home, Dante's moral predicament had been transmuted into Dorothy's lions and tigers and bears. And I was beginning to see a well-paved track through the woods. Surely no respectable god will concern himself with such triviality as my boredom with writing summaries of business books—or if he does, then how can one possibly account for the Nazis, for the Khmer Rouge, for Genghis Khan, for those

Assyrians descending like wolves on the fold? Theodicy, I told myself firmly. The problem of evil. Theology has to take theodicy into account from the beginning. And that's why any philosophically adequate god has to be as Shelley depicts him: remote, serene, indifferent, a generative philosophical principle, perhaps, or maybe some inexplicable creative energy animating the biosphere but not—absolutely not—this passionate God of the Jews. I spent the rest of the day humming "We're Off to See the Wizard."

But such insouciance did not last. I could not make it last. It had once been such a reliable part of my soul, such a dependable part of my intellectual arsenal, but now it was melting away like snow in a February thaw. Over and over again, the same glassy-eyed question was flopping and thrashing in my soul. Why am I going to church? Every time it landed, it splashed me with the waters primeval. I seemed to find myself feeling wetter and wetter.

The Still Small Voice

The other incessant thought was not really a thought at all. No, it was definitely not a thought. It was something more like a perception, more like the first hint of a faint fragrance of baking bread drifting up the stairs toward my study. I might ignore it and keep working, but my mouth would water all the same—like the famous exercise in which a speaker describes a lemon in such sensory detail that everyone in the room salivates. And the perception was this: the undefinable, ineffable unity "organizing" the cosmos or our knowledge of the cosmos is not a concept but a person. A passionate, loving person who really knew who I was and cared about what I had suffered and what I was suffering still. A person as ineffable as any of the rest of us, but more so. Ineffable out to the edges of my most profound experiences of the natural sublime, out to the edges of Rocky Mountains and rosebuds and childbirth—and then some.

I didn't know what to do with this. Concepts can be deconstructed, arguments about concepts can be refuted—but a person standing facing you is a person standing facing you.

Analytical intellect, no matter how fancy or how powerful, cannot make a person disappear. I could not make this person disappear. At best, I could demonstrate that the perception "person" was a metaphor, an analogy of sorts: not that the essence of this perception was comprehended by the word "person" but that it was reasonable in a poetic sort of way to name this strange new reality by borrowing the name appropriately used for human beings or human self-consciousness. It seemed somewhat amused by this effort on my part—but in a familiar, tolerant sort of way, as an old friend you have not seen in years will chuckle at the persistence in you of some small quirky habit she had forgotten about. And that only made the whole situation a whole lot worse, it seemed to me. I felt as if I were running in a panic from something really quite familiar, something intimately known and intimately loved or trusted. But that did not calm me down. It just made me feel like a fool.

I began to worry that perhaps I was hallucinating, that perhaps some crucial psychodynamic structure had just ruptured. But there was no physical aura here, no sensory correlate. And my day-to-day consciousness and behavior seemed quite unchanged: I was keeping up with the laundry, sorting receipts for income tax, editing a paper proposing methods for data collection for quality control in a cardiac intensive care unit. (How do you get those nurses and doctors to fill out the right forms after they get someone back from the brink of death in a cardiac arrest?) I was neither depressed nor even anxious, not really. I seemed as close to sane as I have ever been. I was just confused. And, perhaps, I was spending a little too much time staring out the window.

I got to church a little early one Sunday. Idly, I glanced through the service leaflet with the musical selections and Scripture reading assigned for the day. This week we were going to sing the psalm antiphonally, with the congregation singing the same verse couplet over and over between the verse couplets or triplets sung by the choir. That is a standard form for the Romans, but unusual among the Episcopalians—perhaps because it can so easily damage one's perception of the psalm as a whole. I took a look at the chant line: no wonder. This was really complex stuff. I studied the choir's line, gave up, and concentrated instead on the simpler congregational line. When I thought I could hear the notes, I turned to the psalm verse that went along with the congregational music. It was from Psalm 27:

> *You speak in my heart and say, "Seek my face."*
> *Your face, Lord, will I seek.*

My heart stopped beating. I turned away numbly to the Old Testament reading, which was from the first book of Kings, chapter nineteen:

> Elijah fled to Mount Horeb, and there he came to a cave, and spent the night there. Then the word of the Lord came to him, saying, "What are you doing here, Elijah?" He answered, "I have been very zealous for the Lord, the God of hosts; for the Israelites have forsaken your covenant, thrown down your altars, and killed your prophets with the sword. I alone am left, and they are seeking my life, to take it away." He said, "Go out and stand on the mountain before the Lord, for the Lord is about to pass by." Now there was a great wind, so strong that it was splitting mountains and breaking rocks in pieces before the Lord, but the Lord was not in the wind; and after the wind an earthquake, but the Lord was not in the earthquake; and after the earthquake a fire, but the Lord was not in the fire; and after the fire a still small voice. When Elijah heard it, he wrapped his face in his mantle and went out and stood at the entrance of the cave. Then there came a voice to him that said, "What are you doing here, Elijah?"

I stopped reading and put the leaflet aside. I sat there, one cold hand holding the other, struggling to collect my wits enough to put on my coat and walk out. But Elaine walked by and stopped to say hello.

"I'm preaching this morning," she complained, "and I was up half the night with this stuff, and I'm still not sure what I'm going to say. I wish I knew what God is up to, sometimes. If I give you a copy of this sermon later, will you read it for me?"

We laughed. I said something adeptly allusive about the vagaries of inspiration. Then a woman I had briefly met sat down beside me to ask me to join a women's spirituality group that was getting started . . . and then Pete stopped to confirm plans for a pocket-calendar phone call to find a time to get together.

"Did you know," he asked, "that I used to be an English teacher?—mostly Wordsworth . . ."

The window of opportunity for walking out had closed quite firmly indeed. But that didn't really matter. My mind had entirely shut down: I did not hear a word of the service. I suppose I sang the psalm verse appointed for the congregation, but I have no memory of that one way or another. I came home and tried to stare out the window and get a grip on myself, but it was like a projection screen with no slide in place: white, blank, slightly grainy.

Door County

The door was locked. Of course the door was locked. From the church steps I could see the roof of the cottage we had rented, up beyond the rows of young apple trees with their orange-red fruit—the cottage to which I had brought us in the wrong week, dusty and exhausted, brought myself face to face with the startled agent, with my husband's firm and cautious self-control, with the wailed dismay from backseat prisoners set momentarily free. It was mid-July, peak season, but the agent found us an empty cottage to stay in. For two days now, Warren had guarded the kids at the pool, ushered them through various hikes, played Monopoly, fixed meals. For two days and two nights I had read and slept awhile and then read some more; he had never asked. "Mommy's tired," I heard him say, over and over again. "Let her be."

I knew, of course I knew, that there would be no way to get into this grim old Roman church. What I couldn't fathom was why I tried, or how I had misplaced the third week of July. I could not see why, at this point, these shards of my quotidian consciousness called out to a God who had faded away like the Cheshire Cat. For months this disruptive sense—almost a voice—had disturbed the complacencies of my wholly ordinary life. And now it had disappeared.

But in a resort-town bookstore I found a whole shelf of C. S. Lewis and something titled *Models of God,* a book by an academic theologian named Sallie McFague. McFague argues that all discourse about God is essentially metaphoric, that poetry is the language of God, the language about God, misread and nailed into place by literal-minded religious cops. And C. S. Lewis argues that humans are something like ill-mannered dogs disciplined by th'Almighty into something remotely tolerable—a classicist straight out of T. E. Hulme, *Romanticism and Classicism*. And yet, and yet, there is enormous power in his equally classic critique of those who would deny transcendence, those whose metaphysics comes down to WYSIWYG. It's just that Lewis has dreadful metaphors for the relation between the transcendent and the human. He imagines a God designed for repressed intellectuals terrified and disgusted by their own embodied passions. But he writes well, a classicist in style too.

I read McFague and four by C. S. Lewis in two days, taking refuge in analysis and disputation, tracking Lewis's intellectual and stylistic and theological antecedents, watching my own dispassionate disputation of his metaphors warm to anger and then slowly to outrage, trying desperately to find myself again. I was astounded by Sallie McFague, by the care and self-conscious scholarly polemic of her book and yet—from my literary perspective—at the self-evidence of her underlying claim that nothing in Scripture and tradition can be taken literally, objectively, simply. Centuries ago Blake had argued that the priestly clan misreads, that church tradition literalizes sacred poetry so as to dumb it down, to tame it, and finally to distort it into the service of psychological repression and social control. Didn't these modern theologians know *The Marriage of Heaven and Hell*?

A resort-town bookstore with such titles as these felt like the hand of God. A bookstore as improbable as the locked church was inevitable, as if this Other had some sense of dramatic propriety. On the third day, I went back to the bookstore and bought another bagful of books. The cheap grey plastic bag waited ambiguously on the far side of the front seat as I ate a piece of cherry pie in the hilltop parking lot of a cherry orchard. I calculated odds. Will there be a stone in this fruit, a bone, a germ lurking in this tart sweetness? One well-placed stone, and I will no doubt lose that fractured, patient molar.

"Doesn't this hurt?" the dentist had asked, incredulously, at a routine exam the day before we had left on vacation. I had blinked against the examining light. What? My tooth?

"It all hurts," I did not say.

"A big piece is missing here," he said solemnly and folded his arms. "Be very careful what you eat or you may lose that tooth altogether. How soon can you be back?"

C. S. Lewis and Sallie McFague, God? Okay. Coincidence or magic? And how much else in me is cracked and breaking? This begins to feel like the sprouting of a Dickensian subplot. I don't believe in such things, God, not even in Dickens. Radical subjectivity does not become objective just because others share the delusion. Psychiatric hospitals are full of people who might agree with one another that there is a unicorn in the garden.

But even the most inconsequential scholarly problems can achieve a life of their own, I reminded myself, commanding the same attention as a broken tooth jagged against your tongue: hylozoism, for instance; John Wilkins. I sat there awhile, staring at the plastic bag of books.

But just in case, I bought a pie to take home, to try again to lose altogether this dull ache. That night I fixed dinner, played Monopoly, and organized an after-dinner walk. Warren was tired too: his turn to rest.

5

Across the Waters

WHETHER OR NOT MY EXPERIENCE OF GOD WAS GENUINE, FIRST GRADE conclusively demonstrated the unreality—or sheer irrationality—of any unconscious hope for an end to the conflict between my needs and their needs. Any illusions I might have had about "when they are all in school" were in fact not fact but yet another version of my Someday Dream. I suspect that my life has always been shaped by Someday Dreams, by hopes that life will be a rose garden at some future date—or at least that the roses I already have will have no thorns and no little black spots on their leaves. After I get into college. After I get into graduate school. After I get past prelims. After I get a job. After the book is published. After the baby is born. After the baby is sleeping through the night. After the baby is out of diapers. After whatever seems to constitute the next milestone in life. Someday, someday, someday. Someday life will be easier than life is right now.

But emotionally and morally, the kids' needs were undiminished. Their needs were perhaps even greater: spelling lists, playground bullies, a substitute gym teacher ignorant of asthma who berated them viciously for slowing to a walk when the group was supposed to run laps around the gym. Kids who teased them for eating carrots every day in their lunches, textbooks that were trite or boring or that made mistakes in the naming or drawing of dinosaurs. As all of us remember (although of course we are still trying to forget, all these decades later), life at school can be very hard for kids who are too bright and too perceptive—much less kids whose hearing is iffy and whose airways are unreliable. Schools in the fifties had problems, of course; but everyone knows that schools today have even greater problems. And kids face those problems day after day, relentlessly, with only the emotional resources that a kid has developed.

And, of course, Mommy and Daddy and whatever time-consuming resources we can provide. Bonnie had warned me, of course. When I think about my life, someone has always warned me about my illusions; but I have never wanted to heed the warning. The youngest of Bonnie's four, a daughter, is five years older than Mark. We had dinner together in the spring of the year when that little girl was in first grade and the older three arrayed themselves upward into high school.

"She's gone. And it's great," Bonnie assured me. "But I have got to hit the deck running when they all get in at three. I've got to be there and I've got to have nothing else going on—it's like having a house full of babies again. Except I'm not mopping up spilled milk. Wiping crayons off the wall. I'm helping with algebra and book reports and listening to them talk and talk and talk. By ten, I have *had* it."

I really did not want to hear this. I tried to forget I had heard it. But I remembered that Laura had said exactly the same thing. Her twins are the same age as ours, but when the twins were all two her older kids were ten, twelve, and fifteen. Two-year-olds and teenagers were all too much alike, she sighed.

"It's little babies all day and big babies all night!" she had lamented. "I want to buy them all buttons that say 'I Am Who I Am'—maybe then they'll stop trying to establish their independent identities all over my soul. I don't have the psychic energy to fund all this self-discovery!"

I was at her house that day, drinking tea and watching five toddlers trash her family room, when the three bigger kids burst in the door at three. Laura swung into action with the energy of a linebacker and the delicacy of a glassblower, dispensing brownies, consoling fragile adolescent egos, advising on quadratic equations, drilling on spelling lists, finding soccer shin guards and orthodontic rubber bands, and listening attentively to three chaotic, disjointed accounts of the day offered by three kids, all of whom talked around both braces and brownies in their mouths. I was awed. I had long been amazed by her big kitchen calendar, in which each kid's activities were written in a different color; but seeing a triplet of "big kids" in action was far more sobering than that calendar—terrifying as it was. I tidied the family room, gave Laura a great hug, and fled.

But now I could see for myself the realities that Bonnie and Laura had described. I too realized that all errands and housework and whatever I hoped to do of my writing had to be jammed into the interval between 8:30 A.M. and 3 P.M., because the hours between three and ten were unrelentingly busy. Furthermore, when I signed up for parenthood I did not imagine revisiting the multiplication tables. As a kid myself, I had been baffled by multiplication. As far as I could tell, the law of commutation was black magic, some secret medieval depravity that had found its way into Catholic grade schools: how could 3×7 possibly be the same as 7×3? It had to be a lie. It was inexplicable, impossible, self-evidently incoherent.

In these more enlightened times, I suppose, a kid like me would have found a place in some learning-disabled program. Instead, Mom bought me a pencil box with a slide rule–like slider and numbers printed all over the cover. I could slide the slider and find the answer to any multiplication problem up to 9×9. I was late in fifth grade before relentless repetition began to teach me the answers despite myself. Furthermore, the other kids were teasing me. I did finally learn to multiply—up to 9×9. The elevens are easy, and the twelves I managed by adding.

Mostly I spent math class making up narratives about the adventures of the characters I had created to personify every number. For instance, 2 was shy; 3 was a bit dishonest; 4 was kind but dumb; 5 was adventurous; 6 was always eating and doing anything to be comfortable physically. 25, then, was shy but adventurous. Math was much more interesting this way. I actually had a great set of problems to solve: I had to write a story in my head the resolution of which involved the personality of the answer.

I kept getting little check marks on my report card on the line, "Fails to complete work on time," and sometimes also "Fails to begin work promptly," because I would spend several minutes at first thinking up an adventure to which each problem in that day's set would be related. But my work was correct enough. Doing the narratives required for making corrections involved finding some polite and dramatically effective way to get the wrong answer "off stage." That was hard. I hated doing corrections. So I was very careful. And as any parent of a learning-disabled child will tell you, I was not essentially dumb. My brain was simply miswired for math. I had to turn numbers into people before I could work with them, computation into narrative.

My method succeeded until I hit trigonometry—that was when I finally gave up on the rather daft idea that I would be a scientist. Algebra and geometry had been difficult but fun: equations were such complex plots! Parentheses offered all the dramatic potential of subplots: I added them to every problem with Dickensian abandon. Cartesian graphs introduced parallel stories, like *A Tale of Two Cities* or *Wuthering Heights* or even the multiple universes of Dante and Milton. Figuring all this out was tough, but I had wonderful English teachers leading me through a classical curriculum and I worked very hard. The math nuns were, on the whole, pretty tolerant of what were probably odd questions from me at times. Even in college, my first thought about calculating the area under a curved line on a Cartesian graph was how I could turn all the little rectangles with their little top-piece triangles into a castle. Fortunately for me, this was a history course: I didn't have to *do* calculus.

But as a junior in high school I simply could not fathom what sort of stories trigonometry was really about. I had baffled the nun with my questions. She got me a tutor, but I reduced the tutor to tears at our first meeting. I didn't tell anyone about stories, of course. I'm one of the middle children in a big family: I know when to keep quiet. I just didn't understand anything about trigonometry, not anything at all, because somehow I had never learned the first thing about mathematics.

None of that prepared me very well to console and to help Mark when he was baffled by the demand to memorize anything and bewildered by multiplication. He was, I feared, as immune to mathematics as I had been. In despair, I began to tell him some of the stories I had concocted for myself around particularly problematic equations, like 9 × 3. All three kids were charmed; Warren came out to investigate our laughter. He was dismayed at this poetic approach to multiplication and eager to halt any further transformation of mathematics into narrative: he took over with teaching multiplication tables.

Listening to him, I finally began to understand. We sat with twenty-four teaspoons on the kitchen table, sorting them into groups of threes or fours or sixes or eights. Carol—so passionately the daughter of her father—was delighted, leaping intuitively ahead of his explanations, laughing and gleeful and looking at me reproachfully. I ignored her accusing looks: I was actually beginning to understand multiplication. Commutation is a metaphor!

I kept sorting spoons over and over and over and looking at what I had done. The little kids had left the table but Mark sat there, watching me.

Mark was amazed too. Not at spoons but at me.

"Your Mom is a poet," Warren cautioned him. "Remember that."

In some corner of my soul I remain convinced that what really got Mark over the hump with multiplication tables was my musical metrical arrangements of the results of counting by twos or by threes or by eights. We'd sing together as he set the table and I made salad. After going through that three times over, let me tell you, I can multiply with speed and accuracy. Sister Esmeralda should see me now.

I still don't believe any of it, but that's okay. The kids all go to their father for help. I do the household income taxes, after all: it's not so bad once you figure out the stories. The annual IRS changes feel something like the letters one gets with Christmas cards: guess what the home office deduction did this year! And IRAs learned how . . .

Computational Errors

And "God," whatever I meant by "God," made me feel as multiplication tables had. Something here failed to compute, something was written in the wrong language or demanded a brain differently configured than mine seems to be. The voice as such didn't bother me much: words show up unbidden in my mind all the time. They always have. Words come out of no-where, from some dark silence beyond the reaches of ordinary consciousness. Poems always begin with a line or two arrived from no-where I can trace.

And not only a line or two of poetry. Writing anything, working with anyone on a piece of his or her writing, listening to somebody talk, I can feel the pressure of something that needs formulation, lean back against the shadowy wall of that dark silence, and listen for words that will always come. It's just how I am, how my mind works, how I experience or explain the sensation of my own thinking. Maybe other people experience their own thinking as something they actually *do,* as something they are in charge of somehow. But I never have. It just happens to me, and I listen. Maybe that's why I'm so good with kids: I have no illusion of being in control of anything, not even the insides of my own head.

I am, in short, an excellent example of Oscar Wilde's claim: "Things are because we see them, and what we see, and how we see it, depends upon the arts that have influenced us." Meaning itself—coherence, grace, relationship—is one of the most beautiful things of all. And so my urge to understand is primarily an aesthetic act, an aesthetic need, which is why I turned to literature not philosophy, to gardening not botany. After so many years, my psychic realm is thickly populated by poetry and—like Big Bird trapped in the Metropolitan Museum overnight—I have long ago made friends with texts that are not books on shelves but voices in my soul, voices that powerfully influence my experience of life.

But life inside such a consciousness has demonstrated over and over again that what poets "make," the "lies" poets tell, are in fact the greatest truths and the deepest wisdom I have ever encountered. "There may have been fogs for centuries in London," Wilde observes. "I dare say there were. But no one saw them . . . till art had invented them. Now, it must be admitted, fogs are carried to excess. They have become the mere mannerism of a clique, and the exaggerated realism of their method gives dull people bronchitis." And thus it seemed unlikely that the voice was just subcultural bronchitis, the delayed consequence of a Catholic childhood. I'm not dull and literal-minded, but I am haunted, inhabited as it were by voices of all kinds, voices I welcome and trust. It seemed modestly reasonable that my own spiritual hopes and values might "find voice" in this way.

Nonetheless, I was deeply disconcerted by what this particular voice was "saying," the demands it seemed to be making, the perspectives it was asserting upon my experience. "What is Hecuba to him, or he to Hecuba, that he should weep for her?" Hamlet asks, marveling at the actor's tears. What are these words to me, or my experience to myself, that I should feel so deeply shaken and in fact moved at times to tears? Why did it seem so inadequate—so dishonest, finally—to accept that my sense of a "person" was nothing more than my talking to myself from within the animated resources of the books that had come to populate my soul? All I wanted was to believe that some deep, unruly, creative core identity was fighting—again, again, again—to take control, to wreak some further havoc in my ongoing attempt to lead a reasonable, literal-minded, ordinary life. Why was that familiar conviction so impossible to sustain?

But this voice differed from all the other voices in my head: its aura of the numinous was unmistakable. Words, when there was something that seemed to feel or to show up as words, were merely a cloak, an outer shell, a mere appearance of something else that felt something like a light that was overwhelmingly bright but not for that reason painful physically. Or it was a deep, all-absorbing silence that was nonetheless audible in some interior, nonphysical way. That was, I realized, something like what poetry felt like to me at first, in high school. But this experience was much larger and also utterly without the upwelling pain I had felt then. It was serene. Gracious. Almost reassuring. It felt like an incredible inexplicable demand, but without content and without the least shadow of consequent threat. It seemed almost to be waiting for me when I stopped, as I stopped with increasing regularity, to stare blindly into space.

In short, the whole thing unnerved me severely. And it kept intruding its wry little remarks and sharply pointed observations upon my mundane journal keeping or even the random conversations I had with myself (and whatever array of poets) as I did something mindless like weeding or laundry. As months trailed eerily after months, I reluctantly admitted to myself how utterly consonant these experiences were with the Western mystical tradition as I had skimmed across it doing background for Blake. Or even James, *The Varieties of Religious Experience*. But who, reading such old books, could believe that such experiences might be real? Not delusion, not endorphins, not merely metaphoric expression: real. Not me, at any rate.

But now I felt myself beginning to believe, beginning to abandon the skeptical poise, the noncommittal, intellectual, theoretical distance. I began to feel something deeply compelling about "God" as a name for all this, about "God" as a "person," as a separate, sacred, transcendent, sustaining creator who feels an immediate and deeply personal connection to me and to all the rest of creation as well—to strawberry frogs and autumn clematis and distant nebulae.

One of the Jewish names for this connection is *hesed* or *chesed*, often translated "loving-kindness." *Chesed* is manifest within the great Jewish narratives not as sentimental or romantic love but rather as unflagging fidelity and a deep yet challenging sustenance despite all the suffering consequent upon the vicissitudes of history. I had always admired the vivid character of "God" in these Jewish stories and the densely literary ways in which the book argued with itself in its own many voices about who this God is and what this God is up to in our lives. And now it seemed I was discovering that God is real? Oh no, I found myself saying to myself. Oh, no.

Historical and bureaucratic Christendom seemed no less wildly diverse than it had seemed before, no less commonly either depraved or trivial in its betrayal of or heresy from Jewish thought in the direction of Hellenism and, later, feudalism and, later still, liberal bourgeois capitalism. But some Christian thinkers recognize that Christians are Jews by adoption, albeit patricidal ones. And Christianity as a system of thought or as a Jewish sect "to the nations" now seemed—at least in Pete's and Elaine's sermons—to offer a challenging, comforting, and above all highly nuanced vision of the human condition.

What scared me was not the fact that my own creativity might have such psychological depths that its workings could feel autonomous, like "revelation" or "inspiration." That's standard stuff. I had tamed that terror at some unremembered point—in part just by time and through experience, and in goodly measure through my academic studies in the nature or operation of imagination. With enough concentration, I had always been able to deconstruct my perception of "inspiration"—after it was gone. But those familiar strategies no longer worked. The fact that the voice had my own sense of humor, my own analytical habits, and even my own problems with spelling failed to prove anything at all. The contents of my consciousness were merely, for this voice, something like a collection of the available means of persuasion. Its radical transcendent otherness was not deconstructed by its incarnation within whatever substance my life and reading provided.

The irreducible core of my distress came down to this: the voice seemed to know and to care about me, about me personally, about my own fears and painful memories and quirky associations to things. Pantheism—the locating of the sacred in and as the complex interrelatedness of reality itself—ultimately denies the reality of the individual. Individuality is an illusion, albeit a powerfully persuasive one. We are not separate realities, but part of a cosmic system far too vast for us to grasp in any emotionally real way. Emotionally, all that is real for us is our separate here-and-now progress through linear time-and-place. So we feel that we are real separable entities, but that's just a feeling, an "existence" as illusory as the "absence" of your foot if you sit too long upon your ankles. Nor are time and space linear in the ways perceived by common sense.

Unfortunately, I just couldn't shake this feeling that the "voice" was my own quirky poetic way of experiencing contact with a cosmic reality for whom my individual reality was not illusion. Furthermore, this reality was not acting properly "remote, serene and indifferent," as Shelley puts it. No. It seemed personal and immediate and deeply caring. It was acting like God, in short, as God has always been described by those ancient Hebrew poets and various of their heirs, Christian or Jewish. And in the presence of that reality, my deconstructions and sophistry shriveled into silliness, into something that felt like nothing more than a naive or youthful defense against the reality of passionate sexual response.

Struggling with these currents in my own mind, day after day, I was haunted by two passages from my beloved *Biographia Literaria,* passages I had struggled for months to integrate into my understanding of Coleridge's argument. "In all ages," Coleridge explains, "there have been a few, who measuring and sounding the rivers of the vale at the feet of their furthest inaccessible falls have learnt, that the sources must be far higher and far inward; a few, who even in the level streams have detected elements, which neither the vale itself nor the surrounding mountains could supply." Coleridge takes "the stream of consciousness" as a deliberate metaphor and then uses the metaphor to explain that a personal, loving, creative God constitutes an inexplicable "trace element" in those waters, a trace element that cannot be attributed to the inaccessible mountains of the unconscious but rather comes from some mysterious point "far higher and far inward." That seemed to account for what was happening to me.

But I could not quite find courage enough to grapple with the implications of Coleridge's other thunderous line: "The arguments that at all apply to [the existence of such a God] are in its favor; and there is nothing against it, but its own sublimity. It could not be intellectually more evident without becoming morally less effective; without counteracting its own end by sacrificing the *life* of faith to the cold mechanism of a worthless because compulsory assent." Something in me wilted or faded to black at that claim: God "could not be intellectually more evident without becoming morally less effective."

Part of the problem, I hoped, was that the God who was haunting me bore no resemblance to the God I had learned about growing up. The God of my childhood scored quite well on the Remote Serene Indifferent scale. He was like Mayor Daley but without press conferences and the St. Patrick's Day Parade. God operated through saints and clergy as if through aldermen and precinct captains. God, like the Mayor, really cared only that the system worked, that the schools opened on time, that the streets were plowed and swept and patched. Ordinary folk were to do their jobs, vote early and often, and not ask questions. We were expected to behave; in turn, we could expect both that city buses would run on time and that angels would welcome us at the Pearly Gates.

And if not? If we did not behave? "Sinners in the Hands of an Angry God" might in fact have been written by any of the nuns who ran my grade school. It's a reasonable tactic, I suppose, when there are fifty or sixty kids in each classroom. My oldest brother's first grade class—or so the story goes—had ninety kids. Ninety kids, one nun, and the prospect of eternal damnation.

Years later, the retreat sermon in *Portrait of the Artist as a Young Man* left me breathless with helplessly inappropriate laughter. We spent all of every Friday afternoon during Lent listening to sermons like that, praying the liturgy of the Stations of the Cross, and for each station singing the same long Latin hymns in Gregorian chant. One does not forget: great music and manipulative melodrama were an overwhelming combination for a child like me. If this is what God had done to his own kid, obviously there was not much hope for the rest of us—unless we were very very careful. I always knelt up straight and I never talked in church, never, not once. I even studied my spelling lists—not that studying helped much. My spelling was commonly taken as a sign of my incipient damnation.

I had never imagined being loved like this. Such love was beyond even my wildest fabrication. Maybe that meant it was severely primitive psychological projection? Warren had studied a fair bit of psychodynamic psychology at one point, and I stood one day before his shelves and shelves of primary sources, wondering where to start, where I could find the words I needed to explain away this feeling of being deeply known and intimately loved and inexplicably called to something that remained, for now, entirely unimaginable. But I couldn't figure out where to start reading. That had never stopped me on other projects: if you can't decide, grab anything reasonably central, read it, read all its footnotes, and then read every book to which it refers and all of their footnotes. Pick the three best of these books, and read all their references as well. It would take a few months of book-a-day reading, but I had done it before.

Not that I could go at a book-a-day pace around three kids. Not anymore I couldn't. But mostly, I couldn't imagine explaining away that feeling of being loved without knowing I was lying to myself. No theory has explanatory power equal to the mysterious depths of such love. I can be obtuse at times, and I can be very stubborn. But I'm a terrible liar, especially to myself.

Instead of picking out a book to begin with, I found myself lost in the memory of a dream. Or something like a dream. I don't think I was asleep. During that first fall, the fall of the rainbow and the promise, I had trouble getting to sleep one night.

I was feeling anxious. Just vaguely anxious. We had met with an architect to talk about remodeling the upstairs into something brighter and more useful as study spaces for Warren and me. The costs and the decisions and the responsibility were weighing heavily. So as a relaxation technique I decided to imagine myself floating. It occurred to me how fetal that choice was, yet somehow that recognition didn't bother me.

Neither did the technique work. So I tried imagining myself surrounded by the absolute, unconditional love I have for the kids. I thought about it in those terms. I would never love them more or less, after all, based on how nifty a job they did remodeling their houses, or how much of a mortgage they decided to carry. My love for them is not based on any kind of judgment one way or another. It just is.

And something happened. A sense of overwhelming love, unforced, unqualified, not wanting or needing me to be anything other than I am in my depths or to do anything more than what I most deeply yearn to do but dare not.

And I was certain that this was not a mirror, that this was not my projection shining back into my eyes. No. I was not looking at my love for the kids reflected back at me. I was feeling something for which or of which my love is the reflection, a frail and partial and imperfect human reflection. It was the difference between a teddy bear and a full-grown grizzly emerging from the trees. This love was like a grizzly emerging from the trees. *Chesed*, untainted by the egotism and sentiment that are inevitably part of any human love.

And I also felt it as a breaking through, as something I had been rubbing up against for a long time finally thinning out. As a cervix thins out, perhaps. Because I was most emphatically floating. But the experience set off a violent anxiety attack, like a truck careening out of control and smashing into my little grey Nissan. So I knew I couldn't do this, couldn't dare this, that it was forbidden for me to feel loved as I do struggle to love, forbidden even to think about being loved in that way—much less to imagine such love as a cosmic reality hovering over me.

"Whoops," I thought. "Excuse me." And I ended the floating, and I felt as if I were backing out and closing whatever doorway I had opened by mistake. Sorry. Wrong room. I don't belong here.

And the anxiety instantly resolved, and I went promptly to sleep. That dream, or whatever it was, really bothered me at the time. And that was even before the rainbow and its claims!

What in heaven's name was going on in my head? I thought seriously again about going to a psychoanalyst. But I wasn't exactly afraid, and I wasn't exactly unhappy, and I was certainly not depressed. No. I was in fine spirits and day-to-day life was really going along with no more than the usual chaos. I have questions and issues, sure—who doesn't?—but on the whole I felt pretty sane. And what would I say to a shrink? I think that Somebody up there loves me and I'm sure that's delusion? If it's delusion, after all, then millennia of faithful Christians and Jews have been deluded. Their fidelity—however inconsistent in various places and at various times—offers clear cultural grounds for crediting my experience.

And what was "God" pushing me to do, after all, but to recognize what I was really feeling and to take those feelings seriously, to believe them and trust them and act upon them. "Merely." And if I can't do that, I snarled at myself, then I *do* need a shrink!

But mostly, I admitted wryly, mostly I was feeling curious. Just *curious*. I was willing to play along because I was *curious*. I sat in the kitchen, drinking tea and marveling, amused, at the familiar sparkle of my own relentless curiosity. Well okay then, I decided. I'll do it.

[Do what?] came that voice, wry and quizzical and demanding.

And it was as if Coleridge himself answered for me: the "willing suspension of disbelief for the moment, which constitutes poetic faith." Yeah, right, I thought, thank you very much. Whether or not I believed in God, I was at least willing—for a while anyhow—to suspend my disbelief.

The Wisdom of Solomon

So I bought myself a copy of the *Book of Common Prayer*. It did not come with colored ribbons, as my soft-leather-bound St. Andrew's Missal had, my old missal with its facing pages in Latin and in English. Tongue in cheek, I complained to Elaine. She quite matter-of-factly explained that I could lace eighth-inch ribbon into a strip of plastic needlepoint netting, which would then slide under the outer binding of the spine. And she fished a spare piece of netting from deep within a desk drawer—left over from a church school project some years back. When I stared dumbfounded she began, patiently, to repeat her explanation of how to lace the ribbons through the mesh.

I got quick control of my face and headed out obediently to buy a set of thin ribbons, ribbons in rich satiny liturgical colors, of course, with all the freighted symbolism I barely remembered. Purple for repentance and green, green for what? For hope, for "ordinary time." What lovely ancient wisdom, the formal celebration of the ordinary day. White for eternal life, white that replaced purple for funerals; and flaming silken red, red for grace, red like the flame of the Spirit descending upon the faithful; rose, rose for forgiveness, like the one rose candle among the purple ones on an Advent wreath. Ribbons new and stiff and unfaded, telling tales thousands of years old, the unabashed mythopoesy of the medieval church preserved now more often in polyester than in silk. Nonetheless: I knew a real prayer book needed ribbons!

Nostalgic silliness, I told myself—but I saw nothing particularly hazardous in my own delight in gorgeous colors, beautiful old traditions, and the buying of books. If I were to play along with these strange new currents in my own creative mind, why not play along in style? So I spent a dollar or two on ribbon and carefully followed Elaine's directions.

I pulled out St. Andrew to see where I had once placed the ribbons. Red to the Scripture readings for Sundays, I discovered; white to the litany of the saints—the nuns had us saying that, I swear, every time they needed a few minutes to themselves to think. Blue (for the Virgin, of course) to the Mass. *Introibo ad altare Dei, ad*

Deum qui laetificat juventutem meam: I will go unto the altar of God, to God who gladdens my youth. Purple to the Mass for the Dead. Green, faded now to white beyond the edges of the page, marked the readings assigned for daily Mass. The ribbon was still placed at my birthday, February 8: the Feast of St. John of Matha.

I reread the headnote: he was "the founder of the Trinitarian Order for the ransoming of captives," it explained. "He devoted his whole life and priestly activity to the relief and ransoming of the Christian prisoners of the infidels." The Collect prayer repeated this theme: ". . . that by the suffrage of his merits, we may be delivered by your grace from captivity of soul and body." Oh yeah, John of Matha. I remembered. "Deliver us by your grace from captivity in fifth grade: Amen."

I had discreetly entertained myself through various Latin liturgies by reading around in these headnotes and prayers and Scripture selections devoted to various saints. Some were obviously famous—St. James the Apostle, St. Vincent de Paul (patron saint of rummage sales and basketball, I assumed). But there were also obscure folks, great discoveries for a kid like me who turned arithmetic into storytelling: St. Isidore the Farm Laborer, for instance, was marked with a holy card commemorating the death of my father's mother, an absolute curmudgeon and unquestioned matriarch with thick black eyebrows and a passion for card games. Each grandchild had to sing a song or speak a piece and answer some questions to get a Christmas present from her. The recital seemed to take all afternoon. I set the holy card aside and read that St. Isidore "became famous through various marvelous happenings which accompanied his work in the fields." What do you suppose had happened? I had loved this book—it was the only book I owned, after all, until I was seventeen and convinced my mother that all I wanted for Christmas was a copy of Benet's epic poem, *John Brown's Body*. I hotly resented my missal being replaced by ugly little pamphlets printing the new English liturgy in narrow columns on dusty newsprint that barely survived a month in the pews. The stupid pamphlets offered no place to wander.

I wondered what the *Book of Common Prayer* offered to such wanderers. The usual array of special liturgies was beautifully written and theologically nuanced but not much fun for a bored kid. I turned optimistically to sections headed "Collects for Various Occasions" and "Prayers and Thanksgivings." These offered two or three pithy sentences on dozens of topics to rescue inarticulate clergy asked to lead a prayer for rain or the cessation of rain, for a person recovering from drug abuse, for parents adopting a child or each other's children, or for the proper use of leisure.

None of them held a candle to St. Isidore the Farm Laborer, I decided, although surely there were glorious resources here. Could I, with my more mature and adept imagination, concoct a scene wherein a spouse jealous of televised sports would dare to ask a hapless curate to offer prayer for the proper use of leisure? Or maybe someone on the parish hospitality committee would ask for public prayers for the recovery of those who want whole bean dark-roast coffee instead of cheap decaf at coffee hour? No doubt I could. But I felt a certain sympathy for bored Episcopalian fifth-graders. No wonder the English are such masters at the comedy of manners.

I hunted in vain for the saints who speckle a church calendar with red-letter days, not knowing that the Anglicans print them in a whole separate volume, *Minor Feasts and Fasts.* Someday I would find the saint assigned by the Anglicans for my birthday, I decided, to see who might rival St. John of Matha and his ransoming captives from the infidels. Nothing, I knew, would substitute for him in the scarred recesses of my psyche.

Nor did I find reprinted the Scripture selections assigned for each Sunday—only a schedule. Protestants are presumed to own a Bible, I suppose. At some point after Vatican II, my mother dutifully joined one of the new Bible study groups, resentfully pointing out that my grandmother never owned a Bible and never felt the lack of it, that for the saintly Kate Murphy religion did not mean Bible-thumping. I was never sure what that "Bible-thumping" meant, actually; but I knew better than to ask what might seem like a challenging question in such circumstances. One way or another, I grew up without a Bible in the house: what we had, each of us, were these small leather-bound missals that we carried dutifully to and from the church. My father's zipped closed: I thought that was really neat.

In trying to find a home for the last of my gleaming ribbons, I came upon "The Daily Office Lectionary": Bible excerpts for the day, Elaine explained, not for daily Mass for but a version of the ancient monastic tradition of praying at regular intervals throughout the day. Or—more commonly—for that classic Protestant practice, daily Bible study. My last ribbon found a home: daily Bible study. I felt daringly Protestant.

Entertained by a new book, I began to spend ten minutes each day reading the assigned paragraphs of Scripture. They were ridiculously tiny excerpts. The Gospel selections were so familiar as to be entirely unreadable; the adventures of the disciples as recounted in Acts and in the Epistles still felt like ancient versions of adventures broadcast on the radio when I was very little—except when they read like German philosophy in bad translations. The Old Testament cuts were unintelligible snippets about the adventures of minor kings and obscure prophets with gloriously unpronounceable names. I kept hearing Byron's outrageous anapests:

The Assyrian came down like the wolf on the fold,
And his cohorts were gleaming in purple and gold

The daily pair of psalms, however, were spectacular fun. I kept hearing them echoing backwards, from allusions in English poems I knew better than these originals. Despite the psalms, however, I began to sympathize with Kate Murphy, who never had a Bible and never felt the need of one. She was a woman to quote Keats or Shelley, after all, not Chronicles or Kings or the Gospel of Luke.

I began to feel faintly annoyed with myself or maybe just faintly embarrassed. If I were going to read the Bible, dammit, then I should read the Bible in some respectable fashion, cover to cover or at least whole books at a time, not in stupid little pericopes. The Bible is undeniably the single most influential set of texts in all of Western literature: no need to feel apologetic rereading a masterpiece one knows primarily through fragments sorted out under a year of Sundays and the occasionally improbable saints in the St. Andrew missal. All I had ever read consecutively were the Gospel of John, because Coleridge loved it so, and the selections used in the Great Books course: the first five books of Hebrew Scripture and the Gospel of Luke—which I found strained and quite unconvincing after the grandeur of the Pentateuch. If the Daily Office snippets were stupid, the problem was snippeting, not the book itself. Who could make sense of Milton or Shakespeare, after all, read in sound bites?

I should quit, I decided. But I didn't. One day the Daily Lectionary sent me into the Apocrypha, into books of the Bible whose propriety as scripture is contested by the various canon formation traditions, both Jewish and Christian, that have shaped this Bible over centuries of argument. Here was stuff I'd never heard before. Even the Oxford University Press held these apocryphal books off from the rest of the Bible by beginning anew to number pages—a quaintly medieval bit of numerology, I thought.

And there, in chapter six of The Wisdom of Solomon, this is what I read:

> *Wisdom is radiant and unfading,*
> *and she is easily discerned by those who love her*
> *and is found by those who seek her.*
> *She hastens to make herself known*
> *to those who desire her.*
> *He who rises early to seek her will have no difficulty*
> *for he will find her sitting at his gates.*
> *To fix one's thought on her is perfect understanding*
> *and he who is vigilant on her account*
> *will soon be free from care*
> *because she goes about seeking those worthy of her,*
> *and she graciously appeals to them in their paths,*
> *and meets them in every thought.*
> *The beginning of wisdom*
> *is the most sincere desire for instruction,*
> *and concern for instruction is love of her,*
> *and love of her is the keeping of her laws,*
> *and giving heed to her laws*
> *is assurance of immortality,*
> *and immortality brings one near to God;*
> *so the desire for wisdom leads to a kingdom.*

The page shimmered slightly under my hands. She goes about seeking . . . graciously appealing to them in their paths and meeting them in every thought. Oh. Oh no. Her? This feels like a better-bred version of that elusive dream-image animal, that dog, as if tamed and gentled and not quite so quick with her teeth.

Unless. Unless I'm the one who has been tamed? There's nothing very gracious sounding about anything that meets you in *every* thought. That's the wicked persistence that had recast Sparky's nudging and Prince's delighted leaps into the aggression of a hunting dog when I struggled to find a containing image for this experience battling my own mind . . . and usually losing: giving in, giving up, reading or writing what had to be written or read or even said despite my own calculations of prudence and my own desires.

If the University of Toronto Press had issued amulets with the figure of Northrop Frye, I would have stopped and pinned one to my blouse. No, no, no, I lectured myself. Obviously this is just mythopoetic archetypal symbolism. Don't fall for it. Creativity feels like creativity, and it's all just brain waves and aesthetic exposure at impressionable stages of development. So what: the Wisdom poet, whoever he was, experienced his own creative energies as ineluctable and to some real extent outside his own conscious control. Of course. Go reread "Creative Writers and Daydreaming" and stop this silliness.

But I didn't have a Northrop Frye amulet and I didn't feel much like rereading Freud. I kept reading the Bible, into chapter seven of The Wisdom of Solomon.

> *For in her there is a spirit that is*
> *intelligent, holy,*
> *unique, manifold, subtle,*
> *mobile, clear, unpolluted,*
> *distinct, invulnerable, loving the good, keen,*
> *irresistible, beneficent, humane,*
> *steadfast, sure, free from anxiety,*
> *and penetrating through all spirits*
> *that are intelligent and pure and most subtle.*
> *For wisdom is more mobile than any motion;*
> *and because of her pureness*
> *she pervades and penetrates all things.*

For she is a breath of the power of God,
and a pure emanation of the glory of the Almighty;
therefore nothing defiled gains entrance into her.
For she is a reflection of eternal light,
a spotless mirror of the working of God,
and an image of his goodness.
Though she is but one, she can do all things,
and while remaining in herself, she renews all things;
in every generation she passes into holy souls
and makes them friends of God, and prophets,
for God loves nothing so much
as the man who lives with wisdom.

Her. It had to be her, whoever she was or whatever she meant. I had never had words to describe her so completely. "You have a name!" I heard myself saying aloud. At that, I closed the text: eighteen chapters of such poetry? No thanks. I felt the need of some primitive gesture to ward off unspeakable threat. I stared instead at my hands, motionless and holding closed this blandly printed Oxford University Press edition.

I made some tea and sat staring out the window while the tea, untasted, grew cold. "A pure emanation of the glory of the Almighty?" A mirror of the working of God? This poet, whoever he was, thought that obnoxious animal was *God,* was the Wisdom of God incarnate within humanity? Sophia? She was Sophia? Sophia is all diaphanous Greek drapery. But that overgrown beast had pursued me through every recess of classical Western epistemology, until I had had to admit that something like "God" was a necessary postulate of any morally adequate epistemology. That pursuit had been undelicate and ungracious. I had been deeply annoyed to discover that I had to go read all of Coleridge's theology and take it *seriously* if I was going to understand Coleridge's literary theory.

But why, then, did I feel across the decades the pressure of Sparky's yellow teeth against my wrist, how she would, with a baleful stare, stop nudging and take my entire wrist crosswise into her mouth, locking her fangs and—although never really biting down—refusing to let go until I got up and went out with her? Like Wordsworth pestering Coleridge:

Up! up! my friend, and clear your looks,
Why all this toil and trouble?
Up! up! my friend, and quit your books,
Or surely you'll grow double. . . .
One impulse from a vernal wood
May teach you more of man;
Or moral evil and of good,
Than all the sages can.

Skinny wrists. That obnoxious dog and these stupid skinny wrists. But Wordsworth and Sparky both had a point. I set the Bible aside and went out to garden. Both minds and yards grow weedy, I told myself.

I weeded every free moment for several days without thinking a single thought, filling tall brown bags with seedlings that did not belong in my garden, tugging and yanking and digging things out lest something unwanted set seed and take over the landscape I had planned for myself.

God? *This* poet thinks *that* experience is *God?* It's an apocryphal book of the Bible, I kept telling myself. Nobody believes this, not even those church folks. How heretical. No wonder even Oxford played superstitious—or politically correct—games with pagination.

I asked Elaine nonchalantly about the status of apocryphal books within Anglican canonical tradition.

"Oh sure," she said. "They're considered canonical. They're in the Daily Office Lections . . ." She paused, looking at me sharply. "Take a look sometime. The schedule is in your *Book of Common Prayer.* You might like The Wisdom of Solomon, especially six and seven."

"I will—sometime," I responded with professional blandness.

And something bit down hard on my wrist.

The Lady Behind the Desk, Again

At the next meeting of Elaine's spirituality group, she proposed that we begin to imagine the feminine aspects of God by remembering images of womanly power and authority and insight from our own experience.

The Lady Behind the Desk. God as, as . . . secretary to a dean? God, *the dean's secretary?* I had, I guess, spoken aloud. They were all looking at me, but I was looking at The Lady Behind the Desk, the vision I had so often replayed in all its physical vagueness and emotional clarity. She was there again, watching me with a silent amusement that I could feel rather than see.

I was in tears that I could not explain. I was overwhelmed and appalled, intuitively riveted and yet shaken to my core and unwilling to consider any of this seriously. Surely I was right; surely I was delusional. For all her palpable presence, the Lady and her setting were no more physically detailed than they had been those dozen or more years earlier. And as the Lady watched and then—like the Cheshire Cat—slowly faded away, I tried again to capture control of my shaking voice and to explain myself to the group.

The priest watched me with critical compassion. "It is a mistake," she observed dryly, "to take dreams too seriously." One of the other women, a graduate student at U-Chicago, repeated softly, "God, the *dean's* secretary? The dean's secretary?" She sat back, away from me, retreating into her corner of the couch.

I blew my nose on a piece of the coarse pink tissue found in every church parlor worldwide; I forced myself to steadiness by mapping the priest's discussion-leader options for rescuing this session. How does one continue after a participant starts seeing things? Do they teach that in seminary these days? Apparently not, I concluded: the lines around her eyes were starting to stiffen. Or maybe she was just watching me, waiting and watching with that sharp, critical intelligence I had so admired in her sermons.

Elaine's steady, evaluative gaze finally triggered the self-possession that had been eluding me. I fell back gratefully into the ancient arts of seminar survival, turning the dean's secretary into a comedy routine aimed at the graduate student. My strategy was easily seized by another woman, who had spent several years in the middle seventies doing comedy at Second City. At the mercy of a professional comedian, everyone was laughing before long. Except the priest. She was smiling, but her face had gone from evaluative to wary.

She was still watching me. I was careful not to meet her eyes.

When Ignorance Is Bliss

The only real problem here, I told myself, was that I could find no meaningful support at all for the claim that "the conflict is over." The more I lived with it, the more transparently foolish it seemed and the more self-evident the warnings offered me by Bonnie and by Laura. Yeah, school-age kids can get their own breakfast. They keep themselves reasonably occupied a lot of the time with such middle-size-kid tasks as learning to ride a two-wheel bike or to shoot a basketball or to master the latest computer game. But an ordinary week in an ordinary school leaves them needing help and support with quandaries far more difficult than reaching a yellow box of "gorilla" kept in an overhead cabinet. No one ever outgrows the need for cookies and milk and someone to trust who will listen and care. But children need more of that care, and more often, because they are still constructing for themselves the competence and the confidence that fund a mature and balanced adult autonomy. It was for me an enormous and exhausting achievement to offer that trustworthy attention, that reliable love, not in a therapist's tidy forty-five-minute segments and not in neatly, conveniently scheduled tidbits of quality time, but on demand. Their demand. Consequently, ten or twelve hours a week of freelance writing and editing was honestly all I could manage—fifteen or eighteen at most, and only if no one got sick. I needed more—more of something, anyhow—but they could not thrive with less.

While I was pondering all of this, Warren was elected to a term on the board of directors for one of the Byzantine economic entities at the medical school. For some obscure reason, the agendas and the minutes of board meetings arrived in the mail at home rather than at his office downtown. The tedious work of the board made doing laundry sound exciting, I admit. Certain debates about the governance of the parking facilities marked a low point: what an incredible combination of practical necessity, demonstrable long-range financial impact for the medical center patient base, and utter remoteness from anything about which Warren might genuinely care. He had never realized how complicated it is to manage the medical center's array of parking facilities; and frankly, he was not much interested in learning. But he did. Given a choice, however, he would rather have spent an afternoon weeding or washing clothes. He had also not been given his talents for this, he growled. It was like being stoned to death with popcorn.

But I found myself distinctly jealous that Warren's tedious scut work came first class mail, on good 25 percent rag bond and university letterhead. Once a year, he was invited to a black tie dinner at the Ritz. I could come along as "guest." But nobody shelled and steamed shrimp for me and for women like me. We did not gather once a year for a fancy dinner to celebrate our responsible execution of the tedious scut that forms the substructure of effective leadership and discerning management.

In fact, I found myself repeatedly, helplessly outraged when women like me were described either as wimpettes or as total bimbos. I fumed endlessly that all the self-help wailing about "the wounded inner child" did not translate into ordinary and appropriate respect for the work of women home with their kids, sacrificing all that we sacrificed, working as hard as we worked to attend wisely to the vulnerabilities of the rambunctiously literal child. An essay by Anna Quindlen left me poised uneasily between rage and contempt. In 1988, she wrote a "Life in the 30s" column headlined "Job and a Baby Cannot Still the Nesting Instinct," explaining that all her friends are feeling tempted to have a second baby, quit their jobs, and stay home.

She imagines a housewife's life as one of "lunches, upholsterer appointments, and shopping trips stretched to fill the empty hours"—a life she "ran from with furious little feet when I was growing up. It's something that barely exists now," she continues, "except among the very rich; it's something barely tolerated by men and by women, too. It's not that I would like it as a way of life. I'd just like a little fling at it every once in a while."

In 1988, I would have liked a little fling at it too. My life at home with an eight-year-old and two six-year-olds was distinctly lacking in long empty hours. Furthermore, every household I knew that had a mother home full time did so not from independent wealth but from a deeper, richer independence of spirit—and at considerable economic sacrifice. The only "emptiness" in such lives was in the bank accounts. "Voluntary simplicity," some call it. We called it "making do." And it was hard.

Quindlen sneers that "women who would like to spend just a little more time being homemakers" suffer from "the mistaken belief that this will make everyone happy and safe." But life does not come with guarantees that anyone's efforts will be successful. All anyone can do is try. To refuse to try unless your success is certain suggested to me either some appalling ignorance of logic or some equally astounding failure of maturity. To dismiss as "intolerable" those who dare to dare is to admit, finally, to cowardice in the face of real life.

Pediatricians, neurologists, and developmental psychologists can scream all they want to about the needs of children. Sociologists can fill libraries with studies detailing the impossible predicaments of parents struggling both to provide for their children materially and to care for them emotionally. Report after report can recount how poorly our children perform in school or how shaky their self-esteem, and how dramatically their well-being correlates with sustained parental attention and involvement. The really intolerable fact is that children need far more care, for more years, than we can easily afford to provide—whether as parents or as a society or as an economy. Real lives will be shaped by that fact: the only question is whose. Costly sacrifice cannot be avoided, because there is not, there will never be "world enough, and time."

I sat in my kitchen with Quindlen's column, with the work of a writer I had for so long genuinely admired, fuming and fighting to calm myself down, my anger at her soon surpassed by a helpless rage that I was still so stupidly defensive.

The Housewife and the Scholar

While all this was simmering in my soul—or maybe scorching—I went with Warren to rural Japan, to an international academic conference hosted by the university adjacent to a terrible dioxin accident. I spent the thirteen-hour flight memorizing a couple of dozen Japanese words and phrases—nothing more than the utilitarian stuff a tourist needs. Despite the presence of a university, foreigners were rare in the small city to which we were going. Except for the hotel staff, only high school kids seemed to speak any English at all. Even the street signs were printed only in *kanji*. But Japanese sounds a bit like French, and—unlike the French—the Japanese are tremendously gracious and patient with bad accents and fumbling constructions. Armed with my booklet and essentially on my own most of the time, I had a wonderful time just playing the tourist.

The night after Warren and his partner presented their research, a celebratory group of American epidemiologists went out to dinner to a lovely place that offered the Japanese equivalent of fondue—steaming pots of broth and heaping plates of little bits of things to cook. We got lost on the way, but I smiled at a street vendor and asked for directions. Asked in Japanese, of course, he responded in Japanese, which of course I did not really understand, except for a word here and there. But I matched what I did understand with his gestures, herded the group as directed, and there we were.

No one at the restaurant spoke English; the menu was printed in *kanji*. Warren gestured reassuringly to the anxious faces of his colleagues as I dug a 3×5 out of my purse. A Japanese neighbor had written, in *kanji*, the polite request to select for us a meal of moderate price. I knew how to order a variety of simple meals, but I was not about to tackle a fancy restaurant like this.

So I handed the waitress the card, bowed and apologized in Japanese, asked for her help, and then ordered a round of beer. Later I repeated to the group her instructions about cooking and her cautions about the peppery dipping sauces, once again not because I understood much of what she said, but because the situation itself was a fairly simple one. She was young and beautiful and beautifully dressed; her hands and her eyes were dramatically articulate. I ordered another round of beer. And then I got directions to the bathroom for someone.

I had a wonderful time with that waitress. Everyone else at the table was arguing about statistics, after all—yet another language I do not understand. Both the waitress and I, I suspect, had learned a lot about good-hearted communication from trying to survive life with toddlers.

As we were leaving, the tiny, very elderly maitresse d' asked me, in Japanese, where I had learned to speak Japanese. I answered, in English, that I did not speak Japanese. We stood a moment in the restaurant doorway, mutually bewildered, then bowed and apologized to each other. She repeated her question. Regretting my second beer, I took a deep breath and explained—this time in Japanese—that I did not speak Japanese. And then I felt even sillier. We bowed and apologized to each other a second time.

Suddenly I realized from her face that she understood me to be acknowledging that I was not fluent enough to claim to "speak Japanese." Utterly delighted with the warm approval twinkling in her heavy-lidded eyes, I bowed again, as a young woman and an honored guest to a grandmother presiding in her own house. She smiled and nodded very slightly, accepting my deference with deeply self-possessed maternal grace.

"Are you two done?" Warren asked, bemused and quizzical. "What's going on?" I could not begin to explain.

"Your husband," she said to me in Japanese, her enunciation slow and carefully distinct. "He waits. Go." We left.

As we walked back to the conference hotel, however, one of our dinner partners admitted himself very impressed with my performance that evening. Where had I learned to speak Japanese? I choked with the laughter I had stifled with the maitresse d'. Warren explained—although it didn't really explain anything—that I have a Ph.D. in English.

His colleague joined my laughter and shrugged knowingly. A scholar. Of course. He asked how many languages I had studied, then laughed again when I stopped in my tracks to count. Two beers, after all: I can't count and walk even stone cold sober. Not me.

But learning enough Japanese to fake it with a waitress is far less demanding than managing a successful all-day outing with preschoolers. Why did I feel so keenly the difference in prestige? Full-time mothering demands all the same incredible patience and foresight, the same willing attention to detail that scholarship demands, all the same personal flexibility and intellectual humility and sustained self-discipline. Once outside academia, I had discovered that many people are impressed with quite ordinary evidence—like this smattering of Japanese—of the commonplace scholarly skills. And yet so many people seemed so blind to the closely related but even greater challenges of parenting.

That blindness galled me. Unless, I thought, unless the real blindness here is mine? Unless the real failure here, the painful failure, is in my own pride and sense of worthy achievement? Maybe there's another new language here that I need to master—some phrasebook I need that will help me survive in this land beyond the *terra incognita* of postpartum. After all, plenty of people blithely dismiss academics as dithering fools who cannot cope with the real world. "Those who can, do; those who can't, teach." Yes? Everyone knows that accusation. But I had always ignored it. Ignored it easily, in fact.

And of course plenty of people would have rolled their eyes at my working so hard on seventeenth-century theoretical linguistics, and how those linguistics refracted through the theology of the Cambridge Neoplatonists to support the metaphors linking Coleridge's theology and his literary theory. I had never expected much support or general admiration for that sort of arcana, just as I had in turn never understood what accountants enjoyed about accounting, or what engineers enjoyed about ventilation systems. I had listened, astounded, to an engineer of some sort wax rhapsodic about the technical challenges of evenly heating or cooling very large buildings. We cannot, we do not arbitrarily force people into becoming engineers or accountants or academics, because we appreciate the need for such people to have the specific and creative gifts that the work demands. Real mothering, real nurturing, is exactly the same: not everyone has the deep inner resources demanded by life at home with kids, especially given how likely we are to be unnecessarily isolated socially. And nothing will do more damage to the creative tradition of genuine nurture than the stupid assumption that anyone can do this, just because she has ovaries.

That's it, I thought, that's it. That's the connection here. I can handle life at home because I can handle the isolation, I can handle the solitude, I can handle the lack of structure by turning it into a creative opportunity to generate and to explore my own structures. And not merely tolerate such things: there was much about such unstructured life that I knew I genuinely relished, at least once I had gotten the hang of it. Many of my graduate school classmates fell by the wayside, dropped out or just drifted away, at that massive transition between dutifully attending classes with neat schedules of assignments and the vast terrain of long dangerous months of long empty hours with nothing to do but what you had decided for yourself to do toward preparing for one or another set of major exams. They couldn't handle the lack of a handle on their days, the lack of structure and social contact and regular feedback.

Much less, of course, could most people manage that lack of structure when you added in the noisy incessant demands of utterly oblivious children, of children who suppose—as children so commonly do—that the grownups are doing nothing and have nothing to do, except maybe when the upholstery guy stops in. Well sure, I thought, no wonder all that Quindlen sees is that imaginary world of bonbons and soap operas. That's life at home as it appeared to her when she was a kid. And suddenly her attitude felt naive rather than pernicious, clueless not threatening. I don't suppose she'd much enjoy equally long empty hours in Special Collections, reading a moldy seventeenth-century linguist agonizing that none of us, no matter how carefully we write, can say what we mean, what we want to say, and nothing else.

Sea Changes

The winter of 1988–1989 huffed and puffed and finally drizzled its way into spring. The less satisfied I became with my freelance work, the more I thought about the dilemma of being "just a housewife." And the more I thought about being "just a housewife," the more I realized—grimly, you understand, grimly and reluctantly and angrily—the more I realized how little I had changed after all.

I was still struggling against the need to prove myself. Unless the world took note, my existence itself felt somewhat uncertain: I was still playing to an audience, still keeping an eye on some phantom scoreboard. Furthermore, maybe I wasn't running as fast, maybe I wasn't as late as often, but I still bore too much resemblance to the White Rabbit of *Alice in Wonderland*. Wherever I was, whatever I was doing, I was still too apt to be thinking about being somewhere else, doing something else.

"Life is a banquet," Auntie Mame insists, "and most poor sons-of-bitches are *starving* to death." Indeed I was: caught forever on the thin slice of time between future and past, all my present moments and present activities overshadowed by all that they were *not*. You cannot be who you are, where you are, fully alive to the fully real here-and-now, unless you can banish the powerful spectres of the potential. The sea cannot be the sea until it know the difference between sea and shore.

Maybe I understood intellectually all that I provided my own children, all that I might have for myself of energy to read and to think, to write and to garden. But most of the time, I realized, all that I felt was what I didn't have, what I was not achieving, what the world did not know and value about lives like mine.

Wait. I swatted that thought out of the stream of consciousness like a brown bear getting a salmon for dinner. That's the issue here. The problem here is how I feel, or more precisely how I *don't* feel. I'm not feeling that life is a banquet. I'm not feeling the pleasures and the satisfactions spread before me, the delight of raising homegrown kids, the delight of observing the evolution of consciousness not as an exercise in post-Kantian constructive ontology but as real souls unfolding before me, fragrant with mystery and grace, so often both wise and hilarious beyond my ability to depict. The delight of reading whatever came to hand even if only late at night, without the pressure of publishing to suit the dean; the chance to garden, to sit on park benches swapping stories, to bake my own bread while I supervised homework. "I Got Plenty o' Nuttin'," came the tune, right on cue. I spent the rest of the day singing that song, a favorite of my father's.

At about this point, kids came home wanting me to teach them to jump rope. What I remembered best was not how to jump rope but rather all the jump rope rhymes I had chanted as a girl, there in the alley between church and school, the paved alley that had served as the girls' playground, four hundred or so girls in their identical white shirts and navy blue pleated skirts, standing around or—if someone brought a rope—jumping rope to rhymes. I taught them my favorite:

Tinker, tinker, tinkerman
Sitting on a fence,
Trying to make a dollar
Out of fifteen cents.
He missed, he missed,
He missed like this.

Rhymes keep your balance, I insisted to the kids. Rhymes keep twirlers and jumpers together, especially in fancy games where two or three kids jump, where jumpers move in and out and in again. You can't just *jump*. That's unheard of. Carol was intrigued; the boys were appalled. The jump rope lesson didn't last long, but Carol and I fixed some lemonade and drank it together as I taught her several other rhymes and explained the elaborate variations possible when the rope is long and the jumpers work together. She took a jump rope to school for years thereafter, delightedly learning a polyglot mix of names for the basic games—as well as short chants in Chinese, in Russian, and in Korean.

I had never been much good at jumping rope. I had been great at twirling, however, and that's why I still knew all the words to all the chants. And by golly I could not get the tinkerman out of my mind. Like the tinker, I kept trying to make more hours out of twenty-four, more energy out of the same daily allotment. And failing.

So is family life a zero-sum game? Between kids and careers, a woman can go crazy. But no matter how adeptly managed the house, how few or many the kids, how elaborate or how truncated the career, we can still only do one thing at a time for only a limited number of hours. And unless we can make the cosmic twirlers stop twirling, faster and faster and faster with each passing year, women will jump until we drop dead with exhaustion. But what would it mean, I wondered, to put both feet down at once, stop leaping ropes and simply live, be where I was being, stand here and now in whatever present moment? Or at least, if leaping is a necessary part of life, to leap to a chant of my own devising and at my own pace, to be both the jumper and the twirler myself.

We went to a departmental reception that weekend for some subset of medical residents: smart and handsome folks in their late twenties, with ungrey hair and unlined faces. The usual set of middling and senior faculty, complete with husbands and wives—and all of these spouses, except me, were also medical people. Oh well.

"What's *your* specialty?" one of the bright young things asked me. I startled slightly: four young women stood in a semicircle, politely interested in my reply.

"Early nineteenth century," I replied, without thinking.

It was their turn to startle. They were certain they had misheard. I explained again: British Romantic literary theory. Their faces brightened considerably. Like most academic docs, they were in fact delighted to find someone at a party who was not also a physician. But I was feeling wary. British Romanticism? I hadn't identified myself that way in more than a decade. Huh? And before I had ahold of myself again, one of them recovered sufficiently from her surprise to ask where I taught. Small glances from the others acknowledged her quick thinking, as if this conversation circle were Morning Report on the medical service.

"I don't," I replied with a smile and a shrug, with a self-possessed pizzazz that filled me with an unexpected warmth. "I hung up my Superwoman cape and stayed home with my kids."

They looked impressed. They looked positively awed. They were awash, suddenly, in stories about how they had watched "older women" like me ground into little bits by the conflicts between their careers and their kids. They were uncertain about their own lives but absolutely determined not to get trapped like that.

"You just *did* it?" one of them repeated, still incredulous. "You just walked *away?*"

"I don't know if I could," another chimed, admiringly. "I don't know if I would have what it takes . . ."

I spotted Warren watching me from across the room, visibly amused, visibly amused and with his "How many times have I told you so?" look. I turned back to his residents, to the familiar motherly skill of listening attentively and openly. I was astounded and yet not astounded that subsequent generations of professional women had in fact been watching closely and understanding clearly the lives we "older women" were living. Older women. Oh well. In this crowd I sure felt "older."

Their talk spilled over into a mixed group as the buffet dinner was served: a couple of dozen men and women, speculating and hoping that they could force the professional accommodations demanded by their passionate commitment to the idea of family life, the ideal of personal lives for themselves in which their work was not the sole, all-encompassing reality. Warren and I sat in on the group like elder statesmen, I thought, like real greybeards.

Except I was the one they were looking to and listening to. Not greybeard but crone, wise old woman—of forty-something! Warren sat back mostly silent, observant, deferential, and somehow deeply pleased.

And the next week it happened again. Our architect and his wife discovered that they were pregnant, and suddenly he was full of questions about my working at home.

"In some circles," he explained, "this has a real cachet. Staying home is getting very trendy . . . "

Trendy? Lives like mine were getting *trendy?* Good heavens. I looked up at him, a medical manuscript balanced on a lapboard on my knees because my study was full of carpenters. The kitchen was full of dirty dishes, the basement was full of dirty clothes, the yard was full of kids, and people were hammering on my roof. Trendy?

I called Linda. She edited history books for U-Chicago Press around two boys, the best perennial garden I knew, and a foul-tempered iguana prone to extremely expensive gingivitis. He was the only iguana I knew with his own dentist, whose office was ninety minutes away on the far West Side. Did she know we were trendy? That being home with kids, working catch-as-catch-can around kids, now carried a certain cachet?

"Oh yes," she affirmed. "Didn't you know? You should be a sponsor for baptism class: you'd see. We're quite the thing for new parents these days. Get dedicated lines for a modem and a fax machine and you too can be crazy as a coon, right here at home with the kids and the philodendron. They call it 'telecommuting.'"

I'd never been trendy in all my life. Even the kids realized one day that Warren and I had probably been real nerds when we were kids: they visibly contemplated suing us for divorce and setting themselves out for adoption by parents who were cool. They worried a lot about what to say when teachers asked them what I did, when other kids asked.

"I can't just say you do nothing," Mark complained, mortified that "nothing" was in fact the truth. I had told him to say "editor." He had looked at me as if I were suborning perjury.

"Well *sometimes*," he allowed, grudgingly.

Trendy. Oh heavens. "Telecommuting?" In my mind I kept seeing four cold cups of tea on the kitchen counter and that first baby-sitter, departing in tears in her damp red blouse because Mark had not let her get her papers graded. The *terra incognita* of postpartum, now available on-line . . .

Across the Waters

That night I dreamed. I was standing on a shoreline, looking back across a huge expanse of water. But I was also standing away across back there, a tiny figure on the distant shore. I wanted to go back across the water to myself because "that" was familiar and "this" was not, even though "that" was painful and "this" was not so painful. But I knew I could not go back. I knew I did not really want to go back. It is difficult, after all, to leave the familiar. To leave myself. But I knew I would not go back across the water. With a sigh, I faced forward again.

Santa Claus

By December of 1989, the kids had discovered dinner table conversation as a civilized form: we now had meals instead of feedings. As a result of this exciting new development, Tim regularly interrupted my first bite with a string of several questions about Santa Claus. This reminded me unduly of my doctoral oral exams, at which I choked violently on a swallow of coffee at the first (and exceedingly nasty) such string.

I had always evaded the kids' questions about reindeer, furnaces, and so on by insisting that the whole Santa business is magic. Other than such dodges, I had never talked to them about Santa at all, except for reading "'Twas the Night before Christmas" to them one year. And Santa *is* a kind of magic, after all: quite aside from all the commercial carrying-on, Santa is a game of pretend that the whole culture plays. There is nothing else quite like it. The Easter bunny and the tooth fairy don't even come close. No self-respecting kid buys into the Easter bunny or the tooth fairy.

At various reasonable times, I had also explained that there is no such thing as magic. And I had explained repeatedly that not all one sees on TV is or can be real. We had had wonderful inventive talks about where to hide the camera or how to cut and splice the pictures together. They built ramps out of blocks to restage the leaps on *Dukes of Hazzard,* and they made me come downstairs to admire the space left inside the ramp for the cameraman (an old He-Man doll, as I recall). They had seen magicians, and I had explained about how magicians can hide things. We bought a magic kit, tried magic tricks ourselves, and then sang Mr. Rogers's ditty, "Everything We Do Takes Practice."

Mark had mastered basic syllogistic logic some time previously, and his Santa questions had stopped cold in their tracks. The year before, eyes glistening and face taut with tension, he asked me if Santa was real. Torn by his anxiety, I was inspired by some special guardian angel assigned to mothers who studied too much metaphysics.

"Well, what do you think?" I asked. And out came this impassioned testimonial to Santa's reality, capped by the fact that Johnny's grandma saw him when she was a girl. So it had gone.

This year's dinnertime format became quite predictable. Tim asked about Santa's reality, I replied by asking for others' opinions, Mark and Carol leapt in with testimonies of faith, and I quickly got some more food into my mouth to give Carol a chance to introduce a new topic. If Tim mentioned furnaces and houses without chimneys, Carol always very piously and confidently repeated my assertion that Santa is magic. Mark would watch me and say nothing at all.

At other times of day, Tim asked about the reality of magic tricks, and I repeated that magic is not real. Or Tim asserted that Santa is magic, and I agreed. I think he was perfectly able to put the facts together; but such formal reasoning was a new enough skill for him that he wanted confirmation, especially in such an important matter. Yet I was beginning to feel that perhaps I was playing an academic's game in not answering his question unless he framed it in precisely the right way. Soon enough he did.

"Mommy," he said, very solemnly, "you said Santa is magic. But you said there is no such thing as magic." I looked up from chopping celery and barely missed chopping off my fingertip. "Mommy," he continued, "I want to ask you something."

"Y-e-e-e-s," I said, in my best Mrs. Rogers voice.

"There is a piece of graham cracker here. Can I have it?" He walked out munching.

And the next night he fixed me with his glinty-eyed look and asked if *I* believed in Santa.

"Do *I* believe in Santa? Well now—" Here it goes, I thought; but Mark and Carol rushed in with every defense of the man I had ever heard and then some.

Carol firmly changed the subject to something appropriate to polite company. She fixed Tim with a stare that would have stopped a speeding train. (Miss Manners would have admired her style.)

Later Tim caught me in the dining room, again with his glinty look.

"Santa has to be real," he proclaimed, "or else where would all those presents come from?"

"Where indeed," I replied; and he skipped off giggling.

Christmas week we stopped by Mom's condo. Warren and I were finishing lunch in the dining room when Mark walked in silently and sat down with us. From the kitchen, Mom asked if Santa was ready for Christmas.

"No," I replied.

When Mark's head snapped up, I startled like a guilty thing surprised. Mom stuck her head around the corner, and with polished grace she explained that she had called me Santa because I was so busy getting ready for Christmas. Mom turned effortlessly back to making another pot of tea, and Mark stared at me solemnly.

I was coming to dread dinnertime a bit.

"Have you ever seen flying reindeer?" I replied that I had never seen reindeer that looked as though they could fly. And I compared "'Twas the Night before Christmas" to the series of Santa-based Christmas specials they had watched, attributing the flying reindeer story to that poem, and then Rudolph to the song. I explained about folk traditions and oral traditions. Mark looked like Sherlock Holmes taking relevant testimony; Carol brimmed with tears; Tim was glinty-eyed again.

"Is Santa watching us?" We checked. He wasn't under my chair, nor outside either kitchen window.

"No," I concluded, "Santa is not watching us." Together we sang "Santa Claus Is Coming to Town" and reviewed the reasons I hate that song. My kids will have their literary sources straight, by golly. But with dinnertimes like this, I may die of indigestion first.

"Is God watching us?" Mark asked.

"Yes," I replied, "but God is *real*." Whoops. Tim looked finally satisfied; Mark looked ever more analytical; Carol glowered at me and firmly changed the subject again.

And on Christmas Eve, over our cocoa and cookies, we told silly kid riddles about elephant tracks in the butter and chickens crossing the road. Carol's riddle ended in angry tears. "What if there are no presents tomorrow because there is no Santa and no flying reindeer and no magic or anything!"

No one had an answer, and I felt just awful.

Earlier in the day, Mark had asked Warren if he could sleep on the couch to catch Santa in the act. Warren refused, because he and I would be sitting on the couch after the kids went to bed. Mark then proposed booby-trapping the tree such that an alarm would go off if anyone put a present on the tree skirt. Warren vetoed that too. So Mark organized a game of hide-and-seek upstairs, although the kids are not allowed to play up here. Soon enough he found the closet with stacks of wrapped and unwrapped presents, and of course he shared his find with Tim and Carol.

In the privacy of his room, I had an inappropriately hostile fit at Mark for sneaking around in closets and playing in forbidden territory generally. I said that the kids had been full of Santa questions, but now he had his answer. He agreed to that, crestfallen.

But he was full of Santa-is-coming talk all the rest of the afternoon and evening, seeming to buy into the story much more gleefully than he had for years.

So when I wrapped Warren's gifts, I had each kid fill out a tag "to Dad from Santa." Tim protested that this or that gift was from *him*, not Santa; and I explained that the magic of Christmas—St. Nicholas's magic—was that people want and need to do nice things for others without anyone knowing who did it. We all just say, uh-uh, not me, "Santa." (Carol had been going on about St. Nicholas and leaving her shoes in the hallway all month, because, she explained, "Courtney tried it and it worked! She had candy in her shoes in the morning!" It didn't work in our house, alas.) Tim listened tolerantly, with the same interested but skeptical face he uses for new foods. Mark and Carol wrote their tags in stony silence, proving once again my Daniel Striped Tiger Theorem: plans for serious talk or quality time belong in the Neighborhood of Make-Believe. The only kids you can deal with in such timely and cerebral ways are, in fact, puppets: you are just talking to yourself.

On Christmas morning, Carol fixed her brothers with her most contemptuous "you *boys*" look and announced that obviously Santa was real. Tim whispered to Warren that thus-and-such was really from him. The hyper-observant Mark sat reading directions and never commented on the Toys-Я-Us price tags that for once I had not scraped off. Ho, ho, ho.

Dr. Wallace

In the fall of 1989, I had networked my way through the academic community at church into an adjunct position teaching a single composition course in the upcoming winter term at a local women's college. I'd have earned more frying burgers at McDonalds, but I was desperate to get out of the house and away from my freelance medical editing for a while. Unspeakably awful stuff from an assistant professor at Yale had done me in. If I was doomed to spend my life coping with other people's illiteracy, at least once in a while I wanted to work with those for whom such illiteracy is developmentally appropriate. I had no intention of making my career earning such a pittance in the underground world of part-time faculty, of course: this was just one course for a change of pace.

But just before Christmas, I got a panicky phone call from my new chair: an adoption had suddenly come through for one of the tenured faculty, who had walked in the day before to say she was taking an unpaid personal leave of absence for the next eighteen months. The college—run by Roman Catholic nuns—had no maternity leave policy in place and no arrangements whatever for personal leave. Having waited years for this baby, the woman who left had made a reasonable choice in an unreasonable world; but three courses full of students now had no instructor. Desperate, the chair had reviewed the files of the adjuncts: at least I was somebody somebody knew, Chicago style. And a Michigan Ph.D. no less! Would I consider teaching full-time for five academic quarters, commencing in three weeks?

Warren and I went out to dinner that night, replaying the fateful hot fudge sundaes at Dairy Queen Ann Arbor. I would teach two courses on Tuesdays and Thursdays and a third on either Saturday afternoons or Saturday mornings. I would leave home as the kids left, and I would be home again within minutes after they arrived. Two short days a week, plus half a Saturday. It was a heavy teaching load—the weekday classes met for ninety minutes—but great readings and an incredibly good schedule. I was promised that this quality of schedule would continue, as indeed it did. We ate our dinners, pondered all the imponderables, and voted once again to leap off a cliff. I called the chair the next day, and on that afternoon she delivered a brown paper bag of books.

And in January, I found my name on a door, on a mailbox, on a smudgy list of students' names. I wore my good navy blue suit, only to rediscover why academics always wear earth tones: khaki and tweeds hide the chalk dust. My students called on weekends, asking for "Dr. Wallace." The kids kept handing the phone to their Dad, and my timid, bewildered students kept hanging up in confusion when a man's voice came on the line. Then the kids took to asking, "Which one?" to the equal bewilderment of Warren's junior medical students. For their parts, the kids could not fathom why Warren and I found all of it so amusing. But they were very impressed with my monogrammed canvas briefcase from Lands' End. It was dusty but still whole after ten years in a closet. The Coach leather one I had used as a consultant just didn't hold as many books as comfortably. And like my good suit, it just didn't belong in this friendly, funky little college.

Teaching again was for me the best of times and yet also the worst of times: as Wordsworth complains, I hardly have words for who I was then. Exhausted by the work. Elated by the work. I was something close to drunk with the pleasures of teaching poetry and more than eager to escape from the God questions that had been pursuing me for the last year or so. I hoped that this temporary job would provide respite of several different sorts. But instead I found myself once again working very late into the night and feeling deeply frustrated by an entirely new, entirely unexpected problem.

I found myself frustrated by the fact that the structure of my discipline kept me from offering what I felt my students wanted and legitimately needed the most. Even in a place where students counted for something, a place where my teaching skills won me warm and immediate praise, an English department remains an English department. Poetry names and elicits very deep-set spiritual needs; as always, students came starving for meanings in their lives and for spiritually significant discourse about those meanings and those hungers. But a classroom is not a church. At the end of the term, I still had to give them all grades. And I could not—I would not—deny that grade sheets bracketed our entire relationship. So the real spiritual needs in both their lives and my life remained essentially marginal to the usual enterprise of literary criticism, despite how the poetry itself aroused spiritual issues.

As an English professor, I still felt that it was my task to make their literary heritage accessible to them. I was a professor, not a priest; it was not my place to use literature to meet their spiritual needs. So I taught as I had always taught, some mix of cultural history and fundamental literary reading skills: prosody and plot analysis, character development and figures of speech. Most of these students were graduates from City of Chicago urban public schools: one had to begin at the beginning with almost everything, at least with the younger students.

I taught *Paradise Lost* three times in five quarters, because it had been several years since the department had had anyone willing to do so. I admired Milton's poetic prowess more each time even as I struggled with less and less conviction to explicate the issues behind Milton's God. And despite my pedagogic resolve, I never knew what to feel or what to say when discussions of Milton's God escaped from the text. One day a small, stocky girl named Karyn leapt to her feet, snarling that she hated this punitive, legalistic bastard called "God." Every time her mother beat her, she explained, her mother had said that God demanded that wrongdoing be punished like this.

I let the story hang in midair for a minute. Then I suggested, quietly, that Milton's God is an idea about God, an imaginative construction like any other character, a dramatic portrait.

"Does it match up with some actual reality? Who knows. But *plenty* of folks have always violently disagreed with Milton's portrait of God. Blake, for instance. Or," I added offhandedly, "*me*. I don't buy Milton's portrait for a minute. If that's God, thanks but I'll go to hell. Karyn and me, together." I looked around the room and shrugged. "Yeah, Karyn and me and lots of other folks too."

With but half a glance at me, another woman, heretofore silent, stood up and waited until she had everyone's full attention. With passion and verve right out of Alice Walker, she disputed Milton's theology as refracted through Karyn's mother.

"My momma told me," she concluded, "that God is with me no matter what shit. That's what *my* momma said. And God is." And it was very clear to all of us that Margaret had known some shit worth noting.

When she finished she turned from Karyn to look right at me. Our eyes met and held, hers still bright with conviction but with quickly accumulating lines as this visibly introverted, even shy young woman began to realize what she had dared to do. At the edges of my vision I realized that the class was watching the two of us look at one another.

"Oh God," I thought to myself, "what do I say now?" I nodded, a nod verging toward a bow, and she sat down.

"Yes," I said, as softly as I could and yet be sure my voice would carry. "Yes. That's the alternative. Next quarter, if you stay with this course, we'll read Wordsworth and you'll see that he agrees with Margaret."

I summoned up all the energy I could summon and, pulling another book out of my briefcase, I read them a few key lines from "Tintern Abbey"—

> I have felt
> A Presence that disturbs me . . .
> . . . [and thus] neither evil tongues,
> Rash judgments, nor the sneers of selfish men,
> Nor greetings where no kindness is, nor all
> The dreary intercourse of daily life,
> Shall e'er prevail against us, or disturb
> Our cheerful faith that all which we behold
> Is full of blessing . . .

I stood quietly, holding their attention in some physical way and letting the words slowly settle. Silence ticked away toward the class hour bell. I slipped my books back into my briefcase and zipped it closed.

"Wordsworth calls it 'Nature' and says she is with us always." I said. "Some Christians call it 'Jesus.' He promised to be with us always too. One way or another, the promise is the same, the promise is what Margaret's mother said: no matter what shit, God is there for us, holding us up, like a light inside us that will never go out. Plenty of people see it as Milton does, but plenty of people see it this other way too." And then, just before the bell rang, I reminded them that the subject matter of this class was Milton not God.

I doubt that anyone believed me, of course. Both God and Milton, I thought as I drove home, probably felt quite annoyed with me. I was pretty annoyed with me, myself. But what was I to do? I needed to make sure that question "Who is God?" stayed *their* question, if it stayed at all, and that the answer, if an answer came, felt like their answer too—not mine.

Above all I would not use my authority to enforce any single answer to the question that anyone who comes to Milton must face sooner or later: how does one justify the ways of God to man? Why is life so hard, if God is all-powerful and all-knowing? I was hired to teach poetry, I pleaded to myself, not spirituality and theology. But the distinction had never seemed so shallow, so arbitrary, so "academic" in the very worst meaning of that word. Why bother with poetry, with beauty, if there is no powerful and demanding connection between beauty and truth? I had never been a *l'art pour l'art* decadent, a New Age narcissist.

But on the whole, teaching Milton left me very little energy for questions about why is my own life so hard and what if anything does God have to do with it. Preparing as much as three thousand lines of poetry each week, commuting, spending all of every Monday and all of every Wednesday grading papers at the kitchen table, spending the whole weekend doing laundry and running errands and paying bills, schlepping sick kids with me to wait in my office, curled up on a quilt on the floor, or letting them stay home alone, sullen and resentful and lonely and unsupervised—all that brought me was bifocals and a chronic stomachache and distinctly greyer hair. Whatever the problems of my soul, working like this was clearly no solution.

The conflict is over?

Not a chance, God, not a chance.

6

A Big Blue Frog

As my stint of teaching came to an end, I spent some time just sitting in my study, in the old yellow recliner where I had rocked the babies, where I had read to them, where we slept sitting up all those wheezy, infected nights. I sat there, rocking slightly, staring at my battered, cluttered desk, as if at my own reflection in some soul-mirror. Okay, lady. Okay. So what are you going to do with yourself now, Kate?

It was clear, or clear enough anyhow, that I did not feel the presence of God in my editing for the American Society of Clinical Pathologists. I did not find God in writing summaries of management books. I probably had not even found God in writing that terrific monograph on the *Odyssey* for the textbook company—although perhaps I had come close, or maybe I had merely come close to the memory of the presence of God in my older work with literature, in my scholarly work. Surely God had been in all those places, in all those experiences, because the more I tried to think about it the clearer it seemed that the experience of God is potentially conscious anywhere at all, within any experience, if we can just figure out how to be open to it. And so I had continued with my quotidian freelance work, trusting that I could in time come to feel the presence of God in these words too.

But my little stint back in a classroom, teaching poetry, convinced me I had been fooling myself. God was in hackwork freelance stuff just as God was in housework, sure. But there was available to me something greater, something finer or clearer. In some essential way, I knew that for me the most glorious encounters with God—as I had had in my Coleridge work, in my work with students, in my own writing—would never be available in this kind of work. But what, then? I stared at the top of my desk, at the glass canning jar of pens and pencils, at the calendar in its little two-ring stand, at an empty mug from herbal tea drunk the night before, at miscellaneous piles of paper. If a beloved and familiar desk can feel like a blank impenetrable wall, mine did. Here I was again, here I was still, at the same quandary I had first recognized when Carol and Tim first started preschool: unused skills, unexercised gifts, were accumulating like toxic waste in my soul. How long could I continue to spend so much energy on mothering if my own supply were not somehow replenished?

Well, I had done one piece of rewarding work recently, I remembered. I had done some adult-ed presentations at church, explaining how all of Scripture and all of theological and doctrinal language for and about God is necessarily metaphorical. All namings of the unknowable and unnamable are poetry at heart, I argued, designed to elicit and to evoke our awareness of the sacred but not to capture God in the nets of simple intellect. Language too can be sacramental, holy-making, visionary beyond what deconstruction can destroy. All namings of God are partially true and partially false: Christians need always to remember that we really do not *know* what we are talking about, not in any strict or rigorous sense of that word, to keep all the metaphors in play with all the other metaphors. And then I had looked at two contrasting patterns of metaphors: God as structured orderliness, and God as sustaining presence.

I built a tough and powerful argument, pulling the full range of my philosophic and literary training out of the cardboard boxes stashed in the basement of my soul, lining it up with all the theology I had recently read. I made to them the argument I had felt so unable to make to my college students; I made some amends to God and to Milton both. And in that church parlor I had them, oh I had them indeed, partly trapped by the tight philosophic weave of my argument, and partly held by the passion that drew my verbal abilities to razor-sharp precision. Even Pete had sat engrossed. Perhaps especially Pete.

"But look out," he cautioned me ruefully, some days later. "Everyone grows up believing in Santa Claus, the Easter bunny, and God. Grownups no longer believe in Santa Claus or the Easter bunny. But plenty of people believe in the bunny-rabbit versions of God. Or they don't believe in the bunny-rabbit God, and they have never bothered to wonder if there is any alternative. At any rate, look out for the bunny-rabbit theologians in this place. There are plenty of them, and they have plenty of kick."

I thought his caution inexplicable. I'd take my chances, I decided. He had obviously survived that crowd for fifteen years without looking bruised or even gnawed. Despite his warnings, my fine post-postmodern mysticism seemed to elicit not criticism from the congregation, but increasingly regular and emphatic demands that I should get myself to the seminary and be ordained as priest. Ah yes, I always replied: get another degree for which there are no jobs. No thanks: I have one of those already.

Organized religion, institutionalized religion, struggles more or less successfully to manifest the sacred in major, public, ancient, culturally central ways. These ancient liturgical forms could speak to me at times in powerful, archetypally charged ways. My unconscious or my collective unconscious or my what have you could at times resonate to the old rituals with an energy and a depth that astounded me. But liturgy is not, finally, dancing with the Holy all by myself. Liturgy heightened in me a yearning that only writing satisfied. I am *not* a priest, I argued to the *Book of Common Prayer* sitting atop a heap of notes for my presentation at next Sunday's adult ed. I'm *not* a priest. I'm a poet, I almost said. Almost.

In March of 1991—as a compromise, perhaps?—I did accept Pete's nominating me Director of Adult Education in recognition of how often I was leading the Rector's Forum for him. I offered to volunteer ten hours a week, since I was spending about that much time already; after a year, if I was still interested, we would negotiate both salary and duties in some formal way. It felt like a nice excuse not to phone up the medical journals that had employed me, looking for work. My recent stint of college teaching would end shortly, and I had had about all I could manage of mangled sentences and red pens.

Furthermore, I was coming to feel more and more deeply at home amid the community of folks Elaine and Pete had gathered around themselves during a long and amicable ministry. I had never felt so welcome, so accepted: there was nothing here of the weary combativeness of graduate school or academics, nothing of the grinding isolation of working home alone as a freelance. It was okay here to be the kind of woman I was, a mother devoted to her family, a woman who has ideas and reads books and relishes a lively debate, who knows who she is both personally and intellectually. I had never been anywhere I did not have to fight. But Elaine had already won the fundamental battles about the status of women in church leadership, and I rested gratefully in the broad sweep of her shadow. Suddenly I had many friends, more than I had ever had; suddenly friendships were easy, friendships with men and with women who led all varieties of lives.

Elaine had stopped by the house several times during the winter to drop off brown grocery bags full of books she thought I should read. So as my courses ended, I settled down to finish reading them. I even followed her directions to the seminary bookstore, which is hidden away in the basement of a dormitory. I bought myself yet another bag of books. I had not read in such a sustained way in ten years, and it felt like a homecoming of sorts.

Christianity, I discovered, had some nuanced contemporary thinkers—no one as good as Coleridge, I laughed to myself, but very good people nonetheless, theologians more like Wordsworth than like Milton, people for whom God's essential act was creating and sustaining a new and visionary reality within and among us, not judging and punishing. And there was intriguing, persuasive new scholarship about Jesus, about the gospels, and about the early and radically countercultural Jesus movement in the ancient world. Women's spirituality and women's history were thriving subfields, where top-notch scholars were doing landmark work.

I looked at the titles strewn around my armchair one day, suddenly startled. I was taking all this stuff seriously. What? Dare I think of myself both as a housewife and an observant Christian? It seemed more than flesh could bear—or at least my intellectual pride. That still small voice had never stopped needling me: "What are you doing here? Why are you going to church?" I wasn't sure I could explain. Was I really taking all this seriously not as interesting reading but as real belief? Maybe I was just bored, merely entertaining myself with historical and theological scholarship because, well, because I have the kind of quirky mind that does find such things entertaining. Because I needed something more in my life than child care and laundry and illiterate assistant professors writing garbled paragraphs about tedious pharmacology.

In the mail one day came a catalogue for the "spiritual seeker," offering an array of New Age trinkets. There were no splinters of the True Cross or relics of the holy martyrs, but there were equivalents from an array of Native American and Asian religious traditions, plus books, tapes, bells, benches, candles, incense, plastic statues, and tee shirts variously emblazoned. Stapled into the centerfold was a pitch for yet other catalogues, from which one could buy organic dental floss, oat bran, recycled paper for laser printers, and meditation videotapes. My goose bumps had goose bumps by the time I was finished flipping through the pages. The message was clear: with enough "inner work," you too can achieve peace and perfection, thereby liberating yourself from the human condition. Self-redemption through the mail, with a toll-free call and a credit card.

But there was something so sad about it all. The spiritual hungers of our day are being fed by the vending machine versions of literary masterpieces and philosophically rigorous, psychologically subtle ancient wisdom. Of course the venal have always pandered to the credulous, in every spiritual tradition and in every culture. But spiritual hunger is nonetheless quite real—and the spiritually hungry would starve to death on trash like this.

I remembered a dinner party one time where variously paunchy middle-aged people argued exercise bikes versus rowing machines as if they were giving what the Baptists call "witness." When I admitted to having arthritis and asthma and absolutely no exercise program whatever, I had triggered a cascade of evangelism and, in subsequent weeks, a small flurry of leaflets. It would have been comic were the emotional needs less poignant. I was tempted to send back Thomas Johnson's lovely selected edition of Emily Dickinson, but I doubted that such a gesture would be understood.

Maybe God is real. I could probably get myself as far as a good solid *maybe*. "Poetic faith," yes? That willing suspension of disbelief, for the moment anyhow. But religion—whether institutional churches or these secularized versions—seems also to call out the very screwiest loose screws in the human psyche. If only God didn't feel so real, I could keep a distance from churches and the wholly uncanny aesthetic power of communal worship. I could just stare out of windows and breathe in peace, dismissing everything else as Celtic predispositions intersecting with creativity, introversion, and errant brainwaves. But I had discovered that regular corporate worship powerfully sustained the possibility that this really was an experience of God. And somehow I wanted to sustain that possibility. What an improbable mess. How did smart, well-educated, analytical people like Elaine and Pete nonetheless belong to churches? If only God didn't feel so real . . .

The Opiate of the Anxious

Worse yet, I kept remembering Melissa. In 1973, Melissa found Jesus and stopped worrying about her prelims. But could she be sure, I asked her, that Jesus knew molecular genetics? Not many folks did in 1973: recombinant DNA studies were hot new stuff, undiscovered yet by *Newsweek* or even by *Fortune*. Dusty Palestine, 2000 years ago: did she really trust Jesus to know it?

Melissa was not amused. Melissa was one of the young renegades from physics to biology, and for two years she had been telling tall tales about the research under way in her program. Three of us met now and then for tea in the little shop next to the bank, treasuring our friendship even as our research programs threatened to render us, professionally, almost unintelligible to each other. A mathematician, a literary critic, and this molecular biologist: what a trio we were. But the disparity of our disciplines mattered less than the fact that we were all women in a transparently misogynist setting, that we had been undergraduates together, and together in those days we had found the courage to try what we were now daring to try: that was quite enough to call us together for a cup of tea and a single pecan roll, split three ways. It was enough at least for now.

Melissa had talked about controlling the stuff of life, about the nuclear bomb pioneers, about knowledge and sin and poisoning this garden once and for all, from without and from within. But the work was so exciting. She had seemed to hope that God didn't know, at least not yet. But then Melissa found Jesus and needed nothing else—certainly not Sheila and me.

And by analogy we understood. We had seen other anxious high achievers develop that glassy stare and bright exaggerated affect. Marx's nasty crack made sense in a whole new way. And Jesus apparently knew enough about DNA to get Melissa through prelims. Although I never saw her again, except at a distance, I heard that her research went well: she was done and gone to a fine job before either of us.

Let It Snow

Melissa and her prelims were like the novena said by my high school class when there was no snow in the couple of weeks prior to the class toboggan party at the end of January. The Tuesday before our Saturday trip, it was an incredible 65° outside. But for nine days, the junior class president led us in prayer over the public address system. Very early on the eighth morning, the Thursday before our Saturday plans, big snowflakes began to fall. By the time we got to school, it was clear there would be enough snow for our party. Some of the nuns were visibly jubilant; some of the girls were astounded. And some of us were visibly cautious about revealing the direction of our incredulity.

By noon, the snow was so deep we were all sent home. My pleated uniform skirt wasn't good for much as I waded home from the bus stop through snow that came well above my knees. By evening the city was at a standstill and still the snow kept falling.

It was the Blizzard of 1967, held to account in dozens of deaths citywide. Amidst high winds, twenty-five to twenty-seven inches of snow fell in twenty-four hours.

I remember looking down into the major east-west expressway the next morning. The roofs of hundreds of abandoned cars were barely visible in the blown snow: all I could see for sure were the tops of big trucks. Our one story school building was entirely drifted over in places; like plenty of other folks citywide, the nuns were trapped inside their convent by drifts blocking their doors. They called the president of the Father's Club to get a crew of men to dig them out.

One of the fathers took a picture of snowdrifts blocking the front door of the school. His daughter brought in a copy of the picture as the anniversary of the storm approached. I wanted to print it on the front page of our January issue.

"'Ask and it shall be given to you,'" went my proposed caption, "So last year at this time, the class of '68 prayed for snow for their toboggan party. School closed for a week. Let us pray." We laid out the page, glued it down, and set it out for Sister Patrice to approve—four or five of us, casually pretending not to watch as she proofread the page.

She handed it back to me with her best imitation of properly nun-like severity: I had misspelled *toboggan*. She turned her back on us to retype the line herself, and I almost thought I saw her shoulders shaking.

God as Real Estate Broker

"God is not a vending machine," Zahava had pointed out, pointedly, when I told her the story in 1987, just before we moved away. We were swapping accounts of magical causality from the spiritual formation of our youths, because my mother had rushed into my house the week before, breathless and concerned, with a statue of St. Joseph for me to bury in my garden. Upside down. And in a little plastic bag, to keep him clean. We were selling our first house, and Mom was breathless because she barely made it in the door ahead of the brokers. How dare I have a brokers' open house without St. Joseph?

When the house sold in four days, Mom returned to supervise the exhumation. She didn't trust me, which was wise. Temperatures had plummeted in the first major cold spell of the winter. The ground was now frozen solid: as far as I was concerned, her plastic trinket could stay for the new people to discover when they tried to transplant tomatoes. What if I made a mistake, I wondered as I hacked at the icy dirt. Maybe the buyers' mortgage application would be denied?

I figured I had better not ask: Mom was ostensibly rationalist enough to be quite defensive about enforcing this ritual. I reminded myself, not for the first time, that the Enlightenment never reached Ireland. Probably not even the Renaissance. So, ever the dutiful daughter, I chopped him out, rinsed off the frozen mud, and put the little plastic statue on my kitchen windowsill.

"In the new house, it goes on the *mantel*," Mom insisted as she left. "It needs a position of *honor*. You don't have a mantel here; so that will do. Tell the children, when they get home." She swept out. My house smelled faintly of incense and beeswax: I fled to Zahava's for a cup of tea.

St. Joseph plays this role because he knows about housing problems: can you imagine the scene when he came back out to Mary on that donkey, to tell her the inn had overbooked and they were bumped? Or what about fleeing to Egypt in the middle of the night? Sneaking away from Herod: did they have confirmed reservations? And what happened to their house in Nazareth meanwhile? So here's the saint to broker your prayers about housing. The house we were buying had been on the market for a long time, we knew—and later, when I dug up three plastic statues from the flower beds by the house, I understood why. No bags. I also found a plastic flip-top cap about three inches across, on which someone had printed neatly with a ballpoint pen: "St. Joseph, Please Sell This House." I wondered what the bottle had contained.

My little plastic St. Joseph still sits inside a kitchen cabinet, on a narrow shelf to the right of the sink, next to the jug of Ajax dish detergent. That's not exactly a place of honor, but I find it a useful daily reminder about the power of magic. After all, magic is a theology with deep roots both in biblical religion and in the modern psyche. One of Zahava's Jewish friends called her to call me to get the St. Joseph routine from a real Roman Catholic. Carrying two mortgages will do that to people. A Lutheran friend who hadn't been inside a church in thirty years nonetheless bought a potted plant in which to bury a St. Joseph when an important condo deal ran into expensive deadline problems around a VA mortgage application. Poor cuckolded St. Joseph is the ultimate outsider: he will work a deal for anybody, orthodoxy be damned. You don't have to be Irish or Italian. You don't even have to be Catholic.

All you need is to imagine that the sacred is essentially causality personified, or maybe to project upon the shimmering numinous all of your own deepest, most vulnerable control needs. And when the world proves violent and unfair, as the world so transparently is, then the plastic god you have imagined seems guilty of doing a terrible job of managing causality in ways that are just and loving. In the face of typhoons and tornadoes and epidemics, "his" complaints about human sin seem pretty petty. So we stop believing in "him" and try to take over that control ourselves. Blake describes this process in considerable and passionate detail.

Between a Rock and a Hard Place

In the summer of 1991, Pete announced that he was moving to another parish out-of-state; Elaine said that she would leave as soon as she could find another job. And my commitment to the parish, which had been tentative and peripheral and quite behind the scenes, suddenly moved up front and center: Pete assured everyone repeatedly that the lay professional staff would carry on flawlessly while the parish looked for a new rector. My name abruptly appeared on the masthead of the Sunday leaflets. At coffee hour, at parish parties of one sort of another, suddenly there were plenty of folks inviting me to join their table or engaging me in conversations about their own spiritual lives.

That fall, I found myself in sole command of the Rector's Forum on Sunday mornings—a reprobate group made up mostly of lawyers, chemists, engineers, and senior managers of various sorts—the kind of successful, polished folks who live in the big, elegant homes around the church. The group quickly renamed itself the Heretics' Forum and plainly refused to share responsibility for making presentations on Sunday. Having more than enough of my own spiritual crisis to supply discussion topics, I accepted the role offered me.

One week a German professor cornered me to complain about a misplaced apostrophe the week before. "Don't think you are the only heretic in there!" she objected. Thereafter I proofread service leaflets more attentively.

Elaine left in November, leaving the parish in the hands of various interim and part-time clergy while a formal search committee looked for a new rector. The weekend she left, six people asked me to have lunch with them. Six. I have gone years at a time without six lunch invitations. Elaine had offered a sympathetic ear and sharp eye to plenty of folks in the parish, and at least some nominated me her heir apparent: I gained ten pounds that winter, having lunch two or three times a week with people who needed to talk to someone. One of the Forum regulars, I discovered, had a downtown office half the size of a tennis court, with a glorious view down the river to the lake. But she grieved that she did not see enough of her son, whose father had remarried, had other children with his new wife, and then moved away. We had a lovely lunch on her expense account, and driving back home I realized that if this kept up I would soon weigh at least as much as the charts said I should.

Meanwhile, the interim clergy and various lay leaders quite blithely expected me to take over planning and running every adult education activity in the whole parish. The interim rector was a wiry, pragmatic guy, newly retired and full of stories about a long and colorful career in various churches and parts of the world. He sized me up adeptly, in and around his story telling. In turn, I felt quite reassured by his skill and self-assurance both as theologian and as leader.

I tried to explain that my theological vocabulary and skill were an eclectic mix of Catholic education, Coleridge studies, and random reading. He saw no problem in that, cheerfully demanding that I read John Dominic Crossan's new 700-page tome and buying me huge, expensive reference volumes of Scripture commentary. (I had scandalized him, I think, by offering the Heretics' Forum a comparative plot analysis of the resurrection narratives without at least checking the usual biblical scholar reference books.) He didn't see what I was trying—albeit indirectly—to tell him.

"Look," I interrupted him. "I'm not sure I believe any of this. It's great reading, but—"

He waved me off. He wasn't sure either, he assured me. Nobody with any brains is sure.

"Come off it, Katie," he said one day, a real edge to his voice. "Nobody has answers. None of us are sure about any of this. The church is not a collection of answers. Our job is to teach people to live with the questions, to keep the right questions alive. The only people to worry about, in jobs like yours, are people who are sure, who think they do have answers." He was much more worried, he said, by the fact that I didn't have an exercise program. Or that people were nagging me about ordination. There were no jobs for priests, he insisted: don't let anybody talk me into that. The old joke: by the year 2000, half of all Episcopalians will be ordained.

"Not a chance," I replied. "I'm a poet not a priest." He startled when I said that—so did I—but we both let it go.

Dear Ken. He remains less concerned about my soul than about my coronary arteries. I showed him some of my poetry, and he chewed me out in no uncertain terms for never having sought publication. I had never even considered it. My public self was a scholar or an editor, I struggled to explain, not an artist. He was not persuaded. He told me story after story about a writing course he had taken from W. H. Auden, initiating a persistent debate about the nature of texts that edged into related arguments about the Jesus Seminar and his old friend John Dominic Crossan and narrative conventions in antiquity. And of course about whether or not I had taken a full course of asthma meds and done my aerobic exercise. In time, I suspected, I would be not only fat but also fit. What a thought!

Overnight, it seemed, I had gone from being a literary pagan on the fringes to being a leader in the parish. Heresy sells? One Sunday Linda cornered me, demanding that I reconvene the women's spirituality group. Once a month, fifteen or twenty of us gathered to read something, to swap stories, and to eat Linda's incomparable double chocolate brownies. Then I started tutoring seminarians who were having trouble writing papers in systematic theology or in church music or church history. Every time I turned around, there was something new.

But I was increasing uncomfortable with my new role in the community: this was too much, too fast. My scholarly expertise was getting much too far ahead of my viscera, which were still painfully ambivalent about the whole God business. I was increasingly leery of that voice. The more I engaged of Scripture— whether at Mass or on my own—the more alert and sensitive I became to the Bible's metaphoric mapping of spiritual experience or at least certain parts of the interior terrain of consciousness. And doing so only made the whole book that much more dangerously powerful. It made no sense for me to be teaching when I needed to be learning, to be leading when I ached so for some guidance. But nothing about God had ever accorded with my sense of good sense and common rationality. God seemed transparently crazy, and this job was just more of God's inexplicable craziness.

So although the work itself was seductive fun, I still knew that I was on dangerous ground. When Ken hired himself a curate with very impressive teaching credentials, I proposed that this was an appropriate and graceful moment for me to resign from what had never been officially sanctioned by the vestry in the first place. The new curate could take over the Heretics' Forum, the baptism classes, and everything else into which I had been drawn. I was rapidly developing a major pastoral and administrative role in the parish, I explained, and it seemed to me unprofessional to let such roles proliferate outside of ordinary chains of command and accountability. Either let me out of this, I said, or vote properly to give me a formal half-time position.

The senior warden, a periodic presence in the Forum, could not have been more gracious. She looked over my resume, a report I had written on adult spirituality programs, and a proposed job description.

"You're right," she concluded. "You'd be crazy to volunteer for this. Nobody volunteers this kind of expertise. Either the curate should do it, or you need a contract." And the vestry voted, and I found myself formally on staff. I also found myself in equal measure delighted and dismayed.

But Ken continued to pursue me with engaging arguments about Scripture. And the senior warden—officially in charge of the parish during this interim—always kept in touch thereafter, always quick to hand on some praise she had heard, to offer her own discerning appreciation, or to affirm the vestry's support of my work. As the search process began to narrow the list of rector candidates, she took to reassuring me twice a month that all the candidates were being told that the curate and I were to be kept in place, that working with us was a condition of the job.

So maybe I was confused, but I was having so much fun I managed to ignore my concerns except occasionally, in the dark of the night when I would watch the shadows cast by the moon and the Austrian pine outside the bedroom window. I would watch and wonder a while, and then decide to let things play out a bit further.

Between Ken and the senior warden, something deep within me began to relax, to warm up, to stretch and grow and move freely for the very first time. I had no name for this, whatever it was, for it was all happening at the far liminal edge of consciousness. But it sure felt great.

Spots of Time

Meanwhile, listening to people in the parish was beginning to demonstrate that the questions and doubts and needs haunting my life were the classic spiritual issues. No one seemed to find my life intolerable, least of all me: as the kids headed into puberty, my role at home was transparently vital. Even in my most self-critical moments, I could no longer doubt the decision to put them first and the sacrifices that decision had entailed. But neither did I think about the choice as much as I had once. For me and for the friends I was making at church, the defensive, judgmental tensions of the

'70s and '80s seemed faded now into a common desire to look more closely at our own lives and their meanings: at forty-something, all of us had greying hair and more accepting souls than we had ever had. Even Anna Quindlen, after all, had eventually resigned from the *New York Times* to have more time home with her kids.

In the Heretics' Forum, folks began to share accounts of their own moments of extraordinary spiritual clarity, those inexplicable brief or visionary glimpses in which the world makes sense and our place in it feel both clear and right. As one man put it, "There's more to life than 'He who dies with the most toys wins.'" We spent eight weeks struggling with folks' accounts and understandings of such experiences, experiences that Wordsworth calls "spots of time."

To evoke and sustain such sharing, I told them at least something about William James's *The Varieties of Religious Experience,* about Rudolph Otto's *The Idea of the Holy.* But mostly I told stories. I told them stories from *The Prelude* and from the greater Romantic lyrics, from Dante, Milton, Homer, Shakespeare, Donne, Wallace Stevens. I recited snide snippets of Blake, favorite lines from Tennyson, Hardy, T. S. Eliot, Emily Dickinson, Walt Whitman—all sorts of poets. (Once I even brought in the song of Jonah while he is in the whale, which is some of my favorite biblical poetry—but I was told firmly that Bible Study was the class down the hall. They didn't want Bible from me.) Week after week, it took no more than seven or eight minutes to launch a discussion that sustained itself for the following hour.

But then I insisted that such lucid moments were prayer, and the place erupted. Arguments launched out for yet another eight weeks. I asked what kind of God, what kind of theology, is adequate to these experiences, and off they went yet again. It had been incredible. I would go into Mass afterwards shaking and repeatedly bewildered by how much we are all alike, how deeply common our inner landscapes. Maybe I was fey, as the Irish call it. But so are we all, at least once in a while. Otherwise, I was probably as rock-solid sane as a normal woman can be in these crazy times.

"But is this heresy?" they wanted to know. Haunted still by my recent experience teaching, one Sunday I offered a thoroughly

Blakean and visionary account of orthodox Christian doctrine. Yep, I said. All this is as orthodox as can be. Jesus was a visionary too. These moments, I explained, these incredible coherent moments

> *In which the burthen of the mystery,*
> *In which the heavy and the weary weight*
> *Of all this unintelligible world*
> *Is lightened . . .*

These moments in which we can see "infinity in a grain of sand, eternity in an hour"—these are what Christians mean by "the kingdom of God." At such moments we realize that God is as Coleridge claims:

> *. . . The one Life within us and abroad,*
> *Which meets all motion and becomes its soul,*
> *A light in sound, a sound-like power in light,*
> *Rhythm in all thought, and joyance every where—*
> *Methinks, it should have been impossible*
> *Not to love all things in a world so fill'd;*
> *Where the breeze warbles, and the mute still air*
> *Is Music slumbering on her instrument.*

If life is eternal, I argued, if we are promised eternal life, then it has already begun. The new heaven and the new earth are, more precisely, a new heaven *in* a new earth: God with us, here and now, if we dare to admit, to take seriously our own encounters with the numinous or the holy or the transcendent. These disruptive moments are the very most real of moments. They are our most powerful insights. The question is whether we have the courage to take them seriously.

"Look," I said to them, returning at last to the *Biographia*. "This could not be more obviously true without reducing itself to triviality." I closed my folder of notes and I looked at them. They looked at me—or seemed to. No one seemed to be much oriented to the literal setting, to fifteen people sitting around on the ugly flowered sofas of a church parlor. I sat back into the unreasonable depths of the sofa, my blouse stuck between my shoulder blades. A law professor turned to me abruptly, a tough and aggressive character speaking as aggressively as I had ever known her to speak.

"'The weary weight of all this unintelligible world,'" she snapped. "Who said that? Who?"

"Wordsworth," I told her. She sat back, wrapping her silent thoughts around her like a dark hooded cloak. A pink-cheeked Scotsman chuckled, a passionate and almost red-headed man who was, by the look of him, as Celtic as I.

"I don't know about you," he said, sitting back. "I'm never much sure about *you*, Kate. And until recently I never thought I understood poetry. Or liked it. I'm a chemist. But Wordsworth: him I like. He's got it right." He looked around at the group for affirmation; discussion took off from there.

I felt as if I'd finally made amends for that day with my Milton students.

The Feast of John Chrysostom

Shortly thereafter, my birthday fell on a Saturday. Mom and I went to Mass together before going out for a celebratory brunch. We don't ordinarily go to Mass together like that, but I was feeling overwhelmed by what I was seeing in the parish and what I was feeling about all of it. Maybe it would indeed be wise to spend thirty minutes wondering about where I was headed. Perhaps, I was beginning to think, perhaps my life is not entirely my own work—or even my own to work with.

Maybe I was asking all the wrong questions in trying to figure out what was meant by "the conflict is over." Maybe answers only begin to come when we begin giving up the pretense that we know what questions to ask. As any teacher knows, after all, she who has the power to ask questions defines the universe of possible answers. Maybe I didn't know enough even to recognize my own ignorance. Maybe I should stop asking questions altogether and just listen. It was a disconcerting possibility for a self-respecting intellectual. But this was February of 1992: whatever this was had been going on for more than three years now. For a conflict said to be "over," it was sure taking its own sweet time. It just seemed to get more and more complicated as the months went by.

Mass on the morning of my birthday turned into my own little spot of time. John of Matha in mind, I was intrigued to note that we were to keep the feast of John Chrysostom, a fourth-century bishop famous for his verbal skills. But something in me flinched as I recognized the first reading. It was the call from God to the prophet Jeremiah. In this first chapter Jeremiah speaks prose, but God speaks poetry.

> *Now the word of the Lord came to me, saying*
> "Before I formed you in the womb I knew you,
> and before you were born I consecrated you;
> I appointed you a prophet to the nations."
> *Then I said,* "Ah, Lord God! Behold, I do not know how to speak, for I am only a youth." *But the Lord said to me,*
> "Do not say, 'I am only a youth';
> for to whom I send you you shall go,
> and whatever I command you you shall speak.
> Be not afraid of them,
> for I am with you to deliver you, says the Lord."
> *Then the Lord put forth his hand and touched my mouth; and the Lord said to me,*
> "Behold, I have put my words in your mouth . . ."

I don't remember the other two readings, nor have I ever dared to look them up. Words in my mouth. Like Moses. Like trying to teach that class on Moses, and being unable to speak—as Zechariah had been unable to speak, Zechariah the father of John the Baptist—until I admitted that this finding of words is my particular path to recognizing that I exist, that we all exist, in relation to the Holy. I was being told, on my birthday of all days, that God "knew" me—intimately, passionately, possessively—even before I was born. Surely this is what God had been saying to me all this time. It was not "Look at this" but "Here it is again."

This is, after all, what it means to be a writer. Not just to find words in your mouth, to find in some complex neuronal database the vocabulary or the poetry you filed away there previously. To be a writer is to find words and to feel them not as database retrieval but as gift. In the parallel call of Isaiah, as in countless psalms and other poems, we are told that these found words are as sweet as honey fresh from the honeycomb. Whether the words themselves are the gift or rather my sweet delight in finding them—that's more than I can say. But it does not matter to me, it has never mattered, whether they are my words or Milton's or anyone else's. Moses had Aaron, the story goes, to help him find words. I have English literature. What matters is not where we find the words, but rather that they be the right words, the necessary words, to say what needs saying and to keep silence on the rest.

As we walked out, my mother stopped in the church doorway, blocking the exit of the small Saturday congregation. She waved her finger at me, peremptorily. She had turned and stopped so abruptly that her finger almost brushed my lips.

"Did you hear that? Did you? *Before you were born I consecrated you? Appointed you?* That's true. That is true! In your mother's womb!"

She stopped, startled. She stared at her finger and put it down, and then she looked at me with confusion on her face. And then she blinked once or twice and turned ahead of me down the walk. I watched her for a moment, until someone trapped behind me in the narrow doorway coughed politely.

And we went out to breakfast, Mom and I, and she gossiped in the ordinary ways about friends and family. And neither of us said a word about Jeremiah.

How Dreary to Be Somebody

All weekend long, every time I tried to think about that reading from Jeremiah, I heard the song about Jeremiah the bullfrog, as recorded by Three Dog Night. I didn't understand. I stared out the window for hours on end, struggling and failing to translate the poetic and visionary invitation into something I could understand, something I could locate and evaluate and respond to within the ordinary boundaries of commonsense life. But I couldn't.

All I could manage, finally, was to remember Emily Dickinson's poem on frogs, "I'm Nobody! Who are you?" "How dreary—to be—

Somebody!" she points out. I laughed, as I had at Three Dog Night; but it didn't help. I did not understand. I did not understand, and yet I was deeply moved, and therefore I was both engaged and repelled, both drawn and withdrawing, frozen in amazement and in terror like some small creature startled by the shadow of a hawk.

And it didn't help—it didn't help at all—that one can almost sing the Dickinson lyric to the rock tune, and thus I kept hearing it. Dickinson's poetry is written to the prosodic structures of traditional church hymns, prosodic structures that persist in both folk and rock music. You can find a familiar tune to which to sing any of her poetry, if you know enough prosody. And enough popular music. It's one of those facts that go to prove that ignorance can indeed be bliss. The fit wasn't perfect, but that fact didn't silence the cacophony.

But something else was beginning to stir in me, some resolution of the conflict between Emily Dickinson and Three Dog Night. I sat quietly for a long time, watching the squirrels skidding in the icy snow of the backyard, waiting as I had waited hundreds of times before for an elusive allusion, a half-heard line of poetry, or some other variety of the right words to drift high enough into consciousness for me to hear distinctly.

Another short and flippant song started vibrating deep in my throat, like a radio muted by a wall, like a broadcast coming from too far away to be heard without distortion and static. I sat there, feeling the hum of vibration in my throat and wondering what it was that I was struggling so to sing. And then at last I heard the tune and just a moment later I remembered the words—another frog song, this one recorded by Peter Paul and Mary, "I'm in Love with a Big Blue Frog." I got out of my chair and turned away from the window. If the angel of the Lord had appeared unto me that day, I'd have slugged him.

But I could not deny the energy and depth of my own delight. From all too early an age, I knew that feeling of unsought, unexpected words in my mouth. And if or when I spoke them, people would stare. And sometimes get mad. The hazards were not manageable until I realized that poetry is the work of unsought words, words unsought but waited for, pages blank and tense with the waiting. What I needed to do with such words, I had realized, was to write. And so I had written, and from within the experience of all that writing I began at last to read others' poetry with growing skill and delicate care.

Now it was as if God had finally cornered me, had finally gotten me to credit and to take credit for the truths revealed not in doctrine but in poetry, not in the institutional and bureaucratic church but in the midst of life and in the forms of art. My life. My life and my art, my life here at home with kids and poetry and blank paper purchased several reams at a time.

Unforgotten Dreams and Persistent Desires

Changing the Rector's Forum into the Heretics' Forum was catchy, all right—I was snagging increasing numbers of the forty-somethings who had been undergraduates in the sixties, baby boomers now going grey and thick about the middle. As a cohort, we spent years playing the perpetually critical and perpetually superior outsider: it's always more fun to criticize the status quo in witty ways than to take a real stand in the real world, with all the gritty compromises and practicalities that will demand. But middle age was bringing to all of us enough natural authority that we could no longer sustain that youthful insouciance quite so convincingly.

"Look at us!" one of the guys said one week. "Fat cats! We were going to change the world. Remember that? And look. So what the hell happened?"

No one had an answer. The question hung in midair as we faced one another. We knew. All of us knew. We had sacrificed everything, it seemed on bad days, we had spent our lives and our energies in the pursuit of stuff we said we never wanted in the first place, in the service of material values we had always denied. I let the silence collect for a while, until everyone heard it and felt it clearly, until enough of compassion had been collected and passed around and slowly everyone's eyes had turned to me.

The lines that had floated up this time were Paul Simon's, the lyric he calls "American Tune." I sang a few lines from the first stanza. "What about it?" I asked. "What did we want for ourselves, when we grew up? Maybe Simon is right. I bet he is. I bet we all have shards of old dreams hiding someplace in our souls."

The stories that people told were ordinary stories about the ordinary suffering that comes into all of our lives. But they were also extraordinary revelations from people who were apparently so successful and prosperous and even eminent. Indeed Simon was right. Broken dreams and broken hearts are part of everyone's life.

Under such pressure, the hour seemed to evaporate. I didn't usually provide closure, because there is something so artificial and ultimately controlling about such tidiness. But everyone seemed to be in far too much pain just to walk out in the usual way. So I went back to the song.

Our dreams, Simon insists, are either lost or driven to their knees. But are those alternatives parallel or opposite? What happens to those driven to their knees? Is that humiliation and defeat? Or prayer? In the death of our dreams, he suggests, we can have yet another dream, a dream of rising unexpectedly, of reassurances somehow more potent than the departing or departed Statue of Liberty.

"Furthermore," I concluded, "something has gotten all of us up off our knees and on with our lives. Something." We sat for a moment in silence, then filed out down the hall and into church.

Visions and Revisions

At home after Mass, I stretched out on the sofa and listened to the Simon lyric over and over again on the stereo. The speaker keeps turning away from what he understands to be the truth about his own life. Simon as poet clearly portrays that as a failure of nerve, as a failure to inherit the courage of those who first sailed across uncertain seas to strange new worlds. Maybe I fell asleep on the sofa. I'm not sure. But whether in dream or just in memory, I remembered and relived what had been an entirely real event.

I remembered a time, very early on a summer morning, probably after taking Warren to the six o'clock train. I was standing stock still on the patch of grass encircled by the circular drive, standing there long enough for the morning dew to have soaked into my sneakers.

I had parked on the street, for some reason, not on the driveway. Maybe the car was leaking oil again? Obviously I had been walking across the grass toward the house when I stopped. What drew me back into ordinary reality was the lady across the street. She was walking her dog; she stared at me hard enough to call me back. She wondered what I was looking at.

What was I looking at? I couldn't begin to tell her. I don't remember whether I answered her question at all. I had been, I had been . . . someplace else. Me, God, my reading and writing: together somehow, all of us invisible and in midair. Not my writing for the books-on-tape outfit, for medical journals, for educational publishers, for chemical companies and architecture firms. Not that work. Not even my scholarly writing. No. Not that, not that at all. *My* writing, in my own voice, for my own reasons and not for tenure, stories and poems, tales and tirades that I had always written and always left to accumulate in heedless heaps.

Here was a solution. *This* writing could keep my soul together, here at home with kids and laundry and weeding to do. It wouldn't pay; in all probability nobody would ever know or notice. I'm not Milton: I'm just a wordsmith. I write to hammer the wrinkles out of my soul, to heat something white-hot and shape it and burnish it and let its beauty sing upon a golden bough—whether or not anyone else will ever hear it . This would feed in me what I needed to keep the kids fed. If I dare. If I dare. If I dare to turn, to descend that stair, to defy the observers who would stare and say, "Such a scholar, come to this: only a housewife, dependent on her husband, home with her kids and no life of her own."

I had considered the offer for long enough to taste it, to taste the sweetness there. And then I had turned away. The gods are crazy, I had thought. How completely impossible. Of all the crazy possibilities that I'd ever considered, I'd never stopped for a minute to consider that. Lord, no. That would be too wonderful for words. But it's impossible.

And at that very instant my neighbor had called my name and asked, "What are you doing there?" Why was I standing in the dew-laden grass as if waiting for something that never came?

I remembered shrugging as I smiled at the lady across the street, touching one hand to my temple and gesturing outwards, lightly, laughing, as if to say, *I'm a little fey today; don't worry about me.*

She had laughed and waved and walked on with her dog, that big unruly dog who jumped on everybody.

The Lady, Yet Again

The Lady Behind the Desk appeared that night, this time in a dream. In the dream I'm halfway along the upstairs hallway, walking away from the top of the stairs and toward the door to my study ahead on my right. I'm next to the railing that surrounds the open stairwell.

Suddenly my way is blocked by the Lady and her oaken desk. The desk extends through the railing around the stairs, the right corner floating in the open air of the stairwell. I glance at the Lady, but mostly I'm stunned by how her desk floats through the railing and over the stairs. I'm a bit puzzled by her, but thoroughly astounded by how her big desk has appeared up here, athwart the hallway to my study. Actually, I've been so puzzled by this woman for so many years that I've just about given up wondering about her. Her mysterious furniture blocking my path feels close to outrageous.

I move my gaze away from the free-floating corner of her desk and toward her face, yearning for an explanation that I just know I'll never get. Our eyes meet. After all these puzzling years, I have nothing to say, nothing to feel. Here we are again, she and I, and I will never understand.

I am stunned to recognize that she is me. I've seen her face in such brief, embarrassed glimpses before; before this, I've mostly wondered about what awaits me in that mysterious workplace off to the far right of her desk. I've never really *seen* her face like this before. I was never really thinking about her, but about how she controlled access to the right job.

But she is me, myself, now grey-haired and familiar with how the world works, now almost twenty years older than I had been on that afternoon in Ann Arbor. We stare at one another, amused and recognizant, in full possession of all the memories and struggles and questions we share. That was *me,* that unexpected access to a job that would reward all my hard work. That was *me,* praying that I would show up and calling me an answer to prayer when I turned to myself to find the right kind of work. Me. She was me all along. *I'm* who I've been looking for, not a job.

In the dream, I have no idea what to think, what to do or to say next. Something feels so obvious, so gloriously self-evident. But something also feels unbearably inexplicable, deeply, dangerously mysterious, an uncanny glimpse of realities one cannot see and yet live. The Lady is not merely me; that much is certain. Like the law of commutation, she is a metaphor, an apparent equation between incommensurables.

Nonetheless I look me in the eye, feeling the soul-shaking gulf between what I know and what I know I will one day die without understanding in the least. We understand that too, me and I, there in the hallway: how futile my every effort to understand.

The Lady stands up and moves toward me right through the desk, which ripples around her as she passes. And as she comes she lifts her arms as if to embrace me, her face—my face—transfused with the light of an unbearable love.

I awakened. I awakened in the ordinary dark of an ordinary night in my ordinary bed, recoiling as if from an illusion that had come to steal my soul. I almost wanted to run out into the hall to see if she was still there. I lay awake for an instant, staring at the shadows cast by the moon shining through the windows, the familiar rippled shadows of the ruffles on the cafe curtains. What was this transcendent terror?

But I could neither think nor move. I realized, from the deep, slow, undisturbed rhythm of my breathing, that I was only barely awake. If I closed my eyes, I would be back in the hall again. I almost managed to struggle to find myself within this sleeping body, to reconnect to the hand that lay under the side of my face. But then soft darkness folded over me, and I subsided within it.

I looked into my own eyes, bright and brimming with tears, and lifted my arms in return of embrace, a warm and tearful and enveloping embrace, an embrace at long last, there in the hall by the top of the stairs. And I knew, I could feel without even looking, that the way to my study was no longer blocked. I had found my way at last, at long last, to the place and the work I had finally prayed to find. My gifts—my wordcraft and all these deep unruly passions—were for me, for me to relish and to delight in, gifts given me for the delight of them and not as gold I had to spend in order to survive. They were an invitation to the feast and not the price of admission.

August 1992

But I awakened in the morning to another day. And to another day after that: yet another rosy-fingered dawn on the wine-dark sea. Day after day there came another day, the endless unbroken series of moments in exactly the life I had had before, chaos still slopping in over the gunwales. Were there really time and energy for my own work, there would have been time for a real career. There was not. What good were such visions? I tried to reduce it to nothing more than self-esteem, but that only brought the uncanny to boldface terror once again. No: whoever she was, damn her anyhow, would not be reduced to just that. At most, I supposed, I had been deeply warned that I was what stood in my way. But how many generations of talented women had lamented the all too real burdens of *kinder und kuche?* Good enough to say "the conflict is over"—but who then will do the work that mothers do? However reluctant I once had been to acknowledge the importance of what mothers can provide to children, I was both too observant and too rigorous a thinker to deny it at this point.

Dream-visions do not change anything. I had always known that. Failure to grasp that point is probably what distinguishes psychotics from poets and visionaries, who cut their hands over and over on the sharp edges of dangerous insight. Visions are glimpses that come in disguise, glimpses of possibilities that do not come about unless we find some ordinary way to make them real. I found myself glaring angrily down the hall toward my study, into which I had not stepped in several days. Her and her desk! And me and my dreams, as far out of reach as ever.

Nor did I understand how the vision might accord with my position at church. The pressure of offering so much pastoral counsel and leading both the women's group and the Heretics' Forum had released a torrent of poetry, commonly hundreds of lines each month, and dozens of pages of highly polished prose, fragmentary pieces of a book I hoped to write some day. It would be my own variation upon *Biographia Literaria,* something like a fine post-postmodern "proof" of this uncanny God and a visionary version of the unscrupulous wit that constitutes "God's ways to man." But after a whole year of such productivity, I found myself at the far dangerous edge of exhaustion. I knew I needed, somehow or other, to set a less manic pace in the upcoming year.

But was there a connection between the church work and all this writing? I didn't know; I couldn't tell. I certainly enjoyed both the recognition of my talents and above all the trust and affection with which I was regarded. For the very first time, I felt that I securely belonged to some group larger than my own household. I fit in. I was wanted. It did seem probable that this astounding creative output had its origins in that emotional or psychological security, but it was all much too recent to see clearly. Sorting it out would take time.

My role in the parish was dramatically evident that August. The interim rector had departed in April, leaving the newly ordained curate in sole charge of the place. And then the exhausted curate had taken August off. And then the curate's vacation replacement had himself abruptly departed to bury his mother and attend to her estate. Someone always showed up to say Mass, but the parish as a whole seemed caught in a communal abandonment crisis—in which they turned to me.

In the absence of a familiar priest at the door as they left, people kept coming up to shake hands with me as I stood on the lawn drinking lemonade and gossiping along with everyone else. Any time I looked up, there seemed to be a queue of three or four people "waiting for a word," as folks said when I was a child. People whose names I could not remember, people whose faces I barely recognized, took me aside to confide one or another problem afflicting them that week. One such man took my arm, steered me firmly around the big yew hedge, and gave way to tears.

The crowning moment came when one of the elderly ruling cohort of the Altar Guild cut into the line of people waiting for a word to check with me about something. I demurred. The Guild women knew what they were doing, I insisted, and everyone felt very reassured by their expertise. Women like us had always kept parishes going. Clergy come and go, but the church is the people like us. Everyone knows that. She should do whatever she thought best.

"Well, that's what I thought you'd say!" she snapped, and marched back into the sacristy. I could almost taste apple cider vinegar in the warm August air. But I was delighted. These women were exquisitely attuned to the many-layered discourses of power in the congregation, and I had just been offered a highly encoded encomium, disguised of course inside a test as subtle as any I'd ever taken. And I had passed.

Life at home was no less complicated. Weeds sprouted eagerly as the nights began to cool off, but there were back-to-school sales to which I had to drag reluctant kids—who had also grown like weeds all summer. Three pairs of sneakers. Nine pairs of jeans. Six sets of sweats. Six new gym uniforms. More packages of socks than I could carry to the counter at one time. Utterly endless hunting for acceptable tee shirts. Folders and binders and spiral-bound notebooks, Elmer's glue, tempera paints, looseleaf paper, number 2 pencils by the score. Red pens and blue pens and pink pearl erasers. Hundreds of dollars in book rental fees and lab fees and bus fees. Money poured through my hands like water, and we were not even shopping yet for new winter coats and new boots. I began to think seriously that I needed to reconsider writing audio scripts. My pre-tax salary at church was $830 a month, but I could earn $1500 in two or three days writing business book audio scripts. Corporate communications consulting paid even better, especially now that E-mail was putting executive illiteracy more or less on public display. Teaching at church was fun, but it didn't pay the bills.

As if on cue, the phone began to ring. The American Medical Writers Association called, asking me to lead another workshop at the upcoming annual meeting. Two years of desultory conversations and incomprehensible corporate politics suddenly resolved into an unexpected invitation to sign a retainer for three years of part-time work teaching real rocket scientists how to write technical reports.

An article in the business section said that routine internal audits at a certain company had uncovered embezzlers. I'd worked for the vice president for accounting—I bet she was proud of her staff! For a moment I remembered the soccer player's dad and his SEC reports, and that cocky young auditor whose dangling participles and errors of agreement drove his boss to distraction. Maybe I should call, congratulate the VP, renew the acquaintance?

Or maybe, I pondered, maybe I should stall everyone until my future at church was clearer, or at least until my intuitions had had a chance to sort themselves out. In June, the incoming rector had written to all of the staff, refusing his canonical authority to dismiss us, explaining his hopes for mutual ministry and joint discernment and regular staff retreats—and sending each of us a copy of *Resident Aliens*. I'd never read Hauerwas and Willimon before, and I was extremely impressed both with their devastating wit and with their argument that churches should confront an exploitative, consumerist culture by helping people to develop both the insight and the courage that integrity demands. Maybe, I thought, maybe I need again to find the courage to let my engagement with the parish spin out just a bit further.

And, I realized with deep and sudden anger, maybe I needed to give The Lady Behind the Desk half a chance to prove herself right after all. And so, feeling courageous—or at least impetuous—I called the rocket scientists and the medical writers, politely declining. One way or another, the kids would never go without sneakers: Warren provided. That dependency had bothered me at first; but he depended on me too, in other ways. We had learned each to trust the other's generosity. Money could not cloak the harder questions.

Dancing

One sultry day late in August I rode home through heavy traffic with the sun in my eyes and murder in my heart. My old car was unbearably hot, its air conditioner defunct. I was so hungry I had a headache, but dinner would be late because I had no idea what to fix. I had gone out at the last minute to run some stupid errand that I had meant to do first thing that morning—but I had had one of those days in which interruptions had layered upon interruptions, priorities had been trashed by competing priorities. I had floundered from one petty task to another all day long. I had not gotten into my study to write, but neither had I done anything fun with the kids—an important obligation, in these waning days of summer vacation.

And with sudden illumination I realized: I can't do this. I'm not lazy, I realized; it's not that I am inept at juggling; it's not that I cannot adjudicate competing demands intelligently. There simply is no such ideal balance point, no compromise arrangement whereby all needs are met simultaneously at some just and reasonable and satisfactory level. There are not hours enough in the day for that, not days enough in the week.

Life is not the vaudeville routine in which a man sets a plate spinning on a stick, and then another plate, until he has a whole row of spinning plates that the audience knows will eventually go smash. If life is a series of spinning plates, then I cannot keep my life from going smash.

But the chaos around me is not, in fact, the sound of my life going smash. Nor do I face the prospect of standing in some final defeat, surrounded by shards, while an invisible audience applauds sarcastically. That's not the right image for how my life works.

Life is not a problem in management. Life is a work of art. The pull of all these competing demands is not a problem. It is prerequisite for the art, as the pull of gravity is requisite for dance. Of course I "fail" to be all of me all of the time, because all of me is too much for any one moment to encompass. So yes, I have to fail, to fall, to fall with some sense of grace, day after day, each day differently. In those moments of grace, I can glimpse for a visionary moment by just how much we exceed the limits of our own space-and-time mortality. We cannot do it all, we cannot have it all, within any immediate, limited span of time.

To walk, after all, is to fall in controlled ways. And to dance? Well then, surely to dance is to fall in ways not so much controlled as imaginative, gracious with a grace that comes from the very act of recognizing and shaping the moment-to-moment possibilities of response to the laws of gravity and of motion. The stars in their heavens and me with all my crazy, star-crossed dreams: the whole universe can do nothing better than to fall and to spin graciously, beautifully, in the most sacred of all sacred dance. Even God is dance: the Greek fathers described God's self-awareness, God's relationship to all the creative abundance of God, as *perichoresis*—dancing around.

Relief blew over me like a cool dry breeze, like miraculous repair to the long-defunct compressor. The conflict was ending, right here at a stoplight on Glenview Road with the sun in my eyes. I watched myself, dumbfounded, as the facts arrayed themselves politely but firmly in my mind. The conflict had never been between my needs and the kids' needs, real though that clash can be at times. Nor was it between me and those who judged my scholarship insufficient or my life at home an intolerable waste, despite how deeply those judgments had hurt me. No. The enduring conflict, the inescapable judgments, were entirely inward: I was the one I could never satisfy. And that dissatisfaction interfered far more than housework.

In seeing that truth, I was free at last to see a further truth: what had fueled the conflict was my own passionate vision of perfectly realized grace. In my most visionary moments, I can almost imagine what it might mean to be fully human. Of course I fail to achieve all that I can thus imagine. But that does not discredit what a blessing it is to imagine like this.

Despite the occasional failures of our dreams, we are given the unreasonable grace to keep dreaming, to turn all that falling and failing into dance. We rise again, morning after morning after morning, no matter how dark the night. In every hour of every day, I cannot be who I am: I can't make that identity fit within the narrow limits of space and time. Neither can I abandon that identity, any more than I can abandon my left wrist when my arthritis flares. And surely this is the human predicament, and surely it is possible to live within this predicament joyously.

The tension between stasis and falling, after all, is the domain of dance. The tension between death and living is the art of the impossible rendered not possible but rather gracious and holy. Only with such grace dare I accept the heartbreaking beauty of the parts as parts, the glory of the present moment, the present piece of my life as it unfolds before me and within me. And only from within that sanctuary dare I envision what greater beauty there can be in the whole that remains, most of the time, available only in momentary glimpses, only in the elusive and potent spots of time.

Good enough, God, I thought: it's a deal. And it was, for that blinding moment, until the guy behind me blew his horn, that I was dancing with God. And in the brilliance of that passionate embrace I could dance as angels dance.

EPILOGUE
Another Leap

On Tuesday of the first week in October, the new rector called me into his office, ostensibly to discuss adult education programs. "Before we start," he said, sitting a bit straighter in his armchair, "there is something you should know. The vestry voted last night to make you a volunteer: the salary for your position will be discontinued at the end of December. I know that means you won't be able to do quite as much. But let's begin with a list of what you can continue to do as a volunteer."

I thought about that for a minute, lost in a blank intermediate distance. "I can't," I said, returning to space and time, and I looked at him.

He startled and sat up very straight. "What? The Heretics' Forum? The women's group? Surely the women's group. You can't possibly leave the Forum! All your friends! Think of what you have done in there!"

"I am." I continued to meet his eyes squarely. "That's the point."

We talked. We talked that day and at least a couple of times in the six weeks thereafter, words wasted, squandered, unable to bridge the jagged canyons that can so unexpectedly disrupt the landscape of rational discourse and expectation. I understood, at last, that I did not understand. And neither did he. I suspect we agree on that even now. Incomprehension stood between us, taunting the pretense that we can say just what we mean and nothing more.

The following day, Wednesday in that first week of October, I let myself into his office at 6:30 A.M. I left my keys and my resignation, effective immediately, sitting in the middle of his desk. I thought I was right to expect at least the simple honesty of being plainly fired, rather than made a volunteer by vote of vestry. I supposed it was even reasonable to expect the dignity of a quietly professional request for my resignation, to be followed by some little note of thanks in the parish newsletter. They were presumptuous; I am proud. That's not a good mix. I let myself out the doors that locked behind me and stood for a moment in the long shadows of early morning, wondering what would happen next, wondering whether doors were locked indeed. I checked again: yep, locked.

And I found myself overwhelmed by memories of my exit interview with the dean ten years earlier. The dean had begun by reading to me from the formal Tenure and Promotions report, which warmly praised the depth, range, and maturity of my scholarship and my exemplary record of teaching awards and collegial service. He went on to acknowledge his personal judgment that I had completed and seen through publication a most impressive and quite well-received book that he thought would have taken a mature scholar ten years to do—and this in five years, while beginning my teaching career and giving birth to three children. And so he was puzzled that I seemed to be a somewhat controversial figure in the college. This was supposed to explain why he was denying tenure. A decade later, I still did not understand that situation either.

By the end of November, it was clear that we needed to leave the congregation altogether. I might resign from a particular staff position, but there was no way to resign the leadership that the community had vested in me. The phone had begun to ring incessantly: as Warren put it, I had been elected "opposition leader." That was not a role I wanted. I did not come to church to get embroiled in some updated version of the parish politics endlessly recounted in nineteenth-century British novels. And I had lived all too much of my life, all too successfully, without going to church.

Our last Sunday in church was the last Sunday of Ordinary Time, that green-ribbon season of hope that ends when Advent begins, just after Thanksgiving. I had first come to this church four years earlier, on the first Sunday of Advent in 1988. Somehow it felt much longer than that.

On this last ordinary Sunday, the first reading was from Jeremiah: "Woe to the shepherds who destroy and scatter the sheep of my pasture, says the Lord." Yep, I thought: that's why I'm leaving. It would be wrong to stay and futile besides. Or was he the shepherd, I the destroyed or scattered one? I thought about that for just a minute: not a chance, I realized. Not a chance. I was refusing to fight, not running away. The psalm was no less eloquently comforting, no less pointed in its judgment:

*There is a river whose streams
make glad the city of God,
the holy habitation of the Most High.
God is in the midst of her
she shall not be overthrown;
God shall help her at the break of day.*

The lines wrapped themselves around me like hands, as hands might enfold a yellow duckling. I rested for a moment within the lines, both the hands and the duckling at once, held and holding and safe. I would be okay. This would work out okay.

I closed my eyes and saw the sacred river Alph, five miles meandering from some mysterious source high and inward. And then it was the Huron River, silver and swift, deep and clear and looping in long erotic curves at the bottom of the familiar cliffs. And I was in the midst of the river like that brave little mallard, like a tiny merganser with a bold red crest upon its proud head, like the play of light upon a thousand small ripples, dancing and beautiful, making glad the city of God into which I had flowed from God only knew where, flowing onward both as blessing and as blessed, dark and silent in the night but at the break of day glorious, wearing the wildflowers of the floodplain like a garment, embroidered grass fragrant in the mist.

And I opened my eyes to look around at these people I had loved and trusted, at the oaken reredos, at the vibrant royal blues of the stained glass windows, at the familiar faces of the choir, at what I had gained and what I had lost. I leaned back hard against those strong hands.

And I did not receive communion.

I spent the next week cleaning out my hard drive: printing copies, deleting files and directories, and, in general, scrolling through the literary remains of a most unlikely adventure. I stashed the whole amorphous unsorted heap of photocopies, notes, and manuscripts into the back of a drawer full of old academic files. Then I hauled from the closet the big cardboard carton into which I had been tossing journals and poems and prose fragments for more than ten years. At the bottom, I knew, there were the earliest volumes of my journals—spiral notebooks going back thirty years, to my early teens. The carton was waist high and much too heavy to lift: I had to drag it, and as I did so one cardboard flap tore off in my hands. The sound echoed my feelings precisely. In a despondent and desultory way, I tried sorting through the box. But I had never felt so baffled, so blind, and yet so implacably determined. Like the editor of Diogenes Teufelsdrockh, I could make no sense of these scraps of a life. That would come in time, but not quickly.

I climbed over the piles of paper to go make myself a whole pot of tea. I sat in the living room, staring out the window, more or less praying, more or less hoping to hear that impossible voice and more or less determined never to listen to it again. But instead of the voice I heard, as if in the distance, the keening of funeral bagpipes. As I listened, the wailing slowly turned to words, Wendell Berry's words, a poem titled "A Grace" in which he says, "Though deaf, we dance . . ."

And then George Herbert, as if in reply: "He that liveth in hope dances without Musik."

Amen.

NOTES

Author's Note: In conformity with copyright laws and in compassion for curious readers, below are proper titles for the literary works I cite explicitly. Where I offer no more than the title of a poem, it is a text in the public domain that is also an anthology standard. *The Norton Anthology of English Literature* and *The Norton Anthology of Poetry* have all but a couple of them. Permission is not available, I have discovered, to quote even a few words from such popular-culture figures as Paul Simon or Bill Cosby or Kermit the Frog, so the range of citations is narrower than it might be. I have (with some reluctance) properly attributed to Keats lines of his that I grew up believing were my grandmother's; and I allow to pass without remark the echoes of traditional prayers, liturgies and creeds of Anglican or Roman Catholicism. Biblical citations, which are almost always identified in the text itself, are from the Revised Standard Version. I cannot imagine successfully unearthing all of my submerged literary and religious allusions, such as that on pages 25 and 26–27, above, to Julian of Norwich's famous line, "all shall be well, and all shall be well, and all manner of thing shall be well." Nor do I see much point in doing so. I note just a few that were either particularly important or adjacent to some explicit citation I had already stopped to document. As I have said, like other chronic readers I have a head full of voices, only some of which are truly and entirely my own. If I have missed something that you want identified, please write me in care of Morehouse Publishing.

P. 2 Paul Valéry, "Poetry and Abstract Thought," from *The Art of Poetry,* in *The Collected Words of Paul Valéry,* volume 7, ed. Jackson Matthews, trans. Denise Folliot (Princeton, NJ: Princeton University Press, 1960), pp. 70–71.

William Butler Yeats, "Among School Children," in *The Poems of W. B. Yeats: A New Edition,* ed. Richard J. Finneran (New York: The Macmillan Company, 1928).

Samuel Taylor Coleridge, *Biographia Literaria,* volume 1, ed. James Engell and W. Jackson Bate, *The Collected Works of Samuel Taylor Coleridge,* volume 7, Bollingen Series LXXV (Princeton, NJ: Princeton University Press, 1983), pp. 124–125.

13 Samuel Taylor Coleridge, "Dejection: An Ode" and then *Biographia Literaria,* ed. Engell and Bate, volume 1, p. 203.

"set upon a golden bough": see "Sailing to Byzantium," William Butler Yeats, *The Poems of W. B. Yeats: A New Edition,* ed. Richard J. Finneran (New York: The Macmillan Company, 1928). There is another, rather more submerged reference, on page 241, above.

"enough and more than enough": see William Blake, *The Marriage of Heaven and Hell,* plate 9.

28 William Blake, *The Marriage of Heaven and Hell,* plate 7.

55 John Keats, "Ode on a Grecian Urn" and "Endymion." I follow Jack Stillinger's punctuation of the famous concluding lines of the ode. See *The Poems of John Keats,* ed. Jack Stillinger (Cambridge, MA: The Belknap Press of Harvard University Press, 1978).

T. S. Eliot, "The Love Song of J. Alfred Prufrock" from *Collected Poems 1909–1962* (San Diego: Harcourt Brace Jovanovich, 1963), lines 97–98.

Andrew Marvell, "To His Coy Mistress." The most famous lines from this poem, of course, are these: "But at my back I always hear/ Time's wingèd chariot hurrying near."

56 Richard Lattimore, *The Odyssey of Homer: A Modern Translation* (New York: Harper Torchbooks of Harper and Row, Publishers, 1965, 1967), Book 5, lines 222–223, p. 94.

  Robert Fitzgerald, *The Iliad of Homer,* (Garden City, NY: Anchor Press/ Doubleday, 1974), Book 9, circa line 400 ff., p. 216.

57 William Wordsworth, "The World Is Too Much with Us." My essay in *Philological Quarterly* is in volume 59 (1980): 338–352. It testifies to how much more deeply I was already struggling with God than I recognized at the time. But the fact is that I didn't.

62 The biblical line I quote is approximately Deuteronomy 30:19—"life everlasting" is clearly a New Testament spin. My journals here are plainly inaccurate with regard to the text, but I have not corrected it (as I do, silently, elsewhere) because the inaccuracy tells a truth of its own about the issues I was engaging.

111 James Thurber, "The Unicorn in the Garden," from *Fables for Our Time,* reprinted in *The Thurber Carnival* (New York: Harper and Row, 1975), pp. 268–269.

121 Samuel Taylor Coleridge, "Dejection: An Ode."

128 William Shakespeare, Sonnet 29: "When in disgrace with fortune and men's eyes."

130 Emily Dickinson, "Because I could not stop for death", poem #712 from *The Poems of Emily Dickinson,* ed. Thomas H. Johnson (Cambridge, MA: The Belknap Press of Harvard University Press, 1983). A "trap" is also the name of a particular sort of small, light, horse-drawn vehicle.

  John Milton, "Paradise Lost," Book 1, lines 254–255.

  T. S. Eliot, "The Waste Land" from *Collected Poems 1909–1962* (San Diego: Harcourt Brace Jovanovich, 1963), lines 414–416.

  John Keats, "Ode to a Nightingale."

  William Blake, *The Marriage of Heaven and Hell,* plate 9.

131 Samuel Taylor Coleridge, "Dejection: An Ode."

140 William Wordsworth, "My Heart Leaps Up."

145 Alexander Pope, "An Essay on Criticism," lines 342–343.

  Dr. Johnson's dictum: The curious may look to Boswell's *Life of Johnson,* July 31, 1763, or to the sixteenth edition of *Bartlett's Familiar Quotations,* page 316, entry #3.

150 Sister Mary Robert's threat: a decade later I discovered that she was quoting the gospel according to Luke, chapter 12, verse 48, except that she made the pronoun referent plural rather than singular and therefore masculine/neuter. Which she really did. They all did. When I first read it for myself, the line in Luke jarred something awful. As I've said, I grew up under the care of nuns who were rich, subtle, complicated characters.

151 "the day will come": knowing my grandmother's verbal memory as I have bit by bit reconstructed it, this just about has to be the beginning of a quotation from some poem, hymn, traditional prayer, or Celtic (native Irish) proverb. If you can place it for me—or even finish the line from memory—please write me care of Morehouse: I've been hunting unsuccessfully for decades.

The Book of Common Prayer (1979), p. 372. This prayer is not always or necessarily said: it is one of several options.

152 William Ernest Henley, "Invictus."

164 Andrew Marvell, "To His Coy Mistress." Cf above, page 55 and below, page 199.

180 Oscar Wilde, "The Decay of Lying," reprinted in *Critical Theory Since Plato,* ed. Hazard Adams (New York: Harcourt Brace Jovanovich, Inc., 1971), p. 683.

184 Samuel Taylor Coleridge, *Biographia Literaria,* ed. Engell and Bate, volume 1, p. 239, p. 203.

187 Samuel Taylor Coleridge, *Biographia Literaria,* ed. Engell and Bate, volume 2, p. 6.

191 George Gordon, Lord Byron, "The Destruction of Sennacherib." This one is not in the Norton anthologies, although it can be found for instance in *The Selected Poery and Prose of Byron,* ed. W. H. Auden (New York: Signet Classics of New American Library, 1966).

195 William Wordsworth, "The Tables Turned." This too is not in the usual big anthologies, but it may be found in *Selected Poems and Prefaces by William Wordsworth,* ed. Jack Stillinger (Boston: Houghton Mifflin Company, 1965). If you do look it

up, check also its companion piece, "Expostulation and Reply." The poems appear to recount an argument between plump, arthritic, asthmatic, heart-valve damaged Coleridge and long-legged, athletic Wordsworth about whether to hike or to read; they did a lot of both together, over the years.

199 Andrew Marvell, "To His Coy Mistress." See also above, pages 55 and 164.

204 Jerome Lawrence and Robert E. Lee, *Auntie Mame*, based on the novel by Patrick Dennis; copyright renewed 1988. This is the first line of Mame's last speech in Act 2, Scene 6. In some of the movie versions of the musical version of the original play, this line is very slightly different; I'm citing the script of the original play. The line is not found in Dennis's novel.

"I Got Plenty o' Nuttin'" is a song from *Porgy and Bess* by George Gershwin.

216 William Wordsworth, "Lines Written a Few Miles above Tintern Abbey."

234 William Wordsworth, "Lines Written a Few Miles above Tintern Abbey."

Samuel Taylor Coleridge, "The Aeolian Harp" and *Biographia Literaria*, ed. Engell and Bate, volume 1, p. 203.

237 Emily Dickinson, "I'm Nobody! Who are you?", #288 in *The Poems of Emily Dickinson*, ed. Thomas H. Johnson (Cambridge, MA: The Belknap Press of Harvard University Press, 1983).

253 Jeremiah 23:1; Psalm 46.

Alph: see Samuel Taylor Coleridge, "Kubla Khan, or, A Vision in a Dream. A Fragment"; higher and inwards: see *Biographia Literaria*, ed. Engell and Bate, volume 1, pp. 237–242 and above, page 184.

254 Like a garment: see William Wordsworth, "Sonnet Composed Upon Westminster Bridge, September 3, 1802."

Diogenes Teufelsdröckh: see Thomas Carlyle, *Sartor Resartus*.

Wendell Barry, "A Grace," in *A Part* (San Francisco: North Point Press, a division of Farrer, Straus & Giroux, 1980).

George Herbert, "Outlandish Proverbs," as cited in *The Oxford Dictionary of Quotations,* Third Edition, 1980.

PERMISSIONS

Emily Dickinson, poem #288 and poem #712 reprinted by permission of the publishers and the trustees of Amherst College from *The Poems of Emily Dickinson,* Thomas H. Johnson, ed., Cambridge, Mass.: The Belknap Press of Harvard University Press, Copyright © 1951, 1955, 1979, 1983 by the President and Fellows of Harvard College.

T. S. Eliot, "The Waste Land," copyright © 1922 T. S. Eliot; "The Love Song of J. Alfred Prufrock," copyright © 1917 T. S. Eliot; both from *Collected Poems 1909–1962* (San Diego: Harcourt Brace Jovanovich, 1963). Reprinted by permission of Faber and Faber Ltd., Publishers, London.

Robert Fitzgerald, *The Iliad of Homer.* Copyright © 1974 by Robert Fitzgerald. Reprinted by permission of Doubleday, a division of Random House, Inc.

Richard Lattimore, *The Odyssey of Homer.* Copyright © 1965, 1967 by Richard Lattimore. Copyright renewed. Reprinted with permission of HarperCollins Publisher Inc.

Auntie Mame, Copyright © Renewed 1988, Jerome Lawrence and Robert E. Lee (Revised); Copyright © Renewed 1985, Jerome Lawrence and Robert E. Lee; Copyright © 1960, Jerome Lawrence and Robert E. Lee (Revised); Copyright © 1957, Jerome Lawrence and Robert E. Lee. CAUTION: The reprinting of *Auntie Mame* included in this volume is reprinted by permission of the author and Dramatists Play Service, Inc. The amateur stage performance rights in this play are controlled exclusively by Dramatists Play Service, Inc., 440 Park Avenue South, New York NY 10016. No nonprofessional production of the play may be given without obtaining, in advance, the written permission of Dramatists Play Service, Inc., and paying the requisite fee. Inquiries regarding all other rights should be addressed to Robert A. Freedman Dramatic Agency, Inc., 1501 Broadway, Suite 2310, New York, NY 10036.

Anna Quindlen, "Job and a Baby Cannot Still the Nesting Instinct," *The New York Times,* January 27, 1988, Section A, pp. 17–18. Copyright © 1988 by the New York Times Co. Reprinted by permission.

Valéry, Paul. "Poetry and Abstract Thought," from *The Art of Poetry,* in *The Collected Works of Paul Valéry,* Jackson Matthews, ed., Denise Folliot, trans. Copyright © 1960 by Princeton University Press. Reprinted by permission of Princeton University Press.

William Butler Yeats, "Among School Children" and "Sailing to Byzantium." Reprinted in the U.S. with the permission of Simon & Schuster from *The Poems of W. B. Yeats: A New Edition,* edited by Richard J. Finneran. Copyright © 1928 by Macmillan Publishing Company, renewed 1956 by Georgie Yeats. International reprint rights, exclusive of the U.S., granted by the permission of A. P. Watt Ltd., London, on behalf of Michael B. Yeats.